DAUGHTERS OF

DAUGHTERS OF HAMILTON HALL

Annie Beaumont

Anthea —

Warmest regards,

Annie Beaumont

x

Sept 2018

YOUCAXTON PUBLICATIONS
OXFORD & SHREWSBURY

Copyright © Annie Beaumont 2018

The Author asserts the moral right to
be identified as the author of this work.

ISBN 978-1-912419-36-4
Printed and bound in Great Britain.
Published by YouCaxton Publications 2018

All rights reserved. No part of this publication may be reproduced, stored in a retrieval system, or transmitted in any form or by any means, electronic, mechanical, photocopying, recording or otherwise, without the prior permission of the author.

This book is sold subject to the condition that it shall not, by way of trade or otherwise, be lent, resold, hired out or otherwise circulated without the author's prior consent in any form of binding or cover other than that in which it is published and without a similar condition including this condition being imposed on the subsequent purchaser.

YouCaxton Publications
enquiries@youcaxton.co.uk

Dedication

I dedicate *Daughters of Hamilton Hall*
to Alexander and Oliver, of whom I am immensely proud.

Acknowledgements

Without the encouragement and help of a great number of individuals, this novel would not have been finished. I owe a debt of gratitude to many.

First of all, I thank Ashley Stokes, my tutor at the Unthank School of Writing, for your encouragement, patience and expert guidance.

Many thanks are also due to my fellow 'Unthankers': Sabine, Gill, Lorraine, Jac, Jose, Claudie, Julie, Abigail, Jo, who have all read first draft chapters of *Daughters of Hamilton Hall* and encouraged me enormously. I would never have got this far without you spurring me on!

Simona Caprioli-Cowan, my dear friend, and inspiration for creating an Italian Master of Wines called 'Simona', I thank you not only your valued friendship, but also your impressive knowledge of vintage wines!

Pip Collyer – thank you dear friend for teaching me a little something about house surveys and the horrors that Laura might uncover in a neglected Hamilton Hall!

Marvin Meyers – I am grateful for your help with understanding American military ranks!

Paul Martin – thank you for your special 'bank manager' expertise in the area of applying for a business loan.

Richard Yallop – thank you dear friend for providing me with background knowledge about writing a business plan.

Charles Passant – your childhood memories of the war years in Norfolk were not only fascinating but also invaluable. Thank you for sharing these, dear friend.

Diane Passant – thank you darling, for your enduring encouragement, love and friendship (and for allowing me to use your name for one of my minor characters).

Tony Sweeney – thanks, honey, for helpful discussions about inheritance, heir-hunters and the creative writing process.

Colleen Thomas – thank you for sharing with me your knowledge of young people's street language!

Kenny Gray – thank you for imparting your knowledge of cars, which helped me enormously in writing about *Esther the Fiesta!*

My dear Australian friend, Dr Joanie Phillip, I value our long and enduring friendship and I thank you for casting your keen creative writer's eye over my second draft of *Daughters of Hamilton Hall*.

Hilly Osper, thank you for your long and valued friendship and your excellent beta-reading and help with French. You possess an impressively keen, forensic eye!

Finally, I should like to thank 'Sinead', owner of soft, dulcet Irish tones, who works in a certain credit card company call centre and gave invaluable information and advice when I phoned to ask about credit card fraud.

Contents

1: Summer, 2013	1
2: Sunday morning, 3rd September 1939	4
3: Summer, 2013	6
4: Sunday evening, 3rd September 1939	11
5: Summer, 2013	14
6: June 1940	17
7: Summer, 2013	20
8: July 1940	24
9: Summer, 2013	26
10: 22nd August 1940	29
11: Summer, 2013	32
12: 23rd August 1940	35
13: Summer, 2013	37
14: Saturday, 24th August 1940	41
15: Summer, 2013	43
16: 6pm, 25th August 1940	46
17: Summer, 2013	48
18: 25th August, 1940	52
19: Summer 2013	54
20: 25th August, 1940	58
21: Same day	60
22: 25th August, 1940	64
23: Monday morning	66
24: Sunday, 26th August, 1940	69
25: A few days later	71
26: Monday, 26th August, 1940, Dawn	74
27: The next day	76
28: Late August, 1940	79
29: Later that day	81
30: Saturday, 31st August 1940	84
31: Summer 2013, A few days later	86
32: Saturday, 31st August 1940	88
33: Summer, 2013, that same day	92
34: August, 1940 - Later that evening	95
35: Summer 2013 – same day	97
36: Early September, 1940	101
37: Same day	103
38: End of September 1940	108
39: Summer, 2013, same day, later on	110
40: Early October 1940	113

41: Summer, 2013, same day	115
42: October, 1940, same day	119
43: Summer, 2013, the following morning	121
44: November 1940	124
45: Summer 2013, same morning	126
46: November, 1940	129
47: Summer, 2013 – same day	132
48: November, 1940, the following morning	135
49: Summer, 2013, that evening	137
50: The following morning	140
51: Summer, 2013, same day	143
52: 17th January, 1941	146
53: That evening – In Suffolk...	148
54: April 1941	150
55: The following morning	153
56: Late July, 1941	157
57: Five weeks later...	159
58: 2nd September, 1941	163
59: Early October, 2013	165
60: April, 1942	168
61: October, 2013, the following afternoon	171
62: April, 1942, that afternoon	174
63: A few weeks later	176
64: Some weeks later	179
65: Early November	181
66: June, 1942	185
67: December, 2013	187
68: June, 1942	190
69: December, 2013	192
70: June, 1942	195
71: Late December, 2013	197
72: Mid-July, 1942	203
73: January, 2014	208
74: A year later, 1943	211
75: The next day	215
76: 8th May 1945	221
77: February, 2014	226
78: February, 2015	229
79: April, 2017	240
80: Present day	243

1: Summer, 2013
Suffolk

Laura:
I wasn't exactly dressed for the occasion, as I opened the door on that Thursday morning to the elegant young man standing on my doorstep. Sporting a grubby old purple towelling dressing gown, decorated with egg stains and flour, my hair tied in a messy knot on top of my head, I'd been up since six o'clock that morning, baking cakes and stewing plums to make pies, my donation to the church fête on Saturday afternoon. I'd thought it was the milkman, come for the money for the two-months' worth of milk I'd let slide (*whoops!*) and was now much overdue; or the postie with that new book on special offer from Amazon. But, no. And there he was, this vision of gorgeousness, hair flopping over his eyes, their colour a startling steel grey. He raked his fingers through his raven locks, blinking rapidly, uncertainly. Really, I was quite mesmerised. I mean, they just didn't make them like that when I was his age. He was quite stunning. Clearly, I was born at least a decade too early. He quite took my breath away, dressed in pristine white shirt, sky blue tie and expensive looking navy-blue suit. Not that I knew much about the price of young men's attire, but this was certainly no twenty-quid job from Tesco. Armani, more like. But like I said, I know next to nothing about designer gear for males. And why would I? There's no man in my life and I never had any brothers; no siblings at all, actually. No, none at all; I was the only daughter of my husbandless mother, Sarah White. Mum was killed eight years ago; her life snuffed out like a church candle when a young tearaway on a motorbike failed to stop at a red light. Just like that. Gone. Born in 1957; died 2005. She'd always refused to answer my questions about my father. I am not even sure if she ever married him. There were boxes full of paperwork to sort through after her death, and, despite all these years having passed, I have still never looked at any of it. The papers had been languishing in the loft all this time; for all I knew, the mice had probably eaten the lot.

'Good morning, Madam. I hope I'm not disturbing you?' His eyes looked over me. I pulled my dressing gown tightly around me, self-conscious and not a little embarrassed. I think if I'd been the blushing type I would have been doing so right now.

'I am looking for a ...' he glanced at the manila envelope I'd only just noticed he was holding in his left hand (well, it was those piercing grey eyes, they bored right into me; really, quite disconcerting). Nice hands: clean, manicured nails. 'I'm looking for a Ms Laura White.' Silky smooth voice too. But what the devil did he want with me?

'And you are ...?' He coloured up a bit and it looked rather attractive, made him sort of vulnerable and shy.

'Oh. Apologies. Craig Matthews from Hatch and Horncastle,' he extended his right hand; 'Genealogists. Erm ... I take it you are Ms White?' He cast an appraising eye over me again. I became acutely aware for the second time in the space of sixty seconds of the dreadful sight I must have presented before him. Then, as if it'd only just occurred to him, he whipped out a business card from his jacket pocket and handed it to me, holding it between his index and middle fingers. Yes, very nice clean fingernails. I took the card and read it. Well, it was right enough; that's exactly what it said on the card: *Craig Matthews, Hatch and Horncastle, Genealogists. Finding rightful heirs since 1930.* Then, as if as an afterthought, he opened his jacket to reveal an identity card clipped to his shirt pocket. I peered at the ID tag. Well, yes, it looked like he was telling the truth.

'Yes, I am Laura White. What can I do for you?'

'Erm, it might be easier if I could just step inside for a few moments, Ms White.'

'Well don't stand there like a milk bottle on a doorstep Craig Matthews. Come on in and I'll put the kettle on.' And with that I turned on my heel and led him through to the kitchen at the back of the house, just in time to rescue a dozen fairy cakes from burning in the oven and the plums from boiling over on the hob.

§

'You *what?*' It was two hours later and I was on the phone to my best friend, Kitty. I had it on speaker so that I could move around the kitchen, cleaning up after the morning's cake and pie making.

'You heard. I said this young bloke from an heir-hunters' firm – you know – like that programme on the telly - came here this morning telling me I'd been left a house that used to belong to some old great aunt or other.'

'You're having me on! Come off it, Laura, this is one of your jokes.'

'Kitty Colman, come around here right now and take a look for yourself at the stuff he left me. I've got a load of documents to read tonight and sign in front of the lawyer and a witness tomorrow. They'd hardly leave all these legal papers with me to read if they weren't sure it was me. I had to show him my passport and a utility bill. It's genuine and it is definitely me. Like I just said, some great aunt died ages ago and I'm the rightful heir and, apparently, they've been looking for me for quite a while. God knows how they managed it in the end, but there was this chap standing on my doorstep at nine o'clock this morning, telling me I was the rightful heir to this house. A bloody big house, too, by the sounds of it. Loads of land. I keep thinking I'm dreaming and I'm about to wake up.'

'Hamilton Hall! Crikey Laura! It sounds very posh!' It had taken Kitty all of ten minutes to get from her house to mine after our telephone conversation. 'And is this a photo of it?' She held the brochure in her hands, flicking through the pages.

'Yes, that's it. And it does look grand, doesn't it? It's Grade II listed, whatever that means. But Craig what's-his-name told me it's pretty run down and needs a lot of work doing on it. The gardens look like a jungle, don't they? Apparently, it was requisitioned or something in the war, so the family who'd been living there had to share their home with a load of military bods. And evacuees too, you know, little kids from the cities, to protect them from the bombing. It's been empty for years, and, apparently, it's going to be quite a project if I keep it. And as you know, I'm not exactly loaded, so I've no idea how I would raise the cash to renovate. It will probably cost a fortune. But I'm going over there tomorrow to have a look. I'll need to book a B and B,' I said, drawing breath and reaching for the laptop. Kitty is always telling me I do that. Talk non-stop until my breath runs out.

'It'll probably take a while to sort out all the legal stuff but I can't wait to see it, so I'm not hanging about.'

'What do you mean, *if* you keep it? Do you think you might flog it?'

'It's a possibility, I suppose. I don't really know, to be honest Kitty. It's hardly sunk in. I'll go and have a look around at the weekend and take my time to decide what I'm going to do.'

2: Sunday morning, 3rd September 1939
Hamilton Hall, Norfolk

'...I have to tell you now that no such undertaking has been received, and that consequently this country is at war with Germany.'

Emily:

I heard the chilling words of Mr Chamberlain, emanating from the wireless, as I entered the dining room. My sister, Martha sat staring at the source of the solemn voice: the wireless which stood in the corner. Martha, her mouth gaping, eyes wide with a mixture of alarm, fear and disbelief, looked first at Mother, to her left and then Father, who sat to her right at the oak dining table. No one spoke. An uncomfortable quiet hung in the air. There had been talk of another war in Europe for months now, but no one really believed it would come to anything, did they? Mother looked as if she might cry. Father sat in dignified silence, his expression unfathomable. No one moved.

Now I looked in disbelief at each member of my family sitting there at the table. Nineteen-year-old Martha and I could not, in all honesty, be more unalike. Tall and blonde, with brown eyes, I had inherited my father's looks, whereas my younger sister, Martha, was blessed with Mother's classic French beauty. Although tall, like me, Martha sported sleek, black, waist-length hair, dazzling blue eyes and high cheekbones. My little sister turned heads in any room she walked into. Men of all ages, not only the young ones, were enchanted and she could have taken her pick. Martha Boulais-Hamilton, however, had her heart set on only one: Flying Officer Charles Harwood of Royal Air Force Fighter Command. At twenty-three, Charles cut a dashing figure in his RAF Officer's uniform. Six feet tall, dark brown hair and muddy brown eyes, Charles Harwood's flashing white smile could leave any young girl weak at the knees. Mother and Father, however, were unimpressed by his rakish charm, but their disapproval had made Martha, naturally, and somewhat unsurprisingly, all the more determined to bag him for herself. And she had.

Now, I tried to catch my breath. 'Carter kept saying we would be at war! It's true, then.' No one spoke.

Always an early riser, I loved nothing more than getting my hands dirty in the vegetable patch I had maintained since I was a little girl and only just big enough to hold a hoe or a trowel. Whereas Martha worked as a shorthand typist in the typing pool of the local bank, an occupation considered by our parents to be suitably ladylike. I would always prefer to spend my time with Carter, our now (to us girls at least) quite elderly family gardener, pottering in the greenhouse, or pulling up weeds or harvesting home grown fruits from the trees, to dressing up in an evening gown for a formal event or Sunday best for Chapel. On Sundays, after the service, I would hurry back to change into work clothes. My wild blonde curls, cut short, were tucked behind my ears while a red cotton scarf tied around my head served to keep my hair from falling in my face as I worked. Old brown corduroy slacks, grey sweater with holes at the elbows and green Wellington boots completed the look that left our stylish French mother in a state of utter despair. Martha, on the other hand, was always immaculately attired in calf-length slim skirt, twin set and pearls. Her mane of hair was usually pinned up neatly and fully-fashioned seamed stockings and polished court shoes completed the ensemble. Martha had graduated last year from secretarial college and was quickly accepted at the bank; while I rejected the chance of any type of career training in favour of spending my days maintaining the substantial gardens of Hamilton Hall. Now I had trodden damp earth onto the carpet.

'Oh, *ma chérie!* Do take care. Look what you've brought into the room.' War had just broken out and my darling mother thought a bit of muck on the dining room floor was catastrophic. Martha and I rolled our eyes skyward but otherwise I ignored the scolding.

'So, it's true then?'

'Yes, Em, it's true all right, said Martha. 'Just heard it from old Chamberlain on the wireless. I say, jolly scary, isn't it? Charles will have to fly over to Germany and bomb them all to bits. Then he'll be a hero. Oh, it's so romantic.'

'Martha! That's enough!' Father had spoken at last. 'We shall go to Chapel this evening and pray that this war is soon over.

3: Summer, 2013

Laura:

It was Friday, the day after the visit from the delicious heir-hunter, and I was driving Esther, my prehistoric Fiesta up to Norfolk (yes, *Esther the Fiesta*!). It was only about fifty miles from my humble two-bedroomed terraced cottage in Suffolk to Hamilton Hall (according to Google Maps) but it could take forever in the old jalopy. I just hoped it would last the journey. Thank goodness for the trusty AA Recovery guys. They'd got me out of no end of scrapes over the years when I'd had to call them so many times that I was practically on kissing terms with the car mechanics.

It was the end of my week's holiday from work, so the timing of the arrival of the heir-hunter Adonis on my doorstep yesterday was perfect. I had plenty of time to get myself up to Norfolk and back before going back to work on Monday. Except that I had an essay to finish for my online degree course, and my lovely tutor had already warned me I couldn't have any more extensions, so it had to get done. And I hadn't got around to reading all those legal papers last night, what with celebrating my inheritance with Kitty, so I'll have to take a look before signing them when I meet the lawyer and witness tomorrow. I glanced at the envelope lying on the passenger seat next to me. Just a quick read, that's all it needed. How hard can that be? All right, so that was a thick envelope of stuff, but I'm used to skim-reading.

And, of course, there was also the little matter of the Church fête tomorrow afternoon that I was probably going to miss. But Kitty had agreed to take my cakes and plum pies to the vicar's wife today, so that I could get on the road early. And I had my laptop with me, so I could probably get the final few hundred words of my essay written tonight before meeting the chap from Hatch and Horncastle and the lawyer tomorrow morning to look over the house. I didn't even know if you'd call a place with nine bedrooms, a drawing room, a morning room, a dining room and a library (Crikey, yes, a flipping *library!*), and all the rest a 'house'. Sounded more like a mansion to me, but I'd soon find out. As I drove north along the A11, fantasies of filling the library of Hamilton Hall with academic books, showing off my degree studies (if I ever managed to graduate) crowded my mind. I imagined having dinner parties in the dining room, with staff serving the guests, like on *Downton Abbey*. Or summer garden parties in the 'substantial grounds', that Craig Matthews had so enthusiastically described. Or even a summer ball. There was no end to my ideas.

So, there I was, trundling along in Esther, heading north towards Norwich, when I realised I was getting low on petrol. *Oh, bugger.* I knew there was something crucial I hadn't thought of.

Not to worry, there was a service station not too far ahead and a good thing too, because not only did I need fuel, but I could also murder a cup of coffee.

BBC Radio Norfolk kicked in on the crackly car radio, just as I crossed the Suffolk-Norfolk border and the presenter was talking to some old man, who had found a dilapidated church in Norfolk, ancient it was, and he'd made it his *raison d'être* to renovate it and bring it back to life. Rumour had it that the church had been vandalised by American soldiers and then bombed in the Second World War by the Germans. And later, a pagan cult had taken over and left it in a right mess. The ruined old church was discovered one day a couple of decades ago by this Church Warden guy, and it was covered in a thick growth of trees that had completely smothered it, by the sounds of it. *Crikey. Imagine that!* Give the old boy his due: he took on the task of restoring it. Seems some Satanists didn't like that though, because the poor fellow received death threats. Sounded like a pretty unlucky church, if you ask me, and I wouldn't touch it with a barge pole. Still, I suppose it gave the fellow an interest in life for a few years. Good on him! What I couldn't figure out was why anybody would object to a keen old bloke turning an eyesore into a decent, functioning building again. I thought about Hamilton Hall, and if I did decide to renovate it (I'd figure out later where the dosh would come from, you know, little details like that), then I hoped I wouldn't end up getting death threats from pagans or Satanists or whatever they were, like the ones who objected to the old boy magnanimously doing up an old church. I always thought pagans were kindly people, so I expect that bit of the story was untrue. Surely nice pagans wouldn't wreck a joint and then make death threats to an innocent old man?

The radio interview finished just as I spotted the petrol station and I pulled in. A car whizzed by me and stopped at the pump I was just approaching. Great. *Bloody BMW drivers!* Think they own the road. And all the petrol stations too. I felt like giving the driver a mouthful as he jumped out of the car, but decided my priority at that moment was a coffee and the loo, so thought better of it. Instead I drove over onto the café carpark and parked Esther.

I wasn't too impressed with the standard of cleanliness in the Ladies' facilities and there was no loo roll either. I had to fish around in my handbag for a tissue. I took a cursory glance at my face and hair in the mirror as I washed my hands. No make-up (well, there wasn't time this morning, what with having to pack and sort out the cakes and plum pies for the church to and write a bit more of my dratted essay before leaving) and my hair, naturally a complete mess was in its usual state. No change there. I reached out to the electric hand dryer only to see a handwritten note Blu-Tacked to it: 'Out of Order'. Brilliant. Outstanding service. I shook the excess water off, flicking my fingers, this way and that, then wiped my hands on my skirt.

At the counter, I ordered a cappuccino and toasted teacake and admonished the waitress on the disgusting state of the loos. She had a look of someone who really couldn't care less, with her hair shaved at the sides, eyebrow piercing and nose ring. She had 'Shane' tattooed on the back of her hand and to top it all off, a look of sheer boredom on her face.

To her credit though, she did tell me to go sit down and she'd bring my food and drink to the table, so I let her off not caring about the state of the loos. I paid the bill and looked around for a free table.

The door swung open just as I turned from the counter, heading for a table by the window and in breezed the cocky BMW driver. He was rangy and slim, six feet tall (at least), deep-set dark brown eyes and an expensive-looking cut to his thick, fox-red hair. I bet he was the sort of bloke that has one of those Indian head massages in the hairdressers, and had lots of designer hair products too. I wondered what he was doing, slumming it in a service station greasy spoon joint.

The scruffy waitress plonked the toasted teacake and cappuccino on the table. She'd drawn a little heart shape in chocolate powder on the coffee froth. She'd also spilled coffee into the saucer. Sublime.

Once I'd mopped up the coffee though, the cappuccino and toasted teacake were quite acceptable and I finished them quickly and made for the petrol pumps, which were thankfully a little less busy now. With no flash git BMW drivers around, I filled Esther to the brim and resumed my journey north.

The 'Welcome Home' B and B was a grey brick affair with bay sash windows dressed with blue floral curtains and sat at the end of the main street of the little market town called Wymondham. Colourful flowers in hanging baskets graced the façade, making the building cheerful and appealing. The landlady, Maggie Middleton, was a short, rotund woman in her late fifties, with ruddy cheeks, wispy, mousy brown hair, a strong Norfolk accent and, just as the name of her establishment suggested, a friendly and welcoming demeanour. I warmed to her immediately. I wondered if she had lived in Wymondham very long (if her accent was anything to go by she probably had for all of her life) and made a mental note to pick her brains about Hamilton Hall.

The room she showed me was at the top of winding stairs with ageing dark red carpet and patches of wear and tear on each step. A smell of lavender polish and coffee brewing filled the air and added to the homely ambience of the place. The accommodation was small but adequate (it needed to be; it was all I could afford) and had the added bonus of overlooking a little park at the back. It had an en suite bathroom that probably dated back to the nineteen-seventies with interesting, quirky features to the plumbing: I learned from Maggie Middleton that you had to 'pump the loo handle a few times, my lovely, to make it flush' and you also had to 'be quick into the shower in the morning before all the hot water gets used up by other guests.'

'I expect you'd like a cuppa coffee, wouldn't you, m'dear? And I got some nice lemon cake just out of the oven too. Come down when you're ready and I'll get you some coffee and cake.'

'Thanks, Maggie. That sounds lovely. I'll be down shortly.' And with that I closed the door on her and bounced onto the double bed that creaked and groaned, making me glad that I was alone on this visit and not on a dirty weekend with a sexy hunk like Craig Matthews (fat chance!). My mobile pinged with a text from the said hunk:

> Sorry Laura, but can we possibly meet at the house at 3pm today?
> Double booked tomorrow morning.

I replied that yes, of course, it was fine and began unpacking my small overnight bag. I hung things in the wardrobe, whose door squeaked as I opened and closed it. I used the loo and found that, just as Maggie had instructed, I had to pump the handle up and down a few times to get it to flush. I opened my laptop and, amazingly, the WiFi kicked in automatically. The website had boasted free WiFi at the Welcome Home B and B, but given that the rest of the house seemed to be stuck in a time warp, twenty-first century technology was at odds in this environment.

I checked my emails and found one from my tutor, reminding me there would be no extension for my essay. *OK, I know, I know. You've already made that clear!* I checked my essay and found I had another thousand words to write before the submission deadline, which loomed. I slammed the laptop shut and made my way downstairs to the kitchen. It was already getting on for three o'clock.

Over hot coffee and lemon cake straight from the oven, I broached the subject of Hamilton Hall with Maggie Middleton.

'Oh yes, m'dear. Fascinatin' history, the old place has. Goes back to the seventeenth or eighteenth-century, I think. Been left to rot since the old lady died. Proper sad, that is, proper sad. And all the people what have nowhere to live, and there's the old hall, with all them bedrooms, standing there empty, and ready to rot into the ground. So, what's your interest in it, m'dear? If you don't mind me asking, that is.' She gave me a sideways glance.

'I've just inherited it, actually', I replied, my instincts immediately telling me that this was perhaps a little too much information, too soon. I hardly knew this woman, after all. And as warm and kindly as she seemed to be, she was likely the town gossip for all I knew.

'Inherited it? *Really?* Well, I'm blessed!' And with a countenance that I found difficult to read, Maggie Middleton got up from her pine kitchen chair, gathered her coffee cup and empty plate, and moved over to the sink. 'And what will you be doing with the old place, m'dear, if you don't mind me asking?'

'Not sure yet. I haven't even seen it. I have an appointment at...' - I looked at my watch – 'Oh, in ten minutes from now. Must dash. Thanks ever so much for the coffee and cake. Delicious, Maggie, really good. I'd like the recipe for the lemon cake from you, later, if you wouldn't mind?'

I got up and grabbed my bag and envelope of unread legal documents. As I moved towards the door, a hand gripped my upper arm, forcing me to stop and turn; and the expression on Maggie Middleton's face took a moment to register with me. It had changed from friendly and welcoming to something resembling threatening. 'Just be sure to remember that that old hall has been here a lot longer than any newcomer, young lady.' And with that, she released her hand from my arm and I still felt the imprint of its grip several uncomfortable moments later, as it occurred to me that I might have booked myself into a B and B run by one of those Norfolk Satanists I'd heard about earlier on the radio.

4: Sunday evening, 3rd September 1939
Wymondham, Norfolk

Emily:

'He's wasting his breath. The Germans are coming, like it or not!' Martha stage-whispered to me, and I gave my sister a sharp dig in the ribs with my elbow. Father emitted a little warning cough and Mother's face expressed irritation and annoyance at her daughters' lack of respect for the Lord's house. Not ones for relishing the development of housemaid's knee in a cold chapel, Martha and I endured the hour-long evening service, rolling our eyes at each other as the vicar invoked God to bring an early end to the conflict in Europe.

'Shush!' From the pews behind us could be heard someone tut-tutting and huffing and puffing. More eye-rolling from Martha and me.

As the September sun set my sister and I breathed in the unusually balmy evening air when we emerged, much relieved, from the chill of the little Chapel. We went through the motions of exchanging pleasantries with the local worshippers and the family friends who regularly attended, either under duress (rather like Martha and me) or because they were devout and true believers.

Susie James, twenty, short, plump, ginger-haired, giggly and effusive, approached Martha and me.

'I say, girls, dreadfully scary news, isn't it? Do you think the Germans will invade us? Daddy says it will be all over in a trice, but that's exactly what they all said last time, wasn't it? And that war went on for four years.' Susie sounded more excited than concerned about the anticipation of the impending hostilities and I thought that this was probably the most fun the chubby ginger girl had ever had in her pitiably boring little life. 'Will Charles have to go and fight?' Martha and I exchanged a glance.

'Who knows, Susie?' Martha replied over her shoulder as she walked away, hooking her arm through mine. Heads turned inwards towards each other, we chortled as we made haste down the churchyard path.

'I say, Emily, I ... ' My younger sister hesitated, looked sideways at me, her brow wrinkled in a mixture of sycophancy and worry, an expression she was in the habit of wearing whenever she wanted to wheedle some favour or other out of me.

'What? I know that tone, Martha Boulais-Hamilton. What are you up to?'

'Oh Emily, could you cover for me tonight? I'm meeting - '

'Charles. You're meeting Charles, aren't you? You'll get caught, you know, Martha. You know you will. Susie obviously knows you're still seeing him and she's such a blabbermouth it will be all over Norfolk before you know it. Mummy and Daddy already know you're sweet on him and one of these days they'll notice you're gone and there'll be all hell let loose when they find out about your clandestine little trysts. Never mind bloody Hitler – you won't like the wrath of Daddy raining down on you!'

'Oh, but Em darling, if they were only a little more reasonable. Charles is not the cad they think he is. He's wonderful and he loves me and he's such fun to be with. I want to marry him and live happily ever after. If only I were just two years older and this bloody war wasn't about to start and everything, we could be married by now. Just because he's not some boring old bank manager or lawyer or whatever, they think he's not good enough for a daughter of Hamilton Hall. But he is! He is! Oh please, Em, please say you'll cover for me.'

'OK, just this once. But it has to stop, Martha. I'm warning you, never mind the war in Europe, there'll be a war in Hamilton Hall if our parents find out. And they are bound to, sooner or later. Someone will see you out in that car with him and you know how the locals like to gossip. And his car makes such a racket – I could hear it before it had reached the bottom of our drive the other night. I'm amazed Mummy and Daddy didn't hear it. I knew it was Charles coming along by the sound of the engine, creaking and squeaking and rattling along. Can't he find a decent car?'

'It's an MG, Emily. They all make that noise. Anyway, Mother and Father are always fast asleep by ten and I never go out before then.'

I looked at her sideways under lowered eyelids and raised eyebrows. 'You are being careful, aren't you? You haven't, you know, done anything silly, have you?'

'Whatever do you mean?'

'You know exactly what I mean. Don't play the innocent with me, little sister. You're not letting him, you know, go all the way?'

'Of course not!'

'Of course not, what?' It was Mother's heavily French-accented voice behind us, making both Martha and me start, unaware that our parents had caught up with us.

'Oh nothing, Mummy. Just a little joke.'

'A joke? What about?'

'Oh, just silly old Susie James. She's such a fat pudding,' said Martha.

'Don't be so unkind, Martha dear,' said Mother and we looked quickly at each other. 'Not everyone is as beautiful as you, my child, but it is your inner beauty that is the more important. Looks fade. Don't forget that.'

'Sorry Mummy.' And Martha pressed her lips together to suppress another giggle.

4: SUNDAY EVENING, 3RD SEPTEMBER 1939

We enjoyed a supper of pheasant, roast potatoes and root vegetables grown in the Hamilton Hall garden, followed by pie made with plums and apples from the family orchards, all expertly prepared by Doris, wife of Carter the gardener. Martha feigned a yawn. 'Oh, I'm so tired. I think I'll go to my room and practice my shorthand before I turn in for the night.'

'*Ma petit chéri*, don't stay up too late studying your shorthand. You're looking a little *fatigué*. You must not overdo things,' said Mother.

'I must pass my one hundred and twenty words per minute exam, *Maman,* so that I can get my promotion at the bank.'

'Good girl.' It was Father, looking at her from beneath greying, bushy eyebrows that joined in the middle. 'Although what good a promotion will do you, I can't imagine. You'll only have to leave the job when you eventually find a decent fellow to marry. Still, at least working at the bank keeps you occupied until that day comes.'

Martha gave him a weak smile. 'Goodnight Father. Goodnight Mother. Emily.' She pushed back her chair and stood up, walking towards our parents to peck each of them on the cheek. Martha and I exchanged glances, as my younger sister winked at me and slipped out of the dining room. I heard her skip up the highly polished mahogany staircase to her bedroom.

5: Summer, 2013
Hamilton Hall, Wymondham, Norfolk

Laura:

I'd surely arrived in some kind of alternative reality. This bloody big, posh house could not actually be mine, could it? (Well, all right, it was a bit dilapidated, but let's not split hairs here; it looked pretty posh to me and it certainly was big). I couldn't believe it was actually happening to me. Not me; not Laura White, pushing forty, only daughter of a single mum, scratching a living together working in a care home for seven quid an hour, spending my spare time making cakes for the Church fête and struggling to get an education via an online college degree. Yet there I was. Gazing up at this imposing building, which now belonged to me. With the imprint of Maggie Middleton's tight grip still burning into my arm, it had been with excitement and trepidation in equal measure that I had driven Esther up the sweeping gravel drive that led to a parking area to one side of Hamilton Hall, the house that is now, remarkably, unbelievably, my own.

A separate drive forked off that led to what I could just about see was a rundown stable, the top half of its doors swinging eerily in the breeze. At first glance, I could see that the imposing nineteenth-century grey stone manor house had shabby sash windows in need of more than a lick of paint and dormer windows that poked out from the grey slate, slanted roof. I thought I saw something move behind one of the dormer windows. I blinked and it was gone. A trick of the light? Yes, a trick of the light. No one has - surely - been inside this house for absolutely ages and anyway, there was no other car here, other than Esther. Two chimneys, strategically placed, one at each end of the roof, stood like soldiers on guard. Rhododendron bushes, resplendent in a variety of colours, graced the borders of the drive, along with red and yellow roses, Red Hot Pokers, hydrangeas and purple irises. Amazingly, the flowers had somehow survived despite the efforts of the weeds to choke the life out of them as they funnelled, unrelenting, through the flowerbeds. The florae now displayed a vibrancy of colour in the warm, early summer sun. *Crikey!* There was some backbreaking work to be done here, and all I'd seen so far was the front yard. Perhaps Kitty would help!

From each side of the mansion I could see the 'extensive grounds' that Craig Matthews had mentioned, spreading out beyond the house. Copper beech trees, cedar trees, oak trees, they were all there. An overwhelming sense of history, great substance and continuity swept over me, as I contemplated those trees that had stood for hundreds of years. I felt like a very small and insignificant part of the planet. And there I stood, Laura White, owner of each one of these magnificent specimens.

The engine of an approaching vehicle roared up the drive and the gravel whooshed as the car screeched to a halt next to Esther. A tall, rangy bloke jumped out. He was wearing a dark grey suit, lilac shirt and purple tie; an ensemble that looked like it cost a bob or two. I recognised him instantly: *BMW man!* What the was he doing here? He marched straight over like he was Lord of the flippin' Manor and looked down his nose at me. *Superior git.*

'Can I help you Madam? Might I ask who you are and what you are doing here? Are you lost?'

'And who are *you*, might *I* ask?'

'I am Simon Stewart-Rees, from Archer and Stewart-Rees, estate agents. We are in charge of acquiring a piece of land belonging to the house. This is private property and you have no business being here.' His disdainful gaze looked me up and down. *Condescending git!* 'Now I suggest you leave immediately, as I have a client arriving any moment for a viewing.'

'Have you now. And who, might I ask, has instructed you to sell this land?'

'That, Madam, is none of your business. I think you should leave now.' He fixed me in an icy stare.

'Oh, do you now? Well, let me tell you something, Mr High-and-Mighty. I am not going anywhere. *I* own this bloody house and I am telling you now to get off my land because I am not selling any of it. And even if I was going to sell, you're the last person I'd instruct as an agent. So, I suggest you clear off and don't come back. Oh, and while I'm at it, I'd advise you to stop cutting people up in petrol stations. You and your flash car don't own England you know. And for all your snooty, superior attitude, you've got no manners at all. I don't know where you were brought up, but you obviously didn't manage to graduate from Charm School.' His mouth opened, slightly, his tongue hung loose, making him look like a half-wit.

A blue Mercedes approached and another suited man, hair greying at the temples, mid-to-late forties, got out, accompanied by Craig Matthews. A young woman sat on the back seat of the car and stayed there.

'Hello again, Laura.' Craig's smile was as disarming as it had been on the occasion of our first meeting the previous day. It seemed like months, not hours, since he'd arrived at my door with the astonishing news of my inheritance, and ended up sitting in my kitchen, having tea and hot-out-of-the-oven cakes, originally intended for the Church fête. I'd had to make more after he'd left.

'I see you have met Simon Stewart-Rees. This is Neil Davidson, solicitor acting for you in the matter of your inheritance.' Neil Davidson leaned in towards me, hand outstretched. I shook it. Nice strong handshake. Mum always said you could trust a man with a good, firm handshake. Well, we'd see about that one. I'd rarely met a bloke in a suit that I could trust. Or any bloke, come to that, with or without a suit.

'Pleased to meet you Neil.' I said and nodded towards Stewart-Rees. 'What's he doing here then? He reckons he's in charge of selling my land. What's going on?'

Neil Davidson took a large bunch of keys from his jacket pocket, threw them into the air and caught them with one hand. 'Shall we take a look inside, Laura? And we need to sign the legal stuff.'

He beckoned to the young woman in the car and she got out and walked towards us.

This is my secretary, Tiffany Lawson. She will witness the signatures on the documents.

6: June 1940
Hamilton Hall, Norfolk

"We shall defend our island whatever the cost may be. We shall fight on the beaches, we shall fight on the landing grounds, we shall fight in the fields and in the streets; we shall fight in the hills. We shall never surrender."

Emily:

And so, the whole world now, it seemed, had erupted into total destruction and utter despair. I listened, my heart pounding in my chest, as the Prime Minister spoke over the radio waves.

'All right for you to say, Mr Churchill!' I directed my attack at the wireless that stood in the corner of the dining room. 'You're not the one having to jolly well do the fighting, are you?'

Churchill's speech to Parliament came at the end of a ten-day operation to bring back to Britain allied troops from the beaches of Dunkirk, trapped by the advancing German army. Chaos had reigned on the beach and in the sea where bodies floated in the water and troops were under unrelenting attack from machine gun fire and bombs exploding, shrapnel flying in every direction. I shuddered at the very thought.

Martha stood at the open door of the dining room, her face pale.

'When will it all end, Em? I can't bear it. All those poor boys being hurt and killed. I wish I could do something to help.' She moved across the room and into my arms. We stayed there for several minutes, holding each other.

Eventually, I pulled away, looking into my little sister's face.

'You are doing a good job at the bank, Martha darling. Someone has to keep things moving along normally in amongst all the destruction.'

'I'm glad you think I'm being useful, Em. I'm sure Mummy and Daddy wouldn't say so, but they do want me to carry on working at the bank, despite the war.' Martha replied.

'Well, what else would you prefer to do?'

'Something that's going to help the war effort, that's what. I thought I might join up!'

'Don't even think about it, Martha. Daddy would have a fit!'

'I know. But he couldn't stop me. Charles said he thought I'd look rather splendid in the WAAF uniform!' She attempted a smile.

'You're looking very pale today, Martha. Is it the frightful events of Dunkirk we've been hearing about these last few days, or are you feeling unwell?'

'Oh, my monthly is due, that's all,' said Martha, wiping a tear from her cheek.

'Where is Charles? Has he gone away?' I eyed my sister carefully.

'He's not allowed to tell me where he's going. It's all terribly hush-hush. But he's doing a jolly important job, I know that, protecting us all from the dreaded Germans, and I'm very proud of him. I know he goes on training exercises to some far-flung place or other, but apart than that, I don't know anything. And I always worry that he won't come back. Oh Em, I don't know what I'd do if anything happened to him.' And with that, Martha was in tears again and I folded my arms around her, uttering soothing words of comfort, that I didn't really believe myself.

Doris brought in tea and biscuits and set the tray down on the sideboard. I poured tea and Martha seemed to calm down a bit. I sat down on the upholstered chair that stood next to the wireless in the corner of the room. I unfolded the newspaper that had been lying on top of the wireless.

'It says here that in May, Hitler ordered his troops to invade France,' I read from the newspaper. 'And it says that two days later, German tanks had crossed the Meuse and six days after that they had reached the French side of the English Channel. But the British Government, and the French and Belgians underestimated the strength and power of the German army and this led to the British Expeditionary Force, and French, Canadian and Belgian troops fighting a losing battle as they retreated to the harbour and beaches of Dunkirk.'

'But they must have been sitting like ducks, just ready for the Germans to kill them. How frightful.' Martha let out a sob. 'Oh God, stop it, Emily! It's so bloody awful. I can't bear it.'

I squeezed her hand. 'Trying to pretend it's not happening won't make it go away, Martha. We should keep abreast of what's going on and do what we can to support the war effort.' I turned back to the newspaper and continued to read aloud.

'"Over a thousand sea-going vessels, including ferries, yachts, fishing boats and paddle steamers were checked for their seaworthiness then filled with fuel and taken to Ramsgate, ready to set sail for Dunkirk." Gosh. How brave.'

'I hate it, Em. I know our soldiers are brave, but I really hate it, don't you? Oh! The thought of all those people in those little fishing boats sailing over to Dunkirk to save our soldiers! They must have been terrified. I do so hate Hitler!'

'You are not alone,' I said, and then carried on reading from the newspaper.

'Mm. Apparently, the seawater close to the beach at Dunkirk was really shallow, so the smaller boats had to be deployed as shuttles between the beaches and the larger rescue vessels anchored further out, carrying wounded soldiers out to the rescue ships.'

Martha stifled another sob.

'And, the Royal Air Force acted as protectors, while the rescued troops were sailed back to English soil.'

'Oh!' Martha suddenly perked up. 'I wonder if Charles was flying over the Channel, protecting them,' she said. 'I'd be jolly proud of him if he was.'

I folded the newspaper and placed it back on top of the wireless. I walked over to the window and gazed at the gardens of Hamilton Hall. The grand old oak trees, the cedar trees and copper beeches gave me a feeling of permanence, of stability. The very idea of Germans invading and taking over was beyond the imagination. I turned to face Martha again.

'They're saying around a thousand vessels were used to rescue almost three hundred and fifty thousand men from Dunkirk during that rescue operation. Did you know?'

'Yes. And Mr Churchill called it "Operation Dynamo". They might have rescued a lot of our boys, but lots died.' Martha's eyes glistened with fresh tears.

'Yes, it is really alarming and frightening, Martha, but Daddy says we must think positively. We have strong forces and Mr Churchill has vowed that we will carry on fighting until we win this dreadful war.'

'Yes, but in Wymondham, people are talking of Germans invading and they're all speculating in the pub about what life might be like under Nazi rule,' Martha said as she dried her tears on the lace handkerchief she took from her cardigan pocket. 'I just wish I could do something. Well, don't you, Emily?'

I didn't answer. Instead, I turned back to the window, my arms crossed, and pondered on the newspaper reports and the conversation I'd just had with my sister. Part of me was simply trying to pacify her, but it was true, of course. Absolutely true. The news did make one want to do something to help. I'd thought about joining the WRNS, but Daddy had made clear his total disapproval of the idea.

7: Summer, 2013
Hamilton Hall

Laura:

'What's going on, Craig? Who does he think he is, saying he's trying to buy some of my land for a client? Come on, will someone explain to me, what's happening here?' I was glaring at the heir-hunter and lawyer in turn, from one to the other. Both looked blank.

Simon Stewart-Rees had sloped off towards his BMW and jumped in, slamming the door with attitude.

'Come on, for goodness' sake!' I said. 'Out with it! You both obviously know the guy.'

Neil Davidson spoke. 'The neighbour over there,' he indicated with a nod of his head to the rear left of the house, his words nearly drowned out by the sound of a BMW engine roaring down the drive. 'George Farrington, he's been after extending his property for some time. Before the heir-hunters found you, word got out that there was a possibility the hall might be sold - which it would have been, in the event of no rightful heir being found, and the proceeds would have gone to the state - and Mr Farrington instructed Stewart-Rees to try to negotiate. As I said, that was before Hatch and Horncastle tracked you down. So unfortunately, our estate agent friend was a little too quick off the mark. I must say, his approach is rather like that of a bull at a gate, Ms White. Apologies.'

I did fleetingly wonder why a next-door neighbour would need to view a patch of land when presumably he could just look at it over the garden fence, however, I was now much too impatient to see my inheritance to dwell any further on the obnoxious Simon Stewart-bloody-Rees and his client.

'Now, we need to sign those legal documents,' he said, pointing to the envelope in my hand, 'I take it you have read them thoroughly?'

'Oh yes, yes, of course,' I said, trying to cross my fingers behind my back as I spoke. *Well, OK, so I hadn't read the blessed documents... but I just hadn't had time and anyway, legal documents are so boring.*

'Jolly good. Any questions?'

'Nope. None at all.' Fingers still crossed.

'Then shall we sign and then take a look inside?'

We did so, leaning on the bonnet of his car, our signatures witnessed by Tiffany. Neil gave the envelope to his secretary, who handed him what looked like the details of the house, and placed the signed documents in a briefcase she'd been holding.

'I will copy the documents for our records and post the originals to you in due course, Ms White,' Tiffany said with a smile and got back into the car. I followed Neil and Craig ushered me through the front door.

Craig smiled at me. 'All yours now, Laura!' I felt a definite shiver shoot through my body. Whether it was Craig's mouth-watering smile or the realisation that the house was legally mine, I couldn't say.

As I stepped inside, what I saw just took my breath away. There was a certain grandeur and immediate feel about the place that defied the general state of dilapidation. The reception hall had a stone floor, with a central, mahogany, winding staircase rising to a first-floor landing, which separated into opposite directions. From the reception and to one side there were two doors, one leading to the drawing room and the other to what Neil Davidson described as a 'study/dining room'.

He opened a door for me and I stepped into the drawing room, a massive space sporting two open fireplaces with stone surrounds, one at each end of the room. I walked over and touched the mantelpiece of one, running my fingers along the solid mahogany. I could have written my name in the dust, but nonetheless this was just the most beautiful fireplace I'd ever seen. I gazed around the room, wonderstruck. There was a sizeable oil painting of two people who I assumed were a married couple, hanging over the mantelpiece of one of the fireplaces. They stood side-by-side, rigidly upright, as though each had a clothes pole stuck down their back, and gazed majestically down at me. The man's hands were crossed in front of his waist, the woman's arm hooked loosely through his. He wore a light grey three-piece suit, with a cravat at his neck. She wore an emerald green low-cut taffeta evening gown, exposing the hint of a cleavage, and nipped in to define a slender waist, before the full skirt fell in folds to the floor. A huge emerald, with diamonds surrounding the precious stone, adorned her wedding ring finger. Emerald and diamond earrings hung from her earlobes. A matching large emerald, held on a fine, gold chain, also encircled with diamonds, hung around her neck and fell towards her cleavage. I felt I was in a trance and at once, mesmerised and yet slightly intimidated. I blinked and turned to look at the other fireplace, above which hung another oil painting, of the same couple, but some twenty years younger. My hand shot up and covered my mouth. Tears pricked my eyes. I felt I knew these people; they looked so familiar, yet at the same time, they were strangers.

'Magnificent, isn't it?' Neil Davidson's voice cut into my dreamlike stupor.

'What? Oh, yes. Who are they? Do you know?' I turned and gawped again at the first picture, my mouth open, eyes wide. Suddenly self-conscious, I shut my mouth.

'They, Ms White, are Adalicia and Richard Boulais-Hamilton. Your great-great-grandparents.' My mouth fell open again.

Jesus!' I studied the faces, the features of each Boulais-Hamilton. Adalicia – gosh! *Was this beauty really my blood relative?* It was unbelievable. Yet I could see without a doubt that she bore some resemblance to my poor, dear mother, at least in the colouring. My mum, who had never experienced the fine quality of life that these people had obviously enjoyed, had lived frugally and worked hard all her life to take sole responsibility for me, her only child. *Oh Mum!* The contrast between my mother's simple, but difficult life and the splendour of Adalicia and Richard's lives, hit me like a brick. What had happened that she was no longer part of this affluent family? I felt a tear in the corner of my eye and sniffed to eradicate it. *Get a grip woman! No tears in front of these two blokes!*

'Boulais-Hamilton? So, one of them was French, then?' I asked neither one in particular.

'Yes, Adalicia was French,' Craig said. 'Your great-great-grandfather, Richard Hamilton,' he pointed to the painting, 'was English. But she was French.'

And she was stunning too. Sleek, black hair, neatly styled, swept off her face and piled high up on her head. There was a thin, straight nose, high cheekbones, strong jaw and neat, delicate chin. Dazzling blue eyes looked out directly at me beneath an elegant brow and long, straight black eyelashes. A hint of a sweet, warm smile rested on her lips.

'She looks –' I was unable to finish the sentence. I pressed my lips together and turned away, in the hope of stopping the tears that threatened to escape and run, unchecked, down my cheeks.

'Just like you, Laura.' I turned at the sound of Craig's quiet voice behind me.

'What - ?'

'Adalicia looks just like you.' Craig was gazing intently at me and I can tell you now my hormones were racing. *I mean, honestly, a man has no business being so bloody distractingly good-looking! His very presence set my heart pumping faster. It's just not fair! (Especially when he's probably fifteen years my junior...)*

'Yes, I too, can see the resemblance, Ms White. And why not? You are a direct descendent of Adalicia. There is bound to be a – ' Neil Davidson interrupted my chemically induced internal ramblings.

'I was going to say she looks like my mum, actually.'

A scratching sound interrupted the discussion. My eyes moved to the corner of the room, where a mouse scuttled along the skirting board and behind the floor-to-ceiling burgundy velvet curtains that dressed the glazed French doors. The French doors led to a patio, mottled with patches of green moss and beyond were the far-reaching views of the garden and land.

'*He'll* have to go,' I remarked, referring to the rodent inhabiting the drawing room of Hamilton Hall. 'Otherwise I'll be charging him rent!'

Craig chuckled and Neil Davidson twitched his nose and cleared his throat. 'The local council pest control department will deal with that for you, I'm sure, Ms White,' he offered, not unhelpfully.

I turned my attention back to the portrait of my ancestors and regarded my great-great-grandfather. It was an odd feeling, looking at the only male relative I'd ever come across, and there he was, his image resplendent in oil and surrounded by a gilt-edged frame. Unlike Adalicia, my Mum and indeed myself, he had curly hair, and not black, like the three of us, but a fading yellow blond colour, greying at the temples. Despite his still thick thatch, he looked older than Adalicia, by some ten years at the very least, and where her expression was soft, his was stern. I'd put him at early fifties in this painting, but his wife looked younger; late thirties or forty at the most. About my age, in fact, I realised, with some fascination. It was a weird sensation, looking into the eyes of these two very grand and dignified relatives, from several generations back, and me, probably, the same age now as Adalicia was then.

I walked over to the French doors and gazed out onto the generously sized grounds. The grass was vibrant green, testament to all the rainfall this summer, and it was overgrown. It stretched for what seemed miles, but could probably be measured in hectares. I could see the huge trees I'd noticed from the front drive, copper beech, oak, cedar, and the feeling of substance and continuity swept over me again. Hamilton Hall was mine. I stopped a sob. Perhaps I should have brought Kitty with me to view the house. I could have done with the emotional support of a good mate, as I viewed the house that was to become my home. For this was, indeed, my new home. I knew that now. I had not even seen the rest of it, but knew instinctively that I absolutely could not sell Hamilton Hall. I had no idea where the dosh would come from but I would find a way. Somehow. The anticipation of raising the funds for renovation overwhelmed me and I shook my head as if to dismiss the worry.

8: July 1940
Wymondham

Martha:

The full moon lights my way as I gather my bicycle from the old stable and race down Primrose Lane that leads to the drive of Hamilton Hall, on the outskirts of Wymondham. The still-warm evening breeze blows my long hair behind me and I am filled at once with a mixture of anxiety and thrilling anticipation.

Ahead I see the MG parked on the grass verge, next to the hollow tree, where we always rendezvous. My heart leaps as I approach and see Flying Officer Charles Harwood, resplendent in his RAF blue, throw his cap onto the seat and alight from the car. I jump off the bicycle, throw it onto the grass and run straight into his arms. He covers my face with kisses before finding my mouth, searching it with his tongue. I feel his fingers running through my hair, his hands find my waist, my hips, my buttocks, before cupping my breasts. I wince in pleasurable pain and move his hands away.

'Don't, Charles. We mustn't – not here.'

'I haven't stopped thinking about you for a moment,' he says, now looking straight into my eyes, holding my face in his hands. 'My glorious raven-haired beauty.' He kisses me again, full on the mouth and our tongues find each other again.

We pull away from each other and I finger the pilot wings badge sewn above the left breast pocket of his jacket.

'Where have you been? Were you at Dunkirk? We read about it in the newspaper. Can't you tell me, Charles? I worry about you so much.'

'Darling, you know I can't.' His brow wrinkles into an expression of sincere concern, his gaze soft. 'It's very hush-hush. I could get shot for divulging secrets.' He gives me a lopsided grin and I know that it is in an effort to lighten the mood.

'I wouldn't tell anyone. I just know I would feel better knowing where you were and what you were doing.'

'My love, you are better off not knowing anything. But I promise you, I know what I am doing, I am highly trained in my job and I will always come back safely to you.' He kisses me again, this time gently, softly, on my forehead. I love it when he kisses my head like that. It always gives me a warm feeling and makes me smile.

But this time, through my smile, tears fill my eyes and I am suddenly sobbing.

'Oh Charles, I cannot bear it; all the uncertainty. This bloody awful war. I'm terribly proud of you, but I'm so frightened that something will happen to you. I don't know what ... '

'Don't talk like that, my love. I am here now and when this war is over we will be together for always.' He wipes my tears with his thumbs and kisses me again, harder, with more passion and urgency than I've ever felt from him. We stand there hugging each other tightly, Charles towering above me from his height of six feet and two inches, as he bends to envelope me.

'Come on. Let's go for a drive. We've just got time to get down to the Green Dragon for a quick drink before they call time. Hop in!' He pats my bottom and, recovering rapidly from my raw emotions, I squeal with delight as I climb into the vehicle before Charles starts the engine and the old sports car rattles down Primrose Lane and into the night.

'You've not been out with Charles tonight, have you?' Emily shuts my bedroom door behind her. I shoot her a look. 'Oh, please don't say anything, Em. I haven't seen Charles for absolutely weeks and I found a note from him this morning in the hollow tree. I'd looked in our hiding place for word from him every day for weeks and finally today ... We could only meet for an hour or so, but at least it was something.'

'You've been reading too many Brontë novels!' Emily refers to my frequent visits to the library to lose myself in the literary classics.

'This is sheer lunacy.' Emily isn't giving up. 'You know Daddy will never agree to your marrying Charles. I just don't want you ending up getting hurt, Martha. You are playing with fire, you know,' she lowers her voice to a whisper, 'and if Mummy and Daddy find out...'.

'Well, they haven't yet and you won't tell them, will you? Please Emily darling. Please. I can't give him up. I need to be with him. Promise you won't tell them.'

Emily regards me through lowered eyelids. 'You're all right, aren't you Martha?'

'Yes, of course,' I say. I know exactly what she means. 'Now just let me get ready for bed and leave me in peace. I'm quite exhausted.'

9: Summer, 2013
Hamilton Hall

Laura:

I heard a little cough behind me. 'Shall we look at the rest of the house, Laura?' It was Craig, touching my elbow softly. It felt divine. I was still in the drawing room, gazing out onto the garden. I ran my hand along the edge of one of the velvet curtains, and a dust cloud escaped. I clung on for a while, scrunching it tightly. I lifted the fabric to my face and closed my eyes, staying like that for a moment. This is mine. Hamilton Hall belongs to me. Little Old Laura White! *Yippee!!*

'Yes, sure, let's take a look. Let's see ...' I walked purposefully towards the door, and the two men followed. 'Where next?'

'Well, there's an inner hall, and then a dining room.' Neil Davidson moved in front of me and held open the door of the drawing room. He followed me out, along with Craig. We proceeded through the reception hall and into an inner hall that led to a dining room, which was nearly as big as the drawing room. Like the inner hall, the dining room had stone flag flooring. The walls were half panelled in mahogany and above a dado rail they were papered in thick, embossed paper, that I imagined was once cream coloured, and was now curling at the corners as it came away from the plaster. The large sash windows were dressed in dark green curtains, held back by silken rope tiebacks. A large, oval mahogany table stood on top of a dark green Chinese rug in the middle of the room, with twelve matching chairs placed around it. Neil was describing the details but I wasn't really listening. My eye caught an interesting piece of furniture positioned in the corner of the room and I walked over to take a look. It was a cabinet of some kind. Just like the mantelpieces in the drawing room, it was thick with dust. I ran my fingers over its top and observed the marquetry. There was a beautiful inlaid wood design of roses on the doors. I opened these and realised I was looking at an old-fashioned wireless. I was transported back in time to an era when there were no television sets or devices such as Smartphones or iPads to rule the evenings, but people listened to the wireless or played the piano or read books. Or they spent their time talking to each other. Proper conversations. No 'text speak' in those days, but real, face-to-face conversations. I moved over to the fireplace that still had the remaining ashes of a log fire in the grate. Cobwebs adorned the inside corners of the hearth. Above the mahogany mantelpiece was another oil painting. This was a depiction of two girls, one slightly taller than the other. They looked to be in their early to mid-teens. The older one was blonde, with shoulder length curls, the smaller girl had the same facial features and sleek, straight black hair of Adalicia. The girls' hair was styled with a side parting and a hairclip that kept it off the face. Both wore identical navy-blue twin sets over grey, box-pleated skirts.

'Emily and Martha,' said Neil Davidson.

'The daughters of Adalicia and Richard,' I said. It wasn't a question.

I walked towards the door, eager to explore further. Through the inner hall with stone flag flooring and wood panelling I spotted another door, which apparently led to a cellar. Neil switched on a light at the entrance.

'The electricity is connected! *Great!*'

'Yes, we had it connected for the viewing, and if you do move in, obviously, you'll need it – no point in having it disconnected,' said Neil.

I descended the stone steps and caught the musty smell and row upon row of wine racks. Amongst the empty grooves, I found wine bottles – dozens and dozens of them - thickly coated with dust and cobwebs. I lifted one and blew on it. Clouds of dust mushroomed upwards. *Crikey!* How old was this? Was it even drinkable? I replaced it and patted my hands together to get rid of the dirt. Through a grubby window, I could just make out the garden: grass and shrubs at eye level, and the bottom of tree trunks were also visible from this depth. I shivered, realising I was underground, and turned, ascended the steps and walked across the inner hall again. I opened another door to find a cloakroom with a stone floor and one of those high-level flushing toilets, and an ornate wash hand basin, with scalloped edge. The brass taps were mottled with green water stains and a river of green water damage ran down the basin and towards the plug hole. Instinctively, I pulled on the toilet chain and with a clunk the loo actually flushed.

'Oh, the water's on, as well! Good!' I strode across the inner hall to another door.

Neil read: 'Ah, the Butler's Pantry!' *Butler's pantry? Just like Downton Abbey! Fancy that!*

'I like this,' I said, observing a piece of furniture inside the room.

'It's a Victorian dresser,' Craig said. It had cupboards and a glass fronted cabinet with sliding doors, which I tried out. There was an odd china cup and saucer and silver condiments set inside, along with some assorted silver cutlery. I picked up a tablespoon and stroked the handle and felt myself again taken back to an earlier period in history and wondered what stories this implement could tell, were it able to talk.

I left the pantry and moved along briskly to another door, the two men following on my heel, and as I opened it, Neil read out the description from the brochure details: *Morning Room with French doors to rear terrace.* A 'morning room'? Whatever's a morning room? One that's only used in the morning, perhaps? Bizarre. I walked over to the French doors and peered out. Again, I could see the great centuries-old trees, shrubs and neglected lawns beyond. Excitement grew inside me. I felt elevated and thrilled and shivered with anticipation of what else I might discover. Already, in my mind, I was planning what I could do with each room. *If only I had the money.*

Next, we came across another room with a fireplace with stone surround and what looked like a wood burning stove. I wondered what the Boulais-Hamiltons used this room for? There was some shelving, and floor-to-ceiling sash windows dressed with thick, beige curtains and another deep, curved, bay window with views to paddocks and beyond. To the side, I could see the stables I'd noticed earlier, with the upper part of the stable door swinging on one hinge. There was a wooden ranch fence separating the garden from the paddocks. I was enchanted. I was breathless. In an otherworldly state, somehow detached from the real world. Yesterday I was worrying about not paying the milkman; today I was viewing a manor house that apparently belonged to me. Barely habitable, yes, but nonetheless, mine.

10: 22ⁿᵈ August 1940
Hamilton Hall

Emily:

'You can't stop me seeing him, Daddy! You can't! We love each other and when this war is over we are going to be married. You can't stop us! You can't!' I could hear Martha sobbing through the words that she screamed. I was tidying and weeding in the garden, just beyond the open French windows that looked out from the drawing room. I could have heard my sister's piercing cries a mile away. I had tried to warn her about Charles and her clandestine little trysts, but my darling little sister, as lovable as she is, can be so headstrong and sometimes there's just no reasoning with her.

'Come now, *ma chérie, calmes-toi*. You'll make yourself ill, taking on so.' Mother's soothing voice was having some of the desired effect on my sister, but Father was still furious.

'You defied me, Martha! You deliberately defied me. This will not do! You cannot be seen to be going about with that good-for-nothing.' Father's words set her off again.

'But Daddy. He's an RAF officer. He's from a good home and he loves me, he really does. Just because he doesn't work in a bank –'

'Enough, child! Now go to your room and reflect on your shameful behaviour.'

'But Daddy –'

'No more, Martha! Don't argue with me. I am your father and while you live in this house, under my roof, you will obey me.'

'I hate you! I hate you Daddy!' And with that, I heard Martha storm out of the room and race up the winding stairs, no doubt two at a time as usual, and into her bedroom, where I could just imagine her slamming the door behind her.

'Don't be so hard on her, my dear.' I could hear Mother, as always, trying to defuse the situation. 'She is young and she is in love. You and I were like that once.'

'We never crept out of the house in the middle of the night and brought shame on our families. Your parents would have been furious, Adalicia, had we behaved like that. And quite rightly so. But no. I respected you. We waited till our wedding night –'.

I blinked and looked away. My parents' love life was not something I cared to think about.

'Come, come now, my darling Richard. We don't know that the young man has harmed our daughter in any way. The postmistress was just saying they were seen in the pub together. What's so terrible about that?'

'In the pub! The pub! With all the local riff-raff! My God! The shame! The embarrassment!'

My mother wrapped her arms around Daddy and held him lightly. 'My darling, this war has changed everything. Upper classes are serving in the armed forces alongside those from the lower classes. It has broken through class barriers, as men from different social backgrounds fight and die together. We do not know much about this young man, I realise that. But we should trust that he is a good man for two reasons: our little Martha loves him, and he is serving in the RAF, fighting for our country. That is very honourable, no?' I could see the expression on Daddy's face through the open French window: brooding and obstinate.

As she held him, Mother stroked his back and then stood back, looking into his face. 'Try to be a little understanding, my dear. Of course, you and I waited until our wedding night, but you are twelve years older than I, and times were different then.'

If ever I were to fall in love and marry, it would be a marriage like that of my parents I should hope for. Although Father was very stern and conservative, and Mother his polar opposite, they complemented each other so perfectly; so utterly and completely.

'It's the deceit, I find impossible to accept, Adalicia. She deliberately went behind my back to meet this bounder.'

'Now, now, Richard, my dear.' Mother's voice and the lilt of her French accent had a soothing quality and the desired effect. 'We do not know that he is – how you call him – a bounder. He might be perfectly nice and *agréable*. Let's not make this a bigger mountain than a molehill.'

Peeping from behind the wisteria, I could see that Daddy had softened. Mother's rare linguistic errors always made him melt, even in the most heated of situations and after all these years of marriage. Taking Mother's face in his hands, he kissed both her cheeks, his breathing levelling out, his frown turning to a hint of a smile.

'We will talk about it again when she has calmed down. Now, we must prepare for our trip to London tomorrow and the theatre. I want our silver wedding anniversary to be one to remember.' I saw Daddy pinch Mother's cheek, heard him chuckle slightly then turn serious again.

'But my dear, we cannot let Martha get away with deceiving us and bringing shame and embarrassment on the family name. And when she has reflected on her behaviour and calmed down, we will talk again.'

Oh dear. This little problem was not going to go away so easily. Oh Martha. Martha. Martha. What are we to do with you?

'Emily. Are you eavesdropping?' Father's voice startled me.

'No Daddy. Just tidying the flower beds and wisteria, that's all.' And with that, I picked up the flower basket and secateurs

I'd left lying on the lawn and proceeded to the flowerbeds to pick a bouquet. A sweetly scented arrangement in the drawing room might lift the family mood.

11: Summer, 2013
Hamilton Hall

Laura:

I just had to see the rest of the house. Every square inch of it. Without a word, I left the room and strode across the reception hall to the bottom of the splendid, mahogany winding staircase, the two men hot on my heels. I held onto the dusty bannister with my left hand and took the first step. The stairs were bare wood, whatever carpet there might have been had long gone. I took each step slowly, looking around me as I ascended what was, despite the lack of stair covering, the grandest staircase I'd ever seen in my life. And this was my staircase, in my house. All mine. At the top of the stairs, the landing went both ways, to the left and to the right. I took the right. Behind me, Neil Davidson started reading from the brochure again. I wasn't really listening properly, but I caught his description of the first floor having a landing with stairs to a second floor. Later. Later. I'd look up there later. Because I'd spied an open door leading to a beautiful, huge bedroom with floor-to-ceiling sash windows looking out onto countryside views.

'There are wardrobe cupboards and an original Victorian grate, Ms White. And here is the bathroom, it's en-suite. Take a look.' Neil Davidson sounded more like an estate agent trying to grab a sale in the bag rather than the lawyer appointed to deal with my inheritance. He was beginning to get on my nerves – anybody would think he was the owner of the house, not me! But I shrugged off my irritation and walked into the bathroom to find a room the size of my bedroom at home, with a high-level WC, wash hand basin, with scalloped edges just like in the loo I'd seen downstairs, and a huge freestanding bath. I found myself fantasising about luxuriating in a warm bubble bath, sipping champagne and having my back washed by a gorgeous - *Oh get a grip woman!*

The first few chords of *Beethoven's Fifth* blasted into my thoughts. Neil Davidson muttered and grunted as he lifted his iPhone from his jacket pocket and hurried out of the bathroom. I could hear his side of the conversation: 'Yes, yes, love. No, no of course I hadn't forgotten. Yes, yes, I'm on my way. See you shortly.' He came back to the bathroom door.

'I'm so sorry, Ms White. I'm afraid I have to go. Craig? Can I give you a lift back to your car?' Neil Davidson looked with raised, enquiring eyebrows at us both. Just like that? He gets a phone call and he thinks he can just swan off and leave me there like yesterday's leftovers?

'Hang on a minute. I haven't seen the rest of the house yet.' All right, so he obviously had a family commitment more pressing than showing a mansion house to its new, impoverished owner, but this was a bit much. Bet he wouldn't treat a posh, wealthy client so dismissively. Craig came to the rescue.

'If you need to go, Neil, that's fine. I can finish the viewing with Ms White and perhaps, Laura,' Craig said, looking straight into my eyes with those captivating steel grey ones of his, 'you wouldn't mind giving me a lift back to town in your car?' *Not in the slightest.*

Neil Davidson handed the keys to me and gave the brochure to Craig and took his leave, closing the front door behind him. I could hear his car engine starting and the wheels spinning on the gravel drive.

'Right. Shall we carry on?' We moved to another spacious room with wall-to-wall bookshelves. There really was a library! An upstairs library, like it said in the brochure! How classy is that? I ran my fingers along the book spines, like the keys on a piano, and dust sprinkled to the floor. The books were arranged in alphabetical order by author name and I soon found Jane Austen and the Brontë sisters. I slipped a green Austen volume out from its resting place and turned the pages. I loved the musty smell and the slightly browned edges of the pages. I replaced the book and took another. So very old, and yet these classics had survived the decades. I imagined my ancestors sitting in this library on rainy afternoons, reading these very books. I returned Jane Austen to the shelf and as I did so, I noticed another book, somehow out of keeping with the others. It was small and had a dark blue cover with gold markings on the spine. I lifted it out and turned the pages to find strange looking characters written throughout. Craig noticed my puzzled expression.

'What is it Laura?' I handed the book to him.

'How interesting.' He flicked through the pages. 'It's filled with shorthand writing. Curious!' He smiled, handing the book back to me and I shrugged and returned it to the shelf. I smiled at Craig and we continued to explore my inheritance, and as I happened upon each delightful detail of the house, with every room's viewing came the realisation that what I'd acquired was a superior little money-pit. There would be so much work to do in order to make it habitable. And that would cost money. Money, I just did not have. Yet even so, as the moments passed, the conviction that I wanted to keep the house became all the more emotionally overpowering, alongside the knowledge that I had not a hope in hell of finding the means to renovate and maintain it. The dilemma sat heavily on my mind. My stomach growled with hunger.

'Oh! Time marches on! I must get something to eat. Can we possibly come back again another time, Craig? I'd really love to see all of the house before I go home, but I'm starving now.'

'Sure. Let's go back into Wymondham and let me treat you to a bite to eat. I have some things to go over with you to do with the inheritance paperwork and you have some decisions to make. Do you like Indian food? There's a great little restaurant called *India Village*.' He glanced at his watch. 'It's just after six now so I think they're open. We shouldn't have any trouble getting a table at this time of the evening.'

'OK, sounds great.'

'Or there is an excellent Moroccan restaurant – the *Marrakesh*, I believe it's called – oh, but hang on – ' he looked at his watch – 'it doesn't open until seven. What about the Indian place? Can I tempt you?' *Not half!*

'Yes! I'm ravenous. Indian please, as it's already open. Let's go.' We left the house and I locked up behind us, patting the doorframe affectionately before I searched in my bag for the keys to Esther the Fiesta.

Ah yes. Esther, my (un)trusty Fiesta. Of all the times to refuse to start, Esther really picked her moments. I tried the key in the ignition five times. Nothing. I glanced at Craig apologetically as I reached for my mobile and tapped in the number of the vehicle rescue guys. I really got my money's worth out of the annual premium. I must be their best customer. Or perhaps I was their worst, depending on how you looked at it.

Forty minutes later, Jason, the friendly AA mechanic was shaking his head and sucking air through his teeth like a plumber about to give you an extortionate price for simple job.

'Fuel pump. Kaput I'm afraid. Completely wrecked. This is the fourth time in as many months you've called us out Laura. Perhaps it's time to think about replacing the old girl.' It was true. I'd seen Jason himself twice recently, both times requiring a home start, which resulted in me being late for my shift at the care home. And he was right: there had been two other occasions in recent months when I'd called for assistance.

'How much is a fuel pump going to cost me, Jason?' I was doing arithmetic in my head and as usual my sums were not looking good.

'A hundred and fifty. Plus, VAT and labour at the garage. But then there'll be something else going wrong, so I'd seriously consider investing in a new vehicle.' Happy news.

12: 23rd August 1940
Hamilton Hall

Emily:

'Martha, you can't stay in your room all day. Come down and have some breakfast and say goodbye to Mummy and Daddy. They're leaving this morning for London. Come on, Martha, you can't stay here forever. Don't spoil their anniversary weekend.'

My sister had not left her room since yesterday's row over Charles. Now she was curled up on her bed filling her head with romantic nonsense from her current favourite Brontë book, *Wuthering Heights*.

'Not likely, Em! Daddy was beastly to me yesterday and he will never change his stupid mind about Charles. But I'll show him! I won't speak to him ever again. This is 1940 not 1840! And I am going to marry Charles. We only have to wait two years and then I'll be twenty-one no one can stop us. No one!' Martha's eyes shone with rage and defiance. I could see I was on a mission to nowhere and left her to it.

Breakfast with my parents that morning was a quiet affair. I tried to make light-hearted conversation, but there was a definite tension in the atmosphere and Father looked as though he'd not slept much last night. Poor Daddy. He was a good man and a wonderful father and although he was strict and could be severe, he really only wanted the best for us. Martha had complained that she'd always felt he favoured me over her, but if she'd only behave herself he wouldn't have to scold her so often. I finished eating, excused myself from the table and went to join Carter in the greenhouse. Harry Carter had been the gardener at Hamilton Hall since before my parents were married, so Martha and I had known him and his wife, Doris, who helped out in the house, all our lives. I always found helping Carter, in particular looking after the vegetables and the flowers, worthwhile and rewarding and I learned a lot from him. As a child, I had delighted in planting tomato plants and watching them grow and turn red in the sun. Eating fresh produce from the garden was one of life's most satisfying experiences. As the war progressed, home-grown food was becoming more of a necessity. Today, helping Carter was a welcome break from the strained atmosphere in the house over the past couple of days.

'Another bootiful day, Miss Emily.' Carter greeted me with his broad Norfolk drawl. 'Days like this it's hard to imagine there's a war going on.'

'Yes, Carter. Beautiful weather, but there's a bit of a battle going on indoors, I'm afraid.' Carter looked at me and raised his bushy eyebrows.

'My little sister is as stubborn as a mule. What are we to do with her?' I sighed and shrugged my shoulders. I really thought Martha had gone too far this time. Refusing to eat breakfast with the family or to speak to our parents was just frightful. I couldn't remember being so rebellious when I was nineteen.

'Ah, she's a rum un, is Miss Martha, and that's the truth. But she'll grow out o'that, you'll see. Our Lizzie was a bit of a tearaway when she was that age, but she's married with 'er own family now and me and the missus, well, we couldn't be more proud.'

'Apparently, my sister was seen with a certain RAF officer in the Green Dragon last week and it got back to my parents. They are not best pleased, Carter, I can tell you.'

'Ah, she's only a young un, Miss Emily. You mark my words: she'll be all right when she's got a couple more years on 'er. There's worse things going on in the world these days than a young lady going in a pub. In grand scheme o'things, what with this war - '

'Oh. Mummy and Daddy will be ready to leave. I must drive them to the station. Sorry to interrupt, Carter, but 'I'll be right back, and we can carry on here.'

As my parents got into the car, I glanced up to see Martha looking down through the window, her face half hidden behind her bedroom curtains. She moved away when she realised I'd seen her.

'Don't worry about Martha, Mummy. Daddy.' I looked at each of them in turn as we stood on the platform. The approaching train was slowing down to a halt. 'I'll keep an eye on her and I'm sure she'll be in a better frame of mind when you get back. Just enjoy yourselves at the theatre and we'll see you on Sunday.

Despite Martha's recalcitrance, I wanted to wish Mother and Father a happy anniversary for tomorrow and a wonderful time in London. And I'd planned a special wedding anniversary surprise dinner party for their homecoming on Sunday. I only hoped that Martha would be in a better mood by then.

Late that night, I watched from my bedroom window, as Martha took the bicycle from the old stable and pushed it down the path, then quickly straddled it and rode away into the darkness, the skirt of her pale blue dress ballooning behind her like a parachute. I opened the window and called after her, but it was futile. My words fell silently into the dead of the night.

I slept fitfully, dreaming of planes roaring and bombs dropping, fires, parachutes floating through the skies and little fishing boats filled with injured soldiers. At five in the morning, I woke to the distinctive sound of a rattling car belonging to a certain Flying Officer Charles Harwood. I heard the old stable door clicking shut and my little sister's footsteps crossing the gravel path to the house.

13: Summer, 2013
Hamilton Hall

Laura:

'A hundred and fifty pounds? I haven't got that kind of money. Are you sure you can't fix it for me now, Jason? I've got to get back to Suffolk at the weekend. I'm back at work on Monday. Surely you can do something?'

'Sorry, Laura.' The AA mechanic was shaking his head emphatically, his fatty jowls swinging from side to side. 'Absolutely no way I can fix a dead fuel pump love. You need a new one, no doubt about it.'

Oh great. That was all I needed. I had no idea what I was going to do now. I looked at Craig, who was raking his fingers through his hair.

'Tell you what, Laura. I'll get us a taxi back into town and we can sort out the fuel pump in the morning. Don't worry. We can work this out.' Craig was looking at me with *those eyes* again. I was torn between wanting to kiss him and wishing a sinkhole would suck me into the ground. I was so embarrassed at my old jalopy letting me down yet again. And now Craig was offering to rescue me. Another humiliation. But what could I do? My stomach was yelling for sustenance. There was nothing else for it.

'OK, thanks Craig.'

He took his phone and moved away a few feet to call a local taxi company, while Jason got on with the business of hooking Esther up to his recovery truck. He handed me a card with the details of the Wymondham *Cando Autocentre*. 'Give them a ring in the morning and they can let you know the damage. But whatever it costs to fix, Laura, you really do need to think about replacing the car.' *Yeah, right, Jason. So you keep telling me.*

A taxi arrived and we hopped in. Still early evening, it was relatively quiet and the exotic aromas emanating from the kitchen assaulted my senses. A smiling, welcoming waiter showed us to a table by the window. My stomach rolled again.

We resumed the conversation we'd had the previous day at my Suffolk cottage, with Craig telling me that he'd studied for his history degree at Sussex University.

'I'm doing an online degree myself,' I said, 'My job as a carer is just to fund my studies. I hope I'm not too old to get a graduate job at the end of it!'

'Wow. That's impressive. You're not just a pretty face, and you're not old, either, Laura!' I'm not a blusher normally, but I felt the blood rush to my cheeks. He seemed not to notice, but I bet he did. My face must have resembled an overripe tomato.

'I think my mum might have been proud. She always wanted me to go to university.'

Craig's face broke into a warm smile, which simultaneously reached his eyes and my lady bits. My head knew that, realistically, there was no chance of anything happening between me and Craig, however, my nether regions seemed to disagree. *Down girl. He's probably half your age!* I took a sip of my iced water in an effort to cool myself down. We continued munching our way through the meal in silence.

Appetite sated, we ordered coffee and Craig reached for his briefcase and showed me some paperwork that introduced me to the Boulais-Hamilton lineage and as he started to point out my relatives on the family tree I felt a definite feeling of connection to these people, who had been, after all, my flesh and blood. I came to realise that all my life I had experienced a feeling of disconnection. Being the only daughter of a single mother meant that I had, up until now, known nothing of any relatives, alive or dead. I touched the name – Adalicia – with my fingertips. Adalicia. What a beautiful name. It almost sang to me. And the image of the beautiful, elegant woman, who was my very own great-great-grandmother, with that spectacular emerald necklace sitting around her neck, became vivid in my mind. Next to Adalicia I read Richard's name, then followed the line down to Emily and Martha. A profound sense of belonging overwhelmed me and I lifted the blue linen napkin to my face to mask my emotions and stem a rogue tear that threatened to fall from my eye. A tear for my dear mum, whose life had been one of hard work and relative poverty, in which she just scraped by from one week to the next. A life, which sat in stark contrast to that of the comfortable Boulais-Hamilton family immortalised in oil and hung in the family home. I couldn't bear to look any further.

'Shall we go, Craig?' I spoke through the napkin, pretending to be wiping my mouth. 'That was a lovely meal. Just what I needed. Thanks. I owe you one.'

'Oh, just feed me some more of your delicious cakes and plum pie, Laura!' He laughed.

The bill paid by Craig, we left the *India Village* and strolled down the main street of Wymondham in comfortable silence. It was getting on for nine o'clock and still light. The warm breeze of summer gently blew my hair off my face. My thoughts kept taking me back to Hamilton Hall and the impossible dilemma of how I could find a way to keep it.

'Laura?' Craig's voice interrupted my thoughts.

'Sorry. What did you say?'

'I could pick you up in the morning, and take you back to finish viewing the house, if that suits you?' His expression soft and earnest; his eyebrows raised in enquiry.

'Oh yes. Thanks Craig. That would be great. Especially as Esther is in the motor hospital.' I gave him a crooked smile. 'But I thought you had another appointment tomorrow morning. Isn't that why we rescheduled the viewing to this afternoon? Because you were double-booked?' I said, remembering his text earlier today.

'Yes. But I think I can work something out. Your viewing was cut short today and I know how keen you are to see the rest of the house before you go home tomorrow.'

We reached the front door of Maggie Middleton's 'Welcome home' B and B and stood facing each other. I was feeling self-conscious again now, not quite sure how to initiate the goodbye, when Craig held out his hand to shake mine.

'Good night, Laura.' His smile was warm, yet his body language made him seem like an awkward teenager. I took his hand in mine.

'Thanks for dinner, Craig. Good night. See you tomorrow. About nine, OK?'

I skipped up the front steps and was startled to find myself face-to-face with Maggie Middleton, standing in the hallway. Her arms folded across her ample bosom, she looked me up and down. If she was trying to intimidate me she was succeeding. I really wouldn't want to rattle the cage of this formidable creature. The encounter of earlier that day flooded my mind. She really was a tricky one: serving homemade lemon cake and coffee one minute and warning me off upsetting the locals the next. The memory of her hand clutching my arm and the warning look in her eye as I left to view the house came to the fore. Was she really trying to frighten me off? Her words from this afternoon returned: *Just be sure to remember that the old place has been here a lot longer than any newcomer...*

'Well now, Miss. And what do you think of your inheritance?' The eyebrows raised, creating deep lines above, the head cocked back, the face unsmiling, as she continued: 'You're not going to sell it to some property developer from London, are you?' *The cheek of the woman!* I felt my anger rise. But there was something about her that made me sure I didn't want to antagonise Maggie Middleton. I thought back to the radio programme about Satanists in Norfolk that I'd listened to in the car on the drive up to Wymondham earlier today. An image of me suddenly experiencing inexplicable stabbing pains all over my body, while, somewhere in Norfolk, a certain rotund landlady, stuck needles into a doll that looked a lot like me, sprung alarmingly into my mind.

'Oh hello, Maggie. Not made any decisions yet.' *(Not that it's any of your bloody business, madam!)* 'Good night.' And with that I grabbed the bannister and took the stairs two at a time, shutting my room door firmly behind me and turning the key in the lock.

My heart was pounding in my chest, but whether that was the effect of the flight up the stairs or Maggie Middleton, I wasn't sure.

My eyes scanned the room and rested on my laptop.

OMG! OM-bloody-G! My assignment. I'd forgotten all about it. I hadn't finished my assignment and my tutor had been adamant she was not going to grant me another extension. It had to be submitted electronically by nine in the morning. There was nothing for it. I was going to have to pull an all-nighter. I sat on the bed, pulled the laptop towards me, and typed in my password.

14: Saturday, 24th August 1940
Hamilton Hall

Emily:

I arose early to the sound of the birds singing in the cedar tree outside my bedroom window. I felt less than refreshed from my night's sleep, disturbed, as it had been, by the not unusual nightmares I'd had about the war. Despite trying to maintain a positive outlook, for the sake of my parents and Martha mainly, I did harbour deep fears about how it would all end. No wonder I had bad dreams. A lot of people must have had them too. And then of course at dawn I'd been woken by the sound of my errant little sister returning from her nocturnal assignation with Charles Harwood. What on earth was to be done about Martha?

With a sigh, I slipped into my dark red, velvet dressing gown and pulled on my slippers. It was going to be another exquisitely warm, sunny day, I could tell, even at this early hour. I made for the kitchen, prepared some tea and toast and sat down at the highly scrubbed table. I smiled to myself as I thought of Doris, our much-appreciated domestic help, rigorously scrubbing the table with hot water and soapsuds, sleeves rolled up to her elbows, cotton overall wrapped around her, crossed over at the front and tied at the back. She took a proprietorial approach to her work. Viewing her housekeeping duties as a personal mission, she carried them out like a military operation and with a great deal of pride. She kept the modest flint house down the lane on the edge of Hamilton Hall, that she shared with Carter and their family, equally pristine.

I reached for my list and took up my pencil, ticking off the tasks I had already completed. I wanted tomorrow's surprise dinner party to be perfect for my parents' silver wedding anniversary. They deserved it. I headed for the dining room and opened the sideboard cupboard, taking out the white damask tablecloth, shaking it out. It would need pressing again and I would get Doris to take care of that. I checked the white matching napkins and placed them on top of the sideboard with the tablecloth, for Doris to press. I opened the drawer of the sideboard and took out six white candles, placing them in the candelabra in the centre of the table. I found the Sunday best cutlery set, and opened the lid of the box. The silver would need to be polished again before tomorrow and I made a note to do that myself. I would enjoy sitting at the kitchen table, working on the silver and chatting with Doris while she pressed the table linen. It was to be a small dinner party, twelve in number, including Mother and Father, Martha and me. The dinner, apart from the leg of lamb Doris and Carter had somehow managed to miraculously acquire (it was prudent that I didn't ask questions!) was all from the garden, grown by Carter and myself. I would help Doris in preparing the meal, but knew that she would insist on doing all the cooking herself. Doris's culinary skills were another source of great pride to her. I stepped out of my slippers and pulled on my wellingtons, that I'd left at the kitchen door the day before (Mother always chastised me for treading dirt through the house), and wandered into the garden to choose the flowers that I'd planned to make into a striking arrangement to adorn the centre of the dinner table tomorrow. I checked on the rosemary bush; Doris would want some of the herb for the lamb tomorrow. The mint was growing in abundance in various parts of the garden.

 I sat on the garden bench, turning my face to the morning sun, and thought of my parents in London, relaxing in the elegant hotel and enjoying the theatre. I wondered if the fine London restaurants experienced a shortage of provisions due to the war, like other parts of the country were experiencing. I imagined Mummy's and Daddy's surprised faces as they returned to the house and found eight guests waiting for them, along with me and with Martha too, if she'd stopped sulking by then. I resolved to speak to her once she deigned to emerge from her slumbers.

15: Summer, 2013
Wymondham

Laura:

Choose file. Submit. Done. 4am.

Not my best work, but at least it was finished and I wouldn't get penalised for a late submission. I set the alarm on my phone for 8am and sunk down into the creaking bed. There were five texts from my friend, Kitty, wanting to know all about the old house, but she'd have to wait. *Sleep, take me into your arms...*

Maggie Middleton was right about the plumbing in this place. There was no hot water left by the time I staggered into the shower at 8.05am. The sound of the *Titanic* theme tune had blasted out of my phone and jolted me out of a fitful sleep punctured with dreams of grand libraries, wine cellars, imposing staircases, pinpricks and effigies. I boiled the kettle and used the water to have a strip wash, cleaned my teeth, had a cup of tea while I quickly dressed and grabbed my overnight bag. Dragging open the stiff, heavy fire door of my room, I found myself once again face to face with Satanic Woman herself. *Sugar. I was hoping to slip away quietly.*

'Morning, Maggie! Thanks for everything. Must dash now. Places to go. People to see.'

'What about your breakfast?'

'Oh, that's OK, thanks. Got a breakfast meeting with someone before I head off home. Nice room, Maggie. Enjoyed my stay. Byeee.' I called over my shoulder as I hotfooted it down the stairs and out of the front door.

I scanned the street and spotted 'The Coffee Shop' fifty metres down, with a breakfast menu board on the pavement outside. I headed straight for it. An old-fashioned bell rang over the door, announcing my entrance to the proprietors. Inside, shelves were filled with quaint old teapots and coffee pots and framed watercolour paintings of local scenes adorned the walls: Wymondham's sixteenth century church and the town's market square; Norwich Cathedral; the North Norfolk coastline. Tables and chairs were mismatched and crockery was odd, adding to the charm of the place. I sat at a table by the window and ordered a large coffee, chocolate croissants, fruit and yogurt, then fished my phone out of my bag. A quick text to Craig:

> Checked out of B & B. Having breakfast in The Coffee Shop. Join me here?

Then I took out the garage's business card that Jason had given me yesterday and dialled the number. Line engaged. Bugger.

A folded-up newspaper lay on the empty table next to mine and I reached over for it, hoping the coffee and food would not be long. The bell over the door sounded as the place began to fill up.

The smiling waitress, a kindly woman in her mid-fifties, with fair, wavy hair, streaked with grey, brought my breakfast before I'd had the chance to read beyond the front-page headlines of the local rag. The doorbell clanged again and I looked up to see Craig smiling over at me. That was quick! I'd only texted him a few minutes ago.

'Good morning, Laura. How are you today?' *Actually, ever so slightly wrung out after only four hours' sleep, but thanks for asking, Craig.*

'I'll get myself a coffee and then we can make our way back to the Hall. I've left my car just across the road in the car park, so we can take that. Hopefully your car will be fixed by the time you need to be heading back to Suffolk.'

'I tried to call the garage but the line was engaged. I'll just try again – '

'Oh, have your breakfast first. Plenty of time.' He took the phone from me and laid it on the table, as he fixed me with a smile and those steel grey eyes.

Hamilton Hall loomed ahead as we drove up the gravel drive in Craig's dazzling blue Suzuki jeep and the excitement bubbled up inside me. This time it was me, rather than Neil Davidson, unlocking the solid grey front door. In the kitchen, Craig handed me the brochure taken from his briefcase, which he left on the table.

'Where shall we start?'

I flicked through the brochure and came to the page illustrating the bedrooms. 'Shall we go upstairs?'

I found bedrooms bigger than the whole of the ground floor in my little terraced cottage and en suite bathrooms that would have dwarfed my bedroom. There were dressing rooms with enough space to fit a three-piece suite, along with the wall-to-wall fitted wardrobes. And still playing at the back of my mind: *how can I afford this?* The council tax would probably be equal to my annual salary. But I wanted to keep this house so much. Craig's voice interrupted my thoughts.

'Laura? Are you Okay? You're looking a little pensive if I may say so.'

'I could do with a sit down, actually. Shall we go back down to the kitchen?'

'Yes, of course. I've got some bottles of water in the car. Would you like a drink?'

'Oh, yes, please, Craig. That'd be great.'

We moved towards the stairs and went down to the kitchen. Craig took his car keys from his jacket pocket and made for the front door. I sat at the large pine table in the kitchen. I felt a strong urge to scream out my frustrations, but reined it in. In so many ways, I was incredibly fortunate to have inherited this fabulous house, and the knowledge that it had been passed down through the generations and against great odds, Craig's firm had found me, as the rightful heir, was just overwhelming.

Craig returned and handed me a bottle of water. We sat there unspeaking for a few minutes while I sipped the water then Craig broke the silence.

'Laura. I'm wondering about the book we saw in the library yesterday. The one written in shorthand. A strange find. Might we take another look?'

I got up and walked towards the kitchen door. 'Sure. Why not. I've been wondering about it myself.'

In the library, I reached for the shorthand book and flicked through it again. I handed it to Craig. It meant nothing at all to me. I took a Jane Austen book from the shelf and turned the pages.

'Gosh. This is bloody old. It was published in 1813.'

Craig looked up from the shorthand notebook. 'Can I take a look?' I handed him *Pride and Prejudice* then reached up to take another Austen from the shelf: *Sense and Sensibility*. I heard Craig take a sharp intake of breath. His eyes wide, his mouth too.

'What? *What?*' He didn't reply but carried on flicking through the pages of the book, stroking the spine, running his hands over the hardback cover, then took the other book from me, inspecting that one too.

'For God's sake, Craig! *What?*'

His voice was little more than a whisper. 'Laura. These are rare books.'

'Er, what do you mean? Rare? Everybody's read Jane Austen. How can they be rare?'

'Not in that sense, Laura. No. I mean rare in that they are first editions. And they are in jolly good condition too.'

'So?'

'So, Laura, they are worth a lot of money. And I mean, really, a lot of money. As in, well, this little beauty ...' - he raised *Pride and Prejudice* to eye level – 'is probably worth around fifty thousand.'

'Yeah, right. Pull the other one, Craig. Who'd pay fifty grand for a book?'

'A rare books collector. My uncle – Peter - Dad's brother – he deals in rare books.' He scanned the library, looking up and down, wall to wall. 'And you've got a lot of books in here, Laura. Your money worries could be over. If I'm not very much mistaken, there is a great deal of cash in this very room. And I mean thousands.'

'You mean I could actually keep the house?

16: 6pm, 25th August 1940
Hamilton Hall

Emily:

'Martha. Martha! This cannot carry on. You'll make yourself ill with all this sneaking off in the middle of the night. Get up now!'

My little sister formed a perfectly still mound under the bedclothes, the heavy bedroom curtains still drawn together. I strode across the room and shook her.

'Martha! Wake up now!'

A groan. A slight move. A dark, glossy head bobbed up from under the sheet. 'Oh god. What time is it?' Martha's eyes scrunched up against the dim light of the room.

'It's nearly time to dine, Martha. Mother and Father will be home in an hour. Doris is working away in the kitchen and our guests will be arriving soon.' I walked over to the window and drew back the curtains. The early evening summer light flooded the room and through the window I saw the sun had spread a golden glow over the garden below.

Another groan. 'I won't be joining you, Em. I'm never going to speak to Daddy again. I hate him. Charles and I – '

Anger rose up in my chest. 'Martha! I want to hear no more about Charles and if I see you sneaking off to meet him in the dead of night again I will tell Father. This has been two nights running. You really are too bad, Martha. It is utterly disgraceful behaviour. And Charles really can't have any respect for you if – '

'Oh, shut up Emily! I am nineteen years old and I will see Charles when I want to. Just because you don't have a boy to love you. You're jealous. That's what it is. You're jealous Emily Boulais-Hamilton!'

I felt the sting on the palm of my hand. My sister's head whipped sharply to one side. My hand shot to my mouth. I heard my own gasp before I heard Martha's. Her eyes, wide, glistened with tears. Her hand touched the livid red mark I'd left on her cheek. We stared at each other in shock and disbelief.

I fled the room, descended the stairs and ran into the drawing room, closing the door firmly behind me. I tried to still my erratic breathing and paced the room, wringing my hands. I'd hit my little sister. I'd never been violent in my life and I'd struck my dear Martha. But she could spoil the whole evening by boycotting the anniversary dinner. Doris and I had worked so hard and Martha had not lifted a finger to help. And now she was refusing to join the dinner party. Mummy and Daddy would be so hurt. How could she be so selfish? I was beginning to think Flying Officer Charles-blasted-Harwood must be a cad. He was certainly a bad

16: 6PM, 25TH AUGUST 1940

influence. My sister was playing with fire. She had a good job, working as a shorthand typist at the bank. She had a loving family, a good home. But she could ruin her life. I shrugged as if to shake away the conflict and left the drawing room, moved across the reception hall and into the dining room.

The table looked exquisite. Perfectly set with white damask linen and highly polished silverware, slender white candles to light in the candelabra and plain white porcelain crockery all set off with the vibrant colours of the centre piece flower decoration I'd arranged myself. Doris and I had worked hard on the food preparation and now she had shooed me out of her kitchen so that she could get on with the cooking.

I dared to put my head around the kitchen door as Doris was basting the roasting lamb. Carter was sitting at one end of the kitchen table, drinking tea. The aroma of roasted root vegetables and herbs from the garden played on my senses and for a moment I allowed myself to imagine the pleasure on my parents' faces as they appreciated our efforts for their anniversary celebrations. Except that Martha was going to spoil it all.

'All right, Miss Emily?' Doris's flushed face expressed a look of concern. I suspected she might have heard the altercation with Martha.

'Martha is refusing to come down to dinner. Mother and Father will be so hurt. She's spoiling ev – '

I burst into tears and Doris deftly replaced the roasting lamb into the oven and swept across to me, pulling me into her. 'There, now, Miss Emily, don't take on so. Miss Martha is young and yes, she's a spirited little thing, but she'll grow out o' that.'

She took a muslin cloth from the table and dabbed my wet cheeks. 'There now, Miss. Don't you take on so.'

Carter removed his cap, scratched his head. He rubbed the end of his nose with the palm of his hand and sniffed; something he was in the habit of doing whenever he was unsettled about something.

'But Doris – '

'Oh, but nothin', Miss. You dry your tears and go get ready. Your Ma and Pa and guests'll be here shortly and you don't want them seeing no tears, now do you?'

I snuffled and attempted a thin smile, went up to my room and changed into my bottle green velvet dress, dragged a brush through my hair, dabbed a little *Bourjois Springtime in Paris* perfume behind my ears and slipped my feet into my court shoes. Not a bad effort, but I'd rather be in my Wellington boots any day.

The grandfather clock in the reception hall struck seven.

17: Summer, 2013
Suffolk

Laura:

'You did *what?*' I was sitting with Kitty at her kitchen table, tucking into hot tea and warm plum pie straight from the oven (the plums came from the trees in my little back garden and Kitty and her mum were the grateful beneficiaries of bags full of the bountiful harvest every year). I was bringing her up to speed on my sojourn to Norfolk. The splendid, if neglected, gardens. The magnificent trees, the spacious rooms, the fireplaces, the oil paintings of my ancestors and the rare books in the library. I'd hardly drawn breath since I'd walked in through her front door.

'I kissed his face off.'

And I had. Right there in the library of Hamilton Hall. When Craig had told me the answer to my little cash flow problem lay right there on the bookshelves, I'd felt like I'd just survived a car crash. I mean, was the answer really there, residing in that very house?

'Craig Matthews,' I'd said, 'You're a fucking genius!' And right there and then I took his gorgeous chiselled features (with the sexy full lips and yes, those captivating steel grey eyes) in my hands and kissed the bloody face off him. I mean, what on earth had got into me? *Well, about a hundred thousand quid, for a start, that's what.*

'Laura White! You *Cougar*!' I thought Kitty's jaw was going to lock it was gaping so wide. I slapped her hand playfully and we both giggled and took more bites of plum pie.

'But honestly', I continued, after swallowing another piece of pie, 'one minute I was virtually up a creek full of dung and not a paddle in sight and then the next moment, there was Craig Matthews telling me that I owned a library full of rare books that I could sell to a collector or a dealer and raise shed loads of cash! I mean, what woman wouldn't have kissed him?' Was it really only a couple of days ago, that I'd thought the knock on the door early that morning was the milkman coming to demand payment for two months' worth of milk, and it had turned out to be the heir-hunter?

Through a mouthful of pie, juice running down her chin, Kitty asked, 'So, come on, tell me, what happened? What did he do?'

He ran for it. That's what he did.

I'd heard his footsteps on the stairs and then the sound of a vehicle approaching and I could see from the library window that it was Esther the Fiesta being driven by a stranger. A man in overalls got out of my car and another car was following behind with the name of the garage painted on the bonnet. Craig exchanged a few words with the other two men and swiftly jumped in his jeep, swung it round on the gravel and sped off.

I'd gone to speak to the garage guys and was told that the fuel pump had been fixed, paid for and the car was fit to drive home.

'Who paid for the repair?' I'd asked, only to be told they didn't know, but here was the receipt and all the rest of the paperwork to show that the car was now roadworthy. Then they drove off.

'Jeez, Laura, you couldn't make it up!' Kitty was wiping her chin on a piece of kitchen paper and scraping the last bit of plum pie around her plate, her eyebrows arched.

'I know, but I'm not. It's all as true as I'm sitting here. There were some really odd things happening at Hamilton Hall. Some smarmy git from an estate agent's turned up wanting to negotiate a deal to sell off a bit of the Hall garden to a neighbour and wait till I tell you about my weird landlady at the B and B.' My mind wandered back to Maggie Middleton and her spooky habit of lurking around waiting for me to appear. I described my experiences with the landlady, and with Simon Fancy-pants and Neil Davidson, the lawyer, but tried to avoid any further discussion of Craig. I still couldn't believe I'd done that. Kissed him, I mean. 'Do you think Norfolk people worship Satan, Kit?'

Kitty laughed heartily. 'From what I hear, they do! And Hecate and Herne the Hunter, as well! And they're all high as a kite on mandrake and UKiP! Are you sure you want to go and live up there?'

I had told her about the story I'd listened to in the car driving up to Norfolk, and the noble-spirited old man who had found an old disused Norfolk church almost buried in foliage, and had made it his life's work to restore it, only to be harassed by devil worshipping locals. With Maggie Middleton's words of warning ringing in my ears, I was just wondering if the locals in Wymondham might give me a hard time over Hamilton Hall, when Kitty voiced my very fears.

'You're not worried you'll get the same treatment, are you, if you start doing up the Hall? I was only kidding about Norfolk devil worshippers you know.'

I shrugged and dismissed the very idea. 'Of course not, Kitty! Don't be daft!' But I was.

'So, what are your plans then?' Kitty had got up and put the kettle on again and was waving her purple mug at me. It had a crown and the words *Keep calm and drink tea* on the side. 'More tea?'

I nodded, drank the remaining dregs and pushed the mug across the table towards Kitty.

Kitty Colman had always had something of the sangfroid about her. Unfailingly calm in a crisis and you could always rely on her to spout a few carefully selected words of wisdom whenever the occasion called for it. We had been friends since forever and to me she was the sister I'd never had. She'd started out working for an estate agent, but quickly came to the realisation that there was money to be made as a buy-to-let landlady, and promptly bought her first flat to rent out. Now she owned several rental properties and had long ago given up working for anyone else.

It was Sunday afternoon and we were driving in Esther the Fiesta up the A11 towards Wymondham and Hamilton Hall. I wanted her to see the place I had inherited. And, yes, of course, I couldn't wait to see it again myself.

'Do you think you'll see the heir-hunter again?' I waited until I'd overtaken a lorry on the duel carriageway before I answered. Esther was behaving beautifully. I accelerated and she smoothly and effortlessly left the lorry miles behind. So much for Jason's advice to buy a new car. *Ha!*

'Doubt it. He's done his job now, I think. And why would he want to see a middle-aged woman who'd kissed him inappropriately, anyway?'

'Middle-aged indeed! You're only thirty-eight! How old do you reckon he is?'

'Twenties. Don't really know.' *Oh, Craig Matthews, get out of my head!* 'Anyway, you know me. I don't like to get too involved with blokes.'

And it was true. It was not like me to go all soft over a man, like I did every time I saw or even thought about the heir-hunter. You see, according to Kitty, I'd always been one of what she called 'the world's love rejects'. As soon as I started getting to know a guy I'd get a bit panicky and think it was all going to come crashing down. And of course, then it inevitably did and I'd despatch him unceremoniously from my life. Prophecy neatly fulfilled. Kitty thinks I'm highly intolerant of men *(what me? Intolerant?)*, and she reckons it's something to do with my subconscious and the lack of any male presence in my life as a child. And that bit was true. No father in sight. No grandfather, uncle or brother. No males at all. Just Mum and me. So: in Kitty's opinion, it wasn't any wonder that I always had troublesome relationships with men. No brainer. This was Freudian psychoanalysis, Kitty-style. I thought about the great-great-grandfather whose image in oil hung above the fireplaces in the drawing room of Hamilton Hall. He looked noble, principled and proud and absolutely sure of his high social standing. I imagined him being a stern yet compassionate father. Firm, strict and commanding, yet fair. Any connection between him and myself seemed incongruous, but nonetheless it was fact. I was the direct descendent of Richard Hamilton. I had his blood running through my veins. I wondered what this dignified gentleman would think of his great-great-granddaughter, Laura White.

17: SUMMER, 2013

In no time at all I found myself indicating and turning into the now familiar gravel drive of Hamilton Hall. As I did so, Kitty's voice broke through my contemplations.

'Seems a shame to sell rare books that have been in the family for generations though, don't you think, Laura?'

Kitty's words came out of the blue and shot straight at their intended target. Right, slap bang in the centre of my heart.

18: 25th August, 1940
Hamilton Hall

Emily:

The chimes of the grandfather clock heralded half past seven and I paced the dining room, my hands, sweaty, clasped in front of me. How strange that Mother and Father were not home yet. I unnecessarily adjusted the place names on the table, touched the petals of the roses and tulips and gerberas – *Transvaal daisies*, Carter had proudly called them - in the centre floral arrangement. There was also a sprig or two of lavender for good measure. I tugged gently on the silken robe tieback on the curtains and peered out of the window to the garden. I looked at the painting of Martha and me as schoolgirls on the chimneybreast over the fireplace. I sighed and went to the kitchen. Doris was taking two plum and apple pies out of the oven. She laid them on the kitchen table and looked up at me.

'All right now, Miss Emily?' I could tell she was trying to sound unconcerned and casual, but I knew Doris was well aware that my parents were now more than half an hour late. They'd promised to telephone me from the station so that I could pop down in the car and pick them up.

'I think I'll telephone the station, Doris. It is not like my parents to be late.'

'That's right, Miss. You do that. I expect that train's runnin' a bit late, what with all the disruptions and all these days. Things aren't the same as they used to be, and that's a fact.' She shook her head and raised her eyes to the ceiling. 'Dinner is coming along nicely. That'll all be ready in time, don't you worry.' She wiped her brow with the back of her hand.

Carter had disappeared. Likely in the stables, or tidying up his garden tools in the shed.

'No delays, Miss, no. The London train, no, that's been and gone. That was on time for once.' The Norfolk drawl of the stationmaster's words faded away as I replaced the telephone receiver.

I returned to the kitchen and told Doris. Carter was back from the garden and he exchanged glances with his wife.

'Don't you worry, now, Miss Emily. I can keep the dinner warm and I expect your Ma and Pa'll be on the next train.' There was something unconvincing in her tone, no matter how reassuring the words. 'I can make some tea for the guests if they arrive before your parents get home. Or perhaps they'd like a nice glass o'sherry.'

I went upstairs to Martha's room, tapped lightly on the door. She was sitting on the side of her bed, a look of stubborn defiance swept across her face as she saw me standing there.

18: 25TH AUGUST, 1940

'Martha, I – '

'Get out, Emily! Get out!' These words spat out through clenched teeth.

I took a step towards my sister.

'Martha, no. I am so sorry I hit you. Please – '

'I said get out!' Her eyes blazed at me.

'Martha, Mummy and Daddy are not home yet. I expect they missed the train, so you've got time to bathe and get ready for dinner. Our guests will be here very soon. Oh please, Martha –'

'I told you, Emily. I am not coming down. And why should I care that they missed the train. Just go away and leave me alone.'

She rose suddenly from the bed and moved over to the window, her back stiff and poker straight. Her chin jutted upwards and to one side. Stubborn. Rebellious. Her arms folded across her chest. Recalcitrant.

The grandfather clock chimed a quarter to eight.

19: Summer 2013
Hamilton Hall

Laura:

'Oh my gosh, Laura! It's amazing!'
 I'd parked Esther in front of Hamilton Hall and Kitty had got out of the car and was standing with her eyes on stalks and mouth agape. I pulled the keys to Hamilton Hall out of my bag and walked towards the now familiar grey wooden door. I was coming home. I hesitated and turned to Kitty.

'Actually, come and see the gardens first. The trees are fantastic, Kit.' And I led her round to the back of the house. This was the first time I'd seen the extent of the gardens, apart from looking at them through the drawing room and bedroom windows. I was eager to explore without the presence of the lawyer or Craig.

It had been a warm day with a gentle breeze and the sun still shone, giving the garden a pleasant ambience and adding light and shade to the plants and flowers from the trees. Dappled shadows spread across the lawns, as the sun shone through the leaves and branches of the copper beech tree. We walked over to the old stables and I tugged on the lower half of the door. The upper door swung precariously in the breeze.

'Oh, look at this! A sit-up-and-beg bike!' Kitty was holding the handlebars of an ancient-looking black bicycle with a rotting wicker basket on the front. She tried the rusty bell and it creaked, reluctantly into life. We both laughed.

'I wonder how long that's been here. Looks pre-war, doesn't it?' Kitty said, with a smile.

There were the remains of two horses' stalls and an old, very dirty saddle hung on a rusty nail on the wall. Various corroded garden tools, rakes, a couple of spades and a hoe, were propped up in the corner. It was almost as if they'd been left there while the owner popped home for lunch. And never came back.

'This bike's great, Laura,' said Kitty, trying to wheel it around the stables. The chain fell off, brown and rusty, and swung around the pedals. I chuckled.

'Looks like it's been a long time since anyone rode it,' I said. 'I wonder who it belonged to.'

'Your ancestors, obviously, love. *Duh.*'

'*Smart arse!* Great Aunt Emily was ninety-two when she died in 2010. I can't imagine her riding that thing at her age!' We both laughed again.

'Let's explore the garden.' Kitty leant the old bike against the wall and was talking over her shoulder at me. 'I'd love to see it all.'

We found the remains of a chicken coop; overgrown vegetable patches and an orchard with plum, apple and pear trees.

'Plums! Bloody *plums*!' I squealed. The symmetry. The coincidence. Now I had plum trees growing in *both* my gardens. Here in Hamilton Hall as well as in my little cottage garden in Suffolk. This was so spooky. I shivered. Then I reached up and plucked a fruit from the tree, and another, throwing one to Kitty. We bit into the plums.

'Mmm. I feel like a kid, scrumping!' I said.

'It would only be scrumping if we were stealing. These are your own fruit trees, Laura. All yours.' She beamed at me, her eyes glistening.

We wandered around the gardens, me touching tree trunks, Kitty bending to smell the fragrance of the flowers that, despite the efforts of the progressively growing weeds to choke them, bloomed triumphantly.

We sat down on the long grass underneath the cedar tree and lay our heads back against its thick trunk. Shadows danced around us on the overgrown lawns. It reminded me of us as children, out to play all day during the long summers in Suffolk, dancing around in fields, getting hot and sweaty then resting against some ancient tree in the shade. Kitty's voice cut into my thoughts.

'There's a lot of work to be done in this garden, Laura. What will you do?'

'Don't know yet. Everything has happened so fast. But you're right. I need to get it sorted. Would you – ?'

'Help you?'

'Well I – '

'Course I'll help you! Backbreaking work, but we'll manage. But it will take a long time, what with us both being busy women.'

I leaned over and kissed Kitty's cheek.

'You are such a love!'

'Oh, stop it Laura White! We're mates. We've always been there for each other. You might not have money in the bank but you're not impoverished when it comes to friendship. Let's do it.'

'I'm still wondering about selling some of the books. It would be such sacrilege to get rid of them, but I do so want to keep the house and I have no idea where I'll get the money to renovate it without selling something. I mean the council tax alone - '

'What about selling off some of the land to the neighbour, the one the oily estate agent mentioned to you. Which house is it anyway?'

'I'm guessing it's that place over there.' I pointed to the chimney pot of a house way beyond the copper beech tree, mostly hidden by my wonderful arboretum. 'But I don't really know. One thing is for sure though, I am not going to sell off any of my land to him or anyone else! Come on, let me show you my inheritance.' We got up and walked towards the house.

After a tour of every room, and much 'ooh-ing' and 'ah-ing' from Kitty, we stood on the first-floor landing gazing down at the spacious reception hall below, when a thought suddenly came to me.

'Kitty, I haven't looked in the attic rooms yet. Come on, this way.'

I led her to a solid wooden door, which groaned as I opened it to reveal a set of winding, bare wooden stairs.

'After you, m'Lady,' Kitty mimicked a stately home butler, as she bowed. I rolled my eyes at her attempt to sound ostentatious.

We heard scratching and scuttling as we ascended the stairs and I assured Kitty that it was most likely only mice and not some otherworldly being haunting the place. *It couldn't be anything else because I steadfastly refused to believe in ghosts!*

'I saw a mouse in the drawing room the first time I viewed the place.'

'Just so long as they *are* mice, and not rats!' Kitty laughed.

In one room stood a damaged rocking horse and a child's empty cot, now a muddy yellow. A rocking chair stood by the window where grubby pink curtains hung forlornly. Rugs, evidently homemade, scattered the floorboards. A mouse scampered across the skirting board and disappeared.

'I wonder how long he's been living here!' I said, raising an eyebrow at Kitty. I'll have to get pest control out PDQ!'

'You're right. And apart from that, there really is an awful lot of work to be done, Laura. I can see your dilemma. Let's go back to the library and take another look.'

We left the room, descended the old stairs then crossed the landing to the library.

Inside, we lifted books from the shelves and flicked through them.

'This is incredible, Laura, extraordinary. To think these books must have been in your family for so many generations and are worth a small fortune. But what's amazing is that this house has been empty for so long, since your great aunt died, and the place hasn't been looted! Norfolk people must be pretty honest devil worshippers!'

'That's a point. So: they worship Satan, probably stick pins in dolls, issue threats to outsiders, but apart from that, they're all very friendly, welcoming, law-abiding citizens!' Kitty roared with laughter but Maggie Middleton sprang to mind again and I shuddered.

'What about this, though,' I said, taking the dark blue notebook down from the shelf, and showing her the shorthand writing.

'Oh, yes. It's shorthand, to be sure. Crumbs.' She flicked through the pages. 'It's almost filled, look. There are just a few blank pages at the end. You should get it transcribed. My Mum can probably help you there. Remember, she was a secretary for years before she retired. I know she used to do shorthand. She told me she learnt it at school and she got a better paid job than if she'd only been a typist without the shorthand.'

'Oh, yes, of course! Hadn't occurred to me. That would be great. Do you think she would transcribe it for me? It's probably something really boring, but I'd be interested to find out what it says.' Of course, finding out what it said was, at that very moment, pretty low down on my list of priorities.

Dusk approached as we put the books back on the shelves and left the library, with me shutting the door firmly behind.

'Laura, that bike,' said Kitty, as we descended the grand staircase to the reception hall.

'What about it?'

'Well, I could probably get old Teddy Edwards to take a look at it and make it roadworthy again. Shall we take it back with us? I reckon it will fit into Esther if we put the back seats down.'

'What, that old thing?'

'Yes! Why not? Think about it. If you are going to live here at Hamilton Hall, and you need to save money for the renovations and restorations, having a bike to get around on locally, rather than driving, could be a good idea. How about it?'

Now she had my attention. The thought of belting around the local country lanes on a bicycle that had probably been ridden by my great-aunt or great-grandmother suddenly had a romantic appeal.

'Yes! Great idea Kitty Colman! Come on, let's get it.'

I locked up the house and we adjusted the back seats in the car, before going back to the stable. Kitty tried to put the bicycle chain back in place, while I held the bicycle handlebars. Her hands were getting very dirty but she wasn't having much success.

'Here. You hold the bike and I'll have a go.' I got down on my knees while Kitty held the handlebars.

'Why are we doing this anyway?' Kitty asked, 'I mean, we can't ride it, till Teddy fixes it, so why don't we just carry it to the car?'

'And why don't you just leave the bicycle where it is and put your hands up!'

'*What the –* '

I glanced up from my kneeling position and looked straight into two barrels of a shotgun.

20: 25th August, 1940
Hamilton Hall

Emily:

'Doris, it is nearly eight and no sign of Mummy and Daddy. What could have kept them? Surely they would have telephoned by now if they'd missed the train.'

'Let me get you a nice little glass o'sherry, Miss Emily.'

We were in the kitchen and Doris moved over to the larder and pulled out the sherry bottle and a small glass.

'There you go. You relax and enjoy that.' I took a sip. The doorbell rang.

Checking my reflection in the reception hall mirror, I practised a welcoming smile, before opening the front door to our family doctor, John Beresford, and his shrew-like wife, June.

'Welcome, Dr Beresford, Mrs Beresford. Do come in. Let me take your stole, Mrs Beresford, and your hat, Doctor. I'm afraid it seems Mother and Father have been delayed. They were not on the train I was expecting them to arrive on. But I'm sure they will be here soon, so do take a seat in the drawing room and I will get Doris to make some tea. Or would you prefer sherry?'

John and June Beresford exchanged an indiscernible glance before saying a sherry would be most acceptable and followed me into the drawing room. The doorbell rang again.

'Do excuse me.' I went to open the front door to see Jasper Gurney, our local magistrate, standing there with his wife, Eleanor. Jasper's face already flushed with alcohol and Eleanor's face fixed in an expression of reluctant resignation. I apologised for my parents' absence – *oh where had they got to?* – and ushered the Gurneys into the drawing room to join the Beresfords, before pouring the four guests a glass of sherry from the cabinet.

I excused myself and made for the kitchen, where Doris was busy with the finishing touches of the meal.

'What about Miss Martha?' asked Doris. 'Why don't you let her know the guests are arriving? She's p'raps calmed down a bit now.' Her words were reassuring but the tension in her voice was unmistakeable.

I went upstairs, knocked quietly on Martha's door and entered. She was lying on her bed, still in her nightdress.

'Our guests are arriving, Martha, please get dressed and come down.'

'Go away, Emily.' Her voice was icy. She arose and went to the window. I left. People arriving at the front door would be able to see her standing at the window in her nightclothes, and this won't do, I thought.

20: 25TH AUGUST, 1940

Descending the stairs, I heard the doorbell once again. Dr Beresford had left the drawing room and was walking towards the front door, his expression unreadable as he glanced up at me. Doris and Carter emerged from the kitchen and looked up at me on the stairs. I became aware of a figure approaching the stairs from above and turned to see Martha, ashen-faced, behind me.

John Beresford glanced up at me then opened the door to Arthur Howells, our local police constable.

21: Same day
Hamilton Hall

Laura:
'*Whoa! Hang on a minute. It's dangerous to go pointing things like that at people. Put it down.*' Kitty's tone was no-nonsense, as she moved towards the old man standing at the door of the stable, her hand reaching out for the shotgun he was aiming at us. *Bloody hell. If it wasn't Satan worshipping witches it was a pensioner trying to kill us. What next?*

The old boy held the shotgun with trembling hands, sweeping the gun from me to Kitty and back to me. He had thick, wiry grey hair, curling around his ears and neck and wore a green wax jacket and green wellington boots. A cravat hung incongruously around his neck and his grey jumper had holes where it stretched across his ample belly. Looked like he slept in this getup and wore it all year round.

'Get back. Get back. I'm calling the police. This is private property and you've no right to be here. Get your hands up or I'll shoot.'

'Don't be silly old chap. We are not trespassing. This property belongs to – '

'Me,' I said, my voice trembling. 'This property belongs to me. It's mine, and you're the one trespassing.' I'd finally found my voice a I stood upright. Well, it's not every day you find yourself being threatened by an armed man. It *was* a bit of a shocker. My heart was pounding in my chest.

'*Mine*. Got that?' I continued, vexed. 'Hamilton. Hall. Belongs. To. *Me*.' I staggered up from my kneeling position on the stable floor and moved towards him a couple of steps, pointing a finger at my own chest, in emphasis. 'Hamilton Hall is *mine* and *you* – ' I pointed my finger at him now, making poking motions in the air – '*you* are trespassing, so clear off before *I* call the law.'

'*You? You?* Do you honestly expect me to believe that *you* – ' he looked me up and down – 'own Hamilton Hall? My girl, you are deluded as well as criminal.' His voice was clipped, like an extreme form of Received Pronunciation. A bit like Prince Charles. Only worse. *Posh git.* And who was he to cast aspersions? He wouldn't exactly win *Best Dressed Man of the Year* in that ensemble. He might have a well-to-do accent but he looked like he'd been dressed out of an Oxfam shop.

'Yes, that's right. It belongs to me. And stop pointing that bloody gun at me. It might go off, you silly twit. Who are you, anyway?' I could feel myself getting more than a little bit cross now, my initial terror taken over by indignation and anger. I mean, how dare he be so rude? And on my property too! Threatening me with a firearm and him an uninvited intruder to boot. Bloody cheek. And pointing a gun at us was one thing, but insulting my social background was quite another. Who did he think he was?

'Come on old chap, let's talk about this sensibly,' ventured Kitty, ever the diplomat. 'No need to get aggressive, is there? I'm Kitty Colman.' She offered her hand for him to shake, '... and this is my friend, Laura White. She is indeed the owner of Hamilton Hall and I can vouch for her. What is your name? I don't believe we've met.'

Kitty sounded like she'd been having elocution lessons and if the situation were not so volatile I might have had to suppress a giggle. As it was, I tried to keep a straight face. She was trying to impress the old boy with a hint of class. It seemed to work. He lowered the shotgun and took her hand.

'Farrington. George Farrington, at your service Madam.' He gave a brief nod. 'But how can I be sure your friend is who you say she is? Do you have any identification on you Miss?' He was looking over Kitty's shoulder at me with all the contempt of someone observing an inebriate woman being sick on a number nine bus. Was there no end to the impudence of this bloke?

'Well?' He was eyeing me expectantly. *Oh, hang on a minute, mate, while I just take my passport out of my jeans pocket! I always carry it around with me just in case I need to prove my identity to some random old codger whose marbles seem to have got lost!*

'George Farrington, did you say?' I asked. Bells ringing. Penny dropping.

'I most certainly am. And I've been keeping an eye on the old place since Miss Emily passed on three years ago. Never know what riffraff might come by and try to – '

'So, you're the neighbour who's after buying a plot of my land, then?' I scrutinised his face, a face so heavily lined it looked like an old leather boot, and tried to hold his gaze and read his expression. The memory of the BMW–driving Simon What's-his-double-barrelled-name returned, bringing a sour taste to my mouth.

'Well, yes, that's right. How did you know?'

'Your estate agent was here when I first arrived on Friday to view my inheritance. Cocky so-and-so he was too. Right up himself. And I'll tell *you* what I told *him*: I've no plans to sell any of my land and even if I changed my mind, I certainly wouldn't have any dealings with him.'

'Easy, Laura, he's still holding a gun,' stage-whispered Kitty. I changed tack.

'Tell you what, George Farrington,' I offered, 'we've got to be going now, but why don't I pop by and see you next time

I'm back? Maybe we could talk about the land then?' *Smart thinking, Laura!*

'Yes, good idea.' Kitty nodded. 'I expect we'll be back in a few days and we could give you a knock then? Laura just needs time to think things over, don't you Laura?' *Kitty, you're awesome!*

The old boy scratched his head as if mulling over the proposal in his mind then lifted the shotgun and rested the barrel on his right shoulder. At least he wasn't pointing it at us any longer.

'Very well. Mine's the old place over the fence, just beyond your copper beech tree.' And with that he turned and marched swiftly down my gravel drive, crunching the stones under his wellies as he went.

'Phew!' I suddenly found myself shaking, despite my relief that the gun-wielding geriatric had retreated to his cave.

'Calm yourself, Laura. He was harmless enough.'

'Harmless? *Harmless?* He was pointing a bloody shotgun at us!' (Told you my friend Kitty was the ultimate sangfroid woman, didn't I? Cucumbers have nothing on her.)

'Probably wasn't loaded. Come on, let's get this bike in the car.' Kitty lifted the bicycle, hefted it out of the stable and marched over to the car. I pulled the lower half stable door to and followed on.

'And you really should think carefully about the land, Laura.' She said over her shoulder, as she dropped the old bike into the back of the car and closed the hatchback. 'If you're serious about keeping the house, you need a plan.'

What could I say? Kitty was right of course.

'Tell you what, Laura. Let's just pop back up to the library and fetch that book with the shorthand. I can take it round to Mum's tomorrow and see if she's up for transcribing it.'

'Good thinking!' I took the house keys and headed over to the front door. Kitty slammed the hatchback shut and followed me into the house.

I quickly located the blue notebook and stood once more, gazing in awe at the grand library. I felt what I thought was a warm hand on my arm, expecting it to be Kitty, but when I turned around, she was not standing next to me, but had her back to me, perusing the bookshelves. I shuddered. I don't know why I'd felt a shudder because it was a warm feeling, an almost affectionate touch.

'Come on, Kitty. We need to get going. I've got an eight o'clock start in the morning.'

In no time at all we were driving along the A11 towards Suffolk, the car's CD player blasting out lively 1980s pop music. Kitty hand-danced and nodded her head to the beat. Esther was overtaken by a familiar-looking BMW doing about ninety miles an hour.

21: SAME DAY

'Stupid bugger. What's he trying to prove?'

'He's probably got a very small willy,' Kitty said, turning down the volume on the CD player. She was in the habit of correlating an over-sized male ego with under-sized genitals.

'If it's who I think it is, I reckon you could be right. That looked a lot like the flash-git-estate-agent's car,' I said, and we both collapsed into fits of giggles while I tried to keep control of the steering wheel.

Some three miles further along the road I spotted hazard-warning lights flashing on vehicles ahead and gently reduced my speed.

'Wonder what's going on up here?' Kitty said.

'There's probably a chicken crossing the road,' I said.

'Or a stray cow,' added Kitty. And we giggled.

'Whatever it is, I hope it gets a move on. I need to get home.' I slowed the car to a virtual halt. We both let out a long sigh.

Ambulance and police sirens sounded from behind and in my rear-view mirror I could see blue lights flashing, as cars pulled over to the left, clearing the way for the emergency services to get through.

Some forty minutes later, we started to move slowly and my heart missed a beat and Kitty gasped, as we passed a BMW mangled on the central reservation barrier.

22: 25th August, 1940
Hamilton Hall

Emily:

A scream. A wail. A howl so nerve-shattering that it would haunt me for the rest of my days.

A thud.

'Martha!' I turned to see my sister's limp body tumbling down the stairs towards me. I reached out. A reflex action. I caught her in time to stop her falling the full distance to the reception hall floor. 'Martha!'

The theatre took a direct hit. Hundreds of casualties.

Dr Beresford lunged towards the stairs and in a single, swift movement lifted Martha's wilting body from me as if she were a sleeping child, her white satin nightdress flowing to the floor, and carried her into the drawing room. He laid her gently down on the *chaise longue*. I took a woollen blanket from the leather armchair by the fireplace and covered my sister's pale body. Dr Beresford took her wrist in his hand and checked his pocket watch. Martha's head moved almost unperceptively. Her eyes flickered.

I felt warm hands on my upper arms. I turned to see Diana Passant and her husband Jeremy at her side. I had not heard them arrive. Reverend Johnson entered the room, with his wife, Agnes. I scanned the room. All eight guests had arrived. We were all there, the entire dinner party, apart from Mother and Father, the guests of honour.

Mother and Father. Mummy. Daddy.

The theatre took a direct hit. Hundreds of casualties.

Mummy. Daddy.

Mummy and Daddy are going to be late.

I must tell Doris. The dinner will spoil. The guests are here and the dinner will spoil.

The theatre took a direct hit. Hundreds of casualties.

Why was Constable Howell here? What was he saying?

The theatre took a direct hit. Hundreds of casualties.

What? What was Constable Howell saying?

The theatre took a direct hit. Hundreds of casualties. Hundreds of casualties. Hundreds of casualties.

Martha's wail again. 'No! No! Mummy! Daddy! No! No! No!'

People spoke all at once. Their voices under water. Distorted. I couldn't understand a word. Voices. Voices. I couldn't understand a word. A stomach-churning, nauseating pain gripped my legs. I felt strong arms around my waist and a soothing voice guiding me to the armchair by the fireplace. The day had been warm and sunny; now, the room felt filled with icy, chilly air.

22: 25TH AUGUST, 1940

A direct hit. The theatre took a direct hit. Hundreds of people. Hundreds of people. Didn't stand a chance. Didn't stand a chance. Adalicia and Richard would not have known anything. Didn't stand a chance. Direct hit.

23: Monday morning
Suffolk

Laura:

'Percy has started his nocturnal antics again but that shouldn't affect you as you're on days all this week according to the schedule and he usually snoozes most of the day. Agnes is back to her old trick of dropping Harold into her commode after she's used it. Felicity has quietened down and sleeps a lot during the day, but likes to go walkabout during the night. Lucky for you, you're on days all week. Mary's garbled chatter is still incessant and she's driving David to distraction. He keeps threatening to belt her one, so keep an eye on those two. Welcome back to the madhouse, Laura.'

Sheila Crawford's a senior carer at the Honeysuckle Cottage Care Home for the Elderly where I was reporting back for duty after my week off. It was down to earth with a bang for me as she walked me through the handover in between gaping wide yawns and a great deal of rubbing of the back of her neck. Now she was making circular movements with her shoulders. Must have been a long, hard night.

'You should have a fairly quiet time today. As I say, the boisterous ones are up to their shenanigans at night now. Oh, yes, and Basil Mooney died the other day. Went to bed for his afternoon nap and never woke up. Sarah-Jane - you know, the new girl – skinny little slip of a thing - found him when she went in with his cuppa and biscuit at four o'clock. Said it was her first dead body. Took it well. She'll be a good 'un once she's trained up and got her NVQs. Funeral's a week on Friday.'

I blinked back a tear at the news of the loss of a dear old man of whom I had grown very fond over recent years. I wished I'd been there, holding his hand at the end. I wondered what his final thoughts had been. I would go to his funeral. Pay my respects. There'd probably only be the care home manager and me in attendance. Basil would just slip quietly and unassumingly out of this world.

'Good holiday? Do anything exciting?' Sheila asked, perfunctorily.

Oh, nothing out of the ordinary. Just found out I've inherited a house worth a couple of million quid but can't afford to keep it. Hardly worth mentioning really.

'Not bad, thanks. You get off now and I'll start my rounds. Hope you get some sleep.'

Sheila grabbed her navy-blue fleece from a hook on the back of the office door, took her bag out of the bottom drawer of the filing cabinet and made for the door as, by way of goodbye, she took her car keys out of her pocket and waved them in the air without looking back.

I sat at the desk and pulled the pile of personal files containing individual care plans towards me and flicked through Basil Mooney's profile to see if there was yet a cause of death recorded. Seems his old heart had just given up. Worn out. Poor old Basil. Ninety-one years old. Not a bad age but he'd not only outlived his siblings but his own kids as well so no one ever came to visit him. He was so frail that a slight breeze would have sent him spinning but he was still mentally agile with a brain as sharp as a razor and was as knowledgeable and informative as the Encyclopaedia Britannica. He did *The Times* crossword every morning, as well as a few pages of his book of *Sudoku* every afternoon before his nap. He devoured a new library book every week and eagerly awaited the arrival of the mobile library van every Friday. I had a lot of time for dear old Basil. Now I brushed away a tear and blew my nose as I remembered the times he had teased me about my love life (or lack of it) and asked me about my studies. He'd encouraged me to finish my degree and get what he called a 'proper job with prospects'. It didn't do to get sentimental about the old folks we cared for. They could pop their clogs any day. It was a regular occurrence to turn up for work and be told that one of them had died. Honeysuckle Cottage Care Home would most likely be their final residence. Next stop heaven, if such a place existed. So, we had to keep what we called a 'professional distance'. But old Basil was different. He was what I would call a proper gentleman, with impeccable manners and a kindly, humble nature. Lovely speaking voice too, without sounding at all pretentious or pompous. I would sometimes spend teatime with him while he luxuriated in fond memories of his late wife, his two children who both died without having given him grandchildren, and his life of adventures, travelling the world. I couldn't imagine him ever pulling a shotgun on anyone like that old bugger had in the stable at Hamilton Hall yesterday. I bristled at the memory. I could have sat listening to Basil for hours and often had a chat with him when other service users had their visitors and there was never anyone there for Basil. I heard about his journeys to far flung places, which he brought, vibrantly and vividly alive for me. I had been looking forward to telling him all about Hamilton Hall and felt inordinately sad that now he'd never know. I hoped he'd now gone to a better place and was having a party with his family somewhere up in the heavens or other such place.

I picked up Agnes's file and went down the corridor to her room. She was standing next to her bed facing away from the door, her nightie stuck inside the back of her knickers and her hair standing on end. A common sight with Agnes. Although a slight figure, she seemed to be in robust physical health and was never ill. Not even so much as a bit of a cold. Pity she was completely gaga. Harold was one of a variety of stuffed toys that served not only as her companions but her family. She would lavish care and affection on him and favour him over the others. Agnes could often be heard scolding the other soft toys (her 'children') while Harold could do no wrong. Her care for Harold extended to brushing his 'hair', cleaning his teeth (with her own toothbrush) and sitting him on her commode; unfortunately, she frequently forgot that she'd put him there and he'd invariably topple over and fall in, necessitating the need for a carer (usually me) retrieving him from the unpleasant contents of the pot and putting him through the washing machine and tumble dryer. This was no problem really, except that sometimes his head or a limb would get torn off during the wash and I'd find myself carrying out an intricate surgical operation with the use of the staff sewing kit and surreptitiously returning Harold before his 'mummy' realised he'd gone missing and started getting hysterical or calling the police (it had happened on one occasion; the young policewoman who attended was more than a little bemused when we'd explained to her the nature of the 999 call made by an octogenarian without possession of her marbles. She insisted on meeting Harold to satisfy herself that he was safe and well).

Agnes had one grumpy son in his sixties who deigned to visit her once in a while and used it as an ideal opportunity to complain loudly about everything and everyone before clearing off. Meanwhile, Agnes had no idea who he was.

I went through the motions of delivering the care plan for each individual service user in my care, fed them breakfast, tea or hot chocolate at eleven o'clock, lunch, afternoon tea and dinner. I escorted them to the toilet or helped them onto their commodes, changed their incontinence pads and wiped dribbles of saliva from their chins.

With supreme effort, I managed to persuade David that it was not the best idea to try to knock the block off Mary even though she drove him bonkers with her insensible babbling. Instead I encouraged Mary to engage in a jigsaw puzzle in the hope that it would distract her and give her mouth a rest. I left her trying to fit the pieces of a jigsaw of a John Constable painting into one that was supposed to be a steam train and hoped the impossibility of the task would occupy her until teatime.

At that moment, I knew beyond a shadow of a doubt that I would finish my shift that day and I would never return to work at Honeysuckle Cottage Care Home.

24: Sunday, 26th August, 1940
Hamilton Hall

Emily:

'Martha! Martha!' I am running through the woods, tree and bush branches lashing at my limbs. 'Martha! Martha!' My sister, still in her nightdress and bare feet, flies ahead. 'Martha! Martha!'

I am wading through thick treacle. My legs refuse to move. My voice is silent. I call her again. No sound. She carries on running, flying, running, flying. I scream a silent scream. 'Martha! Martha!'

I feel a warm hand on my brow and a feather light touch on my cheek.

'There now, Miss Emily. There now. It's all right my lovely.'

I try to open my eyes and squint in the sunlight shining through the window. Doris strokes my hair, pushes it back off my face.

'A dream, Miss Emily. Only a dream.'

'Mummy! Daddy!' I feel each breath leave my body, like it is my last. I look around my familiar room. The soft pastel shades of cushions and curtains. I see the four-panelled Edwardian doors; the pale blue blanket draped across the white wicker chair. I glance at the fireplace and the ornate mantelpiece painted white with faded photographs of me with Martha, our younger selves in the summer of 1930, Blakeney beach, the cool breeze blowing our hair sideways. Mummy and Daddy in another sepia picture, walking along the promenade at Southwold, a white lighthouse looming up behind them. I cry softly.

'There, there. Try to sleep some more.'

Sleep. How can I sleep? Mummy and Daddy are gone. *Took a direct hit. Didn't stand a chance.* I cry in earnest now. Hot tears prick my eyes and roll unchecked down my cheeks at the memory of last night's news. I taste the salt as liquid seeps into the corners of my mouth.

Doris dabs at my wet face with a soft, white fluffy towel. Her face is calm but her expression gently concerned and comforting.

The sunlight hurts my eyes. Doris has opened the curtains and I gaze out and wonder why the sun can still shine and the birds still sing when the world as I know it has changed irrevocably? My dear Mother and Father destroyed by a bomb. Gulping sobs make the whole of my body shake. I feel Doris's arms around me, holding me, rocking me. Just like she did when I was a little girl and I'd found my pet rabbit, Bobbie, dead in his hutch. Dear, constant Doris.

'There, there now Miss Emily. You have a good cry. That's right. Cry it all out. That's my girl.'

'Martha. Martha. Where is Martha, Doris?'

'It's all right Miss Emily. Dr Beresford is with your sister. She's going to be all right, you'll see. Dr Beresford has come to give her something to help her sleep. Now you must rest too. Lie down now, there's a love.'

Doris lowers my head onto the soft pillow, pulls the bedclothes up over my shoulders and tucks them under my chin. She slips out of the room and quietly closes the door. Sleep sweeps me into oblivion.

I wake to a darkened room and the sound of footsteps on the gravel drive. My numb body makes its way to the bedroom window.

And there by the moonlight I see Martha, taking the bicycle from the stable. She mounts and I watch as she cycles furiously into the night. The black murkiness of unconsciousness steals me away once again.

25: A few days later
Suffolk

Laura:

It was raining cats and dogs when, ten days after my return to work, I attended the modest and impersonal funeral of Basil Mooney. As I'd imagined, there were only three people in attendance: myself, the care home manager, Janet Green, and a stiff looking middle-aged man in a black Crombie coat and trilby hat, who was a total stranger to me. I wondered who he could be. I'd never seen him at the care home. What was he doing at the funeral of Basil Mooney?

It was all over in a jiffy. The only flowers on the coffin were, predictably, those from myself and an arrangement paid for from the care home funeral fund. But there was also a bouquet of roses and babies' breath that I could only assume came from the mystery man in the black coat. The vicar, a vertically challenged figure, with a paunch and a comb over, a now familiar face at funeral time for Honeysuckle Cottage residents, mumbled his way through the service and, after a hymn sung by him and the three attendees, Basil was despatched to his final resting place.

'Excuse me, madam. I understand you are Ms Laura White? Is that correct?' I was walking out of the church and turned to find the stiff man in the Crombie coat and trilby hat standing before me.

'Yes,' I replied somewhat warily. I eyed him up and down. 'Can I help you?'

'Might we go somewhere quiet for a cup of tea, Ms White? I have something to tell you.'

Jeez. Now what? What on earth could this rather rigid and stern-looking stranger want with me?

'Why? What do you want? And who are you?'

'Apologies, Ms White, I should have properly introduced myself. I am Quinton Stone, solicitor acting on behalf of the late Mr Basil Mooney. I have some news for you but I'd prefer we went elsewhere so that I can have a proper chat with you. Will you join me for a cup of tea? Or you are welcome to come to my offices on Monday morning.' He took a business card out of his inside pocket and handed it to me. I read the card and handed it back to him.

'It's just that I have to dash off promptly to catch the train to London and will be away for the rest of the week. I'd rather talk to you before I leave, if I may?'

So, what else was I going to do that day? Go home. Do some housework, check to see if my tutor had marked my assignment? Weed the garden? Not much at all really. And I was parched. No brainer.

'OK, Mr Stone. I'll join you for a cuppa.' And with that I said goodbye to Janet Green, paying no heed to the fact that I would probably never see her again, opened my umbrella against the rain and led the way to the local teashop, a hundred yards down the road from the church.

As I sipped my tea I was impatient to hear what this stranger had to say for himself. I wanted to get it over with and leave as soon as possible. I felt safe in the busy environment of the teashop, but he was a stranger, after all, and I just wanted to get to the bottom of what this bloke wanted to say to me.

'I'll get to the point, Ms White,' he said, almost reading my mind. *That's a relief. Come on then mate, out with it.* He carefully replaced his cup on the saucer, his pinky finger raised in a crook.

'I am executor of the estate of Mr Basil Mooney. I have to tell you that he has bequeathed a legacy to you. First of all, I need to be sure that you are indeed Ms Laura White. Do you have any identification on you?'

I almost choked. I started spluttering and in the process spilt tea on the green and white gingham tablecloth. Bequeathed? Dear old Basil has bequeathed a legacy to me? *Crikey!*

§

'I don't believe you Laura White! First you inherit a house that you fall in love with, then, just as you're wondering how you can manage to keep it, you foolishly resign from your job without another one to go to, and hey presto, one of your residents passes away and leaves you his money. You couldn't make it up! Are you sure it's legit?'

Kitty was sitting with me at my kitchen table and we were making short work of a bottle of wine and a bowl of cashew nuts.

'I know. But it's legit all right. I'm not making it up, Kitty. It really is true. This Quinton Stone bloke laid out all the papers on the café table and there was Basil's will, stating without a doubt that I was the main beneficiary of his estate. He left a bit for Honeysuckle Cottage and some to cancer research – probably because his wife and his daughter both died of breast cancer - but apart from that, I get the lot. Sixty-two thousand, four hundred and eighty-three quid.' I took a gulp of red wine and grabbed a handful of cashews.

'I'm definitely moving into Hamilton Hall now, Kitty. This money's surely a sign that I am meant to, don't you think?'

'Absolutely. So, when's the big moving day, then?'

'Well, there are things I need to sort out first. And I don't really know where to start. You told me the other day that I need a plan. And you're right. But as yet I don't know what that plan is. I need to figure it out.'

'OK. So, now you've got some ready dosh – when will it be paid into your bank?'

'By the end of next month, he said. I'm overdrawn, but a hundred quid or so will take care of that. It's all happened so fast, I can't think straight. Oh, come on, Kitty, help me. You're the practical one.'

Kitty drained her glass and reached for the wine bottle. She held the neck of the bottle between her thumb and index finger and waved it at me. I shook my head. There was too much to think about and I needed a clear head. She filled her glass and grabbed a handful of nuts.

Through a mouthful of cashews, she said, 'OK, so what will you do with the cottage here? Sell it? Pay off the mortgage? Live on the equity? We need to make a list.' She got up and walked over to the Welsh dresser and opened the drawer. She knew where just about everything was in my house, just as I knew hers. She took out a note pad and a pencil and came back to the table.

'Right. Action plan. Here we go.'

And so, two and a half hours and a couple of bottles of wine later (*well OK, I know I needed to keep a clear head, but you don't know what Kitty and I are like once the vino starts to flow...*) we had it all worked out.

I would rent out my terraced cottage, use the money from that to live on and Basil's money would get me going on fixing up Hamilton Hall. That way, I wouldn't need to work for a while and I could finish my degree studies while the renovations went on.

'You do of course realise, Laura, don't you, that the renovations will be pretty disruptive? There must be a hell of a lot of work to be done. Have you thought about how you will manage to study with all that going on?'

'I know what you mean, but I've managed so far. The builders won't be banging around for twenty-four hours a day, will they? I'm used to studying at odd hours, so I will just carry on as I've always done. Writing my assignments at night if necessary. Talking of which, I wonder if my tutor has marked and returned my assignment yet? Hang on, let me take a look.

I reached for my laptop from the kitchen worktop and logged on.

Yup. She sure had. Eighty-five per cent! I must pull all-nighters whilst stressed out of my brains more often!

26: Monday, 26th August, 1940, Dawn
Hamilton Hall

Emily:
I awoke with a start. Mummy and Daddy had been killed. Their lives extinguished by a bomb. Killed while celebrating their twenty-fifth wedding anniversary. The abject cruelty of it was excruciating and felt like a physical pain in my chest. Oh, this miserable war! How would we continue without our dear, devoted parents? Life, as we knew it, had been destroyed. What should we do?

Martha! A blurred image of Martha riding off into the night on her bicycle formed itself in my fuzzy mind. Had I dreamt it? Had I really seen Martha sneaking off again to rendezvous with Charles Harwood, as she had done on so many nights? No. Surely, not. No. Not on the very night of such devastating news? And hadn't Doris said last night that Dr Beresford was giving Martha a little something to help her sleep? How was she able to get out of bed, let alone ride a bicycle? Yes, it must have been a dream. Just a bad dream. Only a dream.

I threw the bedclothes to one side and with supreme effort lifted my heavy head. I slipped out of bed and grabbed my robe, as I staggered across the room barefoot and along the landing to Martha's room. I tapped lightly on the door. No reply. I tapped again, my hand trembling on the doorknob. Again, I tapped on the door. This time a little louder. And again, one more time.

'Martha? Are you there?'

I opened the door. Tentatively, hesitantly, I stepped softly into the room.

Empty. Gone. My sister's bedclothes lay in a heap on the hearthrug; all that was left on the bed was the crumpled white linen under sheet. A pillow lay on the rug beside the bed.

'Martha!' I gasped, my heart beating like a jungle drum inside my ribcage, my pulse quickening as the deafening sound of blood rushing pounded in my ears. My hand shot up to my mouth, as I took another sharp intake of breath. I thought I might be sick. I dashed to Martha's bathroom and gagged as I did so. Bile rose and rushed into my mouth. I turned on the water tap, swilled my mouth and splashed water onto my face. I took Martha's pink hand towel from the rail beside the porcelain washbasin and dried my face.

I dashed to the bedroom window, drew back the curtains and looked through the soft dawn light down to the gravel drive. Silence. Stillness. Nothing. Nothing.

I sat on the edge of Martha's bed, picked up her pillow from the floor, cradling it, as if it were a baby. My baby sister. Where *is* she?

26: MONDAY, 26TH AUGUST, 1940, DAWN

'Martha?' I called into the stillness of the room.

My thoughts were abruptly interrupted. I jumped. My head jerked towards the bedroom door. What was that? Every nerve in my body was set on edge. There was banging and shouting at the front door. Frantic, feverish banging. Desperate, urgent shouting. Banging. Banging. Banging. Kicking at the door. I glanced at the grandfather clock – twenty-five minutes past five - as I flew down the stairs and unbolted the door.

I opened the door to a young man, and I could see in the new, early morning light, his tousled mousy brown hair, the two distinctive stripes of the rank of RAF Flying Officer on the cuffs of the sleeves of his blue jacket, pilot's wings emblazoned above his breast pocket, his black tie loosened at the neck, his shirt collar open.

In his arms, he held my sister, Martha, limp, lifeless.

27: The next day
Suffolk

Laura:
Two cups of coffee, toast, a couple of paracetamol, a firm resolve never to drink alcohol ever again, and I was beginning to feel almost human as I placed the stepladder on the landing and ascended into the loft. It had been eight years since Mum's death and I'd hardly given the boxes of her stuff a moment's thought, let alone had any inclination to go through them. There were plastic boxes of different colours and a couple of cardboard supermarket ones, once obviously used to transport apples. I was leaning over a plastic storage box, blowing dust away and trying to read the label by shining the torch I'd taken up with me, when I heard a familiar voice coming from downstairs.

'Laura? Laura! Are you there?' Kitty had turned up as she'd promised the night before. I'm amazed she was even out of bed, let alone remembered her drunken offer to help me make a start on sorting out the cottage. It needed a good clear out and some redecoration before putting it on the rental market.

'Up here, Kitty!' I called out then promptly banged my head on a rafter, as I stood upright.

'*Shit!*' That was all I needed, another head ache on top of the alcohol-induced hammering already vigorously taking place inside my skull.

'Oh, you've made a start. Well done that woman! What have you found up there?'

I moved towards the hatch and Kitty was standing at the foot of the stepladder.

'Just as I left them, Kitty, all the storage boxes I picked up from Mum's house after the funeral. Let me see if I can lift one and hand it down to you. We need to get them into Esther. I'll look inside them when I've got time, but right now, I need to clear everything out of the house and get it over to Hamilton Hall.'

'OK, Hun. Give it a go. If you can lift without too much trouble, just hand them one at a time down to me.'

'Hang on then.' I bent my knees and grabbed hold of one of the cardboard boxes, sealed by heavy duty sticky tape. Not too weighty. Good. I moved towards the hatch with it.

'There you go, Kitty. Can you take this? Just pile them all up on the landing for now.'

Once we'd moved all the boxes onto the landing, we took them down to the car and began the loading up process.

'By the way, Laura, I popped into my Mum's on my way round here just now, and gave her that book of shorthand that you found

27: THE NEXT DAY

in the mansion library. She said she'd look at it, but that you've got to understand it's not that easy reading someone else's shorthand, so she might not be a lot of help. And she said it could take some time. I just asked her to do her best.'

'Oh thanks, that's great. I know it might not be anything significant or exciting, but all those pages of dots and squiggles must be about something.'

'And Teddy Edwards phoned this morning and said he can restore the old bike to some semblance of working order.'

'Oh brilliant. Thanks for that too.'

We carried boxes out to Esther, parked at the kerbside and I unlocked the hatchback.

'I hope you're not moving out without paying your milk bill, Laura.' At the sound of the male voice, I straightened up from the hatchback and my head made contact with the hatchback door with an almighty thud. At the moment of impact, I clearly understood the meaning of the term: *I saw bloody stars!*

Rubbing my sore head for the third time that morning, I turned to see Barry the milkman, a portly chap in a green overall, flat cap, and John Lennon glasses on a big nose, raising an eyebrow at me.

'Oh, Hi there, Barry. No, not moving out just shifting some stuff. I'll pay you next week, that OK with you?'

'That's what you always say, and next week never comes. I shouldn't be leaving you milk you know, when you still owe me for six weeks. Any chance of paying me a little something now?'

'Erm, well, I'm a bit strapped for cash at the mo, Barry. Couldn't we just settle up next week? Please?' I tried my winning *(well, all right, sycophantic)* smile, which usually works, but this time failed me.

'I can't keep leaving milk for you – '

'How much is the bill, Barry?' Kitty interrupted, reaching into the back pocket of her jeans.

'Forty-one pounds fifty-eight in total.'

'Forty-one quid?' Kitty's hand stayed on her back pocked as her eyes bulged in shock.

'And fifty-eight pence, yes.'

She glanced back at me with a withering look *(it worked; I felt extremely silly and embarrassed)* and took two twenties out of her back pocket then plunged her hand into the front pocket and brought out a handful of change.

'There you go, Barry,' said Kitty, as she gave him forty pounds and counted out the exact amount of change into his hand, leaving both milkman and me speechless.

Barry took a pint from a crate on his float and handed it to me.

'A pinta for today, Laura?'

'Er no, I think she should take the pay-as-you-go route from now on, and use supermarket milk, but thanks all the same,

Barry.' And with that Kitty picked up a storage box and shoved it into Esther.

'Kitty, I – '

'Oh, shut up. It's forty quid for milk, not a mortgage payment. Pay me back when your Basil money comes through.'

I took her face in my hands and kissed her smack on the cheek. 'Kitty you're a – '

'Oh, don't go mushy on me woman! Come on, we've got work to do!'

That's Kitty for you. Didn't I tell you she's ever the practical one?

The car was full to capacity as I locked up the cottage and we set off for Norfolk. We stopped on the way for petrol *(thank goodness for the credit card!)* and Kitty treated us both to coffee and toasted teacakes at the same greasy spoon joint where I'd first come across the slimy speed merchant in the flash BMW. I shuddered at the memory of seeing an identical car that had crashed into the central reservation barrier as we were on our way back from Hamilton Hall that time. Not for the first time, I wondered if the driver could possibly be Simon Stewart-Rees, the obnoxious estate agent who'd tried to bully me that first day at Hamilton Hall.

I recognised the same pierced and tattooed girl with the hair shaved at the sides who served us in the cafe. How could I forget her? But there was something different about her this time. She sported the remains of a black eye and a bandage around the wrist of the hand emblazoned with 'Shane'.

'Oh dear. What happened to you? Nasty bruise there, you've got.' Kitty said, as the girl brought our food and drinks to the table. Never was one to withhold from enquiry; it was straight to the point, always, with Kitty.

Tears glistened in the girl's eyes and for a very short moment I thought I saw her lips quivering, before she glanced around her and without a word scuttled off back to her workstation. Alarm bells rang in my head as Kitty voiced my private thoughts.

'Looks suspiciously like somebody belted her one and she's ashamed or afraid to talk about it.'

'Mm. Just what I was thinking,' I said, remembering my last psychology assignment about battered woman syndrome and turned to observe the girl behind the counter. On the earlier occasion I'd met her, she had definitely been more on the sullen side than the life and soul of the proverbial party kind, but there was definitely something amiss here today.

We ate and drank in silence then hit the road to Hamilton Hall.

28: Late August, 1940
Hamilton Hall

Emily:

'Oh, my God! Martha!' I step aside to allow the young man to enter the hall. 'What happened to her? What happened? Is she - ?'

'I found her wandering along the lane. It's all right. She's breathing. She's all right. But she needs to lie down.'

'This way.' I say as I move towards the drawing room and open the door. The man carries Martha into the room and lays her down on the *chaise longue*. I cover my sister with the same woollen blanket I had used the night before, and place a cushion under her head.

'I was on my way back to the RAF station from a night out in Norwich and my car ran out of petrol,' says the young man. 'I was walking the rest of the way when I found Martha. I recognised her as the girlfriend of Charles Harwood, a friend of mine.'

'Oh. Right.' I am distracted. In a surreal dream world; not sure where I am. 'But how did you know where to bring her?'

'All the chaps on the camp know where the Boulais-Hamilton sisters live. It's common knowledge. You must be Emily. Maybe we should get your sister something to drink.'

Still reeling, I move out of the drawing room and down to the kitchen. In the pantry, I find some milk to warm on the stove. I shiver.

Back in the drawing room, Martha stirs and her eyes flicker. They fix, unseeing, on me, as I hold a cup of warm milk and honey to her lips.

'Come on Martha. You must try to drink something. Drink something darling.' But Martha's eyes close again and her head falls softly back onto the cushion. I put the cup down and cover up my sister again with the blanket.

I am suddenly aware of the young man still in the room. I turn to him.

'I'm so grateful to you for bringing her home. What is your name?' I ask the young man, now sitting on the edge of the fireside chair.

'Flying Officer Peter Chandler – Pete to my friends. And you're Emily?' He asks again, standing and offering me his right hand to shake. Such good manners and formality are at odds with the world of irreconcilable mental chaos I find myself in. I look at the outstretched hand then look away.

I walk over to the fireplace and place my fingers on the edge of the mantelpiece, squeezing it agitatedly, mentally trying to make sense of recent events.

I am jerked back to my real existence; my cognisant self, by a polite cough. I find my manners.

'Yes. I am Emily Boulais-Hamilton. Our parents were killed in the London bombings on Saturday night.' I say it as if I were remarking on a bus being late, or the weather being unseasonably cold.

'I'm afraid Martha has been terribly upset.' I walk back to the *chaise longue* and stroke my sister's forehead. Martha's cheeks, usually rosy with health are pale and translucent. Her hair, still black and glossy, lies tangled around her shoulders, tumbling down towards her waist. There are scratches on the backs of her hands and on her wrists. Her usually perfect eye makeup is smudged and her lips hold the faint remains of artificial colour.

I fight back a tear and move towards the window. I pull back the curtains and the early morning light drifts into the room.

'I should call Dr Beresford.' I say aloud but to no one in particular. Then I become aware one more time of the man in the room.

'Oh dear. Where are my manners? Would you like a cup of tea, Mr Chandler?'

'Tea later. First, we should call the doctor. Where is your telephone? May I use it to call the doctor? Do you have the number to hand, Miss Boulais-Hamilton?' His voice is soft, gentle, compassionate.

And now they come: the hot, salty tears and jerking sobs. Loud, gasping moans. A hand gently touches my shoulder and I turn around, falling into the arms of Flying Officer Peter Chandler, who holds me tight and strokes my back.

'It's all right, Miss Boulais-Hamilton. It's all right. Terrible shock for you girls. Just ghastly.'

And as I sob the cries of only the utterly desolate, my tears soak the shoulder of the young man's uniform.

29: Later that day
Heading for Wymondham!

Laura:

'Laura, I'm just thinking. Perhaps you should see your bank manager about a loan or overdraft facility to tide you over until your legacy comes through? You'll need something to keep you going. Can't live on fresh air, can you?'

We were still heading up the A11 towards Wymondham to leave Mum's boxes and some other stuff from the cottage at Hamilton Hall.

There'd been a bit of a subdued silence between us since seeing the tattooed waitress with the black eye. She could have walked into a door for all we knew, but both Kitty and I were suspicious and more than a little disconcerted at what we had seen.

'What? Oh, yeah. Right, Kitty. As you say, fresh air never fed a woman. But I can't honestly see my bank agreeing to it. After all, I'm not exactly the most reliable customer.'

'But maybe when you tell the bank manager about inheriting Hamilton Hall and that Basil has bequeathed you a substantial amount of dosh it will swing it. If they know you've got that coming and that you now own two houses, it will make all the difference to their decision. You've got to do something, haven't you? Especially as you so boldly left your employment, without another job to go to. A bit of a hasty move, wasn't it? Leaving without a moment's notice? And at the time, you didn't even know Basil had left you the money. Talk about living life on the edge!'

'Well, yes, all right,' I sighed heavily. 'You've got a point, Kitty, but something told me that it was the right thing to do. I really can't go back to that job. It is shit, it really is. Pay is crap, awful hours and then it is always heart-breaking when one of the old 'uns pops off. You can't help but get fond of them. They don't pay enough for all that grief!'

Kitty just looked at me. I could see her out of the corner of my eye, as I kept my eyes on the road ahead, but she kept quiet. That usually means she doesn't agree, but won't say so, even though she knows she's right.

I indicated to turn off the duel carriageway and felt a flutter in my belly as the lane leading to my new home came into view and I drove down towards Hamilton Hall.

Once there, we worked to get the stuff into the house and left Mum's boxes in the corner of the upstairs library. I unpacked some essentials for the kitchen and stored them in the pantry.

'I could murder a cuppa, Laura,' said Kitty, looking around for a kettle, while I reached for the teabags.

Kitty found a whistling kettle in the corner of the worktop and rinsed it before filling it from the kitchen tap. She located the stove and by some miracle it actually worked. There was also a fridge in the corner of the pantry, unplugged and the door propped open. I placed the plug into a socket and the fridge purred into action.

'Result! The fridge works, Kitty!'

'Great! Where's the milk?'

I pulled a carton of milk from the carrier bag of supplies we'd bought in the convenience store before heading off and placed it on the large oblong pine table in the centre of the kitchen. In a box brought in from the car I found us a couple of mugs, a teaspoon and a packet of chocolate Hobnobs.

'Here we go,' I said, as the kettle began to whistle and I brewed the tea.

We sat at the kitchen table, sipping tea and munching on the chocolate biscuits, as Kitty reflected on the number of calories she swallowed with every bite. Not that she needed to worry. She wasn't exactly obese; in fact, she cut quite the Amazonian figure with her hourglass shape and five feet, eight inches.

'Fancy another cuppa?' I asked, getting up from the table and shaking the kettle. There was still plenty of hot water in it.

'Mm yeah, great. Erm, we said we'd call round to your neighbour, didn't we, to talk about the possibility of selling him a chunk of your land? Shall we go knock on his door while we're here?'

I pondered on this for a moment.

'Well, I know I said I'd go see him, but you know, Kitty, I really don't want to be bullied into selling the land. I'd rather take my time and see how things work out, to be honest.'

'I know what you mean, but it wouldn't hurt to find out how much land he wants and how much money you could raise, would it? I know you've got the sixty-two grand coming your way, but that won't last forever, and there is a helluva lot of work to be done here,' she said, looking around. 'I mean, what if it rains and you find there's a bloody big hole in the roof? Have you even organised a surveyor's report? Do you know the extent of the repairs that might need seeing to?'

Before I could answer, a loud banging on the front door interrupted us.

'Hullo! Anybody in?' I recognised the voice immediately. Speak of the devil...

I got up and moved towards the front door to find George Farrington standing in the reception hall, his un-cocked shotgun slung over his arm. He might have a posh voice, but he certainly didn't have manners to match. Who the bloody hell did he think

29: LATER THAT DAY

he was, coming into my house uninvited? And bringing a weapon in with him too. The cheek of it. But at least he wasn't aiming the shotgun at me this time.

'Oh hello, Mr Farrington. Do come in, why don't you?' I said, with more than a little hint of sarcasm in my voice, which was lost on him. 'What can I do for you?' I placed my knuckles on my hips, my elbows winging out to the sides, a bit like a fishwife; a very stroppy one.

'Ah. It is you.'

'Well of course it is me. Who did you expect to find in my house?'

'One never knows. I keep an eye on the place. Have done since dear old Miss Emily passed on.' *Yes, I know that! It was your excuse for pulling a shotgun on us last time!*

'Well, thanks, Mr Farrington. Very kind and thoughtful of you. Very kind. Would you like a cup of tea?' It was Kitty, with her elocution lessons again, offering the old boy refreshment when all I wanted to do was to get rid of him. *Thanks Kitty!*

I turned and fixed her with a glare that she could not have mistaken for anything but *'shut up!',* which she completely ignored as she moved forward and held out her hand to shake to the old git's before leading him into the kitchen. *Oh, for goodness' sake!*

30: Saturday, 31st August 1940
Wymondham

Martha:

Tonight, I will see him. My darling Charles. By the hollow tree. I comb my hair and put on my lipstick. The red one he likes so much. He says it is delicious and sets off my black hair. He will be there, waiting for me in his little sports car. Just like he said he would. I found his letter in our hiding place in the hollow tree and he said he will be there, waiting for me. Waiting for me. Tonight. He will be waiting for me tonight. And I will run into his outstretched arms and then he will hold me tight and kiss me and I will tell him. I will tell him. I will tell him. And we will be together for always. Always.

Emily is fast asleep. Her bedroom door is ajar. I know she has left it like that so that she can hear me. I see her head on the pillow. Her blonde curls frame her face. She is sleeping soundly and purring like a little kitten. I do love her so. She is my dearest big sister and my best friend. I know she loves me. And she will understand. She will love Charles once she gets to know him. He is a wonderful man and how could she not love the man who is the love of my life?

I creep by, silently, my heart throbbing at the anticipation of falling into the arms of my beloved Charles. Yes. I will be with my darling very soon.

I step down the stairs towards the reception hall, avoiding the creaky step; I know exactly where it is and I move stealthily around it. Through the reception hall I move to the left and find the inner hall leading to the kitchen door. The door squeaks a little as I turn the knob and I hold my breath, standing perfectly still. Emily's door is still ajar and I wait to make sure she has not been disturbed by the sound. I listen. Nothing.

I skip through the kitchen and out of the servants' entrance door, making for the stables. The gravel path crunches beneath my feet and I hold my breath again, hoping that Emily will not wake.

I find my bicycle and wheel it out onto the gravel path. I lift it and tiptoe across the path towards the drive. The bicycle is too heavy. It always is. I put it down again and sit on the saddle. With my foot on the pedal I push down hard and ride down the drive, turn left into the lane and fly along, the wind carrying my hair like a flag behind me. The breeze is still warm. My skin tingles. The stars twinkle and shine in the wide East Anglian navy-blue skies and the moon smiles down on me. My breath quickens and my heart thumps, tapping happily, thrumming, thrumming, thrumming, like rain on a taut canvas tent. Charles. Charles. I am going to see Charles.

30: SATURDAY, 31ST AUGUST 1940

I see it. There it is! The little green car. I see him. There he is. He's sitting in the driver's seat, his officer's cap on his beautiful head. I wonder when he will hear my pedalling and leap from his car to envelop me in his strong, manly arms? Charles, my love. My beloved.

The car grows larger as I get closer.

'Charles!' I call to him.

'Charles!' My breath emits erratically and burns my lungs.

I pedal on and on then pull on the brakes and discard the bicycle on the grass verge, running the final hundred yards.

'Charles!' I call out again and the car door swings open.

'Charles – '

Who is this? In the moonlight, I see a shorter man, more slender than Charles. He walks towards me.

'Charles – '

He speaks my name. 'Martha?'

He's approaching me now. He removes his cap. He's in front of me now. This is a prank. Charles is teasing me. Where is Charles? I look beyond the man to the car. Charles will jump out in a moment and laugh at his silly joke.

'Charles?'

I feel the firm grip of his hands on me. He has put his cap back on his head and he is holding my upper arms, unyielding. He is looking straight into my eyes. He is unsmiling. His eyes glisten in the moonlight.

'Martha. Listen to me old girl. You are going to have to be very brave. It's Charles – '

'Charles? Where is he? Why is he not here and what are you doing in his car?' My breath comes quick and jagged. My lungs are scorched.

31: Summer 2013, A few days later
Hamilton Hall

Laura:
I wanted to stick his head in a vice and slam it shut. Well, no, not quite. Not really. Would I do that? No, of course not. Not just his bloody head, his unmentionables too. The whole bloody lot. I wanted to stamp hard on Quinton Stone's head until I'd flattened it and his bony skull shattered and his wicked scheming brain spilt out.

How could one human being do such calculating, evil things to another? He'd told me so convincingly that Basil Mooney had left me sixty-two thousand quid. Dear old Basil Mooney. He'd turn in his urn if he knew. And that bastard Quinton Stone (I'm sure that's not his real name) coolly took my credit card details right in that bloody café straight after the funeral, saying his firm needed the money up front to cover various fees in order for the funds to be released to me. He even had the nerve to ask me to show him identification to verify I was actually Laura White. I cannot believe I was so stupid. Kitty will go mad. I really believed that Basil had left me his money. Now my bank has just phoned and told me I've been scammed and he has taken several thousand quid out of my credit card. I am up the creek without a paddle. No wonder he wanted to do the deal in a café. He obviously didn't have an office. Of course, he didn't. And the so-called business card he left with me had a false address, email and phone number on it. Quinton Stone was a dirty, lowdown crook and was probably by now on an *easyJet* flight to a life of luxury on the Costa del Crime!

I looked around the drawing room of Hamilton Hall. How was I ever so naïve as to believe that this place could ever be mine? I moved towards the French windows and looked out at the garden with a lump the size of a grapefruit in my throat. Through my tears, I gazed at the beautiful majestic trees, the extensive lawns and the flowers blooming despite the efforts of the weeds to choke them. I felt like one of those flowers, being strangled to death. I let out a wail and pulled at my hair. I screamed again, every foul profanity I could think of, until my throat felt raw.

That was better. Much better.

There was only one thing for it. I was going to have to sell Hamilton Hall.

I reached for my mobile phone.

At that very moment, there was a knock at the front door and I dropped the phone back in my bag. I fantasised it was that scamming bastard come to gloat. I was going to take an axe to his head and split him right down the middle, so that each half of his vile body fell sideways in opposite directions and crashed lifeless to the ground.

I opened the door to Craig Matthews.

32: Saturday, 31st August 1940
Wymondham

Martha:

'You're lying! You're lying, you beast! You are *lying*!' I beat on his chest with my fists, as he holds tight onto my burning forearms. My breath comes in throbbing gasps.

'Martha, Martha, listen to me. I would not lie to you about something like this. I could not be so cruel. Please calm yourself. Charles would not have wanted you to –'

'You wretched man! You are lying to me. Charles would not leave me like this. We are going to be married. Together for a lifetime.' Scolding tears soak my cheeks and the salty liquid that flows unchecked from my eyes blinds me. 'You *are* lying! You are *lying*!' My words come in rasps and grate on my vocal chords.

I feel the sharp sting on my left cheek as my face whips to one side.

'Martha, dear girl. I'm so sorry, but you must pull yourself together.' He's holding my face in his hands and staring into my eyes. 'You are hysterical. You're getting yourself into a state. Now calm yourself. Let me take you home.'

His voice is pacifying, exigent and firm. My legs turn to pulp and my knees hit the ground. I feel the impact. Then oblivion.

One week later...
Emily:

'Your sister is suffering from catatonic depression, Emily.'

Dr Beresford states it simply as he releases Martha's wrist and places her arm back under the bedclothes, gently tucking her in.

'Catatonic - ?'

'Catatonic depression. She's had two terribly traumatic events in her life in a very short space of time and her mind is struggling to process the information. I will give her a sedative injection. Sleep is the best healer. Sleep and rest. She's very young and with some care she should come out of it, but she will need close monitoring, Emily. Can you cope? Do you want me to engage a nurse to help?'

'I think I will be able to manage, Dr Beresford. I have Carter and Doris and I would rather keep it quiet and within the family, if you don't mind. The last thing I want is people gossiping that my sister is mad. Mummy and Daddy would be mortified.'

'As you wish, Emily. I'm afraid there is a great deal of stigma attached to mental problems, so I understand your concerns. However, I will call in to see her every day, and you must telephone me immediately if you see any deterioration in her condition.'

Dr Beresford's voice is warm and reassuring, his expression kindly. But I instinctively know he is deeply concerned.

32: SATURDAY, 31ST AUGUST 1940

As though reading my thoughts, he continues, 'I must warn you that if she does not respond to rest and care then there is a possibility I may have to arrange for her to be hospitalised.'

'A *mental* asylum? A *mad* house? No! I will not have it, Dr Beresford. Absolutely not. I've heard about those places. They'll wire her up to the mains. She could never come out.' I shudder at the very thought. He takes a syringe from his black leather physician's bag and a phial of liquid.

'Well, electroshock treatment is very effective in these cases but let's hope it won't come to that.' He injects Martha's upper arm and returns the empty syringe and phial to his bag. He squeezes my hand warmly. 'I'll pop in tomorrow morning. In the meantime, just keep an eye on her and if she wakes up, try to get her to drink some warm milk and honey. And tempt her to eat something tasty and wholesome, like chicken broth. The grazes on her knees should heal in no time. And remember, telephone me if you are at all concerned, Emily.'

With that, the fatherly family doctor I had known since birth strides out of the room and down the stairs. I follow him and show him out. As he climbs into his black Rover car, he calls over his shoulder: 'Damned hard to get hold of petrol these days. Blast this ruddy war. I'll be visiting patients on my bicycle at this rate!'

I have already been forced to give up driving and father's car stands with an empty petrol tank in the barn. The doctor raises a hand, starts the engine and as he sweeps out of the drive, a familiar, green sports car approaches.

The driver jumps out and walks towards me.

'Hello again, Miss Emily. I hope you don't mind the intrusion, but I was passing and thought I'd drop in to enquire about your sister's health. How is Martha?'

The dapper young RAF Officer, a slightly built man with a gentle yet rakish smile stands before me at the front door.

'She's resting, thank you. The doctor has just left. He says she will be fine once she's had some rest. A good rest is all she needs.'

'And how are you, Miss Emily? Dashed awful time you've been having. Blasted war.'

'We are both fine, thank you,' I say, quite ridiculously, as we are obviously anything but 'fine', and at the same time I am trying to recall whether he had told me his name last week when he had delivered Martha home in the dead of night. Martha seems to be making a habit, these days, of being brought home late at night by various RAF Officers.

'Flight Lieutenant James Morgan', he says, almost reading my mind. 'I wish we had met in happier times, Miss Emily.'

'Please cut the Miss, and call me Emily. Would you like to come in for a glass of apple juice, Flight Lieutenant Morgan?'

'I'd love to Miss – '. He smiles again. 'I mean, Emily. And please, you must call me James.'

I open the front door and he follows me into the reception hall.

'Do come through to the kitchen. I'm afraid I'm not really prepared to entertain guests, but I am so grateful to you for bringing Martha home safely last week. Goodness knows what could have happened to her. The least I can do is offer you some refreshment.'

We sit at the kitchen table that Doris had scrubbed earlier today to within an inch of its life and we sip juice of apples picked from the orchard. I bring cheese and home-baked bread to the table. James regales me with stories of happier times spent with his very good friend, Flying Officer Charles Harwood, who was shot down over Germany shortly after the Luftwaffe had bombed London and blasted my parents to oblivion. He recalls his commanding officer briefing the squadron that the Prime Minister had ordered the RAF to set Germany alight after the atrocious and unexpected bombing of innocent civilians.

'Darned stupid Jerries apparently lost their way. Supposed to bomb airfields and missed their target by a couple of hundred miles.'

So, Mummy and Daddy died as a result of Luftwaffe pilots getting lost. I break out in goose bumps. My heart turns to lead.

James reaches into his inside uniform pocket and pulls out a pale blue Basildon Bond envelope, placing it on the table before me. The name 'Martha' is clearly written in royal blue ink.

'The night Charles flew out on the raid, he gave me this letter and asked me, in the event he should not return, to meet Martha at their usual rendezvous place along the lane here, and give it to her. He gave me the keys and said if he didn't come back the car was mine. I didn't get the chance to give the letter to her, I'm afraid, because she was so distraught, and in all the confusion, I quite forgot. Here it is.' He pushes the envelope towards me.

The forward slanted writing is strong and confident.

I touch the writing with my fingertips. *Martha*.

'I will give it to my sister when she is feeling better. Please, James, would you mind telling me more about Charles? I never knew him, you see, but my sister was – is – terribly in love with him. Adored him. She was convinced they would marry. But our parents – well – it was Daddy really – didn't approve at all.'

James talks at length about his friend and fellow officer. He assures me that my parents, given the chance to get to know Charles, would have loved him, just as everyone else who knew the man held him in great affection. And that Charles Harwood did, indeed, love Martha and intended to marry her.

Hours pass. The evening sun descends through the kitchen window as dusk approaches. The sky is striated in peach and turquoise.

James continues on, until in the end Charles Harwood is no longer a stranger loved by my sister but a man who seems so familiar to me that I might have actually met and known him well. I feel more than a twinge of regret that, from what James tells me, my darling father had it all wrong and that Charles was anything but a 'cad'. My face starts to crumble and I cover it with the palms of my hands as I sob without restraint, forgetting all propriety in the presence of this stranger sitting with me at the kitchen table.

'I say, dear girl, don't take on so. You've been through a lot but this war won't last forever.'

He is up on his feet and I feel his arms around my shoulders. His hands find my face and lift it to his. We gaze into each other's eyes. His face lowers and his lips meet mine.

The kiss is soft and faltering at first then suddenly more urgent and eager as the tip of his tongue explores my lips and mouth and his hands move inside the shoulders of my dress. My skin is on fire at his touch. My hands find the back of his neck and I pull him closer so that now he kisses me harder. His hands squeeze my breasts and I experience sensations hitherto dormant, unexpressed. He takes my hands and gently helps me to my feet. I kick my shoes off and he strips off his jacket, tearing at the rest of his uniform, throwing it to the floor. He raises my dress; I lift my arms and he slips it over my head. He lifts me up by the waist and sits me on the kitchen table. My underwear is pulled aside and his soft fingers find me. My whole body throbs. My breath comes in panting gasps. My legs encircle his waist and I yield to him completely.

33: Summer, 2013, that same day
Hamilton Hall

Laura:

I know. I seemed to be habitually answering the door to the gorgeous Craig Matthews whenever I looked a right mess. The first time I'd met him I was in an old dressing gown covered in baking ingredients, and now here I was looking like an Alice Cooper tribute act. My mascara was running down my cheeks in black rivulets and my black hair was in alarming disarray, having suffered me attempting to pull it out by the roots. Actually, even Alice Cooper would probably be insulted by my impersonation of him. I looked much scarier.

How do I do it? More to the point, how does *he* do it? After all, it was Craig who always managed to arrive at my doorstep at the most inopportune moments. And, quite frankly, I never expected to see him again after the kiss-off incident in the Hamilton Hall library that time he'd told me the first edition books were worth a lot of dosh. That was some while ago, yet here he was, looking as delicious as ever. And that smile was still as disarming and to die for as ever. *Down girl! Throw some ice water on those hormones!*

'Laura! Hello. How are you?'

I was a little bit lost for words. I mean, how *was* I? I'd just found out that some scumbag had ripped off my credit card to the tune of a few grand, so not only was I feeling totally savage about that, but I also felt a complete fool to boot.

I found my voice. 'Oh hi, Craig. I'm not my best, to be honest, just had some really awful news and – '

Oh god, I didn't mean to burst into tears. Really, I didn't. How girly of me!

But I did. Right there on the doorstep, looking like a car crash as it was, then I added more tears to the mix. I tried to compose myself. Then, over a cuppa in the kitchen, explained the situation in rather more detail than Craig needed to know. I would normally, of course, share this with Kitty, but Craig happened to be the one who was there and anyway, it was just such a relief to be able to unload onto someone who would listen and not judge. I really was feeling a right sucker. Bloody idiot in fact. I mean, for god's sake! A stranger approaches me straight after an old man's funeral and I let him loose with my credit card details.

'Have you been to the police, Laura?' Craig asks after some while of me whinging on about it all.

'I haven't had the chance to do anything yet, Craig, because I've only just found out I've been scammed. I didn't even let the person at the bank finish. I hung up.'

Craig pressed his lips together into a grim, thin line. 'Fancy another cup of tea?' He got up from the table and, as though he actually lived in my house, filled the kettle. He took up the mugs, rinsed them under the tap, dried them on the tea towel and placed a teabag in each. He reached for the biscuit barrel and found a tea plate, upon which he placed six Hobnobs. Chocolate ones. Obviously, chocolate biscuits are the only fodder appropriate at a time of crisis like this.

Titanic played out on my mobile. It was Kitty. She was late. She was going to come up to help me make a start on the garden and should have been here half an hour ago.

'Laura. Sorry love. I'm running late. Be there around mid-afternoon. That OK with you? Perhaps I could stay over and we could get on with it again first thing in the morning. How does that sound?'

'OK, Kitty. No problem.'

'You OK, Laura? You sound a bit – '

'Fine, Kitty, fine. See you when you get here.'

'OK. Be there soon.'

I looked over at Craig, as he stirred his tea and pushed the plate full of calories across the table to me. 'Go on, Laura. Nothing chocolate biscuits can't fix.' Something deep inside me stirred as he grinned at me. *Bugger.* I reached for a biscuit and took a bite.

'Terrible blow, Laura, that you've been scammed, but I'm sure the bank will sort it out. Have you thought any more about selling some of your first edition books? I had a word with my uncle – '

'Oh Craig. It's good of you to speak to your uncle and everything, but I hate the thought of those books being in my ancestors' family for generations and me just selling them because I'm broke. It seems criminal somehow. But I really don't know what I am going to do.'

I looked around the kitchen and my mind wandered back to the grand first floor library, the exquisite family oil paintings in the drawing room and the dining room, and my heart turned over. What would those classy people think of me, getting rid of family library books? I just couldn't do it.

'I can hardly afford to feed myself, let alone keep this place on. I really don't see a solution.' I picked up my phone. 'Actually, I was about to find a local estate agent and get someone round to do a valuation. I think I'm going to have to sell Hamilton Hall.' Tears welled up in my eyes again.

'Oh, I am sure it won't come to that. Tell you what, Laura. Let's pop into town for a bite to eat and perhaps we could try to work something out. What do you say?'

He was smiling that winning smile of his again, and his eyebrows were raised, awaiting my reply.

'Craig, I – '

'Lunch is on me. Come on Laura. Just wash your face and comb your hair and you'll be good as new. Shall we?'

'I – '

'I'd enjoy it, Laura. Really, I would. And we can discuss the house. Two heads are better than one. Come on, what do you say?'

'I can't keep letting you take me out for meals, Craig. It's... it's ... well, I feel I owe you.'

'Oh, just make me some of those delicious cakes of yours! Deal?'

Well, put like that...

'OK, give me a minute.' *That smile of his. Jeez. I should bottle it and sell it!*

'And perhaps over lunch I can persuade you to let my uncle value some of your rare books...'

What?

'Is that all you're after Craig? You mean, this is not so much about helping me to work out what to do to keep Hamilton Hall, but more about you securing a sale of my first edition Jane Austen books?'

'Not quite like that, no, Laura, look – '

'Come off it. I'm not that daft. You people are all alike. All out for what you can make out of another person. What if I told your boss at Hatch and bloody Horncastle that you are using clients to do a lucrative deal on the side for your bloody uncle? How would that go down, eh Craig?'

The world was all spinning the wrong way around. God, what next? And there was me, thinking Craig bloody Matthews was a good bloke. Serves me right for falling for a pretty face. I was livid. I'd had enough.

Craig stood up from the kitchen table. 'No, really, Laura, you've got it all wrong. I am not trying to make you do anything you wouldn't want to do. I just want to help you. Really, I do.'

'Yeah, right. Just like that slimy git wanted to help me with picking up a scammy inheritance from some poor departed old boy. And it ended up he just wanted to help himself to my credit card.' I got up from the table. 'Just sod off, Craig. And don't come back! Go. Now!'

We were out in the reception hall now and I pushed him towards the front door. He was staggering backwards, uttering protestations. I gave him one last shove and slammed the door of Hamilton Hall behind him. Then sank to my knees and sobbed into my hands.

34: August, 1940 - Later that evening
Hamilton Hall

Emily:

'Oh, my goodness, whatever was I thinking?' I am adjusting my clothing and James is now getting dressed.

He kisses me again, my face in his hands. Soft, gentle hands that feel good on my warm, flushed cheeks. He runs his fingers through the tight curls of my hair.

'You're beautiful, Emily. You are a beautiful, warm-hearted and lovely girl and that was the most intensely wonderful experience of my life.'

He takes me in his arms, holding me into him, and I feel and hear his heart beat as I rest the side of my head against his chest. His breathing starts to regulate. I feel the stickiness and look down to see the blood. I look at the table. The red liquid stains the pinewood where only this morning, Doris had scrubbed the table clean. I am mortified. I feel unclean and exposed. He sees it.

'My dear girl. You were – I didn't realise - you were a – '

'A virgin, yes, James. What on earth did you expect?' I hear my voice rise by a couple of octaves. Tears prick my eyes.

'Emily, Emily, my lovely girl.' He takes my hand and pulls me into him. 'You are the sweetest girl I've ever known and that was the most momentous experience of my life.' He takes me into his arms again.

We both cry now; soft, quiet sobs. The cry of the young, whose lives are constrained by war-time, who know instinctively that such moments must be snatched and experienced at any opportunity. Unspoken is the knowledge that this could be not only our first, but also our last experience of the expression of adult love. We stay like that for some minutes. Holding each other tightly. Feeling the other's gentle sobs. Both of us caught up in the memory of those shared moments of ecstasy.

'*Martha!* Oh, my goodness, Martha! I must check on her. What *was* I thinking? Dr Beresford told me to keep a close watch on her. James, I'm sorry, I must go.'

'That's no problem, darling. Go and see your sister. I will find us a glass of water for when you come down.'

I light a candle, aware of the rules of the blackout, and go up the winding stairs. I peek into Martha's room to see her still sound asleep. I draw together the blackout curtains and move along the landing to my room, where I place the candle on the dresser, pull together my blackout curtains and remove my underwear. I take a washcloth and clean myself gently at the basin. I feel the soreness but smile at the memory, as I dab the soft towel against my private areas. I open the top drawer and take out clean underwear, carefully dressing myself. I leave my soiled clothes to soak in the washbasin before stepping quietly down the stairs and back into the kitchen.

James has cleaned the table, found two tumblers and filled them from the tap. He is fully dressed now, apart from his uniform jacket, which is hung across the back of a chair. He has closed the shutters at the kitchen window and sits at the table, sipping from his glass. He smiles fondly at me as I enter the room. This was not how I had visualised my first time. He leans forward and takes my head in his hands, bringing it closer to his face, and kisses me gently.

Nine days later, as he was flying on a bombing raid over Germany, an unknown Luftwaffe pilot set alight the Supermarine Spitfire being piloted by Flight Lieutenant James Morgan and sent him crashing to his death.

35: Summer 2013 – same day
Hamilton Hall

Laura:

'*C*hickens!'

'Chickens? What about them, Laura?' Kitty's brow was furrowed, her eyebrows knitted.

'Yes! Chickens! I'll get some chickens. There's already a chicken coop out there and how hard can it be?'

'You are honestly telling me you're thinking of keeping chickens?'

'Why not? Breakfast delivered every morning and then the odd roast dinner thrown in. Can't beat it.' I rubbed my hands together with glee.

Kitty had turned up at Hamilton Hall half an hour after I'd thrown Craig off the premises and found me in a right state. The definitive self-composed, practical person, she'd made me wash my face, comb my hair, pull myself together and tell her all about it. She'd been reluctant to accept that the lovely Craig's dark motive was to make a fast buck out of me so we'd settled on an agreement to differ on that one. On arriving, she'd brandished a carrier bag full of lunch goodies and we'd feasted at the kitchen table before taking a stroll around the garden to survey the full extent of the work that would be involved in tidying things up. For the second time, we had seen the chicken coop. Well, all right, it was a bit on the derelict side, but nothing a little bit of DIY couldn't fix. Hence my brainwave of keeping chickens.

We'd also found an equally dilapidated barn with copious weeds growing knee high around it. It took some huffing and puffing and a great deal of heaving on both our parts to get the door open but then there it was: an ancient looking black car without wheels! With more effort, we'd cranked open the bonnet, only to discover – *yes, really* – no engine! I'd finally come across a car in a worse state than Esther! It was covered in cobwebs and legions of spiders of all sizes marched purposefully and determinedly all over it. I'd wiped the dust and grime from the number plate: JU 4976.

'Well,' I'd said, 'they don't make number plates like that anymore.' And I'd wondered out loud how you could tell the age of the vehicle by the number plate in those days. Neither Kitty nor myself had any idea.

Now we were back in the kitchen, having a cuppa and making a 'to-do' list for the grounds of Hamilton Hall. Any thoughts of selling the house now long forgotten.

'But do you know anything about keeping chickens, Laura? I mean, if you don't then you really ought to find out, don't you think?'

'Oh Kitty. How hard can it be? Stick a few chickens in the coop and feed them every now and again.'

'Don't be daft, there's got to be more to it than – oh – OK, now I see you're joking. Very funny.' she said, sighing, when she looked at the expression on my face.

'Of course, I don't know anything about chickens, except that they lay eggs, and cluck, but you can learn just about anything on the Internet these days. I'll look it up. When I get a chance, that is. Can't be rocket science, surely. But for now, we need to make a start on that garden.'

We both stood up from the kitchen table and started to clear away the detritus of the lunch we'd devoured. I was already feeling much more on an even keel and the memory of Craig's betrayal was fast fading. There was still the little issue of money (or rather lack of it) to deal with, not to mention the fact I'd been scammed, but for now I was able to put it all to the back of my mind.

There was still a light breeze and some warm sunshine as we made our away around the garden. Once again, we came across the orchard, and to my delight found ripe plums and apples hanging in abundance from the trees.

'Look,' said Kitty, pointing at the corner of the orchard, 'blackcurrant bushes! You'll not want for food with a treasure like this in your garden!' I hadn't spotted those, but sure enough, tucked away in the corner of the orchard these were definitely blackcurrants. We also spotted some gooseberry bushes too, but would need to hack away at plentiful weeds and nettles to get to them. Life was actually starting to feel like fun again.

'Yes! And if I get some chickens too, I'll be well away!'

'Tell you what, why don't we pick some of this fruit and do a bit of baking? If we make plenty we can put some in the freezer too. Have you done a shop here yet? Got margarine? Flour? Sugar? Anything like that?'

'No, I haven't actually. Shall we pop out in Esther and go to *Waitrose*? Seems that's the supermarket in vogue around here. No cheap and cheerful *Asda* or *Lidl* in upmarket Wymondham!'

'Come on then, you posh woman!' Kitty beamed at me and I grabbed my keys from my jacket pocket as we made towards Esther.

'Bugger!' I said, as I approached the car.

'What?'

'I've left my bloody sidelights on all night. Duh!!' I jumped in and tried the ignition. Dead as the proverbial door nail.

'Oh crap. Never mind, hop in my car and when we get back we can call the AA out. Come on. We need to get the shopping now.' And with that we sped off down the drive and along the lane into Wymondham.

35: SUMMER 2013 – SAME DAY

As dusk approached, and having produced quantities of apple pies, plum pies, cakes and crumbles in a marathon bake-off with Kitty, I was feeling a lot less murderous towards Craig Matthews and the evil scam merchant. Baking always has that effect on me; well, baking and Kitty, to be honest. There's not much that can't be put right with some homemade baking and a nice hot cuppa with my best friend. She's always been the 'sister' I'd never had and she says I'm her 'sister' too. We opened a tub of thick cream (reduced in Waitrose as it had reached its use-by date, so my ethos of 'waste not want not' meant we had to eat the lot that day; *what a tragedy!*) and spooned it over slices of apple pie. I put the kettle on, fished a couple of mugs out of the kitchen sink and rinsed them under the tap.

The following morning (Kitty had stayed over and we'd shared a creaky double bed with our sleeping bags wrapped around us) I made the phone call to the AA. I got a bit of an ear bashing from the woman in the call centre but I pleaded and must have sounded convincing because within the hour the trusty rescue mechanic, Jason, was once more tinkering with Esther on the drive of Hamilton Hall.

'This could have been avoided, you know, Laura. You really do need to remember to turn your lights off otherwise the battery will be flat as a pancake in the morning, as well you found out. And the AA – '

'Yes, yes, Jason, I know. And I am really, *really* sorry about the lights and the battery. But I've got a lot on my mind at the moment...'

'Have you thought about getting yourself a half-decent car? That would be one less thing to worry about.' He rolled his eyes and shook his head and the fat on his three chins swung from side to side.

'Your Fiesta really is the worst – well, put it this way, you don't find many cars in a worse state than this one on the road these days.' Although Jason admonished me in a roguish but kind-hearted way, the twinkle in his eye told me he was really on my side.

'Oh, don't be mean, Jason. Esther's a good little car. She usually gets me around, with a little help, admittedly, from you and the AA, but she's pretty reliable otherwise.'

Kitty approached us from the house with a tray of teas. 'Actually, Jason, there *is* a car that's in a worse state than Esther. Come on, Laura, let's show him what we found in the old barn.' She parked the tea tray on the bonnet of her car and we took our drinks with us to the barn.

'This I've got to see,' muttered Jason.

We put our mugs down on the ground and prized open the barn doors. It was easier this time and we ushered Jason in.

A long, slow whistle emitted from the car mechanic's pursed lips and he scratched his head. 'Well, well, well! What do we have here? At least Esther's got four wheels. I'll grant you that.'

'And an engine. But look in here!' I lifted the bonnet for Jason to see the empty space beneath.

'This is a 1930s Austin Ten!' Jason let out another long whistle. 'She must have been a real beauty in her day. Classic now. Worth a bob or two.'

'A bob or two? Without wheels or engine? You must be kidding, Jason. It's a wreck. Once I get organised I'm going to get the local scrap yard to come and take it away.'

36: Early September, 1940
Hamilton Hall

Emily:

'Martha darling, you must try to eat something. We need you to get your strength back. Come on now. Doris has made this delicious chicken stew for us. Do have some.'

Martha stares out of the bedroom window. I touch her arm and she turns to me.

'He's gone, Emily.' Her face is pale and still. Her eyes look too big for her sad little face and stare out at me like two huge pools of utter desolation. Where is the vivacious, exuberant Martha, who used to be so full of life? My heart aches for her. But at least she is no longer in a catatonic state. I'm so relieved about that. Dr Beresford had worried me when he'd suggested my sister might end up in a mental hospital. That was some weeks ago and thankfully seems unlikely now.

'I know, my darling. I know. But you are still here and life must go on.' I try to soothe her but my words seem hollow and clichéd.

'How can I go on, Em? Mummy and Daddy, and now Charles. They've all gone. I'll never forgive myself for being so horrid to Daddy just the day before he died. I'm a horrible person.' She sobs; I hold her. Her tears soak the shoulder of my dress. I let her cry and cry. Then I lead her back to her bed and help her onto it. She looks so thin and frail. Her nightdress hangs on her much-diminished body.

'I don't know how we go on when we lose the people we love, Martha. But do I know that we can do only one of two things: we either go on, or we give up and wither and that is just not an option. There are lots of people losing those they love in this dreadful war. But we must keep going. And you're not a horrible person, Martha. You're not to say that. I know Charles loved you as much as you loved him and he was a good man. Daddy would have come around in the end, I just know it.'

I think about James. My first and only love, shot down over Germany. I shudder as if to dismiss the realisation that I will never see him again and the love that promised to blossom was cut down without a chance.

'Come on, now Martha; try to eat something. Mummy and Daddy's memorial service at the chapel is this Sunday. We must get you better so that you can come.'

I take some stew onto the spoon and hold it in front of my sister's face, like a mother feeding her young child.

'Please, Martha, for me.' She obediently takes a small morsel and chews it slowly. 'Good girl. That's it. You'll be well again in no time. You need to get better and get back to work at the bank. We must all carry on and do the best we can.'

Suddenly she throws the sheet to one side and, holding her mouth, makes a dash for the bathroom. I hear her vomiting. I go and kneel by her side and rub her back as the pan fills with regurgitated chicken stew. It is the second time I have heard her vomiting today and she has hardly eaten at all in days. I wipe her mouth with a dampened cloth and hand her a glass of water. Tears from the strain of throwing up stream down her cheeks.

'Emily,' she says in a tiny voice, as I tuck her back into bed, 'I think I'm going to have a baby.'

37: Same day
Hamilton Hall

Laura:

'*No!* Don't do that Laura! I told you, it's a *classic car*. Worth a bit of dosh, if you go to a good classic car dealer. Or an auction, yes, even in this condition.'

Jason took a swig of his tea as he walked around, surveying the old wreck. 'Oh yes, she was a beauty in her day, all right. Wonder what happened to her?'

'Well, it must have belonged to my ancestors. I've just inherited this house, you see. Hamilton Hall now belongs to me, Jason.'

'Well, I'm blessed!' Another whistle. His eyebrows shot up to the heavens. 'Lady of the manor now, are you?'

'Yes, and without a brass farthing to my name. What's the opposite of a cloud with a silver lining?'

'You could get a few grand for this old girl. Have a look on the Internet. You'll see. But for goodness' sake, don't scrap it. And watch out for tricksters. There's plenty of them about and wanting to make money out of you.' *Don't I know it!*

'Just take care, that's my advice. But you mark my words, Laura, there's a bit of money in that car over in that there barn. Just don't scrap it.'

We were making our way back to Esther.

Back at the Fiesta, Jason scribbled a few notes on his pad and passed it to me to sign by the cross he'd made. 'You might get enough from the sale of the classic to treat yourself to a decent car, Laura. You're on dodgy ground with the AA as far as this old car's concerned. You know our fair play policy.'

'Yes, yes, I know, Jason. And you are *very* kind to come out again. I'll take your advice and look up dilapidated classic cars!'

'You do that, Laura. You do that.' And with all the alacrity of a man half his age and six stone lighter, he jumped into his truck, gave a wave of his hand out of the open window, and was gone.

It was dusk and we sat together on the old *chaise longue* in the drawing room. Kitty was gazing up at the oil painting hanging over the fireplace. She stood up and moved across the room and her fingers gently touched the picture.

'This is most remarkable, Laura. Such a beautiful painting and to think these were your great-great-grandparents. You look just like her you know, Laura – what did you say her name was?'

'My great-great-grandmother was French. She was called Adalicia. That's what Craig told me anyway. He showed me the document with the family tree. I think she was far more beautiful than I will ever be.'

'Simply stunning. And so classy. Just look at that gorgeous emerald necklace and the earrings too. And what a figure she had on her. You must feel proud to belong to such a family, Laura.'

'Yes, I think I am, really. They lived in a world far removed from what I've been used to.'

My phone pinged. I saw in the preview window that it was a text from Craig. I immediately deleted it.

'Bloody cheek.' I muttered.

'Problem?'

'No. Nothing really. That was from Craig. No doubt hoping to get back into my good books so he can pull a lucrative deal for his uncle.'

'Now Laura,' said Kitty, looking at me in that reproachful way she does sometimes that always makes me feel like a kid in short, white socks and scuffed shoes, 'you don't know that that's the case. He might genuinely be trying to help you. Why don't you talk to him and find out?'

'We've gone through this before, Kitty. I'd feel guilty selling off my family's precious books just because I'm short of cash. Those books must have been in the family forever, and must have meant a lot to them in their day. Anyway, it was you who pointed that out to me ages ago, remember?'

'I know I did and I take your point, Laura. But sometimes, just sometimes, needs must. You're broke. Just think about it before you dismiss the idea. Now, we've had a look around most of the garden; shall we look around the house and start making a list of jobs? And you never know, we might find some hidden treasure that you wouldn't mind flogging.'

'Good idea,' I said and took my writing pad and pen from my bag and made for the drawing room door, Kitty hot on my trail. 'But I don't expect to find any treasure. If only!'

We both laughed and as we went up the stairs, Kitty recalled that there were nine bedrooms. We decided to start with the attic rooms right at the top and work our way down. That meant climbing another flight of back stairs and ducking our heads as we entered the first bedroom.

'This would have been the servants' bedroom, wouldn't it? What a life they must have had. If *Downton Abbey* is anything to go by, they'd have been up at the crack of dawn, lighting fires and scrubbing floors, poor devils.' Kitty seemed to be in thoughtful mood.

'But all that must have been long, long ago, Kit, because Great Aunt Emily lived alone here at least in the latter stages of her life, according to Craig.' *Stop thinking about him! He was only after your rare books!*

We opened drawers and cupboards and found a huge trunk in the corner of the room. We opened it and as the hinges creaked decades of different smells assaulted my nostrils. There were board games, stuffed toys, an almost bald tennis ball. I wished I could go back in time and spend a day in this nursery, playing as a little girl with my ancestors. As I pulled out items I came across some dressing up clothes.

'Look Kitty. Dressing up clothes!'

Kitty took an item from me. 'No, they're not dressing up clothes at all. These are pieces of uniforms. Servants' uniforms.'

Sure enough. A greying white apron. A rough long grey skirt. These clothes were so very different to the high quality clothes worn by Adalicia and Richard, Emily and Martha in those oil paintings downstairs.

'What a hard life they must have had, Kitty.'

'Yes, in some ways, but at least they had employment and a roof over their heads.'

'What gets me is that if Mum had lived in those times, she would have been sleeping up here and working her fingers to the bone, not living the life of relative luxury like my ancestors living downstairs. I wonder how she came to be estranged from Hamilton Hall?'

'You must have read about it in those documents you signed, Laura.'

'Erm, well...'

'What? What?' She gave me that look again.

'You did read the papers before you signed, didn't you?

I looked down at my shoes.

'Oh Laura. You are the limit! All the information must have been in that envelope. Where is it?'

'Oh, it is still with the lawyer. His PA is going to photocopy and post me the originals.'

'Well make sure you read them when you get them back. Come on, let's look at the other rooms.' She gave me that withering look of hers and I led the way out of the room.

The other attic room had obviously been a nursery at some point and contained the broken rocking horse I'd seen on an earlier viewing and Kitty tried to straddle and ride it.

'Yeehah!' she yelled, as she bobbed up and down.

'Oh, come on, Cowgirl Kitty! Stop messing about. We've got things to do.'

'You know you could have a garage sale of all these bits and pieces. Or what about selling a few things on eBay? Why don't we make an inventory and see what you've got? Some little kid'd be happy with that rocking horse, once it's fixed up. And what about that cot? Just think about what furniture you want to keep and what you want to get rid of. Are you going to bring any of your furniture from the cottage?' Kitty was really getting into her stride now.

We worked our way through each of the bedrooms, making notes as we went.

'Oh, I've had enough. That'll do for now. I think it's wine o'clock,' I said, looking at my watch. After making a few more notes we made our way down to the kitchen and found the wine and nibbles.

'Come on, let's be posh and sit in the drawing room,' Kitty suggested and so we did just that.

We chinked glasses and tucked into olives and cheese and grapes and crisps. Kitty played some relaxing music on her mobile phone and we sat back with our feet up, enjoying the change of pace of the day.

'Have you looked inside any of those boxes of your mum's stuff that we brought over from the cottage?' Kitty asked after taking another sip of wine.

'No. They're still untouched in the library. I'll get around to it one day.'

'Oh Laura! You're hopeless! What's holding you back? You seem very reluctant to see what's inside those boxes. Aren't you even curious as to what's in them? Could be all manner of treasure. They were in your loft nearly a decade before we brought them here.'

'You're not going to do your Freudian gig on me again, are you Kitty dear?' I smiled over at her.

'Now, would I do that dearest Laura? The very idea! No, but I was just wondering why you've never looked at the stuff in all these years.'

'Oh, I don't know. Probably just never found the right moment. There's always something else to do and time just slips by and I never gave the stuff a thought from one year's end to the next. And anyway, it's probably just a load of old photos and stuff like that. Certainly, no treasure, that's for sure.'

A couple of glasses of wine later, the bottle empty and all the nibbles devoured, Kitty jumped up, saying, 'Come on Laura, to the library! We have work to do!'

Taking the empty wine glass from me, she grabbed my hand and pulled me to me feet.

'Oh, why *now*, Kitty? Let's have another bottle of wine and start on the boxes in the morning.'

'Nope. We are doing it right now,' she said over her shoulder and in a tone, that brooked no argument. 'Come on.' *Short, white socks and scuffed shoes!*

We found a pair of scissors in the kitchen and I half-heartedly followed Kitty up the stairs and into the library. The boxes were piled on top of one another and we started by spreading them out on the floor. Kitty took the scissors to one of the boxes and slit it open.

38: End of September 1940
Hamilton Hall

Emily:

'Well, yes, Martha, you are in the family way. No doubt about it.' Doctor Beresford sits on the edge of my sister's bed, having asked some questions and carried out an examination. His tone is matter-of-fact, his attitude non-judgemental. Martha is silent. Barely twenty years of age, my once effervescent, carefree little sister is to become an unmarried mother.

'I would calculate your due date to be around about the end of April, but it's very early days as yet. Anything could happen. Take a ginger biscuit first thing in the morning and the sickness and nausea should ease off soon. Get plenty of rest and remember to eat and drink as usual. You have an infant to think of now. It's not just about you any longer young lady. And remember, you are having a baby, but you are not an invalid. So, while right now you do need your rest, you must try to get up and about as soon as you can.' Our kindly family doctor squeezes Martha's arm and, having replaced his stethoscope in his black bag, gets up from the bed, turns to me and sighs.

'How are you coping, Emily? Do you need any help?'

'We will be fine, Doctor. Just fine. As you say, we'll soon have another little person to think about and we must do the best we can. But, Doctor Beresford, can I ask you something please?'

'Of course, Emily. What is it?' His voice is soft and calm.

'You see, there'd be a terrible scandal if news of Martha's... Martha's... condition got around the neighbourhood. Could we keep it quiet, do you think?'

'Well, I can arrange a home birth, that's no problem, so long as there are no complications. But the baby will have to be registered and you can't keep a child hidden from the outside world for long. But yes, for now we can be discreet. Don't worry.' His smile is warm, but his expression one of concern, as he gently touches my shoulder before moving towards the door and down the stairs.

Two weeks later...

'Emily! *Emily!*'

My sister's screams jolt me awake. I open my eyes to the darkness of the night. The grandfather clock in the reception hall strikes three. My heart leaps. My pulse races. Despite the autumnal chill my nightgown is wet with sweat. *Martha! Oh, my goodness! Martha!*

I rush to my sister's room, stumbling into doorframes as I do so. My mouth and throat are dry. My brow is damp.

Her bed is empty. I see the bright red blood and hear her whimpering in the bathroom. I move swiftly across the room to see her sitting on the edge of the bath, clutching her abdomen; her nightdress stained the same vivid colour as the sheet on her bed. Her face is grey. Her eyes stare with fright.

'Emily! I've lost my baby. My baby. It's gone. My baby is gone. Why is this happening to us?' She searches the ceiling with wide, bewildered eyes. She wails. She sobs. She howls. She trembles.

I catch my breath and gently take her in my arms. My lips quiver. Tears sting my eyes.

'My poor darling. Let me get you into a nice warm bath and clean everything up. I'll make you a hot drink and change your bed. I'll call Doctor Beresford in the morning.' My heart thumps. My pulse races.

'I was going to call him Charles,' she says, and her voice cracks with another heart-breaking sob.

39: Summer, 2013, same day, later on
Hamilton Hall

Laura:

'See! Just as I thought! A load of old photo albums. Nothing much of interest here, Kitty,' I said. 'I might as well put them up in one of the attic rooms and sort through them one day when I've got nothing better to do.'

'We've only opened one box, Laura. Who knows what you'll find in the others?'

'I don't really care what's in them, Kit. Come on; help me take them upstairs and then I can forget about them for a while. There are far more pressing things to think about here, without worrying about Mum's old photos.' I was returning the albums to the box.

'I don't know what it is about you Laura White, but there is something definitely holding you back here. You're so reluctant to even take a quick look. Aren't you even a little bit curious?' Kitty picked up a small photograph album and flicked through it. As she did so, a piece of paper floated to the ground. She picked it up. I was still refilling the box and about to close it up, as she spoke: 'Look at this, Laura!'

She handed me the piece of paper that she had unfolded and I saw immediately it was a premium bond in my name. It was rubber-stamp dated a week after I was born and had a value of five pounds.

'Crikey. I never knew I had a premium bond, Kitty. I don't remember Mum ever telling me. It's probably out of date now.' Kitty took it from me.

'No! They never go out of date, Laura. You should get in touch with *N, S and I* and check to see if you've won anything. You can do it online. You never know, you might have won something.'

'OK, give it here.' I took back the premium bond and stuck it in my jeans pocket. 'I'll check it out, but I don't imagine for one minute there's a fortune waiting for me to claim!' We both laughed.

'Like I said, Laura, you never know.'

We carried the boxes one by one up to the attic and I shut the door firmly behind me. Kitty was right: there was something holding me back from going through those boxes, but I could not for the life of me articulate what it was. One thing I did know was that I just did not want to bring back the horror of the accident that took Mum from me eight years ago. Every year on the anniversary of her death, I relive the day that the police arrived on my doorstep to tell me a motorbike rider had killed my mother. She died way before her time and I miss her every single day. I suppose in a way it's the prospect of looking in those boxes that stirs in me a fear of getting close to her again, only to risk sort of losing her once more. Now that I have this amazing house, I am acutely aware of the lack of comfort in Mum's life. She sacrificed a lot to give me the best she could with her thrifty ways. I remember days when she'd sit me down at the table with only one place set, and put my dinner in front of me. When I'd ask where her dinner was, she'd say she had eaten earlier. I never quite believed her. I feel guilty now for not offering to share my dinner with her. If only she were here now to enjoy this inheritance. At least she could have had a nice comfortable home and me to cook decent meals for her in her later years. Still, no point dwelling on what might have been.

It was still late afternoon as we made our way down the stairs. There was a knock on the front door.

'Oh shit. I hope that's not old George, wanting me to sell him some land again!' I groaned as I walked across the reception hall to open the door. 'He can just sod off, because I'm not being bullied.' I opened the door, about to say as much, only to be met by a tall man in his mid-forties, twinkling blue eyes, smiling down on me. Nice tan, too. He looked a bit familiar, but I had no idea why.

'Hello there. I hope I'm not disturbing you. Laura White, I presume?' Nicely spoken too, without being nauseatingly plummy.

'Erm, well, yes, that's me. And you are?'

'Felix Farrington.' He extended a hand for me to shake.

'Farrington?' I took his outstretched hand, while eyeing him.

'Yes, that's right, Felix Farrington. My old Pa is your nearest neighbour.'

'Oh no,' I said, as the penny dropped. 'Don't tell me you've been sent round to put pressure on me to sell you my land, because if that's the case, you can just bugger off, Felix Farrington. I've just about had a basin full of your dad, and now you're here – '

'Whoa!' He raised his hands, palms facing me, in a gesture of surrender. 'No, no. Not at all. Not in the slightest. Wouldn't dream of it. Actually, I came primarily to apologise for my father. I gather he's been pestering you and I'm truly sorry. If you don't want to sell your land, well, that is your choice. I would not even *try* to persuade you. You see, the thing is – erm, I'm sorry,' he looked to his left and then to his right, 'but would you mind if I popped inside a moment? Easier to talk.'

Kitty was now at my side. She looked at me and gave a slight nod of her head.

'Yes, OK, come on in. Fancy a cuppa?' I held the door open for him and led the way through to the kitchen. 'This is my friend, Kitty.' They exchanged polite greetings.

Kitty put the kettle on while I sat at the kitchen table with Felix Farrington.

'So, what is it you wanted to say?' I looked him straight in the eyes and he held my gaze.

'Well, Pa is getting on a bit, as you will have noticed, and I'm a bit concerned about his health. More to the point, he's worried too. So, he had this idea of buying a bit of your land and building a small bungalow on it, for him to live in, and in the hopes that I'd come home to live in the big house. Then I'd be close enough to keep an eye on him, but he'd still have his independence. He's fiercely independent you know. But the truth is, we don't really need to buy extra land, because we have plenty there already. I'm afraid my father has developed some rather batty ideas in his old age.'

'You're not kidding! He pulled a shotgun on us the first time we met. Said he was keeping an eye on the old place. Worried about squatters or burglars since my great aunt Emily died. Oh!' A sudden thought popped into my head. 'You must have known my great aunt.'

'Emily? Yes, yes, I did indeed. Since I was born, actually.'

40: Early October 1940
Hamilton Hall

Emily:

'But Doctor Beresford, you said I'd had a miscarriage. How can I still be pregnant?'

It is three weeks since Martha's screams had awoken me in the night but she has continued to vomit every day and suffers dizziness and lethargy too.

'Well,' our doctor's voice is calm and benign, 'it seems that you were carrying twins, my dear, and yes, you did miscarry one of them, but you are still holding onto the other little mite. Must be a robust baby.'

I am torn between elation that Martha's heartache following the miscarriage has been assuaged and disappointment that the impending family scandal has not gone away. I must admit, to my shame, that I had been somewhat relieved when Martha had the miscarriage. It seemed to solve a lot of problems. Now the dread and shame of a child being born into the Boulais-Hamilton family out of wedlock overwhelm me. I can just hear the villagers and in particular that awful Nellie Braithwaite in the post office, sniggering behind our backs about the scandal. What am I to do? I look at Martha. She is smiling down at her belly, which she strokes fondly.

'Twins? I was having twins? But I still have one baby?' Now my sister is crying and beaming at the same time and it is the first time I have seen her beautiful, bright smile in months. My heart lifts and I feel guilty at my selfish thoughts. Why should we care about what other people think? There is a horrible war raging across the world and thousands of people are dying every day. A bomb hit even Buckingham Palace last month. The very cheek of those Luftwaffe! The King and Queen survived, but there were casualties. Why should people be concerned about a new life, even if it is a child born out of wedlock? It is so trivial a matter in the grand scheme of things. Anyway, we could pretend that Martha and Charles were married just before he was shot down. I could get her a wedding band and no one will be any the wiser. Once we defeat Hitler, this baby will be part of a new peaceful England. He, or she, will be part of a new generation of children heading for a safer, more hopeful future.

My thoughts are interrupted by Doctor Beresford's voice. 'I think your dizzy spells are probably due to anaemia, Martha. You lost quite a lot of blood with the miscarriage. I will prescribe some iron tablets. Try to eat liver, if you can get it, and plenty of greens. Stay in bed for a few more days, take the iron tablets, but do try to get up and about as soon as you can.'

'Yes, Doctor Beresford, I will do as you say.' Martha's smile has faded now, and she looks anxious. 'I'm so happy to be having Charles's baby, especially after thinking I'd lost it. Imagine! I was having twins! But do you think I might lose the other baby too? I couldn't bear it.' Her face creases with apprehension and concern.

'No reason at all why that should happen, Martha.'

'And how will I cope? I mean: I know nothing about babies. I wish Mummy -'

'You'll soon learn young lady!' The doctor's tone is matter-of-fact.

'It will be fine, Martha. I'm here and Doris and Carter will always help. Don't worry.'

'And you know, Martha, you were one of twins,' said the doctor, 'your mother miscarried your twin, very early on, but you clung on for dear life. You're a survivor!'

'Really, Doctor? I never knew that!' Martha looks first, stunned, then delighted. 'So, twins run in the family!'

'Yes, it seems they do, Martha.' Doctor Beresford takes his pen from his inside jacket pocket and scribbles on his prescription pad, then tears off the page and hands it to me. 'There you are, Emily. Get these from the Chemist's as soon as possible and give her two, first thing, every morning. She must get some iron inside her. And, Martha, carry on taking a ginger biscuit with your morning tea and the nausea will cease very soon, I'm sure.' He gets up from sitting on the side of Martha's bed and moves across the room to the door. There he turns and smiles at us both and leaves the room.

Doris is clearing away after the evening meal and Carter is taking his cap and walking towards the back door of the kitchen. Martha has managed to eat a little food and held it down. She is still resting in bed.

'I'll just clear up them tools before that blackout,' Carter calls over his shoulder, as his hand rests on the doorknob.

'Actually, Carter, I want to speak to you. To both of you.' Doris turns around from the kitchen sink as Carter pauses at the door and turns to face me. He scratches his head and rubs the end of his nose with the palm of his hand.

I look at each of them in turn. 'Can we sit for a moment?' They come back to the table and we all take a seat. Their expressions are difficult to decipher.

I clear my throat.

'You have both been such loyal, constant, kind family members, for as long as Martha and I can remember. And yes, we do see you both as family. Now I have something to tell you and I need your assurance that your usual loyalty and discretion will be unfailing in this matter, as it is of the utmost importance.' Doris and Carter exchange looks.

Doris speaks first.

41: Summer, 2013, same day
Hamilton Hall

Laura:

'Actually, I wondered if you'd like a bit of help with the garden. I've got a ride-on mower in Pa's garage and could get around your lawns in no time at all. Well, a lot quicker than the old push-along type, anyway.' Felix Farrington was on his second cup of tea and still sitting at the kitchen table.

'Wow. That would be really helpful, Felix.' Kitty spoke before I could get a word in. Frankly, I was sceptical. Suspicious even. Yes, getting the grass cut would help a lot, but what was Felix Farrington after? I know we'd downed a few glasses of vino earlier, but my brain wasn't that muddled that I couldn't see an opportunist coming. Or was it my old cynical self, resurfacing? Kitty glanced at me. 'Wouldn't it, Laura?' She was giving me *that look* again.

'Well, yes, it would, actually, Felix, thanks very much, but I wouldn't want to put you to any trouble.' Just because he'd apologised for his barmy dad's behaviour and had a cuppa with us didn't automatically mean I could trust him. Why was he trying to ingratiate himself with me? The plot of land sprung to mind. No brainer; despite the guy's protestations to the contrary, I was unconvinced that he wasn't interested in buying land from me. And I couldn't believe that Kitty hadn't picked up on it. Jeez. First Craig and now Felix. And don't even remind me about the evil scammer. There was always somebody!

'I'm on a month's leave from my VSO post in Northern Sri Lanka.'

'Really? How interesting,' Kitty said, her face alight. 'What are you doing?' OK, so he does charity work. I still don't trust him.

'I've been doing voluntary work there as an Organisation Development Advisor for a local NGO.'

'Wow. That's fantastic,' said Kitty, all bright eyes and enthusiasm. 'How long have you been doing that?'

'Since the war there, we've been working to try and resettle displaced people as well as offering a bit of support for the local communities.'

'That's pretty amazing.' Kitty didn't take her eyes off him.

'As I'm on leave I'll be staying with Pa for a while. I've got some time on my hands and would be happy to help out here. That is, if you don't feel I'd be intruding?' A warm smile lit up his face and laughter lines fanned out from the edges of his eyes. Fine creases, like parentheses, bracketed around the sides of his lips. Well, all right, he was very attractive, but I wasn't going to let a pretty face cloud my judgement. Not again. Not after what happened with the heir-hunter! All knight-in-shining-armour one minute and trying to bag a lucrative deal for his uncle the next. And I was still stinging from that bloody scam. I wasn't going to fall for that sort of thing again.

Felix took a sip of his tea. Then his face darkened, just a trace.

'At some point, I'm likely to have to move back to the old house, as Pa gets on. I think, at the moment, we are just trying to see how things go. As I said, Pa is fiercely independent. And of course, I have my VSO work to think about, but if my father needs me here, I'll have to put that on hold for a while.'

Well, OK, perhaps he wasn't so untrustworthy after all. He was offering to cut the grass, he risked his life doing voluntary service in war torn countries and was obviously concerned about his dad. I started to feel myself warming to this chap – just a little - despite my gut instincts. I mean, as cantankerous as his father might be, Felix Farrington did seem to care about the old boy's welfare. Perhaps I was being a tad over-cautious, in suspecting that the offer of grass cutting meant he had an ulterior motive. Maybe the guy was genuine after all. I mean, I suppose it does take a decent sort of person to do voluntary work in a war zone. And although I had not yet asked him about Emily, nonetheless I was keen to hear about her. I knew absolutely nothing about my family apart from what Craig had filled me in on. And I wouldn't be seeing him again. I was desperate to discover how my mum ended up living on the breadline, with only me for family, while a living relative resided not a million miles away in a place like Hamilton Hall. How *had* she become dislodged from her kin? There were so many questions unanswered. If, as he said, he'd known Emily all his life, perhaps Felix Farrington was the person who could unlock the secrets of my roots. Better than reading boring legal documents anyway!

'I'm just wondering how I came to inherit Hamilton Hall, actually. Do you know? I'm not sure how I am related to Emily.'

'Well, if you don't know, I certainly don't, Laura. I'll ask Pa. He might know.'

'I don't think he believes the place is rightfully mine.'

'Oh well, like I said, don't take my father too seriously. His heart is in the right place, and he was very fond and protective of Emily, especially as she reached advanced years.'

'OK, I'll bear that in mind.' I wasn't entirely convinced, but decided to leave the subject for now.

'Is there anything else you might need help with, while I'm here? If so, just give me a shout.' His face broke into that warm smile again, as he added, 'you know where I live!'

He pushed back the kitchen chair and stood up, his length unfolding until he was towering above me again.

'I'll leave you to it, then. Thanks for the tea.' He offered his right hand and I stood up and shook it. 'Good to meet you, Laura. And you, Kitty.' He nodded at my friend, who shook his hand. 'Have a think about it and, as I said, just pop round if you'd like me to help with the garden.'

His blue eyes sucked me in. For a moment, I stood there looking up into them. Kitty spoke, breaking the spell.

'Thanks so much, Felix. That's really kind of you. And yes, I am sure Laura would appreciate a bit of help, wouldn't you dear?' She had walked around the table and I felt her nudge me on the thigh.

'Yes, thank you, Felix. Actually, yes, yes, I'd really like you to cut the grass, if that's not too much trouble. Kitty and I have been taking an inventory of what needs doing around the place, and getting the lawns sorted out would be a great start. So, yes, thanks. I'd like that. If you wouldn't mind, that is. And so long as it's not too much trouble, of course.' *Oh, just shut up and stop babbling, woman!*

'No trouble at all, Laura. Good to meet you both. I'll be off now.'

And with that, he saw himself out, while Kitty and I stood in the kitchen looking at each other.

Kitty spoke first. 'What a charmer! And kind-hearted too. Lucky you, having such a good neighbour, Laura White!'

'Huh. Don't forget his old man with the propensity to wield a shotgun!' I said, as I walked over to the kitchen window.

The early September sun sunk low and dusk descended, turning the skies into a pattern of striated shades of purple, peach, orange and pink. I felt a sudden chill and shuddered.

'What have we got for dinner, Kitty?' I said as I walked across the room and rooted through the fridge. 'Nothing much in here.'

'What about the freezer? We had that marathon baking session, didn't we? And I think there's a ready meal lasagne lurking in there somewhere.'

I rummaged around in the freezer and we feasted on a microwaved dinner and plum and apple pie.

A thrumming sound pounded in my head and I opened one eye, squinting in the sunlight that shone through the gap in the bedroom curtains. I checked the time on my mobile phone. *7.30? What the -?* The noise stopped and started again. Now it sounded more like a tractor. I shook Kitty, curled up in her sleeping bag next to me.

'Kit, Kit, what's that noise?'

'Uh?' She lifted her head and dropped it again onto the pillow.

'There's a noise out there, like a tractor or something.' I shook her again and she opened her eyes. Then closed them.

She groaned and fell silent again.

'What's that noise? There's a tractor or something out there.' It was no use; I was speaking to a corpse passing itself off as Kitty. I scrambled out of my sleeping bag and staggered over to the bedroom window, drew back the curtains and looked down onto the garden to see Felix Farrington sitting astride his ride-on mower.

42: October, 1940, same day
Hamilton Hall

Emily:

'I think you are about to tell us something we already guessed, Miss Emily. That Miss Martha is in the family way. Isn't that right?' Doris's voice is even and quiet. I listen intently for any tone of disapproval. There is none. She is still the same, stalwart, steadfast Doris I have always known.

'Well, yes, Doris, that is what I was about to tell you. But how did you know?' Surely it cannot have got around Wymondham yet, that Martha, daughter of the respected Richard and Adalicia Boulais-Hamilton is to be an unwed mother? My heart turns over.

'I may not be a woman of the world, Miss Emily, but I ain't no fool and nor am I soft in the head. And I known you girls since the days you was born. In fact, I helped bring you into the world. Both of you. Do you think I'd not notice when one of you is... is... expecting?' Her tone is gentle but firm.

'Of course, yes of course, you are right. I'm sorry, Doris, Carter, I didn't mean to offend.'

'No offence taken, Miss, none at all,' says Doris, and Carter holds his cap, scratches his head and rubs his nose. 'And you want us to keep it quiet, don't you?' Doris continues, 'well, o'course, you can count on that.'

Carter looks at me. 'There's people around Wymondham what don't have much better to do than gahssip. You'd think they hadn't noticed there's a war on, some of 'em. As if we don't have enough to do what with keeping body and soul together without whittling on about things what don't matter. You can count on us, Miss Emily, don't you go worrying none about that.'

'That's right, Miss.' Doris squeezes my arm and her eyes flash as a warm smile sweeps across her face, raising her plump cheeks like rosy apples. Now her face drops, as she continues, 'It's hard enough for you girls mourning for your dear, departed parents, without having to worry about what folks is saying behind your back, so don't you fret now, no one's going to hear about Miss Martha's baby from us. Isn't that right, Carter?' She eyes her husband across the table.

'That's sure as eggs is eggs, Miss Emily. Don't you worry none.' Carter stands up from the table, replaces his cap and makes for the back door. 'I'll get on and sort out them tools now. Back before blackout,' he says, and with that he's gone.

Doris is clearing away the dinner cutlery and crockery.

'Time was when I'd be scraping the plates of you two girls after a meal. Nothing left to scrape these days. Rations is so small. Carter will have to plant more in the garden so we can make ends meet.'

'Yes, Doris, I think that's a very good idea. And we have to share what we have with local folks too. It's the war. We have to help and do our bit. Susie James has gone to join the WAAF, so I heard.'

'That's right, Miss Em. I heard that too, from old busybody Nellie Braithwaite in the Post Office. She knows everything.' She glances at me. 'But don't you go worrying, she won't hear about Miss Martha's baby, that's for sure. Not from Carter nor me, anyways.'

'Thank you, Doris. I don't like to think about a scandal. It would be awful. But I agree with Carter. There's this terrible war going on and people are being killed, yet people still love to gossip and judge others.' I think back to the day my period started, the first one after my romantic encounter with James. I was so relieved, but tears prick the back of my eyes now at the loss of my one and only love. I am aware that it could easily have been me in the family way. As it is, I have to help my little sister through the next months. Things have been noticeably tighter for people in recent weeks and are bound to get worse for us too, as Daddy's money dwindles. I worry about how we will manage with another mouth to feed, especially now that Martha will have to give up work. We will have to tell the bank something. They've been good about her compassionate leave since we lost Mummy and Daddy, but they'll soon be expecting her to return to work.

'I was thinking, Miss Em.' Doris breaks into my thoughts. 'What about us getting some chickens? I knows some people in Wymondham what's done it; pulled up their flower borders to plant veggies, and dug up their lawns too. And got chickens running around. What do you think? It would be good to have fresh eggs, even though we'd have to share them around, and I could do us a nice roast dinner when one of them stops laying.'

'Doris you're a genius!'

43: Summer, 2013, the following morning
Hamilton Hall

Laura:

I could still hear the lawn mower droning on, even after I'd got up, had a soak in the old bathtub with the claw feet, cleaned my teeth and was getting dressed. Felix Farrington was doing a great job. As I was pulling on my jeans, the zip first refused to budge, then broke. Bugger. I peeled them off again and threw them into the corner of the bedroom, which served as a laundry basket for the time being. I found a pair of jogging bottoms in my holdall and pulled them on. Kitty snored away, softly. Yesterday's tee shirt came next. It would have to do. I must get some washing done, I reminded myself. Tying my hair up on top of my head with a scrunchy, I made my way downstairs.

I was now in the kitchen, the kettle on and bread toasting nicely under the grill. I'd clicked on the classical music app on Kitty's phone. She'd left it on charge overnight in the kitchen and now Mendelssohn's *violin concerto* was playing out gently into the morning. Kitty still sleeping at this hour was unusual for her, as she was normally an early riser. She must have needed it so I'd left her to snooze.

I checked my phone: another text from Craig. *Delete!* Taking the toast from under the grill, I spread it thickly with peanut butter and made a cup of coffee. I looked at the lists we'd made the day before. Once again, I was reminded that there was an awful lot of work to be done on the house and in the grounds and it was overwhelming to the point that I felt sick with anxiety. And there was still the question of money hanging over my head. I took a swig of coffee and a bite of toast. That was better.

Titanic played out on my mobile phone, clashing with Mendelssohn. It was the bank. I could feel my heart sink. I'd been rejecting all calls from the bank since the one in which I was informed about the scam. I felt as if I was being sucked into a vacuum from which I'd never emerge. But there was no point in playing the ostrich any longer. I could feel the tremor in my voice as I answered.

'Ms White, this is Sinead calling from the credit card department at the bank.' Her gentle Irish lilt was almost hypnotic. 'I have been trying to get hold of you...' I jumped straight in. No messing about.

'Yes, I know. A scam merchant ripped off my bloody credit card for several thousand quid and I owe you money. Well, let me tell you, Madam, I don't have any money. All right, I was a fool to give that evil swine my credit card details but...'

'No, please, Ms White, just hang on a moment. You don't owe us the money. You got that – '

'*What*? How? What do you mean? A guy from the bank called me the other week and told me I'd been scammed.' This didn't make any sense at all. What the hell was going on?

'That's right, that's right, but I'm trying to tell you that the credit card company will take responsibility for the fraud because you didn't authorise the payment.'

'What? But I gave him my credit card details…'

'Yes, you did, but that is not the same as authorising a payment. It is the credit card company's liability and you owe us nothing. My colleague was trying to tell you that when he phoned, but the call was cut off.' Well, yes, she was quite right. I'd hung up on the guy before he could finish. And not picked up when he'd tried to call back. If only I'd not rejected the bank's calls every time that they'd tried to phone me since. What an idiot I am! I'd got myself into that terrible state for nothing when, had I listened, I'd have saved myself a lot of screaming, angst, disturbed sleep and pulling out of hair.

'You mean to say that I have *not* lost thousands of pounds on my credit card?'

'Yes, Ms White, that is correct. You have *not* lost anything. We will cover it. You did not authorise the payment. What we need is your signature on the disclaimer we sent you last week. Have you received it?'

'Well, no actually, but I am not at home at the moment. Well, actually, yes, I am at home, but not in my Suffolk home. I am in Norfolk, at my Hamilton Hall home. I've inherited it. And I really want to live here but it needs a lot of work doing on it and it's Grade II listed and goodness knows what that will cost to fix it up, let alone what the council tax alone will be, and I don't even want to think about what the utility bills and –'

'Ms White, erm, hello, Ms White? Can I just suggest something?'

'Yes. Sorry. I'm babbling a bit, aren't I?'

'No problem at all, Ms White.' That lovely Irish tone again, calming me down. 'What I'd like to suggest is that you go into the branch and talk to one of our advisors about this. If you've no money, but you say you have two properties, there are ways of raising money to help you. But you need to discuss it all in detail with one of our advisors. Can I make an appointment for you? When would be a convenient time, Ms White?'

I let out a long exhalation of breath. I'd been standing at the kitchen sink, clutching the edge of it with one hand and looking out of the window at the majestic, ancient trees, in all their grace and nobility. *My* trees. Felix was still driving around on his ride-on mower and I could hear the soft humming of its engine, purring away in the background. My heart pounded so hard that I feared it would burst through my ribcage. My phone suddenly felt hot in my hand and my body tingled all over. Here was a faceless voice on the other end of the phone offering me a potential lifeline. I clung hard on to the edge of the sink. The kitchen spun around.

'Well, I can go in later today.' I eventually found my voice.

'At two?'

'Yes, fine. I'll be there. Thanks. Thanks. So much, Sinead. So much.'

We ended the call and I turned from the window to see Kitty standing barefoot in the kitchen doorway in her pyjamas, a wide, beaming smile on her face.

'Morning, Laura. Well, that sounded like a good phone call. Am I right? Good news?'

'Just the best! Coffee?'

I put some more bread under the grill and found a mug for Kitty's coffee. My coffee had gone cold, so I poured it down the sink and, without rinsing the mug, spooned instant coffee granules into both. While the kettle was boiling I filled Kitty in on the details of the phone call. *The Thunder and Lightning Polka* played out on her phone app and we danced an excuse of a polka around the kitchen, twirling around and around until I trod on her bare feet.

'Yow! Laura White, you will never make it onto *Strictly Come Dancing* unless you learn not to crunch people's feet!' We collapsed into fits of giggles, bent double, with stitches in our sides.

And the toast burnt.

As I went to rescue it, I heard a polite little cough and turned around to see Felix Farrington standing in the kitchen doorway.

44: November 1940
Hamilton Hall

Emily:
And that is exactly what we did. Carter got some chicken wire from somewhere (we don't ask awkward questions; we'd rather not know) and old wooden planks and other necessary materials and put together a rather marvellous chicken coop. His cousin, a smallholder from a village on the north side of Norwich, found us five chickens, which, very obligingly, produced breakfast daily. Carter had ridden over twelve miles to collect the chickens from his cousin and carried them back another twelve miles in a cage strapped on the back of his bicycle. It had rained as he made his way back to Hamilton Hall and both he and the chickens looked like drowned rats when they arrived. With the chickens safely ensconced in the coop, Doris fed Carter a bowl of mutton and vegetable broth and hoped he wouldn't catch a chill. Martha has given the chickens human names, as though they were family members (which, I didn't think was a good idea because soon we'll be eating one of the said family members for Christmas dinner) and has taken to ensuring they are all put to bed every evening and fed (usually on peelings from the vegetables that Carter and I have grown in the garden) every morning. They will eat just about anything, except for banana skins apparently, but as it is impossible to find a banana in this war, that is of no consequence. Martha is starting to become more like her old self, apart from odd moments when I can tell she is deep in thought, looking pensive. Sometimes I see a small smile on her face as she strokes her swelling belly. Her sickness has ceased, just as Doctor Beresford said it would. She still spends long hours in the family library, reading Brontë and Austen and the other classics the family has acquired over the years. One day, Carter brought in from the garden a lavender plant, which he had potted last summer, and gave it to Martha as a present to cheer up her bedroom. The gesture brought a smile to Martha's face and a tear to her eye. Doris said that lavender is good for calm and relaxation, which, she says, is just what Martha needs, as an expectant mother.

Martha wrote a letter to her boss at the bank, explaining that with the war on, she had to help around Hamilton Hall with the extra work involved in growing food and, therefore, was not in a position to return to work. Mr Morris, the bank manager, replied without too much comment, except to offer his condolences, once again, on the loss of our beloved parents and Charles, and enclosed her final pay cheque.

And the ghastly war rumbles on and on.

44: NOVEMBER 1940

Susie James came to visit us while she was on a weekend leave pass. I told her that Martha was indisposed, in bed with a nasty cold, and therefore not available to receive company. Susie had heard about Charles being shot down over Germany and made melodramatic motions with her arms and noises of sympathy. She looked quite splendid in her uniform and stayed for a short while, regaling me with stories of her life in the WAAF (you would have thought she was winning the war single-handedly, to hear her speak, though how she could do so working as a clerk, I have no idea). Much to my relief, she made off before it got dark.

Doris was quite right: having ready produced breakfast every morning, as well as fresh eggs for baking and cooking is simply a godsend. The chickens lay well and after taking enough eggs each day for ourselves, we share the rest with the Carters' adult children and the Farringtons, our nearest neighbours, whose son, George, is ten now and growing fast. I only hope that the war is over before he gets called up for military service.

Carter and I have dug up patches of the gardens in preparation for planting more vegetables in the spring. We collected buckets full of apples, including windfalls, and these are stored in the cellar to help us through the winter months. I ache a lot from the hard, manual work, but I am alive and well, and that is something to be grateful for in these dreadful times. We hear of local boys killed in action and services are held in our chapel in their memory.

While Martha reads, wrapped in a blanket in the library, my evenings are spent with Doris and Carter in the warmth of the kitchen. They spend more evenings at Hamilton Hall these days and it makes sense for them to share the warmth of the kitchen with me, rather than being cold in their cottage. Fuel is scarce. Daddy's car stands idle in the barn. Doris and I are knitting socks for soldiers and making up parcels for the Red Cross. Carter reads the paper and makes tutting noises of disapproval and despair, saying things like, 'when will this all end?' He doesn't expect an answer from either Doris or me.

And amongst all of this, we have a new arrival. Tom.

45: Summer 2013, same morning
Hamilton Hall

Laura:

'Well, that will have to do for today. I've made a start on the lawns but I need to go into town now and sort a few things. I hope I'm not interrupting anything?' There was an amused grin on Felix Farrington's face; an eyebrow, raised. Normally, I would have felt ever so slightly silly at being caught cavorting around the kitchen to the *Thunder and Lightning Polka* with my best friend in her PJs, but I was so light headed and elated at the news from the bank that I really couldn't care less what Felix, a relative stranger, albeit a kind and helpful one, thought of me at that very moment.

'Good morning, Felix, and thank you very much for cutting the grass. It really is very helpful of you, *isn't it, Laura?*' *That look again from Kitty. Scuffed shoes. White socks.*

'Yes, it really is, Felix. I do appreciate your efforts. Can I get you a cup of coffee? Toast?'

'Coffee would be great, thanks, Laura. No toast though, I've had breakfast.'

I put the kettle on again and found a clean mug. 'Do take a seat at the table, Felix. Kitty, do you want another coffee?'

They both sat down. Kitty, still in her PJs, didn't seem to bother Felix one little bit.

'It will take a few more sessions before I get the whole lot cut, but it will look much better once I've finished. I'll pile the cuttings into a corner somewhere, and perhaps you could start a compost heap?'

Compost heap? I had more to think about than starting a bloody compost heap, but then I admonished myself for being so mean-spirited. After all, Felix Farrington had known me a matter of hours and already he'd voluntarily made a start on getting the gardens into some semblance of order. I felt I owed him already, and he'd only just begun.

'Actually, Felix,' I started, tentatively, 'I have to pop back to Suffolk today to do some business, but I'll be back in a day or so. I wondered if you'd like to come and have dinner with Kitty and me, once I'm back? Your father is also welcome, if he'd like that.'

The expression on Kitty's face said it all, as her head snapped in my direction. Well, all right, it was a bit of a bold move, given that I'd only just met the guy, and his dad having this penchant for pointing a lethal weapon at me whenever the fancy took him, but I don't like the thought of someone doing me a favour and not showing my appreciation. He *was* my new neighbour, after all. And it wasn't as though it was a date or anything. I'd made it clear that Kitty would be there and his dad could come too.

Surely, he couldn't get the wrong impression, could he? Those blue eyes of his twinkled again. And laughter lines fanned out from them.

'Thanks very much, Laura. That would be really nice. Not sure if Pa would be up for it, but I can ask. I'll give you my mobile number and then you can just let me know when you're coming back, so that we can arrange something.' I put the number straight into my contacts. After swigging his coffee down, he jumped to his feet and saluted us both as he left.

'Crikey, Laura. That was a bit of a shocker. You've hardly met the guy and you're inviting him for dinner. What's got into you? You don't fancy him by any chance, do you?' There was a grin on her face a mile wide. She obviously hadn't noticed what I'd noticed about Felix. He seemed only to have eyes for Kitty.

'Don't be daft! Of *course* I don't. I just want to show my appreciation, that's all. I mean, he was up at dawn and hard at work on the lawns before we were even awake.' I could see she wasn't convinced, so I quickly added, 'And anyway, I want to ask him about Emily.' *That look...*

I started clearing the dirty crockery. 'Anyway, are you coming with me to Suffolk, or do you want to stay here?'

'Oh, I'll come with you. I should really check into my place and make sure everything's OK there and with the rentals. Do you want me to come into the bank with you? Two heads are better than one, and all that.'

'Yes, good idea. There should be plenty of hot water left if you want to have a bath, Kit. And I should collect our dirty washing to take back to the cottage and put a load in the machine. I really ought to get a washing machine in here. Still, can't think about that right now.'

'Tell you what, while I'm in the bath, write a list of the things you need to spend money on here, and that will give the bank something to go on.'

'OK. Good thinking.' I finished collecting the dirty mugs and plates and turned to the sink. 'Hopefully, there will be a light at the end of the tunnel soon, eh, Kit?'

'Well, let's not jump the gun. Best to see what the bank has in mind, first. Right. I'm off into the bath. Shan't be long.' And with that Kitty swanned off upstairs, while I got on with sorting out the kitchen. Then I grabbed a plastic bin bag and scooted up the stairs to the bedroom. Picking up the dirty clothes from the floor in the corner of the room, I found the jeans with the broken zip. I toyed with the idea of ditching them in the bin. Broken zips are such a fiddle to fix. I'd probably need to put a new one in. Could I be bothered? I shrugged, shoved the jeans into the bag and made my way downstairs, leaving the bag at the front door.

In the kitchen, I found my notebook and pen and sat down at the table. Taking the lists that we'd made earlier, I managed to write a rough note of what work I thought needed to take priority, and a guess at the cost. At the bottom of the list, almost as an afterthought, I wrote *Pay for survey*. It was all very well, Kitty and me taking stock, but a qualified surveyor would be able to assess exactly what I faced in terms of renovation works. I crossed out the rest of the list, leaving just one item: *Surveyor's report*.

My phoned pinged. Another text from Craig. *Delete!*

I felt something like a warm hand on my back and turned, expecting to see Kitty standing there. But there was no one. *Huh? What was that?*

Kitty came bouncing into the kitchen. 'OK, I'm ready. Shall we go?'

Ten minutes later, having checked that windows were closed and doors locked, we were headed south to Suffolk. And, hopefully, a helpful bank advisor.

46: November, 1940
Wymondham and Hamilton Hall

Emily:

I had intended to get to the church hall early, but in the event, when I arrived, the allocation process was all but finished. One solitary little boy stood, forlorn, in the corner of the hall. His coat was too small. He had on a school cap, and short trousers. His long socks wrinkled around his ankles. His boots, with broken, odd laces, scuffed. There was a luggage label attached to his coat collar. He scratched his head through his cap and sniffed, wiping his nose on his coat sleeve.

'Ah. Emily! There you are.' Diana Passant called out and waved to me. Eleanor Gurney walked towards me.

'Just one little tyke left,' Eleanor said, *sotto voce*. 'No one else wanted him. Not the most appealing of children. Come and meet him.' I followed her across the bare, wooden floor.

'This is Tom. He's ten and he's from London. This is Miss Emily Boulais-Hamilton, Tom,' she said, turning to the boy. 'She's going to take you home. Now be good and remember your manners. You're very lucky to have been offered a good home.' Eleanor Gurney at her most officious.

'Hello Tom. How do you do? I expect you're tired after your journey.' He gazed up at me momentarily, then looked away.

'Don't worry. We'll be home soon and you can have a nice, warm bath, and something to eat before bed.'

'Don't want a bath, Miss.' His head snapped back towards me.

'Good heavens, of course you do!' Eleanor's eyebrows shot up in indignation.

'It will make you feel better after your long train ride,' I said, 'and there's some delicious potato and leek soup and homemade bread for supper. Shall we go?'

I signed the paperwork with Diana and Eleanor handed me a scruffy cloth bag containing the boy's belongings. I offered Tom my hand to take. He put his hands in his trouser pockets.

'I don't want a bath, Miss. I don't!' We were standing in the bedroom we had made ready for Tom, at the door to the bathroom. He clung onto the door frame steadfastly.

'It's all right, Tom, really it is. If you take your clothes off, I won't look, I promise. You really will feel much better once you've had a soak in a nice, hot bath. It will warm you up.'

He looked far from convinced and wasn't budging from the door frame. 'Then we can have some of that soup Doris made. I can recommend it. It really is quite delicious.' Tom wasn't going to give in without a fight.

'Come along, dear chap. Do jump into the bath before the water gets cold.'

'What's all this fuss about, eh?' We both turned to see Doris standing, arms crossed, at the bedroom door. She moved over towards us. 'Come on my man, let's be having you. If you doesn't want to take your clothes off, then let's get you into the bath with 'em on.'

I was dumbstruck. Would Doris really do that?

Yes, she would.

She grabbed the boy around his waist, picked him up and moved towards the bath, his hands flying off the door frame and waving about in the air.

'No! No!'

'Well, if you won't take them clothes off, you're just gunna have to get in the bath with 'em on. And I can tell you little Mister, you ain't gunna have none of my leek and potato soup till you's out of that bath and nice and clean.'

'All right. All right. But I don't want no wimmin looking at me!'

'That's fine, little Mister. That's just fine. We will look the other way, won't we Miss Emily?'

And we did. We could hear his movements as he removed his clothing then the gentle splash as he entered the bath water. I turned around to face him and so did Doris. His pile of dirty clothes lay pitifully on the bathroom floor. I rooted into his cloth bag and found more of the same: dirty clothes.

'Doris, look. We simply cannot put him into these. Just look at them.'

'You're right there, Miss Em. I'll send Carter over to the Farringtons' kitchen help. Young George is a bit bigger than this little 'un. Maybe they'll have something to spare, what he's grown out of.'

'Good idea, Doris. Good idea. Tell you what, you keep an eye on Tom and I'll find Carter.'

And so, I did. And Carter came back from the Farringtons' with a bundle of perfectly serviceable clothes: short grey trousers, a blue shirt, underwear, socks, darned, but plenty of wear left in them, and a nice warm jumper. They promised to find some boots and a coat and woolly hat and send them round.

Tom looked rather splendid with his hair washed and combed, and his new, clean clothes on. For all his howls of protestation, he did look rather pleased with his fresh appearance, as I observed him looking at himself in the bedroom mirror. Doris had taken the bar of soap and a wash cloth and given him a good going over with those. She had washed his hair and poured jugs of water over his head to rinse the suds away. Despite himself, he seemed to have enjoyed the experience after all.

46: NOVEMBER, 1940

Martha stayed out of sight during all these proceedings.

Later, having tucked into hearty soup and homemade bread, as though he'd not eaten for days, followed by stewed apples and custard, Tom yawned widely. The grandfather clock in the reception hall struck eight. Candles lit the kitchen table.

'I think a certain little Mister is ready for bed, wouldn't you say, Miss Em?' Doris said, as the side of the boy's head made contact with the kitchen table and his eyes drooped to a close.

47: Summer, 2013 – same day
En route to Suffolk

Laura:

We called in for petrol and coffee at the usual place on the way back down to Suffolk. The unfortunate looking waitress was there again, looking less than happy, as we stood at the counter placing our order. Kitty and I exchanged a look.

The girl brought our coffees to the table and Kitty smiled up at her. 'Nice to see you again. How are you today?' I said, but I could detect something in the girl's expression that unnerved me somewhat. I remembered the bruises from an earlier visit and I was sure that Kitty did too.

'OK, thanks.' But she clearly wasn't.

'It's my break now, so I'm going out the back for a fag. 'Scuse me.' And she reached into her overall pocket, pulling out a packet of cigarettes, as she made her way out of the café, furtively looking this way and that as she went.

I looked at Kitty, her eyes following the girl as she left the building.

'There's something about her that really doesn't sit well with me, Laura. I mean, all the bruises she had last time we saw her in here and her scared-rabbitty eyes. Something's wrong, I just know it. It's not our business, I know, but - '

'I agree,' I said quickly and, leaving Kitty and my coffee behind, I followed the girl out.

'Laura – what are you doing?'

'I won't be long,' I called over my shoulder.

Reaching the back of the building, I stopped short, as I watched the girl huddled in the corner, by the refuse bins, lighting a cigarette. *Filthy habit!* She stood, head down, and arms wrapped across the front of her body, unfolding the outer arm to take another drag of the cigarette. I wanted to approach her, have a word. Ask what was troubling her. Mum always said a helping hand and a kindness never did any harm, but could do a lot of good.

As I stood there, observing her for a moment, a male figure appeared through some nearby bushes, approached her from behind. By the looks of him he hadn't had a shower or change of clothes in a while. He was thin and wiry and looked like he could do with a good meal inside him. She jumped, visibly alarmed and frightened. I stood still, watching. Now he made jabbing movements with his index finger, right in her face. She backed off. She was saying something, but I couldn't hear what. Now she was shaking her head and he was pushing her shoulder. She looked paralysed with fear. He was threatening her. He was bloody threatening her.

'Oi! You! Get off! Leave her alone!' I was marching towards the pair and they both turned to look at me.

'Who the fuck're you missus? Fuck off and mind your own fucking business.' *Charming. Impressive vocabulary. Obviously swallowed a dictionary for breakfast this morning.*

'Leave the poor girl alone, you bully. Go on, clear off.' I was moving closer to them now. He was wearing a grubby baseball cap back to front. Probably to hide his lobotomy scar.

'Says who?' He curled up his lip and his teeth were yellow, his skin spotty and blotchy. Dark circles dwelt underneath his eyes and looked as if they'd been there a long time.

'Says me, you little oik. Go on, clear off and leave her alone.' The girl was hunched over, her arms hugging her body, her head lowered. She looked sideways at us, her eyes darting from me to him.

'Get out of my face! What's it got to do with you, bitch? *Fuck off!*' He was making towards me, his arm raised as if to strike me. I dodged out of his way, so that I was now between him and the girl. I stared at him as he stood there, holding my gaze, his lip curled again, his fists clenched. A face-off. His complexion took on a damp, grey pallor. Heroin. Now I could see.

He made towards me again. His hand reached into his jacket pocket. A knife. *Shit! Didn't see that coming.* Adrenaline pumped around my body.

Now sweat broke out and streamed down his face. His nose was dripping mucous. Behind him I could see people from the petrol station forecourt looking over towards us. I looked at the knife in his hand. He swivelled the knife handle. He twitched. I glanced over his shoulder and there she was: Kitty.

Her leg gave a hefty swing and her booted foot made sharp contact with his buttock. He went down, splayed on the ground. The knife left his hand and clanged as it hit the deck. Kitty stood over him. Her foot on the hand that had held the knife. I stood on his other wrist. He yelled and wriggled and swore. As he did so, we pressed our feet down harder. I could hear footsteps rushing towards us. Someone had a mobile phone and was tapping away. People started to applaud and whistle.

A woman in white chef's gear ran over to the girl and put her arms around her.

'All right Kylie. It's all right now.' She soothed, and coaxed the girl back towards the café.

A trembling Kylie whispered, 'Thank you' to me as she walked with her colleague back inside the café.

'The police are on their way', said the man with the mobile phone. I looked at him properly for the first time. *Jeez!* It was Simon Stewart-Rees, the estate agent I'd thought was in an accident all those weeks ago.

'Good god woman! You look like you've just bumped into the Ghost of Christmas Past or some such being,' he said, the shock on my face obviously self-evident.

'Something like that Simon,' I said, drawing a breath, and Kitty looked from me to him.

'Do you two know each other?' Kitty asked and the captive wriggled again, uttering expletives. We trod harder.

'Tell you what,' Simon said, 'I've got some duct tape in my car. Perhaps we could tape his hands behind his back.' The captive wiggled and squirmed and swore some more. Kitty and I looked at each other. It depended on how long the police were going to take to arrive. We couldn't stay like this for long, standing on him. More people arrived. Some were just curious as to what the commotion was about, and went on their way. Others hung around at the scene, as if waiting for a bus or something.

A woman went over towards the knife, that still lay on the ground a few feet away. She reached down towards it. 'Don't touch that! Don't touch it!' Kitty shouted. 'Have you never heard of fingerprints? Leave it where it is, for god's sake!'

The woman shrugged and moved off, jumped in her car and drove away.

Kitty and I exchanged a glance and looked heavenwards. I felt a spot of rain on my face. And another. Great. Now we were going to get soaked.

'Er, Simon, could you get that duct tape you mentioned?' I asked, and off he went to his car. He came back and sat astride the captive's lower back to secure him so that we could release his hands and tape them behind his back. It wasn't easy. He writhed and swore.

Someone from the café came over with a plastic-gloved hand, picked up the knife and put it in a plastic bag.

I made a citizen's arrest. *Yay!* Simon looked at me with a broad grin. He was quite dishy when he wasn't scowling and looking down his nose at me.

Kitty and I pulled the captive to his feet and we all went back into the café.

The police wanted statements.

And I missed the appointment with the bank.

48: November, 1940, the following morning
Hamilton Hall

Emily:

'Tom? Where are you Tom?'

His bed is empty, as is his bathroom.

'Tom?' His clothes are still folded on the chair by the dresser. I leave the room and hurry along the landing and down the stairs. He is nowhere to be seen. Not in the kitchen, nor the drawing room and he's not in the library either, when I rush back upstairs and look in there. I run downstairs and outside into the garden. A thin layer of sparkling frost covers the ground, the trees and the roof, and he will only be in father's shirt that we'd put him in to sleep last night, the sleeves rolled up to the elbow. Dear little fellow had not even stirred from his slumber while Doris and I had undressed him and put him into bed. He will freeze and catch cold if he is out here. I dash over to the barn, calling for him. It is empty apart from Daddy's car, standing idle, the petrol tank still empty. I call Tom's name again, as I run frantically around the gardens. Carter appears from the greenhouse.

'What is it Miss Em?'

'Tom's not in his room. I cannot find him. Have you seen him at all?' Cold air catches in my throat and I shudder. I draw my cardigan tighter around my body. I shiver.

'I ain't seen him out 'ere, Miss. I would have seen him, I'm sure of it. Where have you looked?' He removes his cap, scratches his head, rubs his nose.

I tell him.

'Let's go look again in the house,' he says, in that slow, Norfolk drawl. 'He can't be far.' He follows me at a leisurely pace as I dash back to the house and run up the stairs to Tom's bedroom. Carter follows me and Doris has joined us too. 'He can't have gone far,' says Doris, echoing Carter.

'Tom? Tom? Where are you, dear?' I am beginning to panic. How could I have lost a child after his being in my care for less than twenty-four hours?

'What's the problem, Em?' Martha stands at the bedroom door, yawning and stretching, her little bump just visible.

'We can't find Tom, Martha. Have you seen him?' Silly question. Of course, she has not; she has only just woken up. She follows us into the bedroom.

We look under the bed, and again in the bathroom. Nothing. I walk back to the bed and pull the covers down. And then I see it. A large wet patch.

'Oh dear. Poor little mite.'

Doris moves over to the bed and begins removing the wet sheets. 'I'll get these in the wash, Miss Emily, and get some dry linen on the bed,' she says, and makes to leave the room, her arms full.

I hear a scratching noise. In unison, the four of us look at the wardrobe. Martha and I look at each other. Doris leaves the room, soiled linen in her arms. I tiptoe over and open the wardrobe door. There he is, curled up in the corner of the cupboard, trembling.

'It's all right, Tom,' I say, trying to sound reassuring, 'come along, it's all right.' I reach out for him. He flinches.

'I'm not going to hurt you, Tom. I promise. Come on out and we can get you clean and warmed up. Come along.' I reach out with my hand and he takes it. I turn and signal to Carter and Martha to leave the room.

'Come along, darling. I bet you'd like a nice bath, wouldn't you? Come along. You'll soon be warm and dry. There's nothing to worry about, now.'

He's still tremulous. What on earth has this poor little boy been through?

'Doris has some nice hot porridge waiting for you downstairs, Tom. After breakfast, we can look around the gardens. I can show you all the fruit and vegetables that I helped Carter to grow. And we've got chickens. Perhaps you could help Martha to feed them. Would you like that?'

His soulful eyes gaze at me. He nods. He looks lost in Daddy's old shirt. It envelops him like an enormous tent.

'Splendid. Let's run a nice hot bath for you, and the sooner we have you washed and dressed, the sooner we can have breakfast and I can take you around the gardens. Don't worry about the bed. Accidents happen. It's easily fixed.'

And with that, he smiles, just a little, and we make for the bathroom.

49: Summer, 2013, that evening
back in Suffolk

Laura:

We ended up taking Kylie back to Suffolk with us. She was so shaken up by the incident with the drug addict that her boss had given her the rest of the day off, but she didn't want to be alone. The police had taken the oik away in handcuffs and thanked us for our sense of social responsibility. Simon cleared off in his BMW, but not before giving me another one of his broad grins. That was two in as many hours. *What's got into him?*

I put a blanket ban on fags. No smoking at all in my house or car. I didn't want my car or little cottage filled with stinking smoke. Kylie didn't seem to mind. I made her comfortable in my spare bedroom and Kitty arrived with a Chinese takeaway and a bottle of wine.

Opening the bottle, Kitty said, 'Have you thought of trying some of the wine in the cellar at Hamilton Hall, Laura? Why do we always buy wine when you've got a cellar full?'

'Actually, no, I haven't, Kit. To be honest, I've only been down there once and it gave me the creeps a bit. There's a window and when I looked out I realised I was underground. I felt a bit claustrophobic. But we could look if you like, when we go back. You are coming with me, I presume?'

'Sure. Love to. There's still a lot to do at the old hall,' she said and then Kylie came into the kitchen.

'All right there, Kylie? You'll be OK in that little bedroom for one night, will you?' I said, as I pulled out a kitchen chair and ushered her to sit down. 'What would you like to eat? Kitty's brought us a feast.'

We sat at the kitchen table eating hungrily and drinking wine. Kylie had been quiet and subdued on the drive down to Suffolk and hadn't had much to say since we arrived at the cottage. With food and a glass of wine inside her, I decided to encourage her to talk about herself.

'Where are your parents, Kylie?' I could tell by her accent that she was not a Norfolk girl.

'My dad died in prison and my mum died when I was about six. I was brought up in a kids' care home and had to leave as soon as I turned eighteen, a year and a half ago.' Kitty and I looked at each other and she leaned across and squeezed Kylie's hand.

'I knew Shane – that guy at the café – in the care home. We grew up together in care, see.'

So, he was Shane, of the tattooed knuckles fame. As she spoke, Kylie rubbed at the letters of his name written in blue across the back of her hand, as if trying to erase them.

'We were like, best mates for years when we was growing up in the care home, but after we left, Shane got into drugs and got himself homeless,' she went on. 'I got a rented bedsit and a job, and he kept pestering me for money.'

'Did he hurt you, Kylie?' I asked, and yes, she confirmed that he had been responsible for the black eye and other bruises too. Poor Kylie.

'You've done really well for yourself, Kylie, since you left care. You're keeping yourself and paying your way,' said Kitty, 'you don't need to hang out with the likes of Shane any longer.' She squeezed the girl's arm.

'I s'pose it's a hard habit to break,' said Kylie. 'Me and Shane, we went through thick and thin together in the kids' home, and I thought we'd end up getting married and having kids.' She bit her lip and took a sip of wine, her brow furrowed.

'We all think we will marry our first sweetheart, Kylie, but there is someone much better than Shane out there, just waiting for you, you'll see,' smiled Kitty, 'isn't that right, Laura?'

'Oh yes, absolutely, Kylie. Kitty's right. Don't waste any more energy on Shane. Hopefully they'll get him into rehab and he'll sort himself out. Right now, though, he's on the road to nowhere.'

'He wasn't always like this. He was great until we left care and he got in with the wrong crowd.' Kylie shrugged and took a forkful of chicken chow mein. 'Mm, yummy. This is good!' And her smile lit up the room. Kylie now looked like quite a different person to the sullen girl I'd first encountered in the café, all those weeks ago.

In the morning, I phoned the bank to make another appointment to see the advisor.

'Yes, Ms White, that is fine. We can make another appointment. How about this afternoon? Two o'clock?'

'OK, thanks, I'll be there at two.'

My mobile pinged. Text from Craig. *Delete!*

Kylie wandered into the kitchen as I was making tea and toast. Kitty had gone home after the meal the previous evening and was now on her way back to mine.

'Morning, Kylie. Sleep OK?'

'Yes, thanks, like a top!' She had a pretty face when she smiled, but she needed something done to that hair.

'Looks like your hairstyle is sort of growing out, Kylie. I remember the first time I saw you it was longer on top and shaved at the sides.'

'Yeah. That's right. I need to get it sorted out.' *Too true!*

'Tell you what, there's a great hairdresser who will come to the house and do your hair. Good prices too. Shall I call her and get her to come over and do your hair?'

'Erm, well, I haven't got much money on me.'

'Oh, don't worry. We can sort that out, just this once,' I said. *Well, OK, so I'm skint. So, what?* Just then, Kitty let herself in through the front door.

'Morning ladies!' Kitty called and joined us in the kitchen.

'Hiya, Kit. I'm just going to ring Sharon, to come and do Kylie's hair for her. It will make her feel a lot better, won't it?'

'Yes, good idea. I think I'll get mine trimmed too,' Kitty smiled and sat at the kitchen table, while I poured tea into mugs and put toast onto plates. Then I called Sharon.

'Teddy Edwards has fixed up the push bike. He left a message on my landline. We can pick it up later, if you like,' said Kitty.

'Oh wow! Great!' I was thrilled, until I realised I had no money to pay Teddy for his work. Kitty saw the expression change on my face.

'Don't worry. Teddy said to pay him anytime. He's pretty relaxed about money. Always has been. Does the work and then six months later sends the invoice! I told you, he does it for the love of it, rather than to make any money.'

'That's good, then! Shall we pick it up and take it back to Hamilton Hall?' In my mind, I was already riding that bicycle around the leafy lanes of Wymondham.

At the bank, the first thing the thin, serious-looking chap in a grey suit and rimless specs asked me was how much I earned every month. I was about to quote him my care home salary, and even started rooting in my bag for payslips, when I remembered that, in fact, having left the job, my monthly income was, presently, zero. *Awkward!*

So, the thin, grey man promptly jumped up and opened the door to his office, indicating the meeting was over and I made my way back to the cottage. *Damn!* Yet another setback. There was only one thing for it: I was going to have to sell my beloved terraced cottage in Suffolk. I'd been hoping to get a tenant but the rent I'd achieve wasn't going to be enough to live on at Hamilton Hall, let alone do the renovations it so desperately needed.

'OK, Laura White,' I said out loud to myself as I drove Esther home. 'Back to square one!'

50: The following morning
Hamilton Hall

Emily:
After breakfast, the Farringtons' domestic help, Agnes, arrived at the kitchen door with young George. She had found a selection of shoes and boots, a good coat, woollen scarf and a knitted balaclava. The two boys eyed each other tentatively as we introduce them. Tom tried on the coat, which fit very well and the boots were just perfect. He quickly put on the scarf and balaclava and beamed.

'How splendid you look, Tom!' I said, and then helped him out of the outdoor clothes. 'Shall we all have some hot cocoa? Might as well make the most of it while it lasts. There won't be much more where that came from whilst this dreadful war persists.'

'Oh yes, Miss Emily! That would be super!' George said and Tom shot a wary glance at him.

We drank cocoa, the last of it, as it turned out, and then I took the boys out to the garden to find the chickens, that were moving about in various parts of the grounds, pecking away through the hard, frosty ground looking for grubs and worms. They ate anything they could find and still had room for the peelings that Martha fed them every morning.

The boys began to relax in each other's company and ran around, playing tag, until Tom started to cough and couldn't stop. He looked quite poorly and I took him indoors and up to bed. After a short while, he seemed fine, but it was worrying. Doris thought it was an asthma attack. Tom said it had happened before.

Doctor Beresford visited the following morning and confirmed that Tom suffered from asthma. Apart from breathing in hot steam from a bowl of water under a muslin cloth, there was not too much to be done.

§

And so, the weeks rolled on, the war still raged and soon it was Christmas. Rations were in short supply, despite our being fortunate enough to have stored fruit and vegetables grown in the gardens and the chickens giving us eggs every day. We had to share what we had, and did so willingly with the nearest neighbours and the church, for distribution to parishioners in need.

On Christmas Eve, Carter turned up with a magnificent Christmas tree, cut from the grounds of Hamilton Hall and erected it in the reception hall. Tom and young George helped me to hang baubles and candles on the branches. I fetched the step ladder and helped Tom to climb to the top to place a silver star at the top of the tree. His face lit up.

Martha relaxed with a blanket tucked around her, reading, as usual, in the library. Later, she came down and admired our efforts with the Christmas tree.

On Christmas morning, I took Tom to chapel for the Carol Service and Carter, Doris and their children and grandchildren came too. We made excuses to the other parishioners that Martha was a little under the weather and was staying at home in the warm. We had dinner in the dining room. It was the first time we'd used the room since before the anniversary dinner that mummy and daddy had missed four months ago. Our Christmas dinner party included Martha, Doris and Carter, Tom and the Farringtons. They were the only people, outside of the immediate family and Doctor Beresford, who were privy to Martha's condition. She was now five months into her pregnancy and her baby bump seemed to grow daily. Doris had made her a pretty maternity smock, which Martha wore for the first time on Christmas day. Carter had courageously wrung the neck of one of the chickens (which made Martha wince, rather). Doris had plucked, gutted and roasted it and served it with home-grown vegetables, followed by a magnificent Christmas pudding made by Doris some months ago, and which she'd left in the larder, growing rich and delicious. We poured brandy, found in Daddy's cellar, over the pudding and set fire to it at the table. Tom sat with wide eyes full of wonder at the flames.

After dinner, while Doris and Martha cleared away the detritus of the meal, the rest of us retired to the drawing room and played board games, which young Tom had never seen before. It was the first time that Doris and Carter had sat in the drawing room. Traditions changed with the war. Hierarchies were broken down and we all stood together, as equals.

Later, after the Carters left to visit their children and grandchildren, we lit the candles on the Christmas tree and we all stood around it in the reception hall, singing carols. I handed little gifts to the boys, who opened them excitedly. The Farringtons left and I took Tom up to bed.

As I was tucking him into bed, Tom put his arms around my neck and said, 'Miss Emily, that was a nice Christmas. The best I ever had.' He planted a kiss on my cheek. I felt a tear prick my eye.

'Really, Tom? I'm so glad you enjoyed it. I was worried you'd miss your Mummy today.' I'd been thinking of my own dear parents all day.

'Well, just a bit. But everyone is so nice here, and dinner was really good, it made me feel better.'

'Good night my dear,' I said, 'sweet dreams'.

§

January, 1941

On the seventeenth of January, we received a visitor: Bronwyn Jones, from Wales, the cousin of Tom's deceased father. Diana Passant accompanied her and explained that Tom's mother had been killed by a bomb in London and so 'Aunt' Bronwyn had agreed to adopt the boy.

'But he is very happy here, Diana. Why can't he stay with us, at least until the war is over?' I looked from Diana to Bronwyn Jones and back again. My heart was a clenched fist and there seemed to be a tennis ball trapped in my windpipe. 'He's started school in Wymondham and is getting on so well,' I pleaded. Tom walked in just then and came over to stand behind me, peaking at the visitors. How was I going to break the news that he was now an orphan?

'I'm sorry, Emily, but Mrs Jones and her husband need Tom with them, to help on the farm. Their only son is away in the army, so they need the extra pair of hands.'

'But Diana! He's only a little boy! And he has asthma. He can't possibly work on a farm. Please, let him stay here, at least until – '

'He's *our* family, Miss. He's not yours. You have no right to keep him here.' The woman's face was pinched. Deep lines, like grooves, were etched around her mouth and nose. Two creases like tram lines ran between her eyes, making her look permanently angry.

51: Summer, 2013, same day
Still in Suffolk

Laura:

When I arrived back at the cottage, Kylie and Kitty had been under Sharon's scissors. Kitty's hair was just generally tidied up, but Kylie was transformed. Gone were the tatty, mousy brown locks, to be replaced by a chic new 'pixie cut' style and tawny highlights. Gone also was the metal she'd previously sported in her eyebrow and nose. She smiled at me as I entered the room.

'Kylie, you look lovely!' I said, and she beamed.

'Doesn't she just!' chimed in Kitty, and Kylie glowed even more.

'Kitty treated me,' she said.

They'd done the washing we'd brought back from Hamilton Hall and Kitty was just taking down the ironing board, that hung on a nail behind the kitchen door, ready to attack the clothes with the iron. She picked up my jeans with the broken zip on the ironing board and I remembered the premium bond in the pocket. Before I could react, she flashed me a broad smile. 'How did it go at the bank?'

'Not good. No income, no loan. Simple as that!'

'Oh dear. I hadn't thought of that. Still, it was worth a try. Now what?'

'I think I'm going to sell this place.'

'What? But – '

'I know. But it is debt free now, I finished paying the mortgage a couple of months back and it's the only real asset I have at my disposal. I'm going to have to sell.'

'Oh Laura. It would be the most logical thing to do, but it's such a shame.'

'I know that, Kit, but renting it won't bring in enough for what I need.' I reached for my mobile.

I opened the door the following morning to Simon Stewart-Rees.

'You!'

'Yes, me. What are you doing here? And how did you know where I live?'

'*You* called *us*, remember? My secretary took your call. I'm here to value this place and, hopefully, put it on the market for you.' *I don't believe this!* Of all the estate agents in Suffolk, I had to go and choose Simon bloody-fancy-pants! How had I not made the connection? *Duh!*

'Who is it, Laura?' Kitty was by my side at the door. She looked at Simon. 'Oh, hello. It's you. From the café. You're the one who – '

'Yes. The duct tape,' he said as he held his hand out to Kitty. 'Simon Stewart-Rees. Er Mrs ...?'

'Ms, actually. I prefer Ms. I'm Kitty Colman.' She shook the hand he proffered.

'Well, don't just stand there, come on in and tell me the worst,' I said and with that, we gave Simon Fancy-pants a tour of the cottage.

'OK, so tell me, Ms White. Why are you selling?' Simon was sitting on the sofa with his iPad, ready to make notes. Obviously, a man who doesn't mess about in getting to the point.

'As you know, I've inherited Hamilton Hall. Well, I need to raise some cash to renovate it. And before you piss me off again and ask me to sell some of the land to the neighbours, no, I am definitely *not* going to do that.'

'Fair enough. Old George Farrington is what I'd call an 'on-cloud-nine' type of character, I must say. But he is a client, after all.'

'Yeah, right, OK. But just so's you know, I am *not* selling any of my land to George. Is that clear? I've met his son, and I'm assured that the old chap is one bread roll short of a picnic, so I won't be doing business with him any time soon.'

'Oh, couldn't agree more,' said Simon, 'in fact, acting in your best interests, I'd advise you not to sell the land under any circumstances.'

Well, that was a turn up for the book!

'If you want a quick sale, it might be worth putting the cottage up for auction,' continues Simon. 'I'd suggest a starting price of a hundred-thousand. The place is in good condition. Perhaps a lick of paint might be a good idea, but apart from that, you've kept it well. The fruit trees in the garden are likely to be a good selling point, plus the handy location. If you want to proceed, I can take a few photos now. What do you say?'

It was all becoming a reality now and I felt my heart flip over. I was about to sell my beloved cottage to the highest bidder. It somehow felt very mercenary. Could I actually do it? What would Mum think? She had been so pleased and proud when I'd saved up enough for the deposit and bought the cottage. I knew I was probably being over-sentimental, but that was how I felt. What was I to do?

'Actually,' I said, 'I need to think about this. I'm not so sure I'd be doing the right thing, by selling the cottage.

'But Laura! What else can you do?' It was Kitty, her hand on my arm, her face set in an expression of deep concern.

'Perhaps you do need to think about this, Ms White.' Simon didn't bother to try and hide his exasperation. 'Here's my card, when you decide what to do, give me a ring. In the meantime, I have work to get on with.' This was Simon, back to his old snotty self. I showed him the door, picked up the post from the doormat and left it on the hall table with the rest of the unopened mail.

Over coffee in the kitchen, Kitty, Kylie and I chewed over the pros and cons of selling the cottage and how far the proceeds of sale would go in renovating the old hall.

'I need a surveyor! How can I possibly quantify the costs of renovation without a surveyor's report? Right, that's it.' I reached for my mobile phone.

'Erm, a surveyor is going to need paying, Laura. Remember?' Kitty, practical as ever.

'Well, I bloody need a surveyor's report, don't I?'

Simon's business card lay on the kitchen table. I picked it up. As I did so, my mobile pinged with a text. *Oh, clear off, Craig!*

'Property valuations, surveys, sales and rentals' I read aloud from Simon's card.

Kitty read out the number while I dialled.

'Hello, Simon? Laura White here. Can you do a survey of Hamilton Hall for me? I need a survey so that I can get estimated costs of renovation, and make a decision about whether, or not, to sell the cottage.'

He didn't hang about; he was back at the cottage within fifteen minutes. Kitty let him in. As they entered the kitchen, smiling at each other, Kitty said, 'Talking of auctions, Simon, do you know where we could auction a totally wrecked eighty-year-old car with no wheels or an engine?'

'My firm doesn't actually auction classic cars, only houses, but I could do it for you in another capacity, if that's what you're after. Where's the car?'

'Hi, Simon,' I greeted him. 'It's a 1930s Austin Ten, and it's in the barn at Hamilton Hall. I was advised to auction it, even without wheels or an engine. Seemed a bit batty to me, I mean, who in their right mind would want a car with no engine or wheels? You'd have to be barmy. But I'd be willing to give it a go. What do you think?'

'As a matter of fact, I might be interested in acquiring it for myself,' Simon said.

52: 17th January, 1941
Hamilton Hall

Emily:
Tom promptly sank his teeth into the hand of Mrs Bronwyn Jones that was gripping his wrist, then spat in her face, extricating himself from her grip and running into my arms. He rubbed the sore part she'd been so fiercely clutching.

'Oh, dear, Tom,' I said, 'you really should not do that.' But it was too late. He had already done it and Mrs Jones was squealing like a stuck pig and cursing. Diana admonished her that such behaviour was simply not befitting that of a guardian of an innocent child, then proceeded swiftly to despatch said Mrs Jones from Hamilton Hall, but not before looking over her shoulder, smiling at me and winking at Tom.

'He's a bloody little savage! That's what he is!' We could hear Mrs Jones shouting, 'I don't want him at the farm anyway. You can bloody well keep the little monster!'

'With pleasure, Mrs Jones,' I called after her, 'and please mind your language in front of the child.' Then I turned to Tom, trying to arrange my facial features into a suitably stern expression.

'Tom, I understand you were upset, but please do not ever bite another person again. And spitting is totally unacceptable, too. Please do not do that again either. Do you understand?'

'Yes, Miss Em. I won't do it again. I'm sorry, Miss Em. But she's horrible and I didn't want to go with her.'

'Yes, I know. But there is nothing to be afraid of now. You are safe here with us in Hamilton Hall.' I had yet to break the news about his mother's death to the poor little chap, but when I did, much later, he didn't even shed a tear; just looked momentarily woeful, then melted into my arms for a hug.

Later that afternoon, I heard sobs coming from Martha's bedroom and went in to see her lying on the bed, her face in the pillow.

'Whatever's wrong darling? Tell me, what is it?' I stroked her hair and pushed it away from her face.

'I don't know how I will cope with a child of my own, Emily. Really, I don't. You are so good with young Tom, and George too, but I simply cannot relate to children in the natural way that you do. How on earth am I going to look after a baby? It is too daunting to even contemplate. Oh, if only Charles had not been killed.' She sobbed again.

'You'll be absolutely fine, Martha, don't cry. And you know you will have Doris and me to help. What is there to worry about? Doctor Beresford tells me you are fit and well now, and it is so good that you are up and about and helping around the place, especially with the chickens! You'll be all right, really you will.'

'But Emily, the baby will have no father. I cannot face motherhood alone without Charles.' She sobbed again.

'This is, I'm sure, a normal stage of grief and natural concern about the responsibilities you will face as a mother. But as I have said, you will not be alone. You'll have all of us here to help and the baby will be well looked after and well loved. Don't you worry. Come along, why don't we go downstairs to the kitchen and have tea and cake with Doris? Now, blow your nose and wash your face and come with me.'

'All right, Em.' She smiled a little and went into her bathroom to do as I'd bid her. I walked over to the window and noticed the lavender plant that Carter had potted for her, dry and lifeless on the window sill. Oh, dear, oh dear.

Martha emerged from the bathroom and I held the plant in my hands. 'Martha, whatever have you done with your lovely lavender plant? You do have to water it, you know.'

'Oh no! Look at it! I'm hopeless, aren't I?'

'I'll take it downstairs. Perhaps Carter can do something with it. Come along. I'm sure Doris has some nice plum cake and tea on the go.' And we made our way down to the kitchen, where Doris and Carter, along with Tom, were sitting at the table.

Carter drained his cup and looked at the plant.

'Well, that's a gonner, to be sure. You do need to give a plant a droppa water now and again, you know, Miss Martha,' he said, not unkindly.

'I'm so sorry, Carter,' said Martha, and with that, her tears started again. Tom looked on, with a sad little face and saucer-wide eyes.

'There's nothing to cry about, Miss, really there ain't,' said Carter. 'I'll find you another plant, don't you worry.' He scraped his chair back from the table and got up.

'Oh, my goodness,' cried Martha. 'I can't even look after a plant without killing it! How can I ever take care of a baby?'

Carter stood at the door, plant in one hand, doing his head scratching and nose rubbing with the other.

'Now you don't need to worry about that, Miss Martha. Babies are a lot harder to kill than plants.'

53: That evening – In Suffolk...

Laura:

That evening, while Kitty and Kylie watched telly, I lay in the bath in my Suffolk cottage, with scented candles and a mug of hot chocolate, mulling over the dilemma. What was I to do? I'd inherited a mansion that needed work doing on it and no funds to renovate. How was I going to raise the funds to do the work and keep myself while I finished my degree course and got a proper job? I had no employment (tricky!), a small cottage that was probably worth about a hundred grand, if that, potentially a dilapidated classic car that might bring in a few quid. And a library full of first edition classic books that Craig had offered to relieve me of in exchange for fifty-thousand quid per book. I had at least a dozen reasons why I could not go down the route of selling the cottage or the car or the books. Mostly emotional reasons, but also, I still had trouble believing that the books were actually worth anything. I mean, a load of old books? I made a mental note to look up rare books on the Internet. But even if they were valuable, I wasn't happy about selling them when they'd been in in the Hamilton Hall family for centuries. It just seemed so mercenary to me. And as for my cottage, well, I'd worked hard to buy it, and had Mum not died, I'd have had her living with me in her old age. I had a huge emotional attachment to my little home in Suffolk. There was also the niggling fear that there were evil forces at work in Norfolk. That Maggie Middleton woman was beyond strange. She unnerved me no end, not least because she was so capricious. Nice as pie one minute, threatening me the next. Creepy.

Of course, I had no emotional attachment to the old jalopy. And if Simon Fancy-pants wanted to take it off my hands for a decent sum, he'd be welcome to it. For a price. Even if I could manage to raise the money to renovate (and god knows what horrors Simon might find in the survey!), Hamilton Hall was not going to run itself. The council tax alone, I'd discovered, was just shy of three grand a year. What on earth was I to do? This wasn't just a matter of finding the funds for renovation, I'd then have to find the dosh to run the place. Perhaps the sensible thing to do would be to sell the old hall. But again, sentimentality got in the way.

My head hurt with the effort of thinking things through. Everything was such a muddle. Every time I thought I'd found a solution, doubts flooded my mind and my emotions swamped my 'sensible', 'practical' brain. Avenues that I'd thought would lead me to the funds I needed were all thwarted. It almost felt like there was some jinx or other around every corner. Had Maggie Middleton cast a spell on me? I did wonder. I mean, she had obviously some issue about me inheriting the mansion and what I was going to do with it. Had she been the one to send the fraudster my way to scam me? And then there was the bank loan that didn't materialise. Every time I thought I'd found a possible solution, it was thwarted.

And I doubted that I'd get much for the old classic car, despite what Jason, the mechanic, and Simon had said. Probably a few hundred at the most. That wasn't going to get me very far. Oh, I was in such a muddle! In the meantime, I was living on fresh air. Well, fresh air and Kitty's good nature.

I took a sip of hot chocolate and raised a foot out of the bubbly bath water, flexing it and inspecting my leg muscles. Hmm. I really do need to get back to the gym. And cut my toe nails. And shave my legs. Not that there was anyone in my life who cared about my hairy legs and overgrown toe nails, or untoned leg muscles. Another sip of hot chocolate. Mmm. That was good.

I dunked the bath sponge into the water and squeezed it over my body. Ooh, that felt marvellous. I repeated the process.

There was a tap at the door. Kitty popped her head in.

'Can I come in Laura? I need to use the loo.'

'Sure. Help yourself.' We are so familiar with each other, one in the bath and the other on the loo was nothing new and never an embarrassment. No big deal. Kitty's Mum used to put us in the bath together as children, as did my dear Mum.

'You OK, hon?' Kitty asked, midstream, 'you seem a little pensive.'

'Oh. Just thinking about what to do. I seem to be going around in circles, trying to figure things out. I mean, as soon as I think I've found a way, then something or other, whether emotional or practical, comes along to spoil the idea.' I took another sip from my mug.

'You don't suppose that Maggie Middleton woman has cast an evil spell on me, do you? I mean, she's probably a modern-day witch. I wouldn't put it past her! And what about that old boy I told you about, who received death threats when he renovated that old Norfolk church? There are evil spirits in Norfolk, I just know it.'

'Don't be daft, Laura! There's no such thing, despite me teasing you before about weird Norfolk folk. No, you just need to think things through logically and you'll figure out what to do. Time to make a list again!'

'Not another bloody list! I've made endless lists, and I'm still getting nowhere.'

'You need to focus your mind. One way to do that is to write a list.' Come on, get out of that bath and come downstairs. We can make a start.'

And with that, Kitty stood up, pulled up her knickers, flushed the loo and left the bathroom.

54: April 1941
Hamilton Hall

Emily:

'Come on now, my woman, you can do it. *Push!* Just one more time, now Miss Martha.'

'I can't! I can't do any more. I just can't!' Martha's energy was all but expended but she managed to summon up enough of it to object to Doris's instructions. She had been in labour for some eight hours and it was now just after ten o'clock on the Sunday morning. We had, all three of us, been awake since two and Martha was not the only one suffering from exhaustion.

I bathed my sister's brow with a cold, wet flannel. 'Do come along, Martha darling. The baby is almost here. Just one more push, darling. Please.'

'I want Charles. Where is Charles when I need him? And where is Doctor Beresford? He should be here. You said he was on his way.'

'Darling, don't think about that now. Think about your baby. It needs you to be strong. So, come on, do as Doris tells you and push. Now, Martha. Push!'

And suddenly, there she was: a delightful, pink-faced baby girl, with dazzling blue eyes and a shock of jet black hair, bellowing out her protestations, most indignant at being thrust into the bright lights of the outside world. Doris cut the cord, wrapped the infant in warm, fluffy towels and I took the new-born into my arms.

'Martha, she's beautiful. She's absolutely beautiful. Look at her. Isn't she lovely?' I leaned over Martha and tried to pass the pink bundle into her arms.

Martha stared at the baby as if she wondered what it was and where on earth it had come from. Then the tears fell and she sobbed like a child.

Doris sat on the edge of the bed and took her into her bosom, making soothing noises. 'There, there, Miss Martha. You're a very clever girl and now you have a bootiful baby daugh'er. I'm right proud of you, Miss Martha. Right proud. Now we need to deliver your afterbirth. Just push a little bit more for me. That's my girl.'

I moved across to the cradle and laid the baby down. There was a knock at the door and in walked Doctor Beresford.

'Well, now, seems I'm surplus to requirements! Splendid! Let's take a little look at you both.' John Beresford strode over to the cradle and unwrapped the baby. She protested with another hearty scream as he examined her and the doctor laughed. 'She's a healthy set of lungs on her, that's for sure.'

He moved across the room to Martha's bedside.

'And how are you feeling, Martha? Hard work delivering an infant, yes?'

Martha did not answer but looked over to the window, where the curtains were still drawn.

'What are you going to call your daughter, Martha?' Doctor Beresford lifted her wrist as he spoke and proceeded to take her pulse.

Martha spoke softly. 'I thought it would be a boy and I could call him Charles.'

'Well, you have a little girl who looks just like you. I don't think "Charles" is a fitting name, do you?' The doctor smiled benignly at Martha as he continued with his examinations.

'Charlotte,' came Martha's quiet reply. She turned to face us all. 'Charlotte Adalicia Emily.' Her eyelids drooped and she fell into a deep sleep.

§

'Martha? Martha, wake up darling. Baby wants a feed. Come along dear.'

Martha's eyes snapped open and she looked at me, now squinting, bewildered.

'What? What baby? What are you talking about, Emily?'

'Baby Charlotte. She's crying for a feed. Come along, you need to sit up and try to feed her.'

'Feed her? Feed her? How?'

Doris strode into the room; her manner brooked no nonsense.

'Come on now, my woman. Baby needs her milk. Sit you up now and I'll bring her over. You's a mum now and you has to feed this little one.'

Charlotte continued to air her lungs with great enthusiasm.

Martha looked as if she'd been asked to perform some impossible feat, and that feeding a baby was an utterly preposterous notion. Colour rose in her cheeks and she made to get out of bed. Doris was having none of it. 'No Miss, you stay there and take the baby.'

Despite having been awake all night, chores do not perform themselves and after feeding Tom with boiled egg and dry toast (our meagre ration of butter never lasts the week), we went out to the chicken coop to collect new eggs and feed the hens. The snowdrops peeped optimistically through the cold ground and the crocuses were a splendid blanket of yellow and purple that surrounded the copper beach tree. The weak spring sunshine shone through fluffy clouds. Tom reached into the bucket, took a handful of peelings and proceeded to throw them down for the hens. I told him about the arrival of the baby. He pondered the news for a moment.

'Can I see the new baby, Miss Emily?' Tom's face looked up at me expectantly.

'At the moment, Martha is feeding her and she's very tired, but as soon as she's rested I'll take you up to see the baby. I promise.'

'Can George come to see the baby too?'

'Yes. Of course.'

Tom smiled at the prospect and returned to the business of feeding the hens.

We finished that job then wandered over to the barn and gathered up some potatoes and leaks to make soup for the evening meal. Thank goodness for Carter and his expertise in growing much of our food. How on earth do people manage on rations alone? There was still more work to be done and I took over tasks from Doris that day as she tended to Martha and the baby. We met in the kitchen for tea at four o'clock that afternoon, the previous night's lost sleep etched on our faces. Men were lucky that childbirth was the domain of women!

Afternoon tea in the kitchen was always a looked-forward-to affair with Doris and Carter, myself and Tom sharing snippets of news about our respective days, as we sipped our tea and nibbled small pieces of cake. We tried not to mention the war in front of Tom. Young George would sometimes join us at a weekend and one day he arrived with a chess set and proceeded to teach Tom how to play. Despite the vast differences in their social backgrounds, the two boys shared a strong bond. I often mused in these days that, despite everything, this awful war had brought some welcome changes. Social barriers were worn down and young and old of all classes worked together to make do with what we had.

After tea, I took Carter, Tom and George up to Martha's bedroom to introduce them to Charlotte, who responded with a lung full of air that she screamed out into the room. The boys were somewhat underwhelmed by the sight of the wriggling, writhing, hollering Charlotte as they gazed into the cradle. Carter removed his cap, scratched his head, sniffed and rubbed his nose. Martha lay quietly and we did not stay long.

On the way downstairs, Tom looked up at me as he wiggled a finger in his ear.

'Gor blimey, Miss Em,' he said, 'little babies don't half yell.'

I made a mental note to teach Tom how to speak nicely.

55: The following morning
Hamilton Hall

Laura:

But I didn't. Instead, I stayed in the bath, topping it up with hot water whenever it started to feel cool. Eventually, after I'd bathed myself into something resembling a wrinkly prune, I got out, dried myself and went straight to bed.

The following morning, we filled Esther with more stuff from the cottage, including bedding for Kylie, the vacuum cleaner and some kitchen stuff, collected the bike from Teddy Edwards, thanked him profusely, promised to pay him 'as soon as'. He fixed it to the back of Esther, then the three of us, Kitty, Kylie and I, set off for Hamilton Hall, with fingers crossed that the bike wouldn't fall off en route. We stopped off at the café on the way and asked Kylie's boss if she could have a few more days off. Surprisingly, the woman agreed in an instant, once we explained that Kylie was still shaken up about the incident and worried that some unsavoury acquaintance of Shane's might come looking for her. She needed to lay low for a while and be looked after by two mature women. *Uh? Me and Kitty? Mature?*

'Oh wow! Look at that!' Kylie's mouth was a wide 'O' and her eyes were almost protruding on stalks, as we entered the drive of Hamilton Hall and I parked the car.

'Is this really your place, Laura? All your very own?' Kylie got out of the car and stood, transfixed, as she gazed at the mansion. Oh, yes, it most certainly was 'all my very own'.

I took a deep breath and exhaled slowly as I absorbed the majesty of the house and grounds, the ancient trees and the beautiful flowers, still valiantly pushing up amongst the choking weeds. And along with all its magnificence, came a huge responsibility, which now overwhelmed me more than ever. Before entering the house, we walked around the back to show Kylie more of the gardens.

'Looks like Felix has been back!' Kitty said as we noticed that more of the grass had been cut and the garden was becoming transformed. I felt a glow of something rather nice, rising inside me.

'Who's Felix?' Kylie asked and Kitty explained about our neighbour.

'That reminds me, I promised to invite him to dinner, didn't I?'

'You did indeed!' The voice and a hearty laugh came from behind us and we turned to see Felix standing there with a wide grin on his face and a garden rake in his hand.

'Hello there, Felix. We were just admiring your handy work. Thanks so much for all you've done. It's amazing, the difference you've made.' His smile spread across his entire face, reaching his twinkly eyes and his lips had those now familiar parentheses on either side. *Gorgeous!*

'Not at all, Laura. There's still plenty more to do, though, as you can see. But I'm glad to have something to occupy me whilst I'm on leave. My Pa isn't exactly stimulating company, though I hate to say so.'

Not exactly my experience of the old boy. My stress levels shot up and adrenalin rushed, unstoppable, around my whole system whenever I encountered the incorrigible, shotgun-wielding old bugger. I mean, I never knew what he could get up to next. I think I'd rather deal with the oik at the café!

'This is Kylie, Felix. We've brought her back with us for a little while. She needed a break.' The two nodded at each other.

'So, when are you free to come to dinner, Felix? What about this evening, about seven? And will your Dad come too?' I didn't really want his old Pa to come, but knew I'd extended the invitation, so I felt obliged to follow up.

'Tonight, would be great for me. Don't know about Pa. I'll ask him. But thanks very much for the invitation. See you at seven.'

And I made a mental note to quiz Felix on what he knew about the life of Emily.

§

We found Kylie a bedroom where she could camp out for a few days, and Kitty helped her sort out the bed, while I shopped for dinner. Kylie got busy with a duster and a bottle of *Pledge* and took the vacuum cleaner on her travels around her bedroom and the ground floor of the mansion. That evening, as Kitty showed Kylie around the rest of the gardens, I started to prepare the food. I was setting the table with cutlery brought with us from the cottage, when the two of them entered the kitchen.

'I found this bottle of red in the cellar, Laura. OK if I open it?' Kitty held up a dusty wine bottle. 'There's loads more down there. We shouldn't have to buy wine for years!' And we all laughed at the prospect. I took the bottle from Kitty, blew on the dust and read the label: *Château Lafite Rothschild 1934.*

'Crikey, it's older than you and me, put together, Kit!' I said. 'It's French, look.' I pointed to the bottle. 'My great-great-grandmother, Adalicia was French. Craig told me.

'Yes, I know, Laura. You've already mentioned it a number of times.' Kitty gave me a lopsided smile.

Ignoring her remark, I said, 'OK, let's try it,' and pointed to the corkscrew and the four wine glasses that stood, polished and sparkling, on the worktop. 'It might be a bit vinegary though, if it's that old.'

'It's well creepy down that cellar, isn't it?' Kylie said, and I had to agree, remembering my first viewing of it. I shuddered at the memory.

I could almost smell the mustiness I'd detected down there, and hoped there wasn't an expensive damp problem looming. I pushed the thought aside. Simon was going to come and do a survey in a couple of days and I didn't want to think about what financial horrors he might find.

Kitty said she had shown Kylie the old wheel-less, engine-less car in the barn. Kylie laughed about it, then said, 'You really could get some dosh for that, Laura.'

Bless the girl. She had become aware of my financial dilemma regarding Hamilton Hall and was already trying to think of solutions. What an amazing nineteen-year-old! I hoped she'd seen the last of Shane.

'Well, so I am told, and you heard Simon Fancy-pants going on about it, but I am sceptical, myself.'

'No, honest,' said Kylie, 'I saw a story on the Internet a while ago about an old car like that in America what fetched about eighteen grand at an auction.'

'Really? But it must have had wheels and an engine, surely?'

'No, I don't think it did. I think it was a bit knackered. At the time, I thought, what plonker would pay out eighteen grand for a car that was that knackered, must have more money than sense, but someone did, honest.'

'Hmm. Well, we'll see.'

Felix arrived alone, just as Kitty was opening the wine she'd found in the cellar. He was clutching another bottle of red and a potted plant, which I placed on the worktop, and thanked him. He was wearing a crisp, white, open-necked shirt and black, expensive-looking jeans. His black shoes were highly polished, his fingernails remarkably clean, considering all the gardening he'd been doing. *I do like a man who takes care of himself!*

Kitty poured the cellar wine.

'Cheers everyone!' I said and we chinked glasses and sipped at the wine.

'Mm, not bad!' Kitty said, 'no vinegar!'

'Something smells good!' Felix beamed and I hoped he wouldn't be disappointed with the simple meal of lasagne, salad and garlic bread I'd prepared.

'I want to hear all about my Great Aunt Emily, Felix. What was she like?' I asked, as we all sat down at the table. I was dying to hear all about her.

'Oh, a formidable lady, I can tell you! Quite a character.'

Felix took another sip of his wine, as I brought the food to the table. His brow creased and he twisted his lips to one side.

'Something wrong with the wine, Felix? Kitty and Kylie found it in the cellar. There's dozens of bottles down there. I can open a different one if you don't like it.'

He stood up, strode across the kitchen on those great long legs of his, picked up the opened wine bottle and blew more of the dust off it. Now he was peering closely at the label, his eyes squinting.

'I don't know if you realise, ladies, but we are actually drinking a small fortune here.'

56: Late July, 1941
Hamilton Hall

Emily:

Baby Charlotte's wails woke me with a start at five past four in the morning. I pulled on my robe as the bright moon lit my way along the landing to Martha's room. The cries of Charlotte died away and I overheard Martha's admonishing tone.

'Stop that noise, Charlotte. Stop it this minute. It won't do you any harm to sleep longer. But it would do me a lot of good. Shush now.'

I stood stock still outside the bedroom door.

'Oh, darling Charlotte. Mummy is so sorry. I'm not a very good mother, am I? If only Daddy were here. You'd be so much more content, I just know it.'

Charlotte was quiet now. Through the crack in the partially open door, I saw Martha carrying the little one back to the bed and pulling down her nightdress. Baby suckled hungrily.

'If only you knew, Charlotte. If only you knew. Emily is so much more of a mother than I am. She is so good with you. And with young Tom and even young George. A natural mother. A childless mother, but a wonderful one to all three of you, nonetheless. But me? I am totally inadequate. But I do love you so, my precious little one. I really do. I only want the best for you. Oh, this dreadful war. It has taken away your darling daddy and your grandparents.'

Martha was sobbing now.

'What am I to do? I hate those evil people who robbed us of our dear family. If only I could do something. What kind of a world have I brought you into?'

Charlotte was still suckling away. A floorboard creaked under foot and Martha's head snapped towards the bedroom door.

'Em?' She sniffed.

I entered the room.

'You are doing so well, Martha. Please don't cry. We don't want Charlotte upset, do we?'

Martha caught me in a steely gaze.

'This war has taken away our beloved parents and my daughter's father. And that's only *our* family. Goodness knows how many more have suffered such loss. The devastation is immeasurable, Em. And I feel useless, sitting around here every day, just waiting for the baby to cry for a feed.'

'Don't talk like that Martha!' I sat on the edge of the bed.

'But I do, Em. I really do.'

'Martha, you were very poorly for a long time after Mummy and Daddy were killed and you also lost Charles as well as one of your babies before Charlotte was born. You need time to recover. You were doing well in taking care of the hens every day. Now you have little Charlotte to care for. Don't underestimate the importance of that job. You are nurturing the next generation.'

'For *what*, Emily, for *what?*' Her eyes were ablaze now. 'So that the bloody Germans can bomb the next generation to bits? Shoot them out of the skies?' Her face was set in a furious glare.

I had to see her point; I thought of James and my heart wept for him. But I would not express my agreement. We needed hope for a better future. Instead, I said, 'Change baby over to the other side, now Martha. She's very hungry tonight.' And I held the baby while my sister readjusted her clothing.

1st September 1941

Dearest Emily,
Forgive me.
I have to go. This dreadful war has taken away our beloved parents and the love of my life, Charles. I've joined the WAAF and I'm going to do my bit for the war effort. I have to feel that I can make the world a better place for my darling baby daughter to grow up in. Please take good care of Charlotte for me. I know you will. You are a far better mother than I could ever hope to be. Whatever happens, please love her, protect her and make sure she understands that I love her with all my heart. And always will.
But I simply must do this, Emily. I will write, I promise.
I love you, my darling sister.
Your ever-loving,
Martha X
p.s. I am taking the early morning train. I will ride my bicycle to the station and leave it there. I'm sure you will pick it up when you can. x

57: Five weeks later...
Hamilton Hall

Laura:

'Good morning. I am here to see –' the svelte woman standing at the front door of Hamilton Hall, in a navy-blue velvet trouser suit (skinny fit trousers, *natch!*), white silk top and six-inch killer heels, and with a strong Italian accent, checked her notes. 'Ms Laura White. Is she home?' She arched an eyebrow as she looked me up and down.

I'd opened the door to *Simona de Napoli, Master of Wines, Chalmers and Napoli Wine Group, Virginia Water, Surrey,* according to her business card.

The wine connoisseur had been due to arrive half an hour earlier that morning to check out the contents of the cellar. Better late than never, I suppose. It had taken a fair bit of searching on the Internet (not easy with no Wi-Fi at Hamilton Hall and having to rely on 3G) for a decent expert who would come out to view and value the wine, sooner rather than later, but I found one who was going to be in the area and willing to pop in. And there she was, looking at me as if I were the proverbial cat that had dragged in something utterly disgusting.

'Yes, that's me. And you are Ms de Napoli, are you?' Next to me, she looked like an anorexic stick insect; and I'm not exactly heavyweight.

'*You* are Ms Laura White? *You?*' Her tone dripped condescension and I very nearly sent her on her way, but I thought of all those bottles of (well, potentially) liquid gold in the cellar and invited her in, having assured her that, yes, I was indeed 'Ms Laura White' – and why wouldn't I be?

And so, here we were, Simona de Napoli, Master of Wines and me, standing in the dank, musty cellar of Hamilton Hall while she was busy listing the wines and calculating the price I'd be likely to achieve on each of them. Her attitude had visibly shifted; gone was the disdain and here was a warmth as she started to read out her notes to me, in a voice that was like smooth, liquid, dark brown chocolate.

'*Bene allora,* Ms Laura. You have some vintage wines here. And I see that the bottles have been turned regularly,' she said, inspecting some of the bottle tops. She looked around her, strolling up and down the aisles then reached for a chalk board I'd never noticed before, that was perched on top of one of the racks.

'Aha! Yes, just as I thought. This shows,' she said, tapping the chalk board with a perfectly manicured finger nail, 'that the bottles have been turned and the dates recorded. Corks are not dried out. This means the wine is in good condition. Hm. All looking fine there. See? Dated, recorded and initialled... what does that say? Ah yes, "GF". All in order. This is good when we want to sell. Wine needs to be in good condition. *Splendida!*'

I had absolutely no idea what she was talking about, but let her continue. She took an iPhone out of her (very obviously genuine *Gucci!*) handbag and took a photograph of the chalkboard.

But who was "GF"?

GF ... GF ...

George Farrington!

He really had been keeping an eye on the place since Emily had died. Not such a bad old stick after all... for a shotgun wielding geriatric. I felt somewhat chastened.

The liquid chocolate Italian voice cut through my thoughts.

'If you want to sell, I can give you a help. So, do you wish to sell?' She turned and looked at me. The eyebrows went up.

'Well, yes, it would be nice to make a few quid, if I can.'

'*Splendida!* So, it would be good to start,' she smiled warmly, her eyes bright and focused, sounding a lot like one of my lecturers in a tutorial, 'by clarifying what we mean by the "vintage". You see, Ms Laura, the "vintage" does not just mean the "old". She continued walking up and down the aisles as she spoke, taking photographs on her iPhone.

'OK, I see. So, what does it ...?'

'You see, Ms Laura,' she continued, as if I hadn't spoken, that warm smile still in place, the voice still like runny chocolate, 'in the wine produced on the colder limits of wine production, vintage is often very important, because some seasons will be much warmer and produce riper grapes and better wine.'

'Er, right...'

I just wanted her to tell me how much dosh I could get for the bloody wine, and here she was, giving me a lesson in agriculture. *Come one, Simona, get on with it!*

'On the other hand,' she went on, really getting into her stride now, 'a poor growing season can lead to grapes low in sugar, which will reduce the quality of the resulting wine. Wines of superior vintages from prestigious producers and regions will often command much higher prices than those from average vintages.' *Really? Now you're talking! So, what have I got here, then, in this bloody creepy cellar?*

I wanted to say, *just give me a price!* And hurry her along, but by now I was ever so slightly mesmerized by her impressive knowledge, enthusiasm and, basically, overall Italian style and charm. Not to mention her impossible thinness and that to-die-for velvet suit. And how *ever* did she manage to walk in those heels? She'd positively skipped down the cellar steps in them.

57: FIVE WEEKS LATER

'This is especially the case if wines are likely to improve further with some age in the bottle.' Her voice sliced into my reverie.

'How's that, then?' I wanted her to get a move on, but now she had me gripped. What did this mean? That I might get, say, a hundred quid a bottle if I kept them longer, or what?

'This means, Ms Laura, that before the world war two, when these grapes in these bottles were grown,' she pointed with a bright red talon at the bottle in her hand, her little finger crooked, 'the regions of wine production were more restricted than nowadays, because of a weaker, not so good wine technology. So, the producers had to rely on their skills, and on the annual weather.' *Not another bloody lecture! Do get on with it!*

'The main wine regions in France were: Bordeaux, Burgundy, Champagne and Alsace.' She pointed at the different bottles lying on the shelves. 'The Rioja, here, is from Spain. This Piedmont is from Tuscany, in my country. The Port here, the fortified wine, is of course, from Portugal; and these Madeiras too. The fortified wines, means wines are, of course, fortified, which alcohol content is above seventeen or eighteen percent.' *Fascinating! But can you tell me how much I could get for my bottles of French plonk or not!?*

'Please be aware, that not every old vintage before the world war two has the same value during an auction.' I loved the way she said, "*the* world war two" and not 'world war two' or 'the second world war'. But even so, I was getting exasperated with her.

'OK, fine. So, er, is it possible – I mean, can you -?' I was spitting feathers now, trying to get her to give me an indication of whether, or not, the dusty old bottles in this bloody awful cellar would be worth anything other than for pouring into a spag-bol.

'Can I help you? Yes, Ms Laura. I can.'

Phew!

'Chalmers and Napoli are associated with *Christies* in London. I am sure you will have heard of them?'

Not really, no.

'They are the auctioneers of the wine, you know.'

'Er, right. And?'

'Well, I can ask them to auction your wine for you.' *Goodie!*

'There will be a fee for us, and for the auctioning of the product, of course.' *Of course.*

'Plus, there will be a buyer's premium of seventeen, point five percent, and, naturally, VAT to be added to all bids.' *Naturally!*

'The price excludes auction fees and tax. And, there will be a local sales tax of twenty percent.'

'Yes, yes, all right. But, Simona, what do you think I would get for one of these bottles of wine, here? *That* is what I want to know. Right now. Please.'

That warm smile, again. 'Yes, of course you want to know. That is why I am here.'

She took her mobile phone and started tapping away. Now what? What was she doing and when was she going to tell me if I could get a few hundred quid for the plonk?

'OK, Ms Laura. Here we go. I have done some figures. The next auction will be in March next year and we can take the wine then.' She caught me in her gaze. *Six months away!*

'Now, Ms Laura, it is important to remember that, although it looks that older the wine, more expensive it is, this is not true. No.' As she said "no", she shook her head and raised an index finger, wiggling it from side to side, like she was warning a child against unacceptable behaviour. 'In fact, this *Château Lafite Rothschild 1893 ...*' she held up the bottle, showing me the label '... is priced starting at five thousand two hundred pounds, sterling. That is, unfortunately, four thousand less than another year, as the vintage was not such good as other years. In this case, what people pay for is the *rarity* of this wine as there are not so many bottles left.' *Well, no, I don't suppose there are too many hundred and twenty-year-old bottles of plonk lying around in people's under-stairs cupboards. But hang on a second ...*

'Wait a minute. Did I hear you right? Did you just tell me that that dusty old bottle of plonk in your hand there is worth *five grand*?' (I mean, five thousand quid for a bottle of old vinegar? What idiot would pay that?)

'Oh yes, Ms Laura. It could only realise about five thousand pounds. But it was not a good year, I'm afraid, 1893. If it was a good year, this wine would be worth much more. I am sorry.' She gave me a sympathetic smile, as though she thought that I was going to be disappointed to learn that I owned a bottle of wine worth *only* five thousand pounds.

She strode across the cellar and skipped up the steps, saying over her shoulder, 'I will email you a formal valuation, Ms Laura. Goodbye.' And, with a wink of her perfectly made up eye, she was gone.

58: 2nd September, 1941
Hamilton Hall

Emily:
I scrunch up the letter that had been lying on the bedside table and tears fall, unchecked, down my cheeks.

'Doris! Carter! Where are you?' I call out into the nothingness. 'Doris! Carter!' I run along the landing and down the stairs.

Tears prick at my eyes. My face creases in anguish. *Martha, Oh Martha. What have you done?*

'Carter? Doris?'

A warm hand touches my shoulder. Squeezes it. Rubs it gently. A soft voice: 'What is it, Miss Emily? What's happened?'

Doris. I crumble. She holds me. Warm arms around me.

'Doris. She's gone. She's gone into the WAAF. She's left the baby. Oh Doris.' My breath comes in gasps. Erratic gulps.

I hand her the crumpled letter. I grip the edges of my robe. Shorter than me, Doris reaches up to hold me in a mother's love. Doris. Dear, dear Doris. Stalwart Doris. I drop my hands to my sides.

A small hand slips into mine. 'Miss Emily? Why are you crying?'

Tom.

I sniff and bend down to hug him. 'It's all right, Tom. It will all be all right. It's just that –'

'Come along with me, now, my man, and I'll get you some breakfast. Miss Emily needs a moment to herself.' And with that, Doris leads Tom away to the kitchen, as Charlotte howls again in protest.

Oh, my goodness! The baby! I run upstairs and into Martha's room. Charlotte is red of face and wide of mouth. Her screams pierce my ears.

'There now darling. Come to Aunty. Come to Aunty, darling. Let me find you some milk.'

I hold her tightly to me and take her down to the kitchen, where Carter is drinking tea from an enamel mug and Tom is sitting at the table, waiting for Doris to prepare him something to eat.

'Doris, we need to find the baby some milk. And where are the baby bottles? We need to get some baby milk.' I am trembling and hold Charlotte close to me, her wails loud in my ear.

'Miss Martha has been giving baby some bottle feeds, Miss Em. Don't worry, I'll sort her out.'

'Where is Miss Martha? Why isn't she feeding the baby?' Tom's voice is small and his forehead puckered.

I look at Doris, then at Carter. Carter's hand reaches for Tom's shoulder, as he speaks. 'Miss Martha has had to go off and work for the war effort, Tom. It is up to all of us now to look after the Little Miss.'

He gets up and walks towards the back door. Head scratching and nose rubbing, he leaves for his daily chores.

Doris takes milk from the larder and pours it into a small pan. She reaches into the cupboard and finds a baby's feeding bottle and teat. She looks at Tom.

'You'll have to wait a bit, young Tom, while I look after the little'un,' she says with a kindly smile. 'Then I'll boil you a nice egg and you can go out and see to the chickens, like a big boy.'

'Yes, Miss Doris.' Tom looks at me. He reaches over and touches Charlotte's clenched little fist. She stops fretting momentarily and gazes at the boy.

'Miss Em, can I give the baby her milk, please?'

'Well, I'm not –'

'Come to Tom?' he says, opening his arms to her and the baby leans towards him with outstretched arms.

59: Early October, 2013
Hamilton Hall

Laura:

Oh, my day just got better! Not long after the visit of Simona de Napoli, the wine expert, the jalopy fetched nineteen thousand quid at auction. *Yes! Nineteen grand!* That was nine thousand more than Simon Stewart-Rees had offered me. He'd gone off in a flounce when I'd said I'd rather take my chances at the auction. Jason, the trusty AA mechanic had taken the dilapidated classic car away on his rescue truck and had phoned to tell me the good news. I'd thought it was a windup to start with, I mean, nineteen thousand pounds for an old wreck, but some lovely, obliging idiot paid it. I quickly enrolled on the next module for my online degree course. *Yay!* And now I really should replace *Esther. Double yay!*

But when the survey report from Simon Fancy-pants plopped through the letter box, my day got worse again. The invoice was attached to the front, so I was hardly likely to miss it. Two thousand pounds plus VAT just to look around Hamilton Hall and write a few notes. I've obviously been in the wrong line of work. Should've been a rip-off surveyor!

Kitty opened a bottle of wine (this from Waitrose, *not* the Hamilton Hall cellar!) and we went and sat in the drawing room, to read the report.

'Hamilton Hall is a neglected period house with some nine bedrooms...' it began. Neglected? Bloody cheek! I felt personally offended on behalf of the house. All right, so it needed a bit of doing up. No need to be disparaging.

So, for starters, the survey found several slipped and broken roof slates and the chimney stacks needed *"repointing and lead flashings replaced".*

The gutters and downpipes were full of leaves and leaking at the joints. The downpipes, Simon noted, *"discharged to soakaways in the garden and these had silted up".* Oh, and in the cellar, the musty smell was due, apparently, to a rainwater downpipe leaking at a joint into a light well which served the cellar. *Great! It wasn't a ghost after all!*

'That sounds dodgy, Laura. Water leaking into a light well.' Kitty's forehead creased and her mouth turned down. She took a sip of wine. I read on.

'Oh brilliant! That's just peachy. Now it says here that the leaking gutters have also *"caused damp in the plaster of the upper floor rooms"* and they'll *"need stripping and re-plastering of the damaged areas".* Sounds expensive.'

'Well, that's not so surprising, Laura. We've already seen damp on some of the bedroom walls, haven't we?' Yes, we had.

I looked around the drawing room and took a deep breath. What was I to do? This beauty of a house, with all its flaws, was mine, and I desperately wanted to keep it and live in it, but the renovations were going to be astronomical at this rate. A reality check was kicking in fast. And big time.

The drawing room door opened and Kylie popped her head in. She really did look very nice with that haircut and no metalwork stuck in her face. She'd put on a bit of weight since staying with us for a few weeks and it suited her. She'd even got herself a part-time job serving at the Coffee Shop café in Wymondham, and cycled to work every afternoon. The old bike we'd found in the stable was coming in handy, now that we'd had it fixed. Good old Teddy Edwards! I still hadn't paid him for his work.

Kylie was happy not to be working at the petrol station café any longer, with the risk of heroin addict Shane or one of his druggy mates turning up to hassle her. And she'd moved out of her bedsit and was staying with us for the long term.

'Hi Kylie! You back from work already?' I looked at my watch. Quarter to six.

'Hiya. I was going to ask if you wanted a cuppa, but I see you're on the vino already!' She grinned and I offered her a glass of wine.

'No thanks. Bit early for me. I'll have some tea,' and she disappeared again.

Kitty and I went back to the survey report. It noted that several of the windows had broken sash cords and rotten wooden sills. There was woodworm in some of the roof timbers and in some of the floorboards and joists upstairs. *Bugger!*

'No rising damp, though! A house I once looked at as a potential investment property had rising damp,' Kitty said, 'so I decided against buying it. Glad I did too. It can be very costly to put right.'

'I haven't got to the costs yet, Kitty, but this lot so far looks impossibly expensive. And I've only got the nineteen grand.'

I looked around the room again and my eyes settled on the oil painting of my great-great-grandparents, hanging over the fireplace. Adalicia had been a stunning woman in that emerald green gown and matching emerald jewellery, setting off her black hair. And my great-great-grandfather, Richard, looked as noble and reassuring as he had the first time I'd seen the painting. I so wished I'd known them. What would they have advised me to do? Fleetingly, I wondered who my father was. In the end, I'd given up asking Mum about him.

I looked back at the report. It seemed the wiring had been redone only about ten years ago and so was not old or dangerous *(phew!)*, although there was no central heating. They must have relied upon the open fires and the boiler in the scullery for hot water, which is what we were using, although we hadn't lit a fire yet. Probably need the chimneys swept first, after getting them fixed. The kitchen was old-fashioned, but at least everything worked and I kind of liked the charm of its advanced age.

My mobile phone pinged. Craig.

> Laura, I really must speak to you. Let me explain. Please respond to this text.

OK, I'll respond, Craig. *Piss off!*

> Craig. Stop bothering me with your texts. I will block you! Send.

'Why don't you see what he wants, Laura? He might just want to explain himself.' Kitty always had an alternative viewpoint to balance things.

'That's what he says he wants. To "explain" himself. No way. He probably only wants me to sell him those rare books in the library. Out for a fast buck. Why should I give him the time of day?' But despite my resolve, when I thought of that beautiful face, disarming grey eyes, surrounded by thick black eyelashes, not to mention the engaging charm, I felt something stir inside me. *Get a grip woman! He's only a bloke!*

'Oh well, it was only a suggestion,' said Kitty, 'but you do need to raise some more money.' I gave her a look and turned to the final page of the survey report.

"*The likely cost of renovations could be £200,000 plus, and importantly, there should be a large contingency allowance to cover problems which only become evident once work starts.*"

'What? Two *hundred* grand! And that's just for starters.'

60: April, 1942
Hamilton Hall

Emily:

'Hitler's just trying to dishearten Norwich folks by bombing the Cathedral flat,' said an indignant Carter, as he and I worked in the garden, digging up a corner patch of lawn.

'He'll never do it though,' he continued. 'This is Norfolk. Us Norfolk folks is made of tougher stuff than that.' Two heavy air raids had bombarded Norwich the previous week.

'I hope you're right, Carter. How much longer can we endure these air raid attacks?' I said, although the oxygen in my lungs was better saved, not for talking, but for the strenuous task of preparing the corner of the South West lawn ready for planting yet more vegetables.

'If you want my opinion, Miss Emily,' Carter said, 'I reckon Hitler's jealous of Norwich being home to such a bootiful cathedral.'

I had to smile at his fierce loyalty, but agreed he had a point.

On the first night, the bombing had gone on for over two hours. We were in the cellar, but we could still hear the terrifying noise of the bombs. Miraculously, baby Charlotte, Tom and George, slept soundly throughout.

'Nearly two hundred bombs dropped on Norwich on Monday night,' said Carter. I was impressed not only with his knowledge, but also his lung capacity that allowed him to talk as well as dig.

'And nearly two hundred people killed and hundreds more injured. Bloody bastards. Oh, sorry Miss Emily. Begging your pardon. I was forgetting meself there for a minute. Shouldn't use bad language in front of a lady.'

'That's all right, Carter. I feel like swearing myself sometimes when I think about all this pointless death and destruction.' I wiped the sweat from my brow with the back of my hand. 'It's a miracle that anyone could survive at all.'

'Yes, Miss Emily. You're right.' Carter, sixty years old, grey, stooped and wiry, but still strong as an ox, nodded in agreement then took off his cap, scratched his head, rubbed the end of his nose with the palm of his hand and sniffed.

'And then the blasted Luftwaffe were at it again two nights later.' He said, as if I hadn't been there to witness it myself. He replaced his cap and continued digging. 'And the Americans are stationed at Hethel now. Marching all over Wymondham and Norwich like they own the place. But what use is they? Not done much to stop the bombs, have they?'

Even for the physically strong woman that I had become through maintaining the grounds of Hamilton Hall with Carter, this was hard work. I looked forward to a long, hot bath that evening. Before the war, young casual workers, usually local boys, would help in the gardens for cash payments, but they had all disappeared into the armed forces. Tears pricked my eyes at the thought of the young men who'd lost their lives before they'd hardly begun. I tried not to dwell on James and Charles being shot down over Germany and my parents' death in the first London bombings back in 1940, but these losses were never far from my mind. I recalled, not for the first time, how we had waited and waited that night, for Mother and Father to return from London to the surprise anniversary dinner I'd arranged with Doris. I swallowed hard. A sniff. Must keep positive. Must carry on. *Keep calm and carry on,* the government posters called out to us. Keep calm and carry on. Yes. We must. It was the only possible strategy.

Carter continued his rant. 'Did you hear about the chap what lost his wife and three kiddies in that raid? Three little kiddies, Miss Emily, and one only a tiny baby, just a few months old.'

'Yes, Carter, I did. Nellie in the post office was talking about it yesterday. Apparently, they were in their Anderson shelter and it took a direct hit. Heart-breaking. At least we have some protection in our cellar.'

'Have you heard any news from Miss Martha?'

'No. Not for some time, Carter. Not since she was sent to Scotland for some sort of training.'

A voice called. 'Miss Emily, lunch is ready and the little one has woken from her nap.' Doris, cardigan sleeves rolled up to her elbows and the familiar overall wrapped around her, had baby Charlotte in her arms. Carter's lithe physique contrasted with his wife's corpulent frame and as children Martha and I used to chortle, saying that the couple looked like a Number Ten walking along together – Carter the 'one' and Doris the 'naught'. Now I felt ashamed of our childish, private jokes about them. Doris's devotion to the family was unswerving and she carried out favours over and above the call of duty, as did Carter himself. They were family now and lived with us. Their daughter, son-in-law and children had taken over the Carters' flint cottage, close to the grounds of Hamilton Hall.

'Coming, Doris!' I stuck the garden fork into the soil and arched my back. Carter and I strode towards the house.

Tom was in the Morning Room with George, doing the school work I'd set them. The school house in the village had been bomb-damaged and I had been approached by the education authorities with a request – rather a demand – to run the school from Hamilton Hall. The local children came in the afternoons with their teacher, who held classes in the house. Tom and George joined in the afternoon lessons after home schooling from me in the mornings.

'Come along boys, wash your hands for lunch,' I said and they jumped to it.

After a lunch of Doris's home-made potato and onion soup and freshly baked bread, I lifted Charlotte onto my hip to take her up to the playroom.

As I moved across the reception hall towards the stairs, a loud bang on the front door made me catch my breath and freeze on the spot.

61: October, 2013, the following afternoon
Hamilton Hall

Laura:

'*Ouch!*' I banged my head as I crawled backwards out of the cupboard.

Kitty and I were in the kitchen having a spring (well, autumn) clean and while I'd been crouching down cleaning the lower cupboards, Kitty was on a stepladder, tackling the upper ones. Kylie was still at work at the Coffee Shop, but was due home shortly. As we worked, I'd been thinking aloud about the enormity of the Hamilton Hall project. Once again, it came down to the realisation that the expense was going to be crippling.

'I know Simon's survey report suggested you'll need a couple of hundred grand to fix up the old hall, but you don't have to do it all in one go. Choose one thing to work on and once you find a bit more money, start on another.'

Now I was standing up in the middle of the kitchen, rubbing my lower back. My head still sore. I'd nearly knocked myself out, trying to reverse out of the cupboard, just to hear Kitty stating the obvious. I rubbed my head again.

'OK, I see your point. And it really is the only way to approach the project, isn't it? I mean, even if I sell a few bottles of wine, I'll surely still have nowhere near two hundred thousand in the bank.'

'It's how I do up my buy-to-let properties, you know. I rarely have enough money to do all the work in one go, and none of my houses is anywhere near the size of Hamilton Hall, as you know.'

I reached for the kettle and waved it at Kitty. All this cleaning and chatting was bringing on a mighty thirst. She jumped down from the step ladder as I moved over to the sink, and pulled out a couple of mugs from the cupboard then filled the kettle.

We sat at the kitchen table with tea and apple cake.

'I think the roof, chimney and gutters are most likely to need doing first.' I reached for my mobile. 'I wonder what that would cost?' As I tried to go online using 3G without much success, and resolved to get some Wi-Fi organised, there was a tap on the back door and in came Felix.

'Ladies! Good afternoon!' His smile filled the room. Those delicious parentheses either side of his mouth were captivating, as ever.

I stood up to get another mug and tea plate.

'Hi Felix! Cuppa?'

'Wonderful!' He folded down his lengthy body onto a chair.

'How are you Felix?' Kitty asked. 'I see you've been hard at work in the garden again.'

'I'm great, thanks, Kitty. Laura has enough land here to build a holiday farm!' We both laughed.

'How's your Dad?' Kitty said, smiling up at Felix.

'Pa's not so good. He's deteriorating mentally and I've extended my leave so's to keep an eye on him a bit longer.' *Yes, keep an eye on the old codger, Felix. And confiscate that bloody shotgun!*

'Sorry to hear that, Felix. Anything we can do?' Well, all right, I know old George can be a bit of a bugger, but he had been turning the wine bottles regularly, as evidenced in the chalk board that Simona had shown me, and Felix has been good to me with all the help with the garden and other jobs about the place. I do believe in reciprocity. As Mum used to say, one good turn deserves another and all that.

'Thanks, Laura. But I'm thinking about getting someone in to help with domestic stuff. It would have to be someone good with elderly people, though.'

Kitty looked at me. *No way, Kitty Colman!* I knew what she was thinking, my experience of working at the care home, but despite his good-heartedly keeping the house safe, my heart leapt into my mouth whenever I encountered George. I was at risk of choking on it! There was no way I was going to offer to take care of him.

'Anyway, I popped in to ask if you're around this evening and if so, how about I bring us an Indian takeaway from *India Village*? I ate there one evening last week and it was jolly good.'

My mind wandered back to the time Craig had taken me there, after my first viewing of Hamilton Hall and now something inside me moved. *Stop it Laura! Don't think about Craig bloody Matthews!*

Kitty smiled brightly at Felix (and did I detect a twinkle in her eye?). 'That would be great, Felix, thanks very much!' She beamed at him then shot me a look. Short socks and scuffed shoes sprang to mind.

'Er - yes! Yes. That would be great, Felix. Thanks. And I think I might have a menu here somewhere,' I said, getting up to rummage in my bag. Ah, there it was, crumpled. I knew I'd picked up the takeaway menu as I'd left the restaurant that night with Craig. *Those steel grey eyes... that jet-black hair. That enchanting smile. Oh! Just stop it right now Laura White! Craig Matthews was only after your rare books!*

'Fine. I'll feed Pa and tuck him up in bed before I go for the food. See you about seven, then.' And with that he unfolded his rangy body from the chair and left by the back door.

'Julie at the Coffee Shop fell in the kitchen and broke her wrist this afternoon,' said Kylie, as the four of us tucked into the feast Felix had treated us to that evening.

'Ooh. That sounds painful,' I said, helping myself to more.

'I know. She was yelling a lot and I just knew it was broken, although Mary thought it was only a sprain. Anyway, a bloke having his tea in the café offered to take her to the hospital in his car. Dead cool car it was. A jeep! Bright blue. Metalic blue. Well cool. Wouldn't mind one of those!' *Craig. Drives. A. Bright. Blue. Jeep.*

'Really? A jeep? Mm. So, er, how is Julie then?' I couldn't help wanting to ask Kylie to describe the 'man with the jeep', but thought better of it.

'Well, he brought her back to the café and it is definitely broken. So, then Julie said we need to advertise for someone to make the cakes and pastries and stuff while her wrist mends, and I told her you're a dab hand at doing stuff like that, Laura. And she said can you go see her in the Coffee Shop tomorrow?'

'Really? Me? Tomorrow?'

'Yeah. She was dead happy when I told her and she wants to see you about a job while she gets better.' Kylie took a sip of her Coca Cola. She wasn't, really, much of a one for alcohol, and I'd noticed that she'd never once smoked a cigarette after the day we first took her home to Suffolk with us. She'd obviously given up the filthy things.

'What a good idea!' Kitty was talking through a mouthful of naan bread. Not a good look.

'Yes. Thanks, Kylie. That was thoughtful of you.' I squeezed her arm and smiled at her. I desperately needed to get some more money coming in, rather than living off the jalopy proceeds, Kitty's generosity and waiting for the wine auction next March.

'There is also an opportunity for you to earn some extra money, Kylie, if you are interested.' Felix had been listening quietly to the conversation, just nodding here and there, while he enjoyed his food.

'Really? What's that then?' Kylie's eyes were bright with anticipation.

'Well, as I was explaining to Laura and Kitty earlier this afternoon, my old Pa is getting on a bit and we could do with some help both with him and around the house generally. How do you feel about coming over for a couple of hours in the mornings, to give a hand? I can pay you ten pounds an hour, so twenty pounds a morning. What do you say, Kylie?'

'Oh *wow!*' Kylie's eyes were almost the size of the naan breads on the table. 'That would be mega brilliant! Yes, *please,* Felix! Thanks ever so!'

Felix smiled at her. 'OK, Kylie. Pop over in the morning and I can show you what needs doing and we can have more of a chat then. Although I must warn you, my old Pa can be a bit of a challenge at times. He comes into contact with the real world only very occasionally. And even then, only very fleetingly.'

62: April, 1942, that afternoon
Hamilton Hall

Emily:

'But Major, we have two children and there are five of us living here and the drawing room is already being used as the village school, which was bomb-damaged. I cannot possibly allow numbers of strange men to come and live here too. It would be quite improper.' Requisitioned. Hamilton Hall was to be requisitioned for billeting American air force personnel.

'I'm afraid you have no choice, Ma'am. It's orders from on high. And we must all do our bit for the war effort.'

'But we grow vegetables and give these and eggs from our chickens freely to the village people in need. I do WVS work regularly. My sister is serving in the WAAF. Whatever else can one possibly do for the war effort? And now you say we have to share Hamilton Hall with total strangers.'

'I'm real sorry, Ma'am. But orders are orders. We're expecting more USAAF personnel to arrive in the coming months and they will need somewhere to live. But you have plenty of rooms in this beautiful house, Ma'am. And our men are expected to behave and respect their hosts. We all have to make sacrifices. We're at war, Ma'am.'

I'd opened the front door of Hamilton Hall after lunch that day to Major Marvin Phillips, United States Army Air Force. His substantial presence filled the doorway. He'd removed his cap to reveal thick, wavy, dark brown hair and looked at me with intense, deep-set brown eyes. He stood, I estimated, six feet two inches tall and I guessed his age at early thirties. Charlotte, still on my hip, cried the moment she saw this strange man standing there. Tom and George thought it was hugely exciting to have a 'real American' in the house and later could be heard having whispered conversations together about how many 'Jerries' they thought Major Phillips might have killed. George was later to learn that his home, too, was to be purloined for military accommodation.

The Major took his leave and the village children arrived with their teacher, Miss Carol Simpson, for afternoon lessons. Life at Hamilton Hall was, in one afternoon, first, metaphorically at least, turned upside down then restored to its more familiar state as Tom and George, along with the village children, settled into their school routine with Miss Simpson.

The Billeting Officer arrived the following week to go through the house and inspect every room. He told me which rooms he would take and those we could keep for our own use. He perfunctorily informed me how many people he would put in

Hamilton Hall and made clear to me that I had no say in the matter whatsoever. I was also informed, in terms that brooked no misunderstanding, that I had no recourse and that the British Government had the power to take over Hamilton Hall, with no recompense, should I choose not to co-operate, and we could all be put out onto the streets. He followed that, as if he were doing me a great favour, by saying if we did not have enough beds or blankets for the airmen, then these would be supplied. Free of charge. The following day a service lorry arrived with British and American airmen who marched through the house in their loud boots and put iron bunk beds, thin mattresses and blankets in the requisitioned rooms.

After tea that afternoon, when the village children had left with Miss Simpson, Tom and George went out to play in the late afternoon April sunshine.

Tom arrived home in time for supper with a bulge under his jumper.

'What have you there, Tom?' I asked him, hands on hips and in the most no-nonsense tone I could muster after the testing day I'd had.

'Please, Miss Em. Please can I keep him? I found him in the hollow tree and he's hungry and tired and only a baby. Like Charlotte.'

I lifted my foster son's jumper to find a black and white puppy wriggling underneath.

63: A few weeks later
Hamilton Hall

Laura:

'Glamping!!'

'Huh? What?' I'd woken with a start as Kitty shot bolt upright in bed and uttered that one unintelligible word. Glamping. I squinted at my mobile phone. Five o'clock in the bloody morning! 'What *are* you up to now, Kitty?'

'It's what Felix said yesterday. Remember what he said about the grounds of Hamilton Hall being big enough to build a holiday farm?'

'Er, yes... Vaguely. So?' I said, a big yawn escaping.

'Well, not exactly a holiday farm, but how about building a glamping site?'

'And what, pray, dear Kitty, is "glamping"?'

'Oh, come off it, Laura, you've heard of glamping, surely?' She was wriggling out of her sleeping bag now and making for her dressing gown and slippers. 'Jeez. It doesn't get any warmer in this house, does it?'

'No, I haven't, as it happens,' I said, ignoring her moan about the cold, in *my* house. 'Would you care to enlighten me? And while you're at it, go and put the kettle on. This is the most ungodly hour to be up, Kitty Colman.'

'Come downstairs then and I'll make some tea and tell you about my dream.'

'Your *dream?*' I said, indignant. I slipped out of my sleeping bag and reached for my robe. 'You mean you've woken me up at dawn to share your *dream* with me? Bloody hell, Kitty, have a heart!'

We sat in the Morning Room with blankets wrapped around us, hands wrapped around hot mugs of steaming tea. If I didn't get some heating sorted out soon, I'd have to go back to the cottage for the winter.

'Glamping is the new trend in camping,' said Kitty, her eyes bright with enthusiasm. 'It is camping with all the luxuries you could want, like hot showers, flushing loos, tents with different rooms, separate bedrooms, cooking facilities, heating and so on. All the rage now amongst the well-off. I quite fancy trying it myself, actually.'

'Glamping. Glamping. Mmm. So, basically, it's camping for posh weaklings who lack the emotional or physical stamina to do proper, get-your-hands-dirty camping, is it? Too much of wimps to light their own campfires or squat in the woods for a wee? Whatever will they come up with next?' I rolled my eyes and took a sip of tea.

'Don't scoff. There's a lot of money in it, Laura. You could run it yourself as a business or get someone in to manage it for you. Felix is right, there is a lot of land here and you could put it to good use. You'd need planning permission of course, to convert some of your land, but as there is probably nothing like a glamping site in this immediate area, I shouldn't think you'd have a problem getting it.'

'But I've never run a business in my life, Kitty. I wouldn't know where to start.'

'With a business plan, Laura. You start with a business plan.'

'Then what?'

'Then you go to the bank and ask for a business loan.'

'I went to the bank once before to ask for a loan, remember? And the guy couldn't get rid of me quick enough.'

'But this is different. It would be a different sort of loan. A business loan. Tell you what, I'll make enquiries about getting planning permission while you go to the Coffee Shop about the baking job today, and we can take it from there. Are you game?'

I could only imagine where Kitty got her mental energy from at five-thirty in the bloody morning. I was grumpy and awestruck in equal measure. But that's my best friend Kitty all over. A fearsome force.

'You might have hit on a good idea, there, Kitty. I do have a lot of land here. There's that big paddock beyond the stables and the barn. I think it's about a hundred acres and it's separated from the gardens by hedges and trees, but you can get to it through that gate. So, perhaps...'

'Yes! Great idea! The paddock would be perfect! It was lovely in the summer when it was covered in daisies. And I'm sure it's big enough, from what we've seen of it and it would need to be separate from your own private living space. Excellent idea!'

I pondered on this for a moment.

'And we could have a swimming pool and organised activities like tours of local attractions, cycling, tennis. And barbecues!'

'Yes! Brilliant! Now you're talking, Laura White!' Kitty clapped her hands in glee. 'And how about horse riding? There is no end to the possibilities!'

'I am quite warming to the idea! I think it could work. I just don't know how I would convince a bank to give me a business loan. And there are still all the renovations to do on the house. I feel kind of out of my depth, just thinking about it.'

I got up and looked out of the Morning Room window. I could see the shadows of the trees on the lawn as the light from the room shone out of the window and into the garden. The trees were still magnificent, even as they shed their autumn leaves. The branches danced and swayed in the light breeze. I imagined having spent a whole year in Hamilton Hall so that by then I would have witnessed all four seasons. Not for the first time, I felt overwhelmed by the enormity of what I had inherited, yet I was even more determined to make it work, despite feelings of doubt creeping up on me from time to time.

'There's so much to think about, Kitty. I do feel out of my depth here at times. I want to get it all renovated but there's my degree to finish as well. I do wonder if I will manage it. Everything seems so uncertain, despite having found some of the money.' I felt Kitty's arm around my shoulder and turned to face her. She enveloped me in her arms and hugged me warmly.

'Laura, my dear pal,' she said quietly in my ear. 'I've known you since we were tots together and I know that once you set your mind to something, you will do it. I mean, how many women of your age would work in a care home to fund themselves through university? Most would just take the student loan, but you just plod on, working and studying until you get there. You will achieve your degree, Laura, and you'll sort out Hamilton Hall too. And if you really want to start this glamping thing, well, let's see what we can sort out.'

64: Some weeks later
Hamilton Hall

Emily:

'Oh *please*, Miss Emily! *Please* can I keep him? He's only little and he can eat half of my rations if that would help. Please?'

I looked down at Tom's wide eyes and then at the pup. How could I refuse? I'd already acquired a foster son and a niece, so another little one to look after could hardly make too much difference. Except that the Americans were going to be arriving soon and would no doubt be taking over.

'All right, Tom. You can keep the dog.'

'Oh, thanks Miss Em! Thank you!' Tom threw his free arm around my waist and hugged me tight until I almost toppled over.

'Steady on!' I laughed. 'What will you call him?'

'His name is Patch. I'll call him Patch on account as he's got a white patch over his eye. He looks like a pirate, doesn't he?' Tom's delighted expression warmed my heart after the testing day I'd had.

'Where is George? Did he go home?'

'Yes, Miss Em. He went home when his Mum came back from the Red Cross.' George's father was away in the Army and the boy would spend time with us at Hamilton Hall whenever his mother worked at the Red Cross. Before the war, their lives and ours had been highly privileged. Things had changed so much. War saw to that. 'All right. Let's find Patch some warm milk and something to eat.' I said, ruffling Tom's hair.

The following morning, Doris and I went up to Mother and Father's room. I'd been putting it off since they passed away, but now that the Americans were coming, I needed to move their belongings out and store them somewhere safe. It was necessary for storage space to be found for their things and, very importantly, Mother's jewellery.

I opened Mother's wardrobe and the first thing I saw hanging there was her beautiful emerald green evening gown. As I felt the taffeta, I breathed in her unique aroma and was taken back to the evening she had last worn it, before the war, to attend the annual summer ball which my parents held in huge marquees in the paddocks of Hamilton Hall. A sob escaped and Doris put her arms around me.

'There, there, now Miss Emily. Don't take on so,' she soothed and I took a lace handkerchief from the pocket of my corduroy gardening trousers and blew my nose.

'Sorry, Doris. It's just –'

'I know, Miss Emily, I know. But dry your eyes and let's get on with this job, otherwise it'll never get done.' Dear Doris, ever the practical one. Unshakeable Doris. Comforting Doris.

We folded and wrapped the dress in paper and added some moth balls that Doris found in the chest of drawers. Mother's fur stole came next, along with her woollen winter coat and a selection of hats, gloves and scarves.

'Let's make three piles,' said Doris. One for going away, one for things what might fit you and the third one to go to village people what needs things. That'll save folks having to use their clothing rations, won't it?'

'Good idea, Doris. A very good idea.'

The three piles soon mounted up and then we started on Father's wardrobe. His good shoes, too large for Carter, would be very welcome to some villager, and his jackets, trousers and some of his woolly jumpers too, but not before I put aside a pair of trousers and two jumpers for myself. They would be a bit big but good for wearing while working in the garden. I took two of Mother's skirts and blouses and cardigans for myself. Nothing would fit dear Doris, she was far too rotund to get into Mother's clothes, but I gave her some summer dresses for her married daughter.

We worked on like this until everything was sorted, then we took suitcases from the attic cupboards and filled them with the clothes to go to the village. Other suitcases were filled with the clothes that would be stored.

Last came Mother's jewellery box. I looked through her beautiful pieces, my favourite was the emerald and diamond necklace, that she always wore with the emerald green taffeta gown, and the matching earrings and ring. I placed the jewellery box in the suitcase with the gown and closed the lid, locking it firmly. Then I carried it to the library.

65: Early November
Hamilton Hall

Laura:

'Oh. One of my tenants is moving out next month.' Kitty stood in the kitchen, going through emails on her iPhone.

'Really?' I was only half-listening, somewhat distracted, looking up 'glamping' on the Internet. I'd finally got WiFi installed at Hamilton Hall, along with some bottled gas heaters and was also in the process of getting quotes for fixing the roof and chimneys. And I'd scrapped *Esther* in favour of a 'new' second-hand car. I was sad to see her go. Things were moving now. I seemed to have been dithering forever, but now I was purposeful and determined and – horrors – getting *practical*!

'Yes, it's the chap with his family in the two-bed place on River Road. Apparently, they are expecting their third child and need the extra space. I've got a three-bed coming up to be vacated soon. I'll offer him that.'

'Oh, right.' I glanced at the time displayed on my laptop. Quarter to eleven. 'Oh sugar! I need to get going. Bank manager. Business loan. Gotta go!'

'I'll come with you, if you like, Laura? Er... do you mind?'

'No, of *course,* I don't mind my best friend coming with me to meet the bank manager, who will, no doubt, be as scary and intimidating as hell. I could do with some support. Come on, grab your coat. Let's go.'

In the car, despite Kitty's words of comfort, I could still feel not butterflies but tropical moths tearing around in the pit of my stomach as I mulled things over in my mind. Kitty broke the silence.

'You'll have to show the bank manager that you've got something behind you, before he or she will agree to a business loan, but don't worry, there are various ways we can deal with that.' Kitty looked at me and I took my eyes of the road momentarily to glance back at her.

'Really? Oh. OK. Oh, look, there's the bank. I'll pull in over here.' I indicated and parked the car.

We were shown to a waiting area by a young woman who told us to take a seat and the manager would be along presently.

'Ah. The glamping lady, I presume?' I looked towards the source of the jolly voice. 'I'm more of a traditionalist myself, when it comes to camping,' he continued, 'but glamping is becoming ever more in vogue these days.'

Kitty and I exchanged glances. Perhaps this was going to be a cinch, if the guy is already saying it's a good idea to start a glamping site. 'Yes, I am Laura White,' I said, trying to sound confident and sure of myself, which, truth be known, I was not.

'Come along to my office,' he said and we stood up to follow him.

I've always expected a so-called 'bank manager' to be at least a few years older than me and possibly bearded, or at least old enough to shave, but this one looked about twelve, with his round face, ruddy cheeks and slightly spikey hair. I stood a good two inches taller than him, as we shook hands and he offered me and Kitty a seat in his office. His shirt collar looked too big for him, like he was in his brand-new uniform on his first day at big school. He stuck his fingers down inside the collar and pulled at it as though it was scratching his skin.

'Have you a business plan Ms White?'

'Yes. Here it is.' I handed over the folder with the business plan that Felix, Kitty and I had put together the night before. Eyebrows puckered on the chubby, red face, as the not-yet-quite-grown-up bank manager read the document.

'Well, that seems fairly sound, Ms White, but what is your investment in the project?'

'Investment?' I looked at Kitty, then back at the twelve-year-old and back again at Kitty.

'Well, er –'

'And your projections will need to stand up to critical analysis before the bank could agree to injecting funds.' He didn't even draw breath before continuing, 'the bank will require some security of some sort. Do you have any security?'

'What exactly do you mean by "security"?' My hands started to sweat and I could feel my face flushing and my heart pumping away against my ribcage. I wasn't sure what he meant by *security*, but I had a bloody good idea it was something I probably didn't have. I looked at Kitty again, who had so far been silent throughout the interview, then back at him.

'Well,' said the twelve-year-old, 'some sort of security would be needed so that if you default on the loan, the bank would have some way of recovering the money from you.' *Default on the loan? The cheek of the man!*

'Now look here. You haven't even offered me anything yet and already you are assuming I'll default on the loan. I don't like people like you. You invite customers in with a carrot and then start whacking them with a stick. Well you can shove –'

'*Whoah!* Hold on a minute.' Kitty had her hand on my arm as I started to get up from the chair. She looked back at the twelve-year-old and at the same time tugged at me to sit me down again.

The man (well, I will call him that, but he could hardly be described as an adult) squirmed in his seat and fiddled with his collar again. His neck was looking red and sore.

Kitty spoke: 'What *exactly* are you thinking off, when you say "security"?'

'Well, assuming there are no funds of the customer's own to inject into the venture, this would probably have to be a legal charge over the deeds of the property that Miss - er –' he looked down at the documents before him as if to remind himself of my name. '*Ms* White -' he looked at me and then at Kitty, 'the property that Ms White has inherited.' *What? Give my house to the bank?*

'No *way*! No bloody *way*! I am not handing over Hamilton Hall to you or anyone.' I made to get up and Kitty's hand clamped on my forearm, yanking me down again.

'Actually, - sorry, what did you say your name is?' Kitty smiled benignly at the bank manager.

'Darren Turner.'

'OK, Darren.' She held on to my arm, squeezing it firmly. 'I'd like to invest in this project to the tune of a hundred and fifty thousand pounds. Will that help?' *What?*

'Kitty I – ' She shot me a look that left me in no doubt that she wanted me to shut bloody up and stay that way.

'That *would* help, yes, Mrs - ?'

'Colman. Kitty Colman. And I prefer Ms,' she said, letting go of my arm and reaching out to shake Darren Turner's hand. She'd put that posh voice of hers on again.

'It would, Ms Colman. Yes, it would.'

He returned her smile with all the warmth of a rip-off bank manager about to make a lucrative deal and get himself promoted. Bloody men. Always out to make money. I thought, momentarily, about Craig, my feelings for him now oscillating between hormone-fuelled, undiluted lust and a ferocious need to slap him. But maybe he'd had a point. Perhaps I should consider selling one or two books to help with the renovations, or to start the glamping business. Better than a loan. After all, I'd read all the Brontë sisters' novels ages ago, some of them when I was still at school, as well as Jane Austen's. Perhaps I was just being sentimental and didn't really need to keep some first editions of the same stories.

'You see, Darren,' continued Kitty, 'this would be a joint business venture, with me injecting some cash and Laura and me running it as a team.' *Oh right! Thanks for the clarification, Kitty.*

'Naturally,' Kitty went on, 'I will want to contribute funds. So, if it would make a difference, let's do that then. What do you say?' She glanced at me. *Short, white socks; scuffed shoes.* I kept quiet.

'Well, yes, that puts a whole different slant on things, Ms Colman. But the bank will need to be convinced that the project is viable and that you could see it through to fruition. We need to know that you have considered every foreseeable eventuality, for example, what would you do if you don't complete on time?'

'Yes, I see your point, Darren. There is a lot for us to think about. And we need to go away and give it all some serious consideration. But in the meantime, do we have the offer of a business loan, in principle?' *You've got to hand it to Kitty, she knows how to twist a twelve-year-old bank manager around her little finger. Dead smooth.* I remained silent.

'That's a very sensible idea, Ms Colman. Some other things you might need to consider are the ways that you will promote the business and you will need a unique selling point, that makes your business stand out from the rest.' He stood up and extended his hand to shake Kitty's. 'And yes, you have an offer in principle. Absolutely.'

I sat there in my metaphorical short, white socks and scuffed shoes. Mute.

66: June, 1942
Hamilton Hall

Emily:

'Ouch!' I felt the sharp pinch on my *derrière* as I bent down to take a saucepan from the kitchen cupboard. I straightened up and turned to find an American airman leering at me.

'How dare you? How *dare* you! Keep your dirty little hands to yourself young man, and kindly, in future, knock before entering a room in my home.

'Well now, little miss. No need to get all high and mighty with me. I'm just being kinda friendly. How about a little kiss for a lonely airman who's thousands of miles away from home? You know, maintaining international relations and all.'

'Certainly not! You utterly revolt me,' I said, through gritted teeth. 'Now get out of my kitchen before I hit you with this pot.' I backed away.

'Aw com'on, now, just one little kiss. You know you want to.' He was moving closer to me now, sniggering repulsively.

'I most certainly do not – '

Unbeknown to the assailant, Carter had entered the kitchen via the open back door and, in stockinged feet, was silently, stealthily making his way across to where the man moved closer to me. Carter tapped lightly on the shoulder of the airman, who swung around, alarmed.

'You heard Miss Emily, boy. Now leave the house and get about your duties.'

'Who the hell are you, old-timer, to tell me what to do, huh? I'm serving in the United States Air Force and we are here to save you Limies from the Nazis. Obviously, your own guys are not up to the job, so you need us real men to win the war for you. Butt out.'

The offender's squeals penetrated my ears as Carter, some two to three inches taller, but a lot less solidly built, took a tight hold of the airman's earlobe and led him across the kitchen to the back door.

'I'll be havin' a word with your Major Phillips about this, boy, and we'll see what he has to say about one of his airmen botherin' the lady of the house. That's not good manners to pester young ladies. Not good manners at all. Now get out and stay out. And I should tell you that I keeps a shotgun what I uses to kill rabbits for the dinner table. You needs to watch out, young'un, on account of I'm sometimes not such a good shot and might just miss yon rabbit and get you instead.'

'Thank you, dear Carter,' I said, exhaling in relief, as he shut the kitchen door. 'I would have used this pot to hit him if he'd come an inch closer. What an unpleasant young man.'

'I'm agonner speak with the Major, Miss Emily. It's bad enough you've had your home overrun with the blessed military, but I'm not having no yank being impertinent with you, and that's a fact. Even if they's here for our own good.'

'Carter,' I said, looking at him sideways, 'since when have you used a *shotgun* to kill rabbits for dinner? You use traps to kill rabbits.'

'Well, that dozy so-and-so don't know that now, do he?'

'I'm real sorry to hear that one of my men was overstepping the mark with you earlier today, Miss Boulais-Hamilton. Your man Carter had a word with me and pointed him out. I can assure you the airman in question has been disciplined and you will not have any more problems.'

Major Phillips stood before me, very upright, his cap under his arm. His dark brown eyes, sincere yet stern.

'It was most unpleasant, Major, so I hope you are right. And it is not only me who should be respected. We have children in the house, both our own and the village children who come for school. I cannot allow your airmen to misbehave. It is most inappropriate.' I swayed as I held Charlotte on my hip. She gazed at the Major, a thumb in her mouth, blue eyes wide and vivid, as if trying to work out who or what he was. Poor little girl. I was keenly aware that not only had her mother abandoned her for the war effort, but the child had no father to protect her either.

'By way of an apology, Ma'am, I'd like to invite you to share a drink with me this evening, after dinner. I'd like to demonstrate to you that not every American military man is as uncouth as the airman who insulted you. What do you say?'

67: December, 2013
Hamilton Hall

Laura:

Kylie relieved herself of the bulging Union Jack rucksack she'd been carrying on her back and dumped it on the kitchen table. I'd been at the Coffee Shop most of the day, baking bread, pies and cakes for Julie.

'The flippin' front tyre got a puncture in Norwich, didn't it, and I had to get the train back.'

It was Sunday, two weeks before Christmas and Kylie's day off from the Coffee Shop. Felix had asked her to shop for pyjamas and underwear for old George and she'd been making the most of Sunday opening hours.

'I felt well stupid in *M and S* asking for PJs and undies for an eighty-year-old,' she said. Kitty and I exchanged a grin and a wink. 'If Felix wasn't paying me there's no way I'd do it! Well uncool.' And she started to spread her purchases across the table.

'And this feller helped me on the train with me bike and we got chatting and that – and it turns out he does charity work in Africa, like that Sri Lanka thingy what Felix does.'

'Small world!' Kitty said, and she and I looked at each other, eyebrows raised.

'Yeah, I know,' Kylie said, and reached back into her rucksack, bringing out more packs of underpants and pyjamas. The clothes would outlive George. 'I hope old George likes these. Mind you, he probably won't even notice them. Felix is right. His dad's in a world of his own. Sweet old thing though.'

Sweet? About as sweet as any shotgun-toting old boy can be, I suppose!

'He said he was here on leave visiting his granddad for Christmas, Kylie continued.'

'Who?' I said, confused.

'The bloke who helped me with the bike. And he said he'd come and fix the puncture too. He was well impressed when I told him where I live.'

That evening, as I prepared Italian chicken and pasta for dinner, Felix tapped on the back door and came into the kitchen.

'I've come to collect the shopping Kylie did for Pa. Mm. Something smells good!' Felix was a man after my own heart when it came to food. Kitty was clearing the table ready to set it for dinner and they smiled at each other. Kylie was taking a bath.

I invited Felix to stay for dinner. I always make too much, anyway. He didn't need asking twice.

Felix opened a bottle of wine as Kitty took glasses out of the cupboard. Kylie joined us, wearing jeans, a sweater and a towel wrapped around her head. She gave Felix the shopping for George.

'I've been thinking, Laura,' Felix said, as he poured the wine, 'you asked me some time ago about your Great Aunt Emily and we have never talked about her. You must be sad that you never met her. You'd have liked her, I'm sure.'

'Thank you, Felix. And no, I didn't know her. And I'm still not sure how I came to inherit the house, but the heir-hunter and the lawyer assured me it's mine.'

I stopped for a moment and thought about that. Craig had been showing me the family tree that night in the *India Village* but I'd become so emotional that he only got as far as my great-great-grandparents and their daughters, Emily and Martha. I knew that Emily had stayed living in the house until her death three years ago, but I wondered what had happened to Martha. One of them obviously had children. It must have been Martha, because Emily died without having married, according to Craig. She was still Emily Boulais-Hamilton. The answer lay with Craig, but...

'Laura?' Kitty's hand was on my arm.

'Huh? Oh. Yes. Sorry. Deep in thought for a minute there.'

'Felix is asking about the glamping project,' Kitty said. I realised I must have missed a chunk of conversation about Emily.

Felix looked first at me and then at Kitty. Their eyes met, and did I detect a little frisson? A spark of electricity crackling between them?

'Oh. The glamping. Yes,' I said, distractedly.

Kitty started to fill him in with progress so far. We hadn't seen Felix since our trip to the bank about the business loan. After we'd eaten, I got up and moved towards the kettle.

'Anyone for coffee?' I asked over my shoulder and Kitty and Felix replied 'yes, please' in unison, while Kylie said, 'not for me, thanks.'

'So, Kitty,' said Felix, 'you were telling me about the appointment at the bank.'

'Oh yes, that's right,' said Kitty as I started clearing the plates away, and Kylie filled the washing up bowl with soapy water.

'It's going to be Kitty's business,' I said over my shoulder as I carried the plates to the sink.

'Oh?' Felix raised his eyebrows as he looked back at Kitty.

'That's right,' said Kitty. 'We've worked it all out. Laura is going to rent the meadow to me and then the glamping project will be mine to set up and run. I'll put some money into it from the sale of one of my buy-to-let houses that became vacant recently. And the business loan we put the plan together for is to be in my name, with my buy-to-let properties as collateral, or "security" as the bank calls it.'

'Good idea. I like it. A lot,' said Felix, smiling at Kitty, and there it was again: that twinkle in his eye.

'The bank manager was impressed with the business plan, so thanks for your help with that,' Kitty said, smiling at Felix.

'That's right,' I said, over my shoulder. 'I don't think we'd have got far without your help with the plan, Felix.'

'Happy to help,' came the reply, and he smiled again at Kitty.

'The rent for the land that I'll get from Kitty will help fund the renovations to Hamilton Hall,' I said, as I dried the dishes that Kylie had begun washing.

'And that's it, really,' said Kitty. 'Wish us luck, Felix.'

'I most certainly *do* wish you luck. What a great idea, to rent the land from Laura, and glamping is all the thing these days.'

Kylie finished the washing up and made for the door. 'I hope the shopping is OK for your dad, Felix.'

'I'm sure he'll be delighted, Kylie. Thanks again.'

'I'm off up to my room now. See you all later.'

'Bye, Kylie,' the three of us said, almost simultaneously.

'So, tell me, how's the planning permission coming along?' Felix then asked, looking from Kitty to me.

'So far, so good,' Kitty said. 'Still not had a decision, but we do know that there have been no objections,' (and we hadn't, not even from our nearest neighbours, but they did happen to be Felix and his dad), 'so hopefully it will go through.'

Felix smiled into Kitty's eyes. I just *knew* it! There was *definitely* a fizz between them. Felix looked smitten.

She'd take her time, though. Despite what I jokingly called her 'wheeling and dealing' on the property market, she was not one to jump in with both feet until she was absolutely sure it was going to be a winner.

When it came to men, she was the same. It wasn't as though she hadn't had plenty of offers and (unlike me!) she'd never had her heart broken, but she'd always said she wouldn't take up with a man unless her heart and soul were in it. So far, no man had been able to take possession of her heart, let alone her soul. I think she'd learnt a lot from my past mistakes. Usually, when a man says, "I love you", I'm sure what he really means is "woman, wash my socks, iron my shirts and where's my dinner?"

Nope. I don't think so!

68: June, 1942
Hamilton Hall

Emily:

'Major Phillips, do you *really* think that just because you are an officer and, supposedly, a gentleman, that you will have more success in trying to seduce me than would one of your oafish personnel?' How dare he invite me to have drinks with him? The very idea!

'No, Ma'am. Not at all. I – '

'*This*, may I remind you, Major Phillips, is *my* house. Some of the rooms of which may be *on loan* to the US Air Force, but that does not mean you *own* Hamilton Hall. *I* own Hamilton Hall, and always will, till the day I die. And just because the American Air Force has borrowed some rooms in my house, does not mean that *I* am also on loan. I do *not* come with the territory. Do I make myself clear?'

'No, Ma'am, I mean, yes, Ma'am. I mean, no, Ma'am, you got it all wrong. My intentions are honourable, I assure you. I just wanted to make amends, that's all.'

'Well there is no need. Just keep yourself to yourself and allow me and my family to do the same. And tell your men to keep themselves away too. I will not tolerate impropriety in Hamilton Hall.' Charlotte, still on my hip, reached forward and grabbed the Major's tie, spreading sticky finger marks all over it. Good. It jolly well served him right. I extricated Charlotte's little hand from the Major's tie, while he held his hands up in a gesture of surrender, turned on my heel and strode across the drawing room to the door. Holding it open, I glared at the Major.

'Now kindly leave. And in future, don't forget who this house belongs to. And I ask that you and your personnel remember it and act accordingly.'

The Major's face creased up and he grimaced as he looked sorrowfully at his sticky tie, retrieved his cap from where he'd placed it on the mantelpiece and marched out of the room, saluting as he left.

Doris walked in, looking behind her as she watched the Major disappear. She turned and grinned at me.

'I 'eard that, Miss Emily. Good on you! They's may be staying in Hamilton Hall, but they needs to keep their place and mind their manners. That's not right that they takes advantage. No respect. They got no respect.'

She smiled at me. 'The Major is an 'andsome man, though, that's for sure.'

'Oh Doris, stop it!' I grinned, despite myself. Then I remembered James. 'Oh dear, this horrid war. When will it end, and will we ever get back to normal life?'

'Don't you worry, Miss Em. Mr Churchill is doing a grand job. And now we have the extra help from the Americans, God love 'em, it'll be all over in no time.'

'I do hope so, Doris.'

'I don't suppose you've heard anything from Miss Martha?'

'No. I would have told you right away. After she went to Scotland for some kind of training, I received that short note from her to say she was going away, but couldn't say where. Restricted information. I cannot for the life of me imagine what a shorthand typist does that is so top secret, but there we are.'

'She'll write when she can, Miss Em. You mark my words. She'll be in touch soon.'

'I should get Charlotte cleaned up and get her a drink. The children will finish their games lesson soon and back into the library for their final class before finishing. The baby used the Major's tie to wipe her sticky fingers on.'

Doris's face broke into a huge grin. 'Really? Now that's what I calls poetic justice! I'll clean up the little 'un', she said, taking Charlotte from my arms. 'Come on my woman. Let's be 'avin' yer.' Doris walked towards the drawing room door, chuckling. 'Who's a clever girl, then? Wiping your hands on the Major's tie. That'll show him.'

I walked over to the window and gazed out at the schoolchildren running about on the lawn, squealing with delight as if they had not a care in this war-torn world. Tom and George were inseparable. I watched Tom anxiously, always aware of his asthma. He beamed as he ran around, enjoying the fresh air with his friends before they were to come back indoors for their French lesson, with me. Despite the many restrictions that the war brought, and Tom having been uprooted from the only home he knew to come to Hamilton Hall, he was one of us now. He had lost his parents, but we were his new family. And I could not have loved him more had he been my own son.

A scream jolted me back from my thoughts. *Tom!*

69: December, 2013
Hamilton Hall

Laura:

'I can't, Kylie. Not this afternoon. Sorry. I need to finish my assignment. I don't want to be late with it.'

'OK. I'll go on my own,' she said with a light-hearted shrug of the shoulder.

Kitty was back in Suffolk, getting the vacant house valued and ready to put on the market after the tenant had moved his family out and into one of her bigger properties. I'd really been quite gobsmacked by Kitty in the bank that day, but d'you know what? It was a great idea. It solved so many problems with a win-win scenario for both of us: glamping business for Kitty and Hamilton Hall for me. Selling one of her houses was a great way, I thought, to raise collateral as well as using her other houses as security for a business loan for the glamping park. She was due back in a couple of days and would stay for our first Christmas at Hamilton Hall. Her mother, Kathryn, had booked to go on a cruise for Christmas with a couple of her friends. *What an adventurous woman!* My dear 'Aunty Kath' had worked hard all her life, not least looking after Kitty as well as me, while my Mum was at work, and was now enjoying a bit of "me time", as she called it. She certainly deserved it. I thought about the book of shorthand and wondered how she was getting on with transcribing it. I remembered that Kitty had said that it might be difficult, because apparently reading someone else's shorthand wasn't quite as easy as reading your own. *I wouldn't know.*

Kitty had also insisted on paying me three months' rent for the paddock in advance, so that my cash flow problem was easing somewhat. With that, and the money I earned baking for Julie at the Coffee Shop, I was relieved to realise that I'd have a bit of spare cash to buy Christmas presents. But not today. This afternoon, I wanted to get my assignment submitted so that I could relax and enjoy the Christmas break. Kylie would have to shop alone.

Outside, builders worked on the roof and the chimneys and I hoped they'd be finished, and the chimneys swept, so that we could have real open fires lit for Christmas. Progress was slow, but things were getting done, finally. Pest control had been out and evicted the mice. I'd become so used to the scratching sounds in the night that now the house seemed quiet without them. I'd got quotes for all the work that needed doing and the musty smell in the cellar would be the next job. That would be done – *hopefully!* – in January, then the damp patches in the bedrooms were next on the list. Kylie had – lucky for her – chosen a bedroom with no damp patches or rotten window frames, and she'd started decorating it in pale blues and creams. Turns out she had quite a talent in the interior design department. She'd even found herself a second-hand sewing machine on eBay and was making some curtains for her bedroom. Yes, Kylie was now a permanent fixture at Hamilton Hall. And a very happy one too, especially compared to the sad, distracted, sullen girl we'd first met in the petrol station café all those months ago. The only sad reminder of her earlier life was the tattooed letters on her knuckles, which was a shame. But this girl was blossoming into a lovely young woman.

With the keen help of Kylie, Felix had renovated the old chicken coop and I went online and found the *British Hen Welfare Trust*. Within weeks, we had acquired half a dozen ex-battery hens, and Kylie had taken on the task of naming them all.

She was to be found first thing every morning, feeding the chickens the fruit and veg peelings that we saved in an old bucket, which I'd found in the barn, by the kitchen door, before helping Felix and George in their house. After lunch, she'd jump on the sit-up-and-beg bike and ride off to work at the Coffee Shop. She talked to the hens as though they were her children, scolding Matilda for wandering off too far away from the coop; admonishing Annabella for feather pecking. One morning Kylie had found evidence that a fox had tried to break into the coop and Felix came around to shore up the fencing.

'By the way, Kylie, why don't you pop into the Norwich University of the Arts while you're in the city, and ask about a degree course in art or design or something?' I said, casually looking at my laptop, as I sat at the kitchen table, so as not to look her straight in the eye. It wasn't the first time the idea had cropped up.

'Oh, I dunno. I don't think I'm clever enough to be at university. And anyway, I quite like working at the Coffee Shop and helping out for Felix and George.'

'You're young and intelligent and healthy and talented, Kylie. You can do anything you want, if you set your mind to it.' *God, I sounded like an old biddy!*

'OK, I'll have a think about it.' She sounded doubtful, but at least she'd listened this time.

'Guess what? I thought of a name for the glamping site.'

'Oh yes?'

'Yeah. "Daisyfields". What do you think?'

'*Daisyfields*? Yes, I like it. Why "Daisyfields"?'

'Well, like, when you first brought me here to Hamilton Hall, and Kitty was showing me around that evening, while you cooked, and Felix was coming for dinner, remember?'

'Yes, and...?'

'Well, the paddock, it was covered in daisies then. It was lovely. It looked like a green and yellow and white carpet spread out and I loved it.' *She really did have a keen artistic eye!*

She picked up her Union Jack rucksack and made for the back door. 'Anyway, see you later, then. Good luck with your assignment,' she said, and with a smile, she was gone.

Daisyfields. Mm.

I saved my file, got up and made a cup of coffee and wandered into the drawing room with it. I sat on the *chaise longue* and looked around the room. It was chilly without any heating but at Christmas, with the chimneys swept, I'd be able to light the fire and we'd have drinks and cake and a big, sparkly tree in the corner of the room. Or maybe we'd have the tree in the reception hall, so that people could see it when they walked into the house. Not that many people entered the house by the front door. It was usually the kitchen door that people used. Well, those that knew us anyway. Like Felix.

I stood up and walked over to the fireplace and gazed up at the portrait of Adalicia and Richard. Their eyes always followed me, wherever I was in the room. Every time I looked at their portrait, my great-great-grandmother seemed to be smiling directly at me. Now, I smiled back at her. *Hello, Adalicia. I wonder what you were like? Anything like my Mum? You certainly have her looks, with those beautiful blue eyes and thick, glossy, black hair. The bone structure is quite different though.*

I glanced at my great-great-grandfather. A solid man. Confident. Strong. Kind. *Hello Richard. I wish I'd grown up with a Dad like you in my life.*

And then, from nowhere, it seemed, they came: torrents of tears. I couldn't stop. I put down my coffee cup and sat on the mahogany armchair by the fireplace, with my hands over my face. I tasted the salt, as tears ran down my face and into the corners of my mouth.

70: June, 1942
Hamilton Hall

Emily:

I flung open the French doors and ran out into the garden. Tom was lying on the ground, holding his left shoulder and bellowing loudly. Children surrounded him and Miss Chambers knelt beside him, stroking his head.

I pushed my way through the children and knelt next to Tom.

'What happened?' I asked, looking around at the children's faces. George stepped forward. Tom's face was contorted in agony.

'It was my fault, Miss Emily. I am sorry. I didn't mean to hurt him, but we collided as we played tag and he fell to the ground and landed on his shoulder.' I thought George's heart would break, from the anguished look on his face.

'Let me take a look,' I said, turning back to Tom. 'Don't cry now, darling. I know it hurts, but you must be a brave soldier for me now.'

Patch barked loudly, circling the children before leaping towards Tom, who was still lying on the ground. I took hold of his collar to prevent him from jumping on the boy. The children cooed over the puppy. Hens approached, clucking and pecking at the ground.

'Take the puppy over there, children, and keep him away from Tom.'

'No, Miss Em, please let me have him. He always makes me feel better,' Tom said, wincing, grimacing and holding his painful shoulder. His breath was becoming laboured now and I worried about his asthma.

'Well, now, what's happened here? Do we have a casualty?' The voice of Major Phillips sliced through the cacophony of children's chatter, the dog's barks and the hens' clucking.

'Hi there, Tom. What's up little guy?' He moved towards the boy and hunkered down beside him. I felt his thigh lightly touch against mine, and swiftly moved an inch.

'Looks like you've dislocated your shoulder, Tom, my boy. You need to get that looked at. How far is the hospital Miss Boulais-Hamilton?' Major Phillips' deep brown eyes gazed into mine, a look of quiet concern in them. I almost regretted the dressing down I'd given him earlier, for his over-familiarity.

'It's the Norfolk and Norwich, just a few miles away. But the car is out of action due to the petrol shortage.'

'No problem, Ma'am. My jeep is parked out front.' With that, he scooped Tom up into his arms and we both stood up.

'I'll come with you.'

'Can Patch come too?'

'No, Tom. Dogs are not allowed in hospitals. Miss Simpson, school is dismissed for today. I cannot teach the French class now.' The teacher nodded and gathered the children around her. George took Patch back into the house. The dog was now six months old, house trained, obedient, but still boisterous and excitable.

I climbed into the jeep and Major Phillips helped Tom onto my lap. I hugged him to me, kissing his forehead. 'Don't worry, darling. We'll soon have you in the hospital, and you'll be good as new.'

Tom touched my cheek with the hand of his uninjured arm.

'You are quite right, Miss Boulais-Hamilton. The X-ray shows that the boy has a dislocated shoulder. Nothing broken. We'll put him back together again, pop him into a sling and you can take him home.'

'Thank you, Doctor.' I sighed in relief at hearing that nothing was broken. Nevertheless, I couldn't bear to see Tom in such pain. A nurse with pale skin and light brown hair, in pristine white cap and apron ushered the Major and me back into a waiting room down the green-painted corridor. The hospital had been bombed in a recent raid, destroying operating theatres and patient wards and severely reducing the number of beds available. Had we not been requisitioned for the Americans, we could have billeted the nurses and cleaning personnel who had lost their accommodation in the air raid. Given the choice, I would gladly have taken in nurses and cleaners, rather than the Americans. The bombing evidenced by the devastation of the crumbled buildings, now cordoned off around the hospital grounds, made my heart fill with sorrow.

The nurse left and we sat down on green utility chairs in the sparsely furnished waiting room. The window was cracked. I looked out onto a quadrangle below. A sudden shriek made me start and my hand shot up to cover my mouth as I realised it was Tom. I ran to the door and down the corridor, following the screams until I found him lying on a stretcher behind a makeshift curtain.

'Tom! Darling!'

The doctor turned to me. 'Leave us, please Miss Boulais-Hamilton. We need to return the boy's shoulder back into its socket. It's painful but we cannot do our work with a woman fussing around us.'

'He's my *son* doctor! I cannot –' I felt an arm around my shoulders. Major Phillips' voice was warm, calm and reassuring.

'Come on, Ma'am. Let's go back to the waiting room and let these guys do their job.' Tom's eyes beseeched me to stay, but the doctor's stare countenanced no argument.

'Be brave darling. I'll only be down the corridor.'

'Yes, Mummy. I'll be brave.' But his lower lip trembled. His brow wrinkled.

Mummy. He called me "Mummy".

71: Late December, 2013
Hamilton Hall

Laura:

'I really don't know how you fit into the Hamilton Hall family, Laura. But if the heir-hunter says you inherited the house, then it must be correct.'

Thomas had arrived that afternoon with his grandfather, Tom, who, we'd discovered, had been evacuated to Hamilton Hall. Once we realised that Tom had once lived in the house, I could hardly wait to meet him. Now, on the first Sunday after Christmas, Kitty and I, Kylie and Thomas, sat with Tom in the drawing room, having tea and listening to the reminiscences of this amazing octogenarian. His snow-white hair, thick and wavy, defied his years. His smooth, clean-shaven face was relatively wrinkle-free, apart from the laughter lines that fanned out from the edges of his eyes. His voice was calm, quiet, confident. There was a gentleness about him.

'Have you met George Farrington? He lives over in the big house near the paddock. He's losing his marbles a bit these days, but he and I, we've been best pals since I arrived here as a kid.' *Oh yes, I'd met shotgun-toting George, all right! And "losing his marbles" wasn't how I'd describe him. He'd mislaid them long ago!*

'Yes, we have met George, and his son, Felix too. Felix helps a lot in the garden.' I said, although I was more interested in finding out about my ancestors. 'Did you know Martha, Tom? People say I look like her, from the oil paintings, that is.'

He glanced at the painting of Adalicia and Richard.

'Tom?'

'Martha? Oh yes. She never returned after the war, m'dear. Charlotte – that was Martha's daughter - never knew her. She was only about a year – probably less than that – when her mother left. Charlotte took Emily to be her mother and me her brother, although she did know the truth, always. Her dad was a pilot. Killed in the war before Charlotte was born. I remember her being born.' His eyes glazed over and he looked in the far distance, through the drawing room French doors, as if he was pondering on this. *So, Charlotte was my grandmother.*

'So, why did Martha leave?' I hated to bring him back from his thoughts, and I tried not to pressurise or push it too far, but I was keen to learn the facts of my parentage.

'Joined up. Emily later said – when I was more grown up, that is - it was because she wanted to avenge the deaths of their parents – that's them in that picture.' He nodded towards the painting. 'And, of course, Charles - that was Charlotte's dad.' *Things were beginning to... my great-grandfather – an RAF pilot! A war hero.*

He leaned forward and took up his cup from the table, taking a sip of tea. 'Emily said their parents were killed in the first bombing raid on London.'

'Oh god, no.' I felt the pain of loss shoot through me. I looked at the painting of Adalicia and Richard. Those beautiful people destroyed by a bomb.

'What were they doing in London?'

'Well now, that I'm not sure about. But Doris and Carter did say something about a celebration.' I wondered who 'Doris and Carter' could be, but didn't want to interrupt the flow of his reminiscences. I would ask later.

'How horribly sad.' I leaned in and touched Tom's hand, as we sat side by side on the *chaise longue*. His hand felt soft, even though it looked a bit like crumpled brown paper. His hands looked older than his face.

'Yes. There was a lot of sadness around in those war years. I was lucky. I got evacuated out of London to Hamilton Hall and I came to accept Emily as my true mum. She was a wonderful woman. Very warm, kind and very determined. Wouldn't take any nonsense from anyone, that's for sure.'

I heard a little chortle from Kitty and glanced over at her.

'That seems to run in the family, then,' said Kitty and I shot her a look.

Tom tapped his forehead with his index finger. 'Smart too.' His face lit up. 'She was one of the first mature students to go to that new university when it opened in Norwich, you know, the University of East Anglia?'

'How amazing –'

'Yes, Mum – Emily that is – was one of the best. She got a First-Class degree, you know.'

I was stunned and thrilled in equal measure. '*Really?* What did she study? Do you know?'

'English Studies, it was. You can't get better than a First, can you?'

Without waiting for a reply, he continued, 'I went to her graduation. And a very proud day it was too. Yes, I was very lucky, to have her as my adopted mum. Very lucky in lots of ways. And the war was over before I was old enough to be conscripted. And because of my asthma, I didn't get called to National Service, either.'

'What happened to your parents, Tom?'

'Oh. They were killed in the war. That's how I came to be evacuated up here and stayed here when the war was over.' He gazed across the room and glanced out of the window again.

'I'm so sorry, Tom. That must have been horrible for you, to lose your parents when you were so young.'

'Oh, I don't remember too much about them, Laura, but I do know - always did know - that I was better off up here with Miss Em.

'What happened to Charlotte?'

'Charlotte? Oh, now, that was terribly sad. They went back to France.'

'They?'

'Charlotte and her husband, Jean-Baptiste.' *So, was my grandfather French, too?*

'They went to lay flowers on Martha's grave. For her birthday, it was. She was buried in France, you see.'

'France?'

'Yes. They went over on the ferry. Charlotte wasn't keen on flying because she knew her father had been killed in a plane, shot down over Germany, so they took the ferry. It was nineteen-eighty-seven. February.' Tears sprung to his eyes. He looked away.

I gasped. Kitty, who had sat, unspeaking, throughout the conversation, covered her mouth with her hand and screwed up her eyes tight shut. Kylie and Thomas looked up from the iPad they'd been absorbed in.

'Oh, my god!' I gasped. 'So, are you saying that they died in the Zeebrugge ferry disaster? I remember it being on the news, when I was a kid.'

'Yes. That's right. It was tragic. They'd gone over to France to lay flowers, as I said, on Martha's grave, and were lost in the ferry disaster as they travelled home. You know, Martha might have been a flighty little madam – well, that's what old Carter used to say, anyway, but your great-grandmother died a war heroine, Laura.'

'A heroine?'

'Well, yes. She was in the SOE, you know.'

Kylie and Thomas had been quietly listening to the conversation with one ear while preoccupied with something on the iPad. Now Kylie's head whipped up and her eyebrows shot up in surprised delight.

'The SOE?' she squealed. 'Really? Oh *wow*! That was the Special Operations Executive and they were real heroines, those SOE women. I saw a black and white film about it once. This woman, called Violette, was an SOE spy and that and she was captured by the Germans and they tortured her and everything and she never told them any secrets or anything.' Kylie's face was ablaze with excitement.

Tom smiled at her, his eyes twinkling. 'Yes, yes, I've seen the same film, many a time, myself, Kylie. And, coincidentally, Violette had an English father and a French mother, just like Martha.'

Kitty and I looked at each other. I reflected for a moment on what Tom had said. This was my ancestor, Martha, we were talking about. One minute, a little madam; the next a war heroine. My head was spinning. I was finding it hard to keep up. That little girl, whose image, along with that of her sister, hung over the fireplace in the grand dining room. The smaller of the two. The darker of the two. A World War Two heroine.

'And she never came home.' I said, quietly.

'No. Mum - well, Emily that is – she was mightily upset when she got the news. The Americans were still here.' Tom looked through the drawing room window and into the far distance. His eyes watered. He blinked and then came back to us. *The Americans were still here, he'd said... Oh, yes, the Americans. Craig had told me that Hamilton Hall had been requisitioned. Could I possibly be American? Surely not!*

'Tom,' I hardly knew how to broach the subject, but wanted to know more about Martha. 'You said something about Martha being a bit of a madam. That description hardly fits with the picture of a war heroine, does it?'

'Well, you know, Laura, you've got to remember, like I said, I was a ten-year-old when I arrived at Hamilton Hall. I was hardly capable of forming an accurate opinion of a grown-up. But I have vague memories of Martha. She was very sad most of the time. Even after baby Charlotte was born. Emily told me she wasn't always like that. It was Carter and Doris who used to say she was spirited. They loved her though. I do know that. So, don't get me wrong. I think she just had so different a personality to that of her older sister.' *Carter and Doris, again ... who were they?*

'Are you tired? Do you mind me asking more questions? We can leave it if you're tired. And I don't want to upset you.'

'Oh, no problem, at all, Laura. I am happy to be back in the old hall, reminiscing. I had many a happy year living here.' He smiled but his eyes glistened with the threat of a tear.

'Thank you, Tom.' I squeezed his hand again. Shall we have some more tea?'

Kylie jumped up and offered to make the tea and Thomas followed her out. She called over her shoulder, 'I'll bring the yummy Christmas cake in too!' Kitty winked at me with a smile.

I looked at Tom, then at Kitty, and back to Tom.

He took a perfectly ironed, folded handkerchief from his jacket pocket and wiped his moist eyes, then blew his nose.

Composing himself, he added, 'You see, Martha's baby, Charlotte, was my baby sister, to all intents and purposes. I remember the day she was born.'

'Yes, of course. So, who exactly were Carter and Doris?'

'Carter and Doris? Oh, they were the gardener and the housekeeper here. Me and Emily, and Charlotte and old Carter and Doris, we were a family unit.'

'Yes, from what you've told us, I can see that, Tom. Your own constructed family.'

I envied them.

'Can you tell me anything more about Charlotte and Jean-Baptiste? He was French, too, with a name like that?'

71: LATE DECEMBER, 2013

'Yes, that's right. You see, he was a kid in France when Miss Martha went over as an SOE and she stayed hidden in his family's house. He told us she used to teach him English and tell him stories in French and that she was writing a diary, which she hid up the chimney so the Germans wouldn't find it if she got captured. One day, when Charlotte was about sixteen, Miss Emily received a letter from Jean-Baptiste – addressed to *"Family Boulais-Hamilton, Hamilton Hall, Norfolk, England"* – I'll never forget it - that's all it said on the envelope, but it found her - saying he'd found the diary and wanted to return it to the family. Emily, well, she was overjoyed to hear from someone who'd known Martha during her service in France, and invited him over to stay.'

'Do you know what happened to the diary, Tom?' Kitty said.

'Well, that was strange. Because it wasn't in any language really. It was just a load of dots and lines and marks and things, as I recall. But Jean-Baptiste insisted that it was Martha's diary, and that he'd watched her writing it and that she had told him she was a Boulais-Hamilton from Hamilton Hall. And he had remembered all that.'

Kitty and I exchanged a look, almost reading each other's mind. We let Tom carry on, without comment.

'And wouldn't you know it, but Charlotte – who was only sixteen at the time, like I say – and Jean-Baptiste – in his early-twenties - fell for each other! Emily agreed to them getting married – it was a whirlwind romance and a really quick wedding – because, she said, she didn't want a repeat of what had happened with Martha. They had a son, Carl, born within a year of their marriage.'

'What happened to their son?'

'I don't know, exactly. You see, after he graduated university, he left to go and work abroad and never came back, although I think he did write to Emily quite regularly. He was in Thailand at the time of that tsunami...' Tom gazed into the fire, his eyes glistening. 'And we never heard from him after that. And then, after seven years ... '

Tom's chin creased and he pressed his lips together, then covered his face with his hands. My heart felt as if an iron fist had grabbed it and squeezed it. A feeling of guilt swept over me at the sight of this gentle person visibly upset.

'Presumed dead.' Kitty said, softly. It wasn't a question. We knew what he meant.

'Yes.' Tom looked up and sniffed. 'And he was my nephew, really, see? Adopted nephew, I know, but still, I was the only uncle he knew. Charlotte and Jean-Baptiste, they didn't have any more children.'

He leaned back in his chair and sighed.

'I don't know if Carl ever married. Well, he could've done, I suppose, but if he did, we never heard. So, like I say, I don't know how you come to belong to Hamilton Hall, Laura. But obviously, you do.'

It seemed to me that Tom himself had more right than I, to live in Hamilton Hall. He had, after all, grown up here. Was I an interloper? So many unanswered questions, but the one at the forefront of my mind was: how did my mother fit into the Hamilton Hall family? I cleared my throat before speaking.

'Tom, my mother's name was Sarah. Did you know her at all?'

'Sarah? No, no, there was never a Sarah here, not to my knowledge.'

Confusion now engulfed me. If Charlotte only had a son, who had no children, and there was no 'Sarah' at Hamilton Hall, how on earth could I be at all connected to this ancestral home? Tom was a man of advanced years. Could we trust his memory? Kitty and I exchanged a glance. Then she turned to Tom.

'What happened to Carter and Doris?' Kitty asked, as Kylie and Thomas returned with two crowded tea trays.

'Well, they lived a long and happy life together, after the war ended. They died in the early nineteen-seventies. First Carter and then Doris a few years later. I married their granddaughter, Claire.'

72: Mid-July, 1942
Hamilton Hall

Emily:

'There's a German in the cedar tree!' Tom's breath came in gasps, his eyes agape. I feared he was on the verge of an asthma attack. The bucket of food for the hens was still in his hand. I took it from him and placed it on the floor near the back door of the kitchen.

'Come and see, Mummy. Come and see!' His words came between his wheezes. He tugged at my hand.

'Calm down, dear.' I moved him to the kitchen table and sat him down. Patch followed, barking, bouncing about. Tom's dislocated shoulder had recovered, but I still worried that he might hurt himself again, and we'd be back at the hospital. A lone American airman appeared, scratching his head, unaware of the unfolding drama. Doris tutted and told the airman to take a seat at the kitchen table and she would find him something to eat.

Carter scraped his chair back and got up from the breakfast table, and, scratching his head and rubbing the end of his nose with the palm of his hand, took his air rifle from the locked cupboard in the pantry and loped towards the back door. Tom made to get up from the table, but I firmly pressed my hands down on his shoulders to ensure he stayed put.

'Come on Tom, I'll get you some warm milk,' said Doris, taking the whole thing in her stride. Nothing new there.

I followed Carter and Patch came too, barking even more urgently.

The voluminous white parachute spread, entwined around the cedar tree's branches, the pilot's legs and booted feet dangled like those of a hanged man. He groaned.

'Just stay still. We are going to help get you down,' I said, wondering if he understood a word. '*Guten morgen*,' I ventured, my German language skills woefully limited.

Carter ran over to the stables and appeared again with a ladder.

'Are you in any pain?' I called up to the pilot. Another groan.

'Let me get up there and see what state he's in, Miss Emily,' Carter's voice reassuringly calm, as ever.

'He's a *real* German, isn't he Mummy?' Tom was at my side, eyes like saucers, eyebrows arched. Patch continued to bark, wagging his tail enthusiastically. 'We could take him hostage!'

'Stop that, Tom! He may be German, but he is a frightened and possibly injured human being. We must be kind.'

'But Mummy. The Germans bomb us nearly every night. That's not kind.'

What could I say? The boy was right. We'd spent the night before in the cellar as the bombs rained down on Norwich. We were yet to discover the extent of the damage, but the bombing had seemed less fierce than earlier raids. Nevertheless, I could see that the boy in the tree was just that. A mere boy.

Carter took a penknife from his jacket pocket and cut the strings of the parachute – not an easy task, undertaken from a branch of the tree that he now sat astride – and together we managed to disentangle the Luftwaffe pilot, who screamed and squirmed throughout the process and it did not take long to see that his leg was broken.

'Just try to stay calm. We are going to help you.' The young man reached into his tunic pocket, screaming incoherently as he did so.

I understood barely a word of German, but his demeanour told me everything I needed to know. Carter hooked his arm into the crook of the pilot's elbow and grabbed his other hand. Sure enough, the German had a pistol.

'No need for that, young'un. We's only gonna help you.'

I took up the air rifle that Carter had left against the trunk of the tree and aimed it at the German.

'Just stay calm, now, young man, and we will get you medical help. Carter, give me his pistol.'

Carter wrenched the pistol from the German's hand. Still as strong as an ox, despite being in his early sixties, Carter maintained a firm grip on the younger man. He handed me the pistol and I placed it in the pocket of the brown, corduroy trousers – inherited from Daddy - that I always wore for working in the gardens.

'All right, Ma'am, we can take things from here.' Major Phillips stood by my side. His deep brown eyes bored right through me. Four of his airmen stood behind him.

'Major Phillips, he is injured. We need to get him medical attention. You cannot simply take him away.' I handed him the pistol.

'Like I said, Ma'am. We can take over from here.'

'And like *I* said, Major, this young man is injured. He may well have spent the entire night hanging in the cedar tree. It would be inhuman not to get him to the hospital.'

'Sure, Ma'am. And he probably spent the hours before he landed in the tree, bombing the hell out of your country.'

'Major, we are at war with Germany. And yes, the Luftwaffe are bombing night after night, however, that does not mean we English should behave like barbarians. This is *not* the Wild West! Now kindly help me get this casualty to the hospital. Where is your jeep?'

'OK, Ma'am. We'll take him to the hospital, but we'll have him under armed guard all the way. And then he will be dealt with as a prisoner of war. Understood?'

'*Understood? Understood?* How dare you take that tone with me! Yet again, I remind you that you and your airmen are living in *my* home. Kindly remember that and show some respect. I do not take orders from you or from anyone. Now get your men to bring the jeep round and I will get a blanket from the house to carry the casualty over to the vehicle.'

I could feel my face flush and the veins in my neck protrude as rage engulfed me.

Carter touched my arm. 'Let me get the blanket, Miss Emily. Come on Tom, you come indoors with me.' And with that, his hand on Tom's shoulder, he marched back into the house, leaving the Major and me glaring into each other's eyes, and the German groaning in pain on the ground.

Patch, appeared again, boisterous as ever, and jumped on the German, licking his face with gusto. *'Hallo hündchen!'* The pilot smiled, despite himself, as he ruffled the dog's head and ears, and patted his back. We got him into the jeep and made our way to the hospital in Norwich.

The hospital doctor confirmed that the Luftwaffe pilot had indeed suffered a broken leg. He was transferred under guard to the USAAF hospital at RAF Morley, and the Major drove me back to Hamilton Hall. I had hardly spoken a word to the American throughout the journey or at the hospital, but now he cleared his throat.

'Miss Boulais-Hamilton, I am *real* sorry if I spoke out of line earlier. I didn't mean to insult or disrespect you, but as allied forces here in your country we have a certain duty.'

'Clearly. But there is no need to try and inflict your bullish impulses on me and my family, Major. And that young German was lost and frightened and injured. Despite the fact that we are at war with his country, we should observe proprieties and behave with decency, courtesy and respect.'

I let out a sigh of exasperation. Oh, this tiresome, troublesome, futile war! When would it end?

'Yes, Ma'am. Understood, loud and clear.' With a rakish grin, he doffed his cap at me.

When we arrived back at Hamilton Hall, Tom was in the garden, playing the celebrity, regaling George and his other school friends with the events of the morning and the "real live German" he had found in the tree. My heart warmed. The little imp!

Smiling, I turned to walk into the house and coming out through the kitchen door, Carter and Doris met me.

And I knew immediately.

They didn't have to say a word.

I just knew.

Instinctively.

Telegram.
Martha.

§

My body is burning. On fire. My legs are leaden. My arms are limp. My throat is dry. I have no saliva. I cannot speak. I cannot cry. I feel arms around me. Warm arms, encircling my trembling, scorching body. I am being picked up like a small child and I am being carried up the stairs and along the landing. I am being taken into my room. I am being - ever so gently - laid down on my bed. Blankets cover me. A soft hand strokes my brow. Still, I cannot speak. I cannot see the room. I can see nothing. Nothing, except Martha: Martha, six years old, clutching her rag doll; Martha riding the rocking horse in our nursery; Martha, running in the garden; Martha, chasing her rabbit; Martha, playing snakes and ladders with me by the fire; Martha, helping Doris bake cakes in the kitchen and getting more on the floor than in the baking tin. Martha in the library, reading Jane Austen. Martha. Her wild, blue, defiant eyes and long black, glossy hair. Martha, riding her bicycle to meet Charles late at night. Martha, stealing back into the house at dawn. Martha, giving birth to her beautiful baby daughter. Martha. My little Martha.

I feel dead inside.

I hear the warm, soft voice of Doris. Whispers between herself and Carter. I feel the little hand of Tom, stroking my face. I breathe in his unique aroma. My fine boy.

The sun has set, leaving my bedroom in semi-darkness. There is a soft, light tap on the door and it opens just a little. The Major. On his face: concern; in those deep, dark brown eyes: warmth.

'How're you doing Ma'am? Can I tempt you with a drink? Some tea? A sherry perhaps? For the shock?' His gentle smile almost, but not quite, reaches his eyes. I do not reply. He quietly closes the door behind him and walks towards me.

In silence, I remove the blankets and slowly swing my feet and legs to the floor. I try to lift my upper body and flop back down again.

'Let me help you.' The Major's arms encircle me, as he tenderly helps me off the bed. My knees buckle, as my feet touch the floor. The Major holds me, warmly, firmly. I feel soothed.

'I'll be fine, Major.' I hear my voice but it belongs to someone else, it seems.

'Sure, you will, Miss Emily.' His words, warm, reassuring, make tears roll down my cheeks. I wipe my face, ineffectually, with the back of my hands. More tears flow, unabated.

'There now, let it all out.' His arm is around me and I feel his warm hand stroking my back.

'She was my baby sister. Killed fighting for freedom and peace. I thought only the men were sent to war. What was she doing? Why did they send her to France? She'd have been safe here, at home with me.' I sob, uncontrollably. Tears unrelenting.

'You must be real proud, Miss Emily. Your sister fought for your country. She must have been one, sassy, courageous girl.'

He holds my chin in the space – the shape of a 'V' - between his thumb and index finger. I feel the warmth of his hand. He moves his hand to the back of my neck, strokes my hair. He lowers his face to mine. His lips lightly brush my forehead. Then my lips.

His head whips to one side as I step back and my palm makes contact with his face with a loud crack. I feel the sharp sting to my hand. He touches his cheek with one hand, his eyes scrunched up tight. *'Ouch!'*

'How *dare* you patronise me! How dare you try to take advantage of my situation! How *dare* you!'

And in the very fraction of a moment, my hands take hold of the sides of his face and I am kissing his lips furiously, fervidly, intensely, hungrily. My tongue searches his. I hold his neck, his head, my fingers brush through his dark brown, wavy hair. His arms are around me, his hands explore my breasts, he groans. I slip out of the corduroy trousers, pull the blouse over my head. He is removing his uniform jacket, his tie, his shirt. We are moving – me stepping backwards - onto the bed. We make loud, animalistic noises as he pushes into me. I scratch him, bite him. Kiss him. Kiss him. Hold him. Own him.

We are lying naked in each other's arms. Replete. Soaked in each other's sweat. He takes my face in one of his hands and turns me to look at him. He strokes my hair, pushes it back off my face, combing it through with his fingers. He is looking straight into my eyes.

'I love you.'

'Don't...' I put my finger to his lips. 'Just don't.'

73: January, 2014
Hamilton Hall

Laura:
I'd not yet lit the fire that day and it grew very cold in the drawing room. I'd been having feelings of something... not quite sadness, but an emotion I couldn't quite define, on every occasion that I found myself alone. Stupid, really. It was after meeting Tom and hearing his stories that, whenever I looked closely at the oil paintings of my great-great-grandparents and those of Martha and Emily, I experienced a momentary feeling of getting in contact with my own ancestry. It was fleeting. Intangible. Not quite within my reach. And suddenly I'd find myself a blubbering wreck. *Pull yourself together woman! Get on with your studies!* I blew my nose, gathered up my empty tea mug and walked across the reception hall and into the kitchen, where, on my laptop, another essay waited to be finished.

It was warmer in the kitchen with the winter sun shining through the big sash windows. I sat at the table and looked at my laptop. I was almost there with my assignment. Just a bit more to write and I'd be done. I sniffed and started typing.

§

Why did looking at my ancestors evoke such raw emotions? Of course, I knew the answer to that! It was my father. You know, *the one that got away!*

I wished that Mum had told me more – or at least something – about him. Not for the first time, I wondered what had happened to him. Tom seemed to have no idea who my father was. Whenever I introduced the subject to him, he seemed to draw a blank. I was so confused and whenever I was alone, I found myself preoccupied with these thoughts.

Later, I tossed around in my bed, trying to eradicate the thoughts from my mind. I looked at my mobile phone: *ten to three in the bloody morning!* Sleep. I must sleep. But I was wide, wide awake. And no wonder. For one thing, I couldn't get the faces of my ancestors out of my mind. Every time I looked at their images in those oil paintings I felt that they were speaking to me. But what were they trying to say? I so desperately wanted to know. And then there was the renovations project, which just seemed enormous.

Rationally, I knew everything was working out fine; just like Kitty had always said it would. The glamping business was ready to take off. Some money was coming in. I had a little job. Julie at

The Coffee Shop had recovered from her broken wrist, but she was so happy with my baking that she'd asked me to stay on. My bread, pies and cakes were – quite literally – selling like hot cakes! My degree was nearing completion and I was heading for a good grade. It pleased and encouraged me to know that, as Tom had told me, Emily had also studied for a degree as a mature student. It gave me yet another sense of connection to her. Tom had also said she'd later become a lecturer at the University. Graduating could also mean more opportunities open to me for a well-paid job. That could, just could, mean being able to afford to run Hamilton Hall. At least, I hoped so.

The work on the house was getting tackled, bit by bit. As long as the basic repairs were done, the rest – mere aesthetics – could wait. I had everything to be happy and optimistic about. So, why did I feel so glum? I wanted to know who my father was. That was why. And how was I entitled to inherit Hamilton Hall when, as Tom had said, there was no 'Sarah' that he remembered? And this Carl fellow had apparently been childless and lost in the Tsunami. I supposed the information could probably be found within those documents that I was instructed to read before signing them, but didn't. Well, they just seemed to be boring legal papers. I didn't really expect to read anything revelatory in them. I thought I was just signing to say I was the rightful heir. I really should take a look. The lawyer had said his secretary would photocopy the papers and post them back to me. I flicked through a pile of unopened post that languished on the hall table, but there was nothing there from the lawyers. Perhaps they'd been sent to the cottage. Or perhaps they'd been lost in the post. Craig would have the information, but I could hardly ask him now. I'd already threatened to block him if he contacted me again. And it seemed he had respected my position. I hadn't heard from him. Not a word. I didn't know if I was happy or sad about that. Well, all right I admit it, I *did* know. I missed him. *I bloody missed him!* Why did he have to turn out to be a bloody money-grabber? I tried to put him out of my mind, but sneakily, when I least expected it, the memory of the heart-melting heir-hunter would creep into my thoughts. *Oh, get a grip woman! Get to sleep!*

I needed to do some research on one of those ancestry websites. After all, I had the names of my great-great-grandparents. How hard could it be?

I wriggled out of bed and reached for my robe. I glanced over at Kitty's side of the bed. She'd popped back to Suffolk again and was not due back until the morning. I made my way down to the kitchen and put the kettle on. I took my tea and laptop into the morning room. I'd brought that old rocking chair down from one of the attic rooms and found a pillow for it. One day, I'd repaint it. Right now, its history was etched with scratchy words on the wooden arms. I sat down and opened my laptop. Dead as a door nail. I closed it and reached for the charger. My ancestry research could wait till the morning.

I sipped my tea and leaned back in the chair. The tea was too hot. I placed the mug on the floor and leaned back again, pulling my robe around me tighter, my eyelids grew heavy. Heavy. Heavier. Heavier. Just resting my eyes. Resting my eyes. *Resting my eyes. Resting my eyes...*

Laura... Laura... Laura... the boxes, Laura. The boxes... The attic room, Laura... the boxes... the boxes... the boxes... The attic room, Laura.

I feel chilled to the bone as I move up the stairs, carefully, slowly, one at a time. One at a time. I think that I can feel something like a hand on my back, gently pushing me forward. I look behind me. I see no one. The attic room door creaks as I open it wide. I see the boxes. One is still partially open, from the time that Kitty and I had started looking through it. Only old photos of me and Mum in that one. I reach over to another box and feel a warmth embrace me. I look around for something sharp to cut the sticky tape. Nothing. I feel in the pocket of my robe and find an abandoned hair clip. I sit on the wooden floor and start to cut away at the tape and it starts to give way. I tear at it. Tear at it. Hack at it. Tear at it. There. It is cut through now and I strip it away from the cardboard. I open the flaps of the box.

I take out items and a white envelope lies, sealed, beneath a pale pink, silk pashmina. My hands tremble, yet now I feel warm. Warm. Warm. A warm hand, still on my back. I turn around. No one is there. I lift the envelope...

I'm reading the words aloud now; the handwriting is very familiar.

"To Laura:" it says. *"To be opened in the event of my death".*

74: A year later, 1943
Hamilton Hall

Emily:

'Mum...'

'Yes, darling?' I'd been wiping down the kitchen table, working around Tom as he sat and ate his breakfast. I was supervising Charlotte as she ate a soft-boiled egg. Her success was a rather hit and miss affair.

'What's a "litamate little basket"?'

'Pardon?' I straightened up in horror as I heard Tom's words. Yes, he had mispronounced the word, but there was no doubt what he meant. I exchanged a glance with Doris, then Carter, who scratched his head, sniffed and rubbed the end of his nose.

'Where did you hear those words, Tom?' I looked straight at him, 'who did you hear saying them?'

'It was Jimmy. He said his big brother said Miss Nellie in the post office said that Charlotte is a – '

'Yes, yes, all right, Tom. I know what you said. Now finish your breakfast and go and feed the hens. Then it will be time for George to arrive and you'll both have your morning lessons. I'll have a word with young Jimmy when he comes to school this afternoon. And you're not to use those words again. Hear me? They're bad words.'

'Yes, Mum.'

So, Nellie Braithwaite had finally got wind of Charlotte's arrival and the absence of any father, and was obviously spreading gossip around the village. I would ride the bicycle over to the post office later, and have words with the horrid woman.

First though, I needed to check the barn door, that seemed to have been swinging and banging unrelenting in the breeze all night. Carter came with me.

'Well,' he said, as we wandered over the grass towards the barn, 'that'll be old Nellie spreading gossip all right. Might've known nothing would get by her. Nosey old b–'

'Yes, yes, Carter, I know. But it must have been the children coming here for school lessons who started it. They see Charlotte every day. It was bound to get out.'

'Well, yes, Miss Em, that's true, and you can't blame young'uns for talking about what they see, but that Braithwaite woman's got a poison tongue in her head and there ain't no cause for her to go calling little Miss Charlotte a ba –'

'Don't say it, Carter,' I said, raising my hand, as if to stop the traffic. 'I just cannot bear to hear the word!'

'I was going to say "basket", Miss Em.'

'Yes, yes, Carter, but we both know what that word stands for - Oh! My goodness! What has happened?'

Approaching the barn, I'd seen that, rather than the door swinging because it had been left open, it was hanging off its hinges, broken. Strange.

'Stay here a minute, Miss Em. Let me go take a look.' Dear old Carter. Ever the protective one. He stuck his head through the broken door and then stepped inside.

'Well, the thieving buggers!'

I moved swiftly into the barn, only to see Daddy's car, bonnet up, engine gone and all four wheels missing.

'Thieving buggers indeed, Carter!'

I sighed. 'Come on, let's get the door fixed.'

We couldn't drive the car anyway; the petrol shortage saw to that. I left it as it was, never to drive it again.

'I must say, Miss Emily, you do deal with problems calmly, for one so young. Any nasty, unpleasant thing what happens, you never let it affect you.' If only, I thought. If only. On the outside, I may have seemed calm and serene as a swan, yet underneath, at times, my emotions smouldered like a seething cauldron. And Martha's death was a grief so raw it still felt like razor blades cutting through my heart.

'I'm right proud of you Miss,' Carter continued. 'And I know your Mother and Father would have been too.'

We walked back to the house, where Doris was in the kitchen, cleaning Charlotte's face and hands.

'Them potatoes is getting a bit low, now,' she said, looking up, 'Carter my man, take a look in the pantry and see if them potato peelings has sprouted enough yet. We's gonner need them planting soon.' It had been Carter's idea for us to save potato peelings with "eyes" in them, in the darkened pantry. This would encourage the "eyes" to sprout and he could plant them for new potatoes to grow. Quite ingenious, I thought... and it worked too.

Doris was equally inventive. She had purloined the disentangled German silk parachute from the cedar tree and had been busy making white blouses out of it for her daughters and a Sunday best dress for her granddaughter, Claire. For the less well-off young women of the village, she had made blouses and nightdresses.

There was a loud knock at the front door. Patch barked excitedly and I shushed him as I walked across the reception hall, with him jumping around at my ankles. He's not much of a watchdog, I mused, thinking that he let thieves strip father's car without raising the alarm. I opened the door to Mary, the vicar's wife, fury written all over her face, fists clenched by her sides.

'Mary? What is it? What's happened?' I took her elbow and led her into the reception hall.

'It's the chapel, Emily. The chapel of all places!'
'The chapel? What about it?'
'It's been vandalised, that's what. Vandalised! Ruined. Absolutely ruined. And I can tell you now, who is responsible. Those dreadful Americans. That's who.'

'That's terrible. How awful. Do come into the morning room, Mary and let me get you a cup of tea.' I placed my hand on the small of her back and led her through. 'What makes you think it was Americans who did it?' I did not want to think of Marvin's men being implicated.

'They left their calling card, Emily, that's how. A packet of chewing gum and an airman's cap!'

Sure enough, the chapel had been ruined and there were no funds available to restore it. Once again, Hamilton Hall had to be utilised: this time as a makeshift place of worship. Doris, Carter and I set to work in the drawing room, rearranging the furniture and bringing in all manner of seating to use as pews. An altar was fashioned in front of one of the fireplaces. The portrait of Mother and Father was removed temporarily to make way for a crucifix. The chalice went on the mantelpiece.

Marvin arrived back after three months of duty elsewhere. He was unable to tell me the exact location, but by now, after years of war, I was perfectly aware that I could not, under any circumstances, be privy to such classified information. *Careless talk costs lives*, we were admonished from posters displayed on public buildings.

'Emily, honey!' Marvin had entered the library as I was tidying up the children's books after school and swept me into his arms, kissing me full and long on the lips. By now, despite our best efforts at discretion, we were fooling no one by trying to appear as nothing more than cool acquaintances. We were a couple and very much in love. I knew that Marvin loved me deeply. He told me so. Constantly. I, however, had never returned the sentiment. What would be the point? I knew from bitter experience that love can be cast asunder at the blink of an eye. Mummy and Daddy. Charles. James. Martha... my dear Martha.

'God, I've missed you! Let me take a look at you, my beautiful English lady!' He held me at arms' length and cast his eyes over me. 'Mmm. Just as lovely as ever.' And with that, he hugged me tight again.

A light knock on the library door made us separate and stand a few inches apart from each other. Doris came in, giving a discreet little cough.

'It's Constable Howells, Miss Emily, come to talk to the Major about the chapel and the car.'

'Oh, thank you, Doris. Please could you show him into the drawing room? We'll be down in a trice.'

'O'course I will.' She gave a little smile, first at me, then at the Major, nodded and left the room.

A quizzical frown crossed Marvin's brow. 'The chapel? Why would the local policeman want to talk with me about the chapel? And what's this about a car? Whose car?'

I told him of the damage to the chapel and of the suspicions that some of his airmen were responsible for that, as well as the wheels and engine being stolen from Father's car.

'OK, let's get to the bottom of this,' he said in his serious Major's voice, and strode purposefully out of the library and down the stairs.

The culprit – indeed the ringleader, it turned out – was the same airman who had tried to force himself onto me in the kitchen shortly after the arrival of the USAAF at Hamilton Hall. Fuelled by much too much alcohol consumed in the Green Dragon public house in Wymondham, he had persuaded some of his fellow servicemen to help him 'teach these bloody Limies a thing or two'. He and the others were promptly dealt with and, after having spent some time locked up on RAF Hethel camp with privileges withdrawn, despatched from Norfolk to who knew where? And jolly good riddance too!

75: The next day
Hamilton Hall

Laura:

'*L*aura? Laura... are you there, Laura?'

Footsteps approaching. I try to move. I am paralyzed, it seems. I try to move my fingers. I feel the crumpled paper in my hand. I try to lift my head. My neck is stiff and refuses to move. I am still sitting on the floor, my head resting on the box.

'*Laura? Where are you?* Oh! There you are! What on earth are you doing up here?' Kitty, puffing, out of breath, kneels beside me, her arm around my shoulders. I try to speak. My mouth refuses to move. I feel Kitty's fingers combing through my hair, stroking my forehead.

'Laura darling? What are you doing here? You must be frozen. Come downstairs and I'll make you a hot drink.' Still, I cannot move. I cannot speak.

Kitty takes up the silk pashmina from the floor and wraps it around my shoulders. I shudder and suppress a sob.

'Why did you come up here, Laura? It's bloody freezing.'

I look up at Kitty. 'I was... I... I had a dream. This dream. It was like a dream... I'm not sure... It seemed so ... sort of ethereal... And someone was telling me to come up here. And I suddenly ...'

'What, Laura? What?'

'Oh Kitty. My poor mum. My poor, poor mum.' I am sobbing now. The hot tears like rivulets running down my cheeks. 'She didn't have to ...'

'What is it, love?'

Kitty sees the paper in my hand and uncurls my fingers. She takes it and begins to read aloud.

15th April 1997

Laura, my darling,

I have long wanted to talk to you about where you came from, but regrettably, I never found the courage. I write this on your 21st birthday, and I feel it is time. If you are reading this, it is because I am no longer alive. First, I'd like to start by telling you that you are the best thing that ever happened to me. I was barely eighteen when I found myself pregnant, and life, as you know, has not been easy. But for you, my lovely Laura, I would do it all again in a heartbeat.

'Oh, my god! Laura. This is just... Oh, my god!'
'Kitty. She didn't have to...'
'Oh Laura. Why didn't you call me last night? You know I'd

have come straight away.' She strokes my cheeks, wiping away tears. I point to the letter.

'She... I didn't know. I never knew...' I cannot continue. I point again to the letter. Kitty reads again.

I grew up with a very cold father, who liked to beat me and my mother whenever the fancy took him.

Kitty shudders. 'How despicable. What a bastard.'

My mother died just before I turned seventeen and I left home straight after the funeral and went to live in a hostel. It was a tough place to live, but at least I was not living in fear of being beaten every night by a drunken father.

'Oh Laura. I had no idea. Your poor, poor mum!' Kitty takes my hand in hers and squeezes it, then turns back to the letter.

I had a job working in a factory. The hours were long and the work hard. But I could work nights for extra pay and that meant I could get some sleep back at the hostel during the day, when the other residents were out. Night times in the hostel were rarely quiet. It also meant I could get a warm bath when I woke up in the afternoon, before the others got in and took all the hot water.

'This is heart-breaking, Laura. Absolutely heart-breaking. I had no idea your mum had such a sad young life. She never spoke about this.'

'I know.' My voice a croak, I shiver again. Kitty pulls the pashmina tighter around me.

'Look, Kitty,' I point to the letter. 'She talks about your mum.' Kitty continues to read.

I made friends with another girl at work, Kathryn, a few years older than me. She worked in the factory office. And, yes, she is the mother of your dear friend, Kitty.

'I think we knew they met at work, didn't we? They used to talk about it. But I only have vague memories,' Kitty said. She turned back to the letter.

I worked hard and saved my money so that I could rent a place of my own. After a year, I could just about afford to move into the little cottage in Suffolk, where I raised you.

My normally self-composed friend now has tears in her eyes. We look at each other. My chin begins to quiver. Another sob escapes.

Kitty sniffs. Gathers herself. 'Come on, darling, let's go downstairs to the kitchen where it's warmer, and I'll make us a hot drink.' She stands up and tries to pull me to my feet. My body has other ideas and refuses to cooperate.

'How long have you been sitting here on the floor, Laura? Come along. Try to stand up.' I make a monumental effort and my joints begin to creak into life. Slowly, I get up from the floor, feeling like a baby giraffe, stiff, unsure of my limbs, my body like someone else's, not my own.

75: THE NEXT DAY

'You're too old to go spending the night on a cold attic floor!' she says, trying to get me to my feet.

'Oh, shut up!' I dig her in the ribs with an elbow.

She manages a little giggle and we leave the attic room.

Downstairs, I sit in the rocking chair in the morning room, tucked into a blanket, the pashmina still around my shoulders. Kitty places a mug of hot chocolate in my hands.

'There you go. That'll thaw you out.' She tucks a stray strand of hair behind my ear, then sits opposite me, picks up the letter and carries on reading, words I read last night. Words so hard to hear.

I realized just before I moved into the cottage in 1975 that I had enough money left to go on a little holiday. I wanted some sunshine so I went to Spain, and stayed in a cheap room.

I spent my days on the beach and the evenings strolling along the promenade. I can still feel to this day the warm sun and the breeze on my face and arms as I walked along. I will never forget the aqua blue of the Mediterranean Sea and the big, yellow, warm Spanish sunshine. The sounds and smells of Spain are delicious. There were lots of couples, walking along the sand, holding hands. I envied them. I was all alone.

'She must have felt so lonely, Laura. She could only have been about eighteen,' says Kitty.

'I know. Bloody eighteen. And all alone.' The tears flowed again. I wave a hand at the letter. 'Go on. Read it, Kitty.'

Then, on the third day of my holiday, I was sitting on a bench by the beach when a very handsome young man came to sit next to me. He was tall, with shiny black hair and intense blue eyes, almost the colour of the Mediterranean itself. His name was Carl Hamilton-Blanc and he came from Norfolk.

'Charlotte's son! Carl Hamilton-bloody-Blanc! Oh my god, Laura. Carl was your father. So, this is how you came to inherit Hamilton Hall. Through your father. Not through your mum, at all.' I nod. Mute.

Yes, Carl Hamilton-Blanc! Very posh! I had never met anyone with a double-barrelled name before. He was very nicely spoken and confident, but also a little shy, I thought. I found that very endearing. We spent every moment of the rest of the holiday together and he showed me the sights of Barcelona, excursions I could never have afforded to do alone, and he knew all about the history of the magnificent buildings we visited. Those days were the happiest I'd ever had, and I will treasure them forever.

I gaze into the nothingness of the morning. The happiest days of her life. At least she'd had that. Kitty continued to read from the letter.

He told me about his family and that his father was French and as a boy had known Carl's grandmother, when she was a spy in occupied

France during the war. His parents met when his father came over from France to visit Martha's family to bring them something that had belonged to her. Carl said that his parents had a whirlwind romance and married within three months, even though his mother was only sixteen at the time, and his father twenty-four. Carl had been a honeymoon baby. It sounded very romantic.

'It all fits in with what Tom told us, doesn't it? But it seems that Carl didn't survive the tsunami in Thailand.' My father is dead. I will never meet him. The mystery man I have longed to meet all my life. Dead.

'Yes. And Tom did seem very lucid, despite his advanced years, unlike old George. I did feel we could trust his memory, that day he came to tea, Laura, even though you had your doubts.' She leans in and squeezes my arm, and I wave my hand at the letter. Kitty begins reading again.

Carl was wonderful and I easily fell in love with him. He said he loved me too and wanted to keep in touch once the holiday was over. But I didn't think that would be possible because I knew he came from a very upper-class family and lived in a big mansion house, called Hamilton Hall. I thought his family would not accept me. Why would they? I was a working-class kid from a council estate, worked in a factory and my father had been a drunken bully.

'No wonder Mum was tee-total, with a father like that. I think I'll do the same.'

'No need to go that far, Laura!' And she laughs, despite herself.

And anyway, we were very young and he was going off to university to study Spanish at the end of the summer holiday. I didn't want to disrupt his studies. I envied him the chance to go to university. It is something I'd always wanted to do. Carl was my one (and only) boyfriend. We were both eighteen, but that was where our similarities ended. We were from very different worlds.

'Jesus Christ, Laura. Your lovely mum really thought she wasn't good enough to be a Hamilton. From what Tom has told us, the Hamilton Hall family were warm, welcoming and thoroughly decent. I mean, they took in Tom, didn't they? And Emily looked after Charlotte too. If she only knew! What a different life she could have had.'

'I know, Kitty. I know.' And my tears flow now, uncontrollably. 'She suffered and struggled so much in her life. But it could all have been so different.'

'Well, with a father like she had, I'm not surprised your mum grew up with a feeling that she wasn't good enough. Oh Laura. I am so sorry.' She looks back at the letter.

But on that holiday in Spain, my darling Laura, Carl Hamilton-Blanc gave me the most precious gift: you. Carl Hamilton-Blanc, from Hamilton Hall, Norfolk is your father. Go and find him, Laura. Find your father.

'Oh, Laura.' Kitty sniffs, glances back at the letter.

When you were born, I gave you the English translation of his surname: White. And I changed my surname too, so that we were both called White. I pretended I was a widow.

And now Kitty is kneeling on the rug in front of me, her arms around me, as we hug and cry, the chair rocking back and forth as we do so. I gather myself, take the letter from Kitty's hand, and continue reading.

I have never told a soul, of the identity of your father, and apart from writing this confession to you, I will take my secret to the grave.

'Confession, Kitty! *Confession!* She makes herself sound like a fucking criminal! Like she was bloody ashamed or something!' I screw up the letter and throw it to the floor. 'Oh Kitty, if only she could be here with us now. She had nothing to be ashamed of. She was the best mum I could have wished for.'

Kitty gets up, walks through to the kitchen and comes back with the kitchen roll, which she holds in front of me. I tear off a piece of paper and blow my very red nose, while Kitty mops her own tears. She picks up the crumbled letter, opens it, smooths it out and reads aloud.

Know that you were born from love, young love, and although it was not always easy, bringing you up alone, I would not have changed a thing.

The kitchen paper works hard now, to mop up our copious tears. We sit holding each other. I've never seen Kitty looking so discombobulated.

'I could scream at the injustice of it all, Laura.'

'Don't. You'll wake up the chickens!'

Now Kitty and I are laughing and crying at the same time. She looks down at the letter. Reads the final words aloud.

I hope you find this letter after my death and that my words comfort you. I was always reluctant to divulge your father's identity to you. I did it for the best of reasons. I didn't want you rejected by his family. That was my greatest fear.

I love you Laura. Thank you for 21 wonderful years of you. I am immensely proud to call you my daughter. Follow your dreams and make a success of your life. Be imaginative. Whatever you set your mind to do, you can achieve.

All my love, always,

Mum xxx

'I know, Mum. I know,' I say, into the room. 'I know and I will.'

§

Later, after a hot bath, a breakfast of toast and boiled eggs, with plentiful mugs of coffee, it suddenly occurred to me that we hadn't seen Kylie all morning.

'Where is she?' I called over my shoulder to Kitty as I skipped up the stairs. 'Sleeping in?'

I tapped on Kylie's bedroom door and stuck my head into the room. Her bed was empty. My heart thudded. My mouth turned dry.

'Kylie!' Oh god, where was she? Shane the oik sprang to mind.

I ran from the room and headed for the stairs, to be met by Kylie, taking the steps two at a time.

'Morning Laura! Got to dash – late for work at George's ...'

'Kylie - where have you –'

I heard a little cough. Kitty was standing at the bottom of the stairs, shaking her head and putting a conspiratorial finger to her smiling lips.

Oh yes.

Of course.

Thomas.

76: 8th May 1945
Hamilton Hall

Emily:

'It *is* over! The war is really over!' We read the headlines – *Victory over Europe!* - and I scrunched up the newspaper and threw the pages into the air.

'It's over!! It's over!! Oh Marvin, it is …'

Marvin picked me up and swung me around the drawing room, kissing my face, over and over.

The war in Europe is over and Hamilton Hall has survived. A new family has been constructed following the deaths of Mummy, Daddy and Martha. I am so proud to have Tom as my son.

Now, Carter, Doris and I are planning a celebration dinner/dance in the paddock. Marvin is organising extra victuals – steaks, sausages, chocolate and beer - from the USAAF base where he has been stationed since the arrival of the Americans three years ago. At any one time, there have been some fifty thousand USAAF personnel posted around the Norwich area. Their departure will be a source of great sadness for some, but a welcome relief for others.

Marvin and I were in the drawing room, finalising plans for the celebratory dinner/dance to be held tomorrow evening.

He put down his pencil and took my hands in his.

'Emily honey...'

'Don't, Marvin.'

'You don't know what I was going to say...'

'No, but I can guess. We have had this conversation before. I will not leave Hamilton Hall and go to America with you. No doubt a lot of English girls will leave with their American fiancés, but I will not be joining them.'

He touched my face. His dark eyes boring into me.

'How can you walk away from our love like this?' His words cut through my heart like a surgeon's scalpel.

'I am not walking away, Marvin. I am recognising that everything has a season and ours is drawing to a close. I cannot possibly leave Hamilton Hall. You know that.'

'But Emily, have these past years meant nothing to you?'

I bit my lip. Of course, our time together has meant the world to me but that does not induce me to leave Hamilton Hall behind and follow Marvin to a country I have never even visited. And into a culture so strange and different from my own. It would be sheer folly. And who would look after Hamilton Hall and the family?

'Yes, Marvin. Our time together means a lot to me. But it is time to acknowledge that it was a wonderful interlude in our lives and soon it will be over.'

'But Emily, I – '

There was a tap on the door and Doris entered.

'Begging your pardon, Miss Emily, but we need you now in the marquee.'

'I'm coming, Doris. I'm coming now.' And with that I followed her out of the drawing room, leaving Marvin raking his fingers through his hair in exasperation.

The dinner/dance was a splendid affair. The Americans did us proud with their contributions of food and beer, not forgetting chocolate Hershey bars and sodas for the children. American airmen danced the night away with the local girls and the children danced and played together. Their excitement uncontainable. Some of them ate the equivalent of their own body weight, it seemed, in chocolate. Everyone wore a smile on their face as wide as an ocean. It was a most memorable night. The end of hostilities in Europe. The beginning of a much better world for our children to inhabit.

That evening, after the celebrations were over and Marvin and I lay in my bed, he took me in his arms and held me tight.

'Emily, please promise me you will think about it.' I knew to what he was referring.

'I will think about it Marvin. But I know that I will not change my mind.' I took his face in my hands and kissed him softly. 'Why don't you stay here with me in Hamilton Hall?'

Marvin pulled back from me, looking straight into my eyes.

'I'm a guy, Emily. I cannot live in a woman's house. It is against the natural order of things. A man needs to be the provider for his wife and family.'

Indignation arose in my chest. I wanted to slap him but resisted the urge.

'You *cannot* live in a woman's house? And what, Major Phillips, have you been doing these past three years?'

'But that's different honey. It was the war. Now that the war is over, it is time for me to provide for you. Please, Emily, come to the States with me. I'll buy some land. We will build a big house, even bigger than Hamilton Hall.' The very thought repelled me. As if 'bigger' automatically meant 'better'.

'Just as I thought. You were perfectly happy living in my house when the war made it convenient for you to do so, but now that the war is over, the status quo has to change? Is that what you are saying? That I have to live according to *your* needs and desires and no consideration whatsoever for my own? How *dare* you?' I slid off the bed and pulled my robe around me.

'No, honey. That's not it at all – '

'No, Marvin, that is *exactly* it. You honestly expect me to leave everything I know and love here in Norfolk and move to America with you, to a life that would be so culturally and socially alien to me, that I can only imagine what it would be like. And build a *new* home? How ghastly. Hamilton Hall has been in my family for generations. It has substance and stability. Not even through two world wars could the Germans destroy Hamilton Hall. It stands and remains standing through all manner of difficulties and struggles. I will not leave it.' My breath came in short gasps now, my anger rising with every syllable.

'But Emily, I *love* you! I want you to be my wife, goddam it!'

'Fine words, Major Phillips,' I countered, feeling so incensed I could have spat. 'Fine words. But what is the difference between you staying here and me moving to America? I'll tell you what the difference is, Major Phillips. Biology. That's what. You think because you have the anatomy of a man that you are entitled to the perfectly natural, social expectation that I, a mere woman, will follow you. Well, no, Major Marvin Phillips, I will not. And that is the end of the matter.'

§

1955...

And so, the Americans stayed at Hamilton Hall until the war had all but ended. After their departure, there was much weeping and wailing by lovesick local girls, and disappointment amongst housewives, who had made extra cash by taking in airmen's laundry, and now wondered how they would make ends meet. Some had not heard from their husbands for some while and did not know whether or not their loved ones would return safely.

Local children missed the Hershey bars, the chewing gum and rides on the handlebars of bicycles, the preferred mode of transport of American personnel in Norfolk.

On the fourteenth of August 1945, Victory over Japan was declared. It had been almost six years since that fateful day when the voice of our then Prime Minister, Mr Neville Chamberlain had come through our wireless and into our dining room, and announced that we were at war with Germany. This time, celebrations were hosted by USAAF camps and were well attended. USAAF bands played late into the night as local girls danced with airmen and much alcohol consumed. A surprising number of babies were born in Norfolk exactly nine months later. In some cases, weddings were hastily arranged, while the mothers of some newborns faced the prospect of putting their infants up for adoption, the fathers long gone.

Our British troops started to return home and huge emotional adjustments had to be made within families. Returning soldiers were reunited with children who, having grown up without their fathers, were virtual strangers. Husbands and wives had the not inconsiderable task of getting to know each other all over again. Some marriages blossomed. Others floundered. Some fathers, sons, brothers, boyfriends never returned. Those who returned but were not the same person as when they had left. War leaves emotional and mental scars as well as physical ones.

The Hamilton Hall library continued to be used as a makeshift school room, and the drawing room as a chapel until, just before the war ended, when services were moved to the Abbey. Moving services to the Abbey meant a longer walk for some local worshippers, but overall, most were happy with the arrangement. After the end of the war, the school was rebuilt and the Hamilton Hall library returned to its original use. The chapel has never been restored, following the vandalism incident. It was damaged further by a German bomb and lies derelict to this day.

Tom grew taller and stronger and made me proud in so many ways. Always keen to help with household and gardening chores, he happily built, mended, dug and planted under the direction of Carter. Throughout, he maintained his devotion to the hens, feeding them and collecting eggs from the coop every morning. Tom's dog, Patch, was never far from his side. Tom left school with good grades in his School Certificate examinations and went to college to train in mechanical and electrical engineering. Last year he and Claire, granddaughter of Doris and Carter, married. We had a wonderful summer wedding reception in a huge marquee in the Hamilton Hall paddock. It reminded me of the summer balls that Mother and Father had held every year, before the war changed all of our lives.

I signed over the flint cottage, which belonged to me as part of the Hamilton Hall estate, to Tom and Claire as a wedding present. They moved in after the wedding, along with Patch. This year saw the birth of their first son. On that day, an elderly and very tired Patch slowly climbed the stairs of the flint cottage. Well aware that he was never allowed up there, he disobeyed this rule, as he lay down outside the bedroom while Claire laboured for seven hours to bring her son into the world. Patch remained there, unmoving, until he'd heard the baby's first cry. Then, and only then, did he rest his head on his front paws, close his eyes and take his final breath. But Patch had sired pups, and his daughter and son, Bessie and Scrap, still live in the cottage. Tom and Claire named their first-born child Richard Marvin Thomas. I shed a tear when I heard that Tom had named his son after my father and Major Phillips. Marvin had, in many ways, been like a father to Tom. I felt a deep sense of guilt engulf me whenever I admitted to myself that I had not only rejected the man who loved me but who also loved my son.

The excruciating emotional pain of losing Martha and my parents eased somewhat but never fully healed and I feel it keenly to this day. Charlotte has grown into a stunningly beautiful young girl, who strikingly resembles Martha. Sometimes, I witness a defiance in her nature, obviously inherited from her mother, but Charlotte is intelligent and charming and mature beyond her years. Tom has always regarded her as his baby sister and she seems to accept and enjoy that, never questioning his true origins. She delighted in being a bridesmaid at his wedding last year and looked pretty as a picture in her pink dress.

Major Marvin Phillips had continued to beg me to return to the United States with him right up until the time had been imminent for the Americans to leave. However, I was not prepared to leave my home. Letters from America still arrive with almost predictable regularity and even now, all these years after the war ended, Marvin persists in his attempts to persuade me to join him across the Atlantic.

However, I am a daughter of Hamilton Hall and here is where I shall stay, until I breathe my last.

77: February, 2014
Hamilton Hall

Laura:

I stared at the face smiling from the front page of the *Wymondham Mercury*, and froze. I felt like a glass figurine that had been smashed to smithereens with a sledge-hammer and there had been nothing I could have done to stop it. *Norfolk man, 28,* the headline read, *wakes from four weeks in a coma!* I stood there, transfixed by the unmistakably recognisable steel grey eyes of Craig Matthews.

So that was it! The reason he'd stopped texting me was probably not that he was respecting my wishes (or, rather, my threat to block him!) but because he couldn't. He had been in a collision with a van on the A47 and had sustained a head injury. The van driver had got away with a whiplash – plus a hefty fine and a ban - after being found guilty of driving without due care and attention. Apparently got off light because he pleaded guilty and it was his first offence. Hmm!

The photograph showed Craig sitting up in his hospital bed, now out of intensive care and on the regular ward.

The neurosurgeon in charge of Craig's case had explained in an interview with the *Mercury* reporter: *"There is a tendency for an injured brain to swell. Inflammation will make the brain push against the skull and this causes pressure to increase, with the consequent risk of the blood supply being cut off. It can lead to serious consequences, possibly death. We put such a patient in a medically-induced coma in order to rest the brain and allow it to heal ..."*

Oh my god! It was a miracle he was still alive. He could have died! My hand shot up to my mouth. My eyes agape. Nausea swept over me. I checked the newspaper report again, for the date of the accident. Then I checked through my 'sent' text messages. With typical tardiness, I hadn't deleted any. Just as I feared: the accident had happened not long after I'd sent the vitriolic text to Craig, telling him to lay off or I'd block him. *Laura. White. You. Are. A. Heartless. Cow.*

I grabbed my car keys from the table, my coat from the back of a kitchen chair, wrapped my scarf round my neck and I ran out through the back door, calling out to Kitty, 'I'll be back later. I have something I need to do.' And with that I jumped in my car and was tearing down the drive, into the lane and on my way to the hospital, as fast as the law would allow me.

'Are you a relative?' The receptionist raised an enquiring eyebrow at me.

'Not quite. I'm his fiancée, though,' I said, crossing my fingers behind my back. 'Does that count?'

A thin smile. She hit the keyboard in front of her.

'He's on this ward,' she handed me a piece of paper with the name of the ward that she'd written on it, 'follow the signs along the corridor and turn ...' I was gone before she could finish the sentence.

'*Laura!*' A mixture of surprise, delight and embarrassment spread across Craig's face as I walked into the ward.

'Craig, I – '

'It is so good to see you Laura. How did you...? As you can see, I've been a bit in the wars, as they say.' He gave me a delicious, lop-sided smile.

'I didn't know until this morning. You're all over the *Wymondham Mercury*!'

'That doesn't matter. You're here now and I am so glad to see you. Does this mean I'm forgiven?'

'Forgiven? What for, Craig? For trying to use me to make money? Is that what you're talking about?'

'Well yes, but – '

'So, you admit it then? You were trying to use me?' I felt the hairs stand up on the back of my neck. It seemed I was right. He was a con artist after all.

'No, no. I mean, you were obviously very angry with me but...' His voice trailed off and he looked away.

'But what, Craig?' I wasn't letting him get away with it. I needed to know. Part of me also wanted to see him squirm. Just a bit. Well, all right, I know, I am mean. But it was important to me to know whether or not I could trust this man with the gorgeous looks and the winning smile.

'I wasn't trying to use you, Laura. Really, I wasn't. I was just trying to help.'

'Help? Help who? Me, or you, or your uncle?'

'You, Laura. Of course, you. Only you.'

'Why should I believe that?'

'Because it is true. I wouldn't try to trick you, Laura. I'd never do that. I was just a bit ... I don't know... clumsy, I suppose, in the way I approached it.' He rubbed his head. 'Ouch!'

'What's up? Are you in pain Craig? Shall I call someone?'

'No, it's OK darling. I'm due my medication soon. I'll wait.' *Darling. He called me darling!*

'Are you sure? I can easily call the nurse...'

'Yes, I am sure, Laura.' He tried to smile again but I could see it was a supreme effort. He was just putting a brave face on it. That gorgeous face now sported a tiny scar just above the left eyebrow, I noticed. I turned and headed for the nurses' station.

'I'm visiting Craig Matthews and he seems to be in quite a lot of pain at the moment. Can someone take a look, please?'

A nurse wearing a navy-blue uniform and dark brown hair tied up in a messy bun looked at her computer screen.

'He's due for his pain killers in half an hour. Are you a relative?'

'I'm his fiancée ...' I said, lying through my teeth for the second time that morning.

'Oh, really? He never mentioned...'

"Oh, I expect it was that bump on his head... forgotten ... haha!'

'OK, I'll come and see him.' And I don't suppose for one moment that she believed my story. However, she didn't say anything but swanned off towards Craig with me following in her path. I arrived at the bedside just in time to hear the nurse telling Craig that his fiancée was worried.

'Fiancée?' Craig's brow scrunched up in an expression of total confusion.

'Sorry darling. I was worried. You seemed to be in such pain,' I quickly said, my face feeling very hot and red. *Just keep your mouth shut Laura White!*

An impish smile spread across Craig's face.

The nurse (who turned out to be the ward sister) checked Craig over, suggested he wait for the medicine rounds and smartly left the room.

'*Fiancée*, Laura?'

'Well, I had to say that to get in. They only let relatives in at this time of the day, so I ...'

He took my hand in his. 'Laura, I do like the sound of it.' *Did he, now?*

'Craig, you haven't answered my question.'

78: February, 2015
Norfolk

Laura:
After a week, Craig was discharged and I brought him home to Hamilton Hall and nursed him back to full health. Well, I like to *think* I had something to do with his complete recovery, but actually, the truth is, he was always going to make one.

Six months after that I married him.

Well, what else was I supposed to do? The man, albeit ten years my junior, absolutely worshipped the bloody ground I walked on. And it was mutual, so why deny myself the pleasure of looking into those delicious steel grey eyes every morning for the rest of my life?

Craig had not, it turns out, been scheming to make money out of my rare books after all. He was genuinely trying to help me, in his own sweet way, to raise funds for me to renovate and live in Hamilton Hall. And also, as it turned out, it had been Craig who had paid for old Esther the Fiesta (remember her?) to be fixed that time she broke down after I'd first viewed Hamilton Hall. A man is hardly going to do that if he's hell bent on making money out of a woman, now is he? And one of the reasons he was persevering in trying to get in touch with me – apart from the fact that he was (can I really say this?) falling for me hook, line and sinker – was that he wanted to finish going through the family tree with me. Had I not been so obdurate, I'd have known a long time ago that Carl Hamilton-Blanc was my father. Well that, and had I read those legal documents I signed before taking possession of Hamilton Hall. *Duh!* Come to think of it, the originals that the lawyer had promised to return to me hadn't arrived yet. But I did know that Carl was my father, so what did it matter now? Craig had in his file a letter found unopened in Hamilton Hall, after the death of Emily. It had been written by my mother, addressed to 'Carl Hamilton-Blanc, Hamilton Hall, Norfolk', telling him that he was my father and should anything happen to her, would he please take care of me.

Kitty had been right all along: I needed to learn to put my trust in a man for once in my life. So, I'd decided it was time for me to channel my inner power goddess, take the bull by the horns, and marry Craig before I lost him again. *(And before you go all cynical on me – no, he is NOT after Hamilton Hall ... he happens to be quite well-heeled in his own right, thank you very much!)*

We got married in the little chapel close to the grounds of Hamilton Hall, which turned out to be the one renovated by the old boy I'd heard being interviewed on the radio as I drove up to view my inheritance for the first time. Apparently, generations of the Boulais-Hamiltons had worshipped there. Now, I am not in the least bit religious, but Craig's mum really wanted her son to be married in a church, so we obliged.

And Kitty and Felix did the same (well, they're not married yet – but it's only a matter of time). *Didn't I say there was a definite spark between them?* She found a tenant for her Suffolk home and moved in with Felix.

True to her word, Simona de Napoli returned in the March and took the vintage wines to auction. This turned out to be a highly lucrative 'nice little earner' as some would put it, and we now have sufficient funds to finish the renovations, pay the council tax and eat for a while.

The *Daisyfields* project *(Kitty loved Kylie's suggestion for the name!)* is making excellent progress and business should be up and running with first 'Glampers' arriving in the summer of next year. Kitty was in her element.

Between them, Felix, Kitty and Kylie take care of Old George, and Tom is a regular visitor at their house, as well as at Hamilton Hall. He arrived one afternoon with a seven-week-old puppy, a direct descendent of a dog called Patch that he said he'd found in a hollow tree when he was a kid. We called the pup Patch, in honour of the original dog.

Once the shock of my mother's letter had dissipated somewhat, the revelation about my parentage turned into relief that, at last, I knew my true heritage and actually belonged at Hamilton Hall. However, a niggling feeling still played at the back of my mind, aided and abetted by an inbuilt, unshakable belief that I, Laura White, was not deserving of such good fortune. I felt a sense of extreme loss whenever I thought about Carl, my father. A terrible tsunami, that happened thousands of miles away, took him from me long before I ever knew who he was. I sometimes had dreams about him, where he was standing a few metres away from me and I tried to run into his arms but my legs wouldn't move.

Kylie continued to live at Hamilton Hall and her friendship with Thomas blossomed into a very sweet relationship *(well, Kitty and I thought so!)* that saw her flourish and after she finishes her degree course in art and design (she *did* eventually enrol to study - *yay!*), she is planning to join him doing voluntary work overseas. *Oh yes, Thomas was a much better bet than the drug-addled oik at the petrol station café!*

And Kylie turned out to be a real asset to Hamilton Hall, with her flair for artistic design. As each renovation project was completed, she set to work, dreaming up colour schemes and soft furnishings for each room. She was a dab hand with a paint brush too, and thought nothing of donning old clothing, acquired at one of the many charity shops dotted around Wymondham, and attacking a room with a tin of paint and pretty fabrics. Well, not literally *attacking*, but you get my drift. Tom had told me that two of his sons were builders, and another was a plumber, so I used their family business to do a lot of the works that Simon Fancy-pants had highlighted in the survey report. It seemed fitting to keep it all in the Hamilton Hall family. As far as I was concerned, we all belonged to the house.

I kept some of the original furniture that had been in the house, sold some pieces – thanks to eBay - and gradually – again via eBay – bought more pieces in keeping with the style and age of Hamilton Hall. So yes, I saw my plans coming to fruition, slowly but surely. It had taken a lot of hard work, blood, sweat, tears and stress, but now I wondered what I'd been so worried about.

One day, Kylie, Kitty and I decided to have a spring clean in the library. I was setting to with a can of *Pledge*, when the duster snagged on something as I polished a bookshelf. Looking closer, I discovered a tiny hook. Looking up and down the shelves, I saw several more hooks.

'Hey, look at these!' I said and Kitty and Kylie came to examine what I was looking at. We started lifting the hooks, and Kylie stood on the stepladder, to reach the higher ones nearer to the ceiling. She started to lose her footing and grabbed the bookcase to steady herself. It moved backwards, nearly taking Kylie with it. And that's when we discovered it. A secret storeroom. We could walk into it. Strange that Simon the rip-off-surveyor hadn't found it when he was on walkabout for his expensive surveyor's report.

We pulled out boxes and suitcases and started opening them. Family treasures were unearthed, including women's clothes, personal documents – they would make interesting reading at some point – and – oh my gosh! - the emerald green evening gown, emerald necklace and matching earrings and ring, worn by my great-great-grandmother in the oil painting that hung in the drawing room. I held the gown to my face and breathed in the family history, along with a very strong smell of mothballs. I took the beautiful jewellery in my hands.

'Oh, these are exquisite. Just look at them.' I could hardly breathe.

'You'll need to keep them in a safe, or at the bank, Laura. They look very much like the real thing to me,' said Kitty, ever the practical one, as she squeezed my shoulder. I put the pieces back in the jewellery box, closed it and ran my fingers over the carved wood. As I did so, it occurred to me that all the time that I had been worried about how I could renovate and keep Hamilton Hall, the house itself was harbouring enough vintage wine and jewellery to cover all costs and give me a good living for some years to come. While I was happy, however, to sell off the wine, the jewellery and the rare books would stay in the family, where they have always belonged.

I stroked the glorious green garment gently, as if it were a family pet. Then I thought we really had discovered a (dead) family pet when Kylie exclaimed, 'Hey, look at this!' as she pulled a fur stole out of the same suitcase and wrapped it around her shoulders, parading around the library like a catwalk model. We squealed with delight at every new item we retrieved from its storage place.

§

I decided to keep a business head (the new, *level-headed* Laura!) and prepare my Suffolk cottage for a tenant. After all, I couldn't live in two places at once. It meant sorting out anything that I was absolutely sure I didn't need any more and ruthlessly disposing of it. The charity shops did well out of me in the two weeks I stayed at the cottage with Kitty and Kylie. We stripped it bare, keeping only those things that I absolutely knew I couldn't live without. This was no time for sentimentalities. Together we redecorated and I used Kitty's letting agent to find me a decent tenant. During the proceedings, I came across a piece of paper I'd completely forgotten about, tucked behind a candlestick on the mantelpiece: the old premium bond I'd found in the box of Mum's stuff in the attic. Kylie jumped to it and looked up the *N S & I* website on her smartphone and I thought she was having a laugh when she announced that I'd won a thousand pounds.

'No, really, you have, Laura. Look!' And she shoved the phone in my face so that I could see it with my own eyes. 'See, that's the correct number, yeah?'

Correct.

I decided there and then to gift half of the prize to Kylie, in recognition of all her hard work, both in the cottage and in Hamilton Hall. She immediately said she was going to use some of the money to have the tattooed letters laser-removed from her knuckles. The rest of the money I used to book a weekend break in Paris for Kitty and Felix. Kitty objected, but I was adamant because I wanted to show my appreciation for all she and Felix had done. Which, where Kitty was concerned, was just being there for me, really. And Felix had worked miracles, making the gardens of Hamilton Hall look beautiful. We'd recruited the help of a few local boys, who were glad of the extra cash, but Felix had refused any financial reward whatsoever.

I had already paid for a cruise for Aunty Kath the previous year, with some of the wine money. She was really getting into the swing of sailing around the Mediterranean like Lady Muck! And she deserved it after all the love and care she had given to me all my life, and the friendship she'd shared with Mum.

So, it seemed that all my ships were coming in, along with all my Christmases and birthdays. If only Mum had lived long enough to share it with me. My dear mother. Despite being short of material things, I'd never lacked love and affection, not to mention encouragement and sheer devotion, from her. Her belief in me was unwavering. The day I graduated with my First-Class Honours degree last year was bittersweet. On the one hand, I was happy and proud, but on the other, I felt a huge sadness that Mum could not be there to share in celebrating my success.

With the cottage refurbishments finished and a tenant lined up, we popped in to see Aunty Kath, before heading back to Norfolk.

After tea and sandwiches, she looked at me.

'Laura, dear, I've something for you,' Kathryn said, reaching behind her to a highly polished mahogany writing bureau. I knew immediately what it would be.

'It took me a while, but I have finished transcribing the shorthand book you gave me. Here it is.' She handed me a typescript, along with the blue notebook.

I smiled at Kathryn and squeezed her hand. 'You're such a love,' I said, softly.

'It seems your great-grandmother was in the SOE in France during the war. And this was her diary.' Of course, she was only confirming what Tom had already told me last Christmas, but it was magical to see the actual words of my great-grandmother typed by Aunty Kath and printed on crisp, white paper.

'Martha was a clever girl,' Kathryn said. 'She made sure the enemy wouldn't be able to decipher the notes by using a sort of a code. You see, with shorthand, a word can be written above the line, on the line or through the line. Where it is placed, depends upon the vowel sounds. As I said, it took me a while to figure out what she'd done, but once I had, reading the shorthand wasn't so bad. I'm rather pleased that I can still read shorthand after all these years!'

'You're a genius Aunt Kath!'

'Your great-grandmother's boyfriend was an RAF pilot, shot down over Germany before she realised that she was pregnant.'

Despite knowing this already, tears sprung, unbidden, to my eyes and I felt my chin crease and tremble.

'I know, Aunt Kath, my great-grandfather was a war hero too,' I managed to say.

Kitty reached out and held my hand.

Kylie came over and put her arm around my shoulder. 'Ah, bless,' she said, giving me a little squeeze. 'You've got a well cool family, Laura.' And in that moment, I realised that the only family

Kylie had ever known was our own: me, Kitty, Felix and even the shotgun-wielding old codger, George. And, of course, Thomas and Tom. And Craig, now, too. An extended family, and all of us, in some way, belonging to Hamilton Hall.

Later that night, as I sat alone in the morning room going through unopened post that I had picked up from my Suffolk cottage, I looked for those legal documents I had signed all those months ago and was supposed to have read, but hadn't. They were not in the pile of mail from Suffolk and they hadn't been delivered to Hamilton Hall either. Strange. Hadn't Neil Davidson told me that his secretary would copy the documents and post the originals to me? Oh well. I shrugged my shoulders and, making a mental note to call the lawyer in the morning, picked up the transcript of Martha's diary and began reading.

Codename Veronique. I am Veronique. Shorthand will fox those bloody Jerries. What's more, I can write a lot more in shorthand than I can in longhand. And if the idiot Gestapo do get a hold of it, they will not understand a word.
I joined the WAAF to help the war effort. Ostensibly. But my heart is black with anger and hate for the enemy who took away my dear parents whilst they innocently celebrated their silver wedding anniversary. And the same enemy that also killed Charles, the love of my life, robbing my darling daughter, Charlotte of her daddy. It was a stroke of luck, the WAAF accepting me. I was worried that my mental weakness might be discovered, but I lied about my health and they took me. I also lied about Charlotte, telling them I was single and childless. Now I am to avenge the deaths of my loved ones. I carry the hate in my heart like a stone.

§

Basic training in the WAAF was a bit of an eye-opener. Rising at dawn, cleaning out toilets, scrubbing floors, marching around the parade ground at unearthly hours, being screamed at by the WAAF Flight Sergeant. And what use such activities could be to me when I got through training and went on to work as a secretary for some station commander, I simply could not fathom. But they said we had to be broken down before we could be built up again. And filthy work was good for the soul, according to our sadistic Flight Sergeant WAAF!
I swore at her one day. In French. I was ordered to the Station Commander's office, pronto, for what I assumed would be a jolly good dressing down. But he proceeded to speak to me in French, and I, quite naturally, replied in

French. With Mummy being French, and Daddy being English, unsurprisingly, Emily and I were brought up with the two languages. The twenty-minute conversation with the station commander was conducted entirely in French with me standing to attention and the result was that I was sent to Scotland for special training before being parachuted one night into Brittany and landing in a lavender field. When I woke up and smelt the lavender, I thought I was in the gardens of Hamilton Hall. I tried to move. Searing pain shot through my ankle. I tried to look around me but my head felt as if it was cracking in two and the sun in my eyes was blinding.

§

I must have passed out again and when a shadow fell over me, for a moment, I expected to hear Carter asking me what on earth I was doing in the lavender bushes. I opened one eye, squinting, to see a little boy gazing down at me.

'Bonjour Madame. Vous n'avez rien?'
'Bonjour mon petit, comment t'appelles-tu?'

Another shadow fell over me and this time it was a young man, his complexion nut-brown, sun-kissed. Handsome, rugged, muscular, tall. A black beret covered his dark brown hair. He was unsmiling. Lifting me, wordlessly, he carried me as though I were a stuffed cloth doll through the purple fields towards a farmhouse with smoke escaping from its chimney. I winced again as the pain seared through my ankle. I clung steadfastly to my radio suitcase. I held onto him with my free arm and felt the undulation of his muscles beneath his black jumper. The boy told me his name - Jean-Baptiste - and that he lives at the farmhouse with his big brother, Benoît – who had carried me to the house - and grandparents. They are farmers and Benoît manages the lavender fields. Jean-Baptiste told me his parents were killed by the Gestapo. Benoît is not only a lavender farm worker but also a resistance fighter. He is a man of few words. He is twenty-two. His little brother idolises him. Jean-Baptiste reminds me so much of young Tom at home in Hamilton Hall. He is perhaps a year or so younger. After I had been in the attic room of the farmhouse – my hiding place - for three days, Jean-Baptiste started coming up to keep me company while my ankle healed. He brings me bread and cheese and water. The grandmother comes up occasionally and empties the pot from under the bed. I tell

Jean-Baptiste stories about England and my home in Norfolk. I tell him we have lots of lavender growing in Norfolk, just like here. I am teaching him to speak English but have made him swear not to speak it to anyone else but me. It could be a matter of life and death. He saw me writing my diary. He laughed at the funny dots and squiggles on the page. I hid it up the chimney and told him it was a secret diary.

§

I have a Type 3 Mark II (B2) SOE Suitcase Radio and a pistol, which I have also hidden up the chimney.
I have made contact with London and they've given me my orders: I am to ensure that British servicemen escape from German custody and back to England. I am ordered to help *La Résistance Française* to blow up a bridge that is approximately two kilometres from the farmhouse and which is expected to be used to transport German artillery trucks and a lot of German soldiers into the immediate area. I am also ordered by London to assist *La Résistance Française* with the planning, coordination and execution of the sabotage of electrical power grids and telecommunications. My brief is monumentally challenging and highly dangerous, and I am scared. Of course, I am scared; but if we succeed, we will defeat the blasted Nazis and help bring this frightful war to an end. Crucially, I will have avenged the deaths of my beloved parents, and Charles, at the hands of the murderous Nazis, and hopefully make the world a safer place for my daughter.
There is a secret trap door in the corner of the attic room, and Benoît has told me that when my ankle is healed enough, I must practice getting into it and hiding, should the Germans come to the farmhouse.

§

Benoît is quiet, monosyllabic and moody. During the day, he is away working in the lavender fields, and *he* disappears again after the evening meal. He has been up to the attic to see me only once since I arrived. I have to stay in the attic in case the Germans arrive and I don't have time to move quickly enough to hide. There is little for me to do but to wait for coded messages to come through from London, but I cannot do anything until my badly sprained ankle heals.

§

Jean-Baptiste still comes up to the attic to see me every day after school. I tell him stories in English and in French and he asks me constantly about England, a truly exotic land to him. I tell him about Charlotte and how the Germans shot down her father. I still cannot believe that Charles is dead. In my dreams, vivid dreams, he is at home with me, living in Hamilton Hall, with my dear sister, Emily, with Doris and Carter, and most importantly, with Charlotte.

§

My ankle is better and it is a beautiful, warm, sunny day. I moved carefully down the attic ladder and found myself in a single room that is, all in one, a kitchen, a dining room and a sitting room. There was no one about. I looked through a cracked window. In the distance, I could see a lone figure, working in the lavender field. I knew it must be Benoît. He must be tired. He works all day in the fields and is often out by cover of darkness on *La Résistance Française* business. When does he rest?
I lifted the latch on the farmhouse door and stepped outside. What harm could it do? I look French. I sound French. I am French. I am Veronique from Normandy, visiting my family in Brittany. That is my cover story. I will stick to it.
The fresh air hit me and the sun warmed my face. I felt enveloped in a gentle breeze. It had been some weeks since I was out of doors. I breathed in the aroma of the lavender and was transported, once more, back to the gardens of Hamilton Hall.
I strolled towards the lavender field and as I got closer I recognised Benoit. He turned and scowled at me. 'What are you doing here?' His face was hard, granite. 'You should be in hiding, you little fool!'
'It is a lovely day and I need some air. And don't you dare call me a fool. I am here to help *La Résistance!* Remember that.'
How dared he speak to me like that?
'So. We French peasants are to be eternally grateful to you British, then, is that it?'
'That is not what I am saying. But courtesy costs nothing.'
I turned and walked away, towards a small copse, some fifty metres ahead. He called after me and I ignored him, carried on walking. The breeze was welcome after the stuffy attic. The sun still warm on my face. I thought of Charles and of Charlotte; Emily, my parents, Carter and Doris. And little Tom.

Veronique! You are Veronique! I chided myself, mentally. Do not think about your family. Focus on your mission.
I entered the cool shade of the thicket and sat on the ground by a tree, resting my back against its trunk.
I heard the snap of a twig and instinctively felt for my pistol, looking around me. Footsteps. Feet cracked the undergrowth. Then I saw him. Standing there.
'You're a spirited little *mademoiselle*, aren't you? I'll give you that.' There was, as he approached – not a smile – this man never smiles - but a smirk on Benoît's face. 'And leave your pistol where it is. You won't be needing it, *petite fille.*'
I took my hand off the gun in my pocket and stood up to face him. 'To you, Monsieur Benoît,' I said, looking him straight in the eye, 'I am Veronique, SOE agent, and *not* a little girl. Kindly have some respect.'
'Like I said, *spirited!*'
I walked past him and towards the edge of the thicket. I heard him following me.

§

In the past week, we have secured the escape of five British airmen and two soldiers, one English and one Dutch. I have reported back to London. While I was on the radio, I heard strange voices downstairs and hid the equipment up the chimney. Later, Benoît came up to tell me the visitors had gone. He refused to tell me who they were, except to say that we had been close to discovery. I took the radio equipment from the chimney and reported back to London, successfully.

§

Plans for the blowing up of the bridge are under way. I went out last night with Benoît to survey the area. Intelligence from London suggests the German artillery trucks are due to cross the bridge in two nights' time. Strategic planning is of the essence. We must succeed in our mission.

§

Mission accomplished! We ran like the wind, away from the bridge, through the lavender fields with Benoît holding my arm, pulling me behind him. The explosion had been thunderous. The bridge, ablaze, had collapsed like a construction made of children's wooden building blocks. La Résistance fighters had cheered at the top of their lungs, slapping each other on the back, but were unheard. We charged through the lavender fields and into the thicket. Benoît pushed me against a tree and pulled me into his arms. Silently, he kissed me on the mouth. Fiercely at first, then softly. Gently. His tongue found mine. He pulled my hair out from its bun and it tumbled down to my waist. He ran his fingers through it. This was the first man to kiss me since…

What am I doing? I am promised to Charles. My mind races back to the lane that led to Hamilton Hall. The little MG in which Charles sat waiting for me. Charles, in his uniform, jumping from the car. Charles holding me. Kissing me.

But Charles is dead. Benoît is alive. Very much alive. And warm. And vital. And here. And he wants me. Here. Now. And I want him.

§

Much later, and now, sated, we lay in the undergrowth, our arms and legs entwined, until dawn broke and we wandered, hand in hand, back to the farmhouse.

§

I can hear voices. German voices. My heart pounds; beats like a drum. I pack my radio suitcase and stuff it up the chimney. My diary will follow.

Run Jean-Baptiste! Run for your life!

79: April, 2017
Hamilton Hall

Laura:
There was a strange sense that I recognised the face. It seemed quite familiar but I couldn't think why. Then the eyes. Vivid blue. And the sleek, black hair, shot through with grey. And something – quite – imperceptible - in the gaze. And everything around me faded away into a kind of mist. And all I could see was this face. A bodiless face. And now with a kindly, warm, enquiring expression. A face I somehow knew that I knew, yet knew that I didn't know. He took a step forward and I heard the gravel, then, on the drive, crunching underfoot. And all around him seemed to be a warm mist and above, in the sky, a huge orange ball. The sun, encircled by a fading halo that now seemed like the edges of a stream, rippling around it.

Crunching. Crunching. Crunching on the gravel. His eyes never left mine. His lips opened into a wide, wide smile. His teeth, straight. Straight and dazzlingly white. His body now, in view: upright, tall, toned, long-limbed. His back straight. Like a rod. His eyes glistened with threatened tears. Still the smile was there. Wide. Warm.

I searched my mind for an elusive memory. Arrows shot here and there criss-crossing both hemispheres of my brain. Searching. Searching. It was like one of those moments when you are tongue-tied or can't quite remember a word and say something like: *Oh! It's on the tip of my tongue but I can't say it ...*

And it was in a deep corner of my brain but I couldn't access it. This face: so very strange, yet so very recognizable.

Then, suddenly, it was as though dark clouds were assembling all around, and a storm threatened, as a chill wind groaned around Hamilton Hall.

Patch ran out of the house, bouncing around excitedly, barking. I snapped at him to stop.

Craig came out of the house, carrying our toddler twins. He stopped in his tracks.

'Can I help you?' As he said it he lowered first Clarissa, then Carlotta to the ground. I looked from him to the dark-haired stranger.

I picked up Carlotta and held her close. She grabbed a handful of my hair and tried to chew on it.

The familiar stranger stood, motionless. His expression now changed, impossible to read. The dark clouds began to disperse and the sun now shone. He gazed at the twins, one and then the other and his face softened and he smiled again - a wide, bright smile – first at me, and then at them.

'I'm looking for Laura.' His voice was clear and crisp and clipped. He sounded 'nicely spoken', as Mum would have said, without being too 'posh'.

'I'm Laura,' I said. Carlotta grabbed another chunk of my hair and pulled hard. I held her hand, trying to disentangle it from my ponytail.

'Yes, you are. Of *course*, you are.' That wide smile.

I squinted in the sun, unravelled my hair from the clutches of the little one in my arms.

'Do we know each other?' I say.

'Well, yes. And, no.'

Craig moved towards me and placed a reassuring arm around my shoulders. In his other arm, he now held Clarissa.

The girls reached out for each other, patting hands, conversing in the private, unique language known only to toddler twins.

I handed Carlotta to her Daddy, moved towards the car and shut the hatchback door. I don't know why. We hadn't even finished packing the car yet.

I turned to face the familiar stranger. I was closer to him now. And I could see. It was unmistakeable. The bone structure: the jawline, the cheekbones. The eyes. The hair. The man standing before me was the male version of Adalicia. And he fit - exactly - the description I'd read in Mum's letter. The letter I'd found in the box in the attic three years ago.

Something akin to an electric shock shot through me. A stray lock of hair escaped and blew across my face. Still squinting in the April sun, I tucked the errant strand behind my ear. Slowly, the realisation dawned and I instinctively knew, without doubt, that the rightful heir to Hamilton Hall was not me after all, but the man who now stood before me.

'You ... you're ... my – '

I looked from him and back to Craig, and back again. My breath came in short gasps. My heart beat like thunder inside my ribcage. Despite the mild, spring morning, sweat soaked my hands and my brow.

'I think so, Laura. I think I am. Your mother was Sarah Williams, wasn't she?' I nodded.

'Where – where have y – ' My breath came in jagged bursts. 'I thought – I thought – '

He was stepping, tentatively now, towards me. I turned and Craig was there, behind me. Kitty came out of the house, followed by Kylie and Thomas. My head shot back to look at him.

The twins stood on the driveway, where Craig had now placed them, oblivious to the unfolding drama. They scampered around, examining handfuls of gravel, pulling at flower petals.

And I crumbled. Just crumbled. Just like that. My knees gave way and would have hit the gravel driveway with a hefty thud, had it not been for Craig's rapid action. His arms embraced me steadily.

And suddenly, they were all around me. Kylie picked up Clarissa and Thomas took Carlotta. Kitty took my hand. Warm. Comforting. Reassuring. Craig, steadfast, held me securely.

'Shall we all go inside?' It was Kitty's voice, but it seemed to be coming through a tunnel. 'I think a nice hot drink might do us all good.'

'I'm Craig Matthews,' said my husband, in his confident, assured voice, letting go of me with one hand and reaching out to the older man. 'I gather you are – '

'Carl Hamilton-Blanc. I believe Laura is my daughter.'

80: Present day
Hamilton Hall

Laura:

'*I never knew of your existence, Laura.*' Carl sat in the mahogany armchair next to the fireplace, looking very much like he belonged there. Craig sat to one side of me on the *chaise longue*. Kitty sat on the other side, holding my hand. We were all back in the house and sitting in the drawing room, having tea. Kylie and Thomas were out on the lawn, keeping the twins and the dog amused, our planned outing to the north Norfolk coast put on hold.

'And I am so very sad and sorry to hear that Sarah has passed away.' I saw the pain in his eyes, as I explained that Mum was no longer with us, his lips pressed tightly together, deep worry lines etched on his forehead. He looked around the room and I wondered if he remembered much about it. The room had been redecorated in pale lilacs and shades of ecru and I'd had new curtains made and hung, but much of the furniture remained unchanged. The oil paintings of my great-great-grandparents hung, as ever, over each of the fireplaces. To the side of one chimney breast, hung a new oil painting, this one of me with Craig. In it I am wearing the very same emerald green gown, with matching jewellery belonging to Adalicia, that Kitty, Kylie and I had found that day in the secret store cupboard behind the bookcase in the library.

Craig handed Mum's letter addressed to "Carl Hamilton-Blanc, Hamilton Hall, Norfolk" to the man I now knew to be my father.

He read aloud, '*I don't want anything from you Carl, and I don't want you to know our whereabouts, but I do want you to know that you have a beautiful daughter. Our daughter. Laura. Please take care of her if anything happens to me. In such an event, you will be notified.*' He looked up, tears filling his eyes.

'If only I'd known. But Emily stopped writing and sending on post ....' His voice trailed off. The lawyer, Neil Davidson, had found the unopened letter when the heir-hunters and legal team had gained access to Hamilton Hall after Emily's death. He'd forgotten about it (the incompetent idiot!) and the letter had languished at the bottom of his briefcase for some time before he found it and passed it on to Craig.

Kitty handed a tissue box to Carl. He took one, thanked her and wiped his eyes, then smiled.

'I'd have known you anywhere, Laura. This letter from Sarah merely confirms what I'd guessed the moment I first saw you out there.' He reached out and squeezed my hand. It felt ... good.

'And I thought that you were lost in the tsunami,' I said after some time. 'That is what Tom had assumed. Do you remember

Tom? That's his grandson, Thomas – out there with Kylie,' I made a gesture towards the French doors leading to the garden, 'looking after the twins.' Patch and the twins were rolling around on the grass, Carlotta now trying to ride the dog as if it were a horse.

'Yes. I see the resemblance. I used to call him 'Uncle Tom'. Of course, to all intents and purposes, he was my uncle.' He smiled. Just a little. 'He was wonderful. I'm so glad he's still around. I feel bad for not keeping in closer touch. I used to write to Emily, but after a while, her replies ... well, she didn't reply.'

'So, what about the tsunami? Were you affected by it?' Craig's voice sliced into the silence that had followed.

'Oh yes. Absolutely. I was in Thailand at the time the tsunami hit. I was very lucky to be in the right place at the right time, high up in the hills. I had recently retired from Chulalongkorn University in Bangkok – where I taught – '

'Oh really? What did you teach?' Craig interrupted. I didn't think it mattered right now, what Carl had taught. I just wanted to understand more about why I'd gone without a father all my life.

'Spanish language and literature.'

Mum's letter sprang up in my mind. She'd said Carl was going to study Spanish ...

'Laura did a degree, you know. She graduated with a First-Class Honours. Like Emily, we gather?' Craig said, smiling proudly, although I wished my lovely, uxorious husband would stop interrupting.

'Oh, that is wonderful, Laura. Well done you!' I felt a warm glow. Here was my father, praising his little girl. It felt strangely ... poignant. 'And yes, Emily was a mature student. The first intake at the university in Norwich.'

The French doors opened and Kylie popped her head in. 'We're going to take the girls to see the hens, OK?'

'Oh sure. Don't stay too long though. Are the twins warm enough?' Craig always said I was like a clucking hen when it came to Carlotta and Clarissa.

'Yes, I'm sure they're fine,' Kylie reassured me. 'We've been running about,' and she closed the door behind her.

'So, Carl, what happened in the tsunami? Where exactly were you?' Craig squeezed my hand as he spoke.

'I was in the hills in Phuket on a week's meditation retreat, actually. The first I knew that danger was imminent was when elephants started running up the hills from sea level.'

'Elephants?' Kitty cut in. I was sitting gazing at Carl's face: those vivid blue eyes - just like those of Adalicia in the oil painting - and the little wrinkles – laughter lines – that fanned out from them. The familiar glossy, black hair, just like Adalicia's and Martha's –

and mine. His hair was streaked with grey. My father was older now than our female ancestors had been when their images had been painted in oil.

'Yes. Elephants are very clever creatures,' he continued. 'They can hear danger from a long way off. They started running up the hills, long before anyone knew what was about to happen.'

He looked across the drawing room and into the distance. His mind now six thousand miles away.

'I was heavily involved in – well - first, the rescue operations – everyone who could help, did something – feeding, offering shelter, clothes, etcetera – getting medical attention for the injured – burying the ... well ... after that I helped in the rebuilding of communities. It was a busy time.'

I couldn't help wondering why he and Emily had not kept in touch, but there were so many questions, it would be impossible to ask him all of them now.

But, what a striking man, I now thought, taking in his facial features once again. I could see why Mum was so enamoured. He would have been a looker when they met, and already I could tell this was a man of exceptional character. A man who could be relied upon to do the right thing. People talk about seeing "auras" – like some kind of light or energy field surrounding another person. I don't know if I buy that sort of stuff, but if Carl Hamilton-Blanc had an aura, I'd imagine it to be pure gold. As a little girl, growing up without a dad, I'd often wondered what my father was like. I'd had dreams of meeting him one day and how it would be so emotionally charged, with me running into his arms and him embracing me tight, never to let me go. Just like in the films. Now this man sat next to me: my father. Yet, despite the admiration I already had for the man, I felt none of those imagined emotions I'd dreamt up as a child. Nothing like a film at all. And the question on my mind, despite what I'd read in Mum's letter...

'Why didn't you try to find my mum? I know how you met – she left a letter for me too, explaining everything about you – that she didn't think your family would accept her, she felt she wasn't good enough - so she didn't give you her contact details – but even so, if she'd meant anything to you – anything at all - well, I know you were both very young – but you could have tried, if you'd really wanted to.'

I sounded harsh. I know I did. And I was ranting a bit. But it was true. And it needed to be said. Why *didn't* my father want to find my mother?

'Oh, Laura, I did. Believe me, I tried very hard to find Sarah. But you have to remember that there was no Internet in those days. It was very difficult to find someone who didn't want to be found. And anyway, when I could eventually search the Internet,

I was looking for Sarah Williams, not Sarah White. I had no idea she'd changed her name. And anyway, there was every chance that she had married.'

'She never married. And she changed her name to the English version of your name, Blanc. That's what she said.'

'It means so much to me that she did that, Laura.'

'So, how did you find out about me?'

Carl let out a gentle laugh that sang out into the room.

'Why, the village gossip, of course! A woman by the name of Maggie Middleton. I saw her in the high street as I walked up from the train station, and she recognised me. After all these years, she recognised me! Called me a dead man walking, if you please! Couldn't wait to tell me that I'd been pipped at the post and that you were living here. Said something about cats and pigeons when you found out I was alive. If you want anything to get around, just tell Maggie and she will do the job for you at lightning speed! I remember her at school. She was just as bad then.'

I raised a hand to my mouth and stifled a giggle. 'I've met Maggie Middleton. Is she a witch? She unnerves me every time I see her.'

'A witch? Goodness me, no. But you'd be forgiven for thinking so. I think she'd give witches a bad name that they don't deserve!' At this, we all chuckled, and the laughter rippled around the room. 'No, she's just the village gossip, it runs in her family, and she's kept the tradition going, it seems. Her aunt – Nellie, I think she was called - used to run the village post office and apparently was the wellspring of all "knowledge", according to Uncle Tom.'

We all laughed at this.

'So, did Maggie tell you that I was your daughter?'

'Oh no. She just said "some young woman called Laura" had inherited Hamilton Hall. No, she didn't tell me, but the moment I saw you there on the drive, I knew. I just knew.'

'And ... will you ...?' It was a question I needed to be answered. But a difficult one to ask.

'Will I what?'

'Well, Hamilton Hall. It's not really mine now, is it? It's ... yours.'

He looked around the room.

'Mine? No, Laura. No. Hamilton Hall is undeniably yours. I left a long time ago.'

And not only had I inherited this wonderful mansion, but – even better – I'd found the lovely father I had wondered about all my life. Not for the first time in Hamilton Hall, I felt a strong sense of continuity and belonging. If only my mum ...

I glanced at the oil painting of my great-great-grandmother hanging above the fireplace... and then at the portrait of me and

80: PRESENT DAY

Craig that hung next to it. Carl followed my gaze and looked at it too. Craig had commissioned the portrait for our first wedding anniversary.

'People say I look like Adalicia.'

'Yes, you do, Laura. As do your girls. You three are most certainly the daughters of Hamilton Hall. But you are your mother's daughter, all right. When I first set eyes on you, on the drive earlier, I thought I was seeing Sarah all over again. Your movements, your mannerisms. Even the timbre of your voice. Just like Sarah. Look.' He reached for his wallet from his jacket pocket and produced a faded, dog-eared black and white photograph. Despite the age of the image, there was no doubt at all that these two were my mother and Carl. Yes, the photograph was pale and discoloured now, but it still showed their bright smiles, hugging each other tight, looking very happy together. And very young. There they were: my parents. For the first and only time, I was seeing my parents together albeit on an old black and white photograph. I felt a lump in my throat and bit my lip.

'Tell you what,' said Carl, lightening the mood, 'why don't I take us all out for a meal? There's a splendid Thai restaurant here in the village. *The Suphannahong*. I remember it from years ago, and it's still there. I saw it as I walked up from the station.'

My tummy rumbled. 'Mm. Yes. That sounds like a plan! I think we practically lived on Thai takeaways when the twins were first born. That Thai chicken green curry is to die for!' And anyway, we still we had a lot more catching up to do.

Kitty and Craig agreed. Kitty picked up her mobile to call Felix. Might as well make an occasion of it!

Kylie, Thomas and the twins were back on the lawn, hands joined in a circle and singing nursery rhymes. Patch scampered about, running in and out of the human ring formed.

'Would you like a proper introduction to your granddaughters?' Craig said, as he stood up and walked across the room to open the French doors.

'Clarissa. Carlotta. Come here, my darlings. Come and meet Grandpa!'